FORT DA

a report

W9-BEW-891

FORT DA

a report

elisabeth sheffield

TUSCALOOSA

The University of Alabama Press
Tuscaloosa, Alabama 35487-0380

Copyright 2009 by Elisabeth Sheffield
All rights reserved
First Edition

Published by FC2, an imprint of the University of Alabama Press, with support provided by Florida State University, the Publications Unit of the Department of English at Illinois State University, and the School of Arts and Sciences, University of Houston–Victoria

Address all editorial inquiries to: Fiction Collective Two, University of Houston–Victoria, School of Arts and Sciences, Victoria, TX 77901-5731

⊗

The paper on which this book is printed meets the minimum requirements of American National Standard for Information Sciences—Permanence of Paper for Printed Library Materials, ANSI Z39.48–1984

Library of Congress Cataloging-in-Publication Data
Sheffield, Elisabeth.
  Fort Da : a report / Elisabeth Sheffield. — 1st ed.
    p. cm.
  ISBN-13: 978-1-57366-150-8 (pbk. : alk. paper)
  ISBN-10: 1-57366-150-3 (pbk. : alk. paper)
  1. Neurologists—Fiction. 2. Americans—Germany—Fiction. 3. Boys—Fiction. 4. Cypriots—Germany—Fiction. 5. Psychological fiction. 6. Experimental fiction. I. Title.
  PS3619.H4515F67 2009
  813'.6—dc22

                            2009010732

Book Design: Julia Drauden and Tara Reeser
Cover Design: Lou Robinson
Typeface: Baskerville
Produced and printed in the United States of America

Much thanks to Patrick Greaney, for making the German clean and sauber, and also for his astute observations and suggestions overall. My gratitude goes as well to Patricia Ackerman for an insightful reading of the book as it neared completion; to Sam Gerstenzang, for many good games of backgammon; and to Katherine Eggert, Marcia Douglas, Stephen Graham Jones and Mark Winokur, for their intelligence and support. Mark Winokur especially I would like to thank for asking a crucial question in the early stages of this project: "what about the consciousness of the boy?" Thanks also to Dan Waterman, Brenda Mills, Amanda Wicks, and Carmen Edington; to Tara Reeser and Lou Robinson for their smart and imaginative design work; and to Lance Olson for his kind and encouraging words. Finally, I'd like to thank Jeffrey DeShell ("my sin, my soul…"), without whom this book could not have been written.

For J.D.

"[W]e cannot now, outside ourselves, approach and behold again what inside our mind seems so beautiful, what excites in us a desire to see it again (a desire apparently so individual), save by seeking it in a person of the same age, by seeking it, that is to say, in a different person."

Marcel Proust
Time Regained
1037

"I believe people see something alien in me and the real reason for this is that in my youth I was never young and now that I am entering the age of maturity I cannot mature properly."

Sigmund Freud
Freud Museum
Vienna

"Nothing could be finer than shagging with a minor."

Dean Martin

.

Contents

I.

1. There Are No Pain Receptors in the Brain

A person doesn't want to be unreasonable, Ms. Wall. She doesn't want to be unreasonable and therefore she will attempt to be reasonable. Therefore she will attempt to give her explanation in a reasonable manner, that being a manner in which chronological sequence is clear and events are precisely delineated. She will not fudge or tinker. Of course it is possible that good intentions will be conquered by neuroanatomy, by the ancient megaliths of the mammalian brain that sit at the foundation of consciousness. For we know that at this stage in evolution, the amygdala has a greater influence on the cortex than the cortex has on the amygdala—allowing emotional arousal to dominate and control thinking. A person doesn't want to be unreasonable, but feeling is a variable that cannot be discounted.

Another is the nature of memory. The inherent inexactitude of the internal record of external events—this must be acknowledged. Yes it must be acknowledged that the neuronal record of reality is selective, if not capricious, a spotty chronicle at best. The flavor of *Sachertorte*, for instance, will be available, but not the name of the café on the Ringstrasse in which the cake was consumed. Also, it must be conceded that an illness such as cerebral malaria can diminish the reliability of the record even further, smearing the ink, so to speak, deleting entire pages. It must be conceded that there is no memory of the months following the excursion to Africa, and additionally, that bits and pieces of all the years previous may have been lost as well.[1]

---

[1] *Cerebral malaria* complicates about 2 percent of cases of *falciparum malaria*. Quinine, chloroquine and related drugs are curative if the cerebral symptoms are not pronounced, but once coma and convulsions supervene, 20 to 30 percent

Therefore this account will probably fail as an etiology—the sequence of cause and effect being incomplete. Nevertheless, it will be as rigorous as possible. And she will try not to cry.

She will try not to cry, Ms. Wall, not only because of the adverse relation between lachrymal secretions and paper fiber, but also because of the negative response in this household to emotional display. If Osman sees her red eyes, he may confiscate the gunmetal gray PowerBook 100 obtained for twenty British pounds from an American professor departing from the University and the Island. Using a quaint nomenclature cobbled together out of eastern mysticism and Freud, Osman will claim that the "cathexis" is channeling outward energy that needs to be turned inward, "to be enlisted in the forces of healing." But the fact is that he and the old woman, his mother, dislike emotional display, being themselves—contrary to the popular image of Mediterranean peoples—exceptionally unemotive. The face of each is generally blank, like the exterior of this penthouse apartment. For example, an observer looking up from the roadside at the windows on the western face of the top story could see only an impenetrable gleam, similar to that presented by a pair

---

of patients do not survive. In patients who do survive the acute phase of the disease, long term and even permanent cognitive impairment (including memory loss) is often seen.

   Given that sub-Saharan Africa was never part of the global malaria eradication program, probably due to the high costs and complications of eradicating the disease over such a large and politically unstable landmass, it was a mistake to flee with the boy from North Cyprus to a malaria-endemic area like Mozambique. So why even go there? No doubt (to be painfully honest), the hope at the time was to exploit the "off the radar" attitude that had allowed *Anopheles gambiae complex* (the mosquito that transmits, via the female of the species, the protozoan responsible for malaria) to continue to flourish in such places.

of wraparound sunglasses. An observer looking out and down, on the other hand, could see not only the person below, but also the line of eucalyptuses along the far side of the road, the row of kebab shops and stationary stores on the near, the stream of ancient Mercedes taxis and battered Renaults between, and the white towers of the university beyond. Or, by stepping over to the windows on the eastern face, he or she could look out over an expanse of flat concrete roof tops spiked with rusted iron poles (supports, Osman says, for second and third stories that will never be built), to the shimmering blue green waters of the Mediterranean beyond. Further, with the aid of binoculars or the zoom lens of an expensive camera, he or she could take in details of the view scarcely visible to the naked eye—a dust coated foot in a blue plastic sandal on its way to the beach, the fly speckled carcass of a dog that isn't going anywhere. All this could be seen by the penthouse observer, while the one on the ground would be unable to discern so much as a shape in the window.

She will try not to cry even though to the observer on the ground, it is as if she does not exist. While the observer on the ground may try to imagine who resides at the top of the tallest building in Gazimağosa, he or she is unlikely to conjure up a thirty-nine-year-old American woman—more specifically, a perimenopausal neurologist with an acute cardiac condition. More likely, an observer would envision some Turkish Cypriot bigwig or raki-gutted playboy like Sabri in *Bitter Lemons*, the memoir by the novelist Lawrence Durrell, and he or she would not be far off, in that Osman is a bigwig if not a raki-gutted playboy, lacking both excess adipose tissue and the requisite sportiness. He or she might also install a nubile wife with light olive skin and dark olive eyes, and in this case would miss the mark entirely, as Osman has no wife—his domestic, if not his sexual needs, are fulfilled by his mother, Sibel, a stout but by no means obese woman who, like others of her age and class, does her errands with her dyed black hair uncovered, but wears a silver beaded hairnet when she is engaged in housework or cooking. Right now, for example, as Sibel is polishing the row of windows on the other side of the room, her arm sweeping over the glass in a one-sided breaststroke, the beads of her hairnet flash and then blur, flash and then blur, like the dorsal side of a dolphin, rising and submerging, rising and submerging.

This won't do. Self-control must be restored, if your support is to be gained. Support does not, of course, mean financial support—the woman's savings will cover any bills the *Schlafzentrum* in Kiel refuses to settle, or strategic—a Turkish Cypriot *avukat*, a Mr. Mehmet Kamil, as well as a German *Rechtsanwalt* and an American attorney, will provide legal counsel.[2] Further, the woman's sibling, the Admirable Miranda Boynton (né Ramee), who acquired an accounting degree from Russell Sage College before ceding to the maternal instinct and producing progeny, has offered her money management skills. So material and tactical support are no problem. What lacks is understanding. This can be inferred from the way they all avoid the woman's eyes, from the way the woman is spoken over and around, like a body on a dissecting table, a body to be incised, searched, sampled and sutured back up again. A body to be dismissed as a meaningless

---

[2] To be honest (once again), it is still very unclear what transgressions have occurred and what kind of penalties or punishment could result. Child protection laws are complex, with important particulars that vary from country to country.

aberration, histological analysis of the extirpated tissue having proved inconclusive. Thus Miranda felt free to write, words
penned in big block letters (as if the woman's sexual proclivity,
like the late stages of syphilis, had made her blind), that "YOU
MUST BE SOME KIND OF MONSTER." In fact, it is suspected that the only reason the Admirable Miranda has offered
to supervise the estate is that she hopes to eventually procure
it for her numerous offspring. Given that in the eyes of others
the woman has become less than human, a nest egg at best, the
woman cannot help but feel that at present, emotional support
is insufficient. Without understanding, without the knowledge
that at least one other person recognizes her loss, she shall die.

Stop.

It is possible you found the utterance about the need for
understanding surprising, given the scientific background of
its source. After all, there have been no studies showing that
empathy, like oxygen or carbon, is a necessary element to sustain cellular metabolism. Indeed, there are no pain receptors
in the brain. Then again, there is some truth in the colloquial
phrase "to die of a broken heart." It has been observed, for
instance, that bereavement leads to a depression of the immune
system such that individuals are more prone to infection and,
consequently, more likely to develop certain types of cancer.
Whether empathy can counter such a depression and increase
immunocompetence of course remains to be seen. But that is
not the point. That is not the point because the point is…the
point is…

Oh, what is the point?

You said that literature was the point, that stories provide
life with meaning. This declaration was met with resistance, in

retrospect stemming from a need to discredit you after you dismissed a creative writing project as derivative. Which it was. The story was clearly dependent on the fantastical world created by the writer C.S. Lewis. Although you could have been more tactful. You said, it is recalled, that the project was "thoughtlessly escapist" and that the writer needed to be more "honest," to draw from her own "reality" rather than "the Christian allegory of a dead Cambridge don" (Lewis's allegory, it must be admitted, had gone unperceived). Indeed, you feared that it was already too late, that the writer was already an "incorrigible fantasist." Yes, you could have phrased all this less bluntly. Then again, your own honesty at Hudson High, twenty-four years ago (more precisely, in AP English 10, Fall 1976) leads to the assumption that you will appreciate an attempt at honesty now. An attempt at a true story. If not at literature (indeed, all aspirations in that area were relinquished long ago). A true story that will faithfully present yours truly, without distortion or bias. To this end, a detached style has been adopted, one that will hopefully facilitate accurate reportage. The intent of this style is to step outside Rosemarie Ramee in order to more accurately observe her (and not, Strunk and White forbid, to annoy you with passive verb forms, which it is well remembered were a source of contention in high school). Yes, and maybe if the observations are presented with great care, with the greatest possible degree of honesty and precision, in the end empathy will be received. Yes, maybe if a full report is given, or as complete a report as the situation allows, understanding, if not identification, will follow. This is the hope that is clung to, the lifeline along which the story will be strung.

2. An Irreversible and Profoundly Regretted Excretion

Rosemarie Romeo Ramee had a brother. An openhanded beginning. Yes, because three facts, before this kept close, have been shared. And now an additional admission (palms up, arms spread wide): these three until now unshared facts were secrets. However, no concealing stratagems (i.e., any kind of "cover-up") will be conceded. For all has always been there for the record— even though all is no longer, strictly speaking, here. Thus you found the despised middle name on your roster for AP English 10 at Hudson High, and on the first day of class, proclaimed it out loud, giving sonorous emphasis to each syllable. Which is not to imply, by the way, that that initial, brutal enunciation went unappreciated. How cathartic to be so exposed, like a duck wing sucked down to the aerodynamic bone. To be sure, when later on you counseled, re: the assignment to write a fictional short story or even a novella, "let your imagination soar," the flight ended with a stunned plunge. However, no blame can be assigned. No blame can be assigned because Rosemarie Romeo Ramee flew smack into the self's creative limits in your AP English 10 class. Fortunately the present project, being a true story—actually no more than a report—need not observe such bounds.

But to return to the more pertinent two of the three facts presented above: RR (for now that a full nominal disclosure has been made, Occam's razor can be employed) *had* a brother. That is, there was a brother and now there is no more. As there was a brother before there was no longer a brother, this report shall proceed chronologically. Hence there was a brother, named Tomas Tomaszewski Ramee at the insistence of the maternal progenitor, née Teresa Tomaszewski Tomasino, despite the stuttering objections of her husband, Raymond, a dysarthric former carpet layer turned carpet purveyor who could no longer contend with consonance.[3] An obstacle to paternal articulation but otherwise a source of unchecked pride, both maternal and paternal, Tomas Tomaszewski Ramee was born at Columbia Hospital, in Hudson, New York, in February of 1965, three and a half years after yours truly, and thirty-two years after Tomas Tomaszewski, maternal uncle of Teresa, cut the ropes of the life raft tied to the bulwarks of a New York bound Polish cargo ship with the miniature pocket knife bestowed upon him for his sixth birthday and launched it (and himself) overboard. But to reinstate the current subject of this report (though that subject, like his deceased namesake, is himself no longer present), Tomas Tomaszewski Ramee was born in 1965. Born in Hudson, New York in February of 1965, three and a half years after yours truly and six after the Admirable Miranda, he was a source of unlimited pride, both maternal and paternal, until his death at the age of fourteen. Yes, Tomas Tomaszewski Ramee died in 1979, a fact that is completely true but also completely unsatisfying. Because little can be inferred from this fact—the datum is insufficient to solve the problem. The problem of the monster. Yes, because yet another admission must be made: there is a

---

[3] The act of speaking involves a highly coordinated sequence of contractions of the respiratory musculature, larynx, pharynx, palate, tongue and lips. These structures are innervated by the vagal, hypoglossal, facial and phrenic nerves, the nuclei of which are controlled by both motor cortices through the corticobulbar tracts. Disease of these nuclei may lead to weakness or paralysis of the articulatory muscles and therefore to speech impediment. It may be noted here that neurologic disease has been linked with the chronic inhalation of fumes containing toluene (usually in glue, contact cement or certain brands of spray paint).

monster. There is a monster even though the term is surely less than germane. The term is surely less than germane because a monster by definition is unnatural (either physically, mentally or morally), but a person who acts in accordance with his or her natural disposition is not, per se, unnatural. A disposition that, by the way, only became apparent in Kiel, and further, would never have manifested itself without the provocations of a certain green-eyed proviso.

A person thus roused who then acts in accordance with his or her natural disposition is no more monstrous than the fly-teased spider, driven to secrete its tacky snare. Then again, human beings must also act in accordance with social conventions, and to the degree that a person's disposition compelled deviation from said conventions, it could be said that that person was a monster. Is a monster—in the original sense of a formal or structural aberration, like the sphinx with its lion's body, eagle's wings and woman's head and breasts, or to give a more contemporary example, the goat genetically altered to lactate the protein for spider's silk. On the other hand, in the sphinx-riddled society of ancient Greece a disposition towards adolescent and even prepubescent males was considered natural, comprehensible and even virtuous. Moreover, the fact that today such a disposition is considered unnatural, incomprehensible, and certainly not virtuous, as evidenced by recent expensive judicial decisions against the Catholic church, illustrates that the boundaries of the natural are not only flexible, but redefinable, and suggests that the silk-spinning goat may someday be a familiar component of Old MacDonald's farm.

Consequently, while there is clearly a monster by contemporary standards, the term should be used with an appreciation for the transitory, shifting character of cultural mores as to-day's paragon may become tomorrow's pariah, and vice versa. This recommendation is motivated by a commitment to objective truth, a commitment predicated on the recognition of a diachronic as well as synchronic dimension to reality. Or as the maternal antecedent of the monster, Teresa Tomaszewski Tomasino Ramee, used to advise, "life, my children, is a path of treachery. The future is a bandit who hides in the trees up ahead and the past is a dog that will come to bite you from behind." Indeed, to proceed somewhat less histrionically in the figurative direction established by Teresa, it is with one eye on the road, and the other on the rearview mirror, that this report shall be delivered.

Which means resuming the route established above (although, admittedly, a detour has been taken). Therefore, RR had a younger male sibling, Tomas, a.k.a. "the Titmouse"—a hypocorism coined by Raymond, in reference to the infant boy's proclivity for Teresa's mammary glands. Indeed, the Titmouse remained more or less attached to said glands for his first three years, to which Teresa had no objections. On the contrary—the day that the Titmouse suddenly released Teresa's nipple, folded his frail arms and fell limply over, she sank into a nine-month depression. According to Teresa, during this extended period of lactation she had felt not only like a "real woman" but "a Madonna," although according to the maternal bloodline dictate of Mosaic law, she was, technically, Jewish.

In the meantime, the Titmouse seemed to grow greater with each feeding, to the extent that he more resembled a species of parasite such as *Ixodes scapularis* or the common deer tick, specimens of which regularly could be found embedded in the gray plush of the familial feline, Smokey—taut pellets that popped when pinched, smearing the fingers with a waxy, primary red. Yes, like a tick the Titmouse appeared to grow greater with each feeding, as the chests of his biological antecedents concomitantly swelled with pride. Yes, the chests of Raymond and Teresa filled with pride, along with additional milk in the case of the latter, as the Titmouse flourished, as if the augmentation of his flesh was proof that their two sets of chromosomes had been successfully traded, the chiasmus completed. As if they didn't have two offspring already.

Yet upon private inspection, no distinguishing feature could be found. No distinguishing feature as he slumbered in his outgrown bassinet while Teresa downed whey protein shakes in the kitchen below to prepare for the next round. Nothing to place him in his own cozy taxon, other than the rubbery nub between his legs—which seemed of little consequence. Indeed, as has been noted elsewhere, the Freudian concept of penis envy has no empirical support. Nothing special could be discerned, no unique feature or capacity, other than the ability to ingest large amounts of Teresa's milk. Consequently, the Titmouse was of small interest. Yes, RR had a brother, but so what? Until one fall afternoon, about nine months after the boy's unremarkable birth. Usually, afternoons were relegated to playing "House," the Admirable Miranda's favorite game. However, "House" calls for a household, or a social unit of those living together in the same dwelling, and that p.m. the AM was at a Brownie meeting. And while RR regularly performed the parts of both husband and baby for Miranda, alternating between the two in precocious recognition of the fact that these roles are interchangeable in a domestic system where "mother" is the center, she could not do it all. No choice therefore but to shuffle, purposelessly, from room to room. When, at the foot of the stairs, Mother Teresa's voice was heard, wafting down from the connubial sleeping quarters, afloat on the liquid notes of *Fi la nana, e mi bel fiol, dormi ben, e mi bel fiol,* an Italian version of the parental musical imperative to stop crying and to go to sleep. Indeed, endowed with an Italianate paternal heritage, in addition to the Polish Judaic maternal one, Teresa Tomaszewski Tomasino Ramee drew from a supply of folk songs, peasant traditions, primitive lore and village idiocies as seemingly abundant as her milk. Therefore, an old country lullaby of some kind always followed lactation, which in turn invariably triggered somnolence in the Titmouse. Which meant that Mother Teresa would be, for a brief period, available for play. So as soon as the Titmouse was fully insensate, a game of "House" or better yet, "Thing," could ensue.

Later, as a preteen fascinated by Greek mythology (a fascination coincident with immersion in the classically inspired world of C.S. Lewis), RR would learn that "Thing" was a ludic version of the myth of Proteus. But at present, it was simply a fun game. A fun game infrequently played, as the Admirable Miranda preferred "House." When the Admirable Miranda did consent to play, she always took the role of the "Master" who told the blob-like thing what form to take. However, because nothing was more enjoyable than the grip of the *Ding an sich,* the momentary loss of self in the loose leathery lurch of an elephant, or in the adhesive swipe of an anteater's tongue (a predilection which, along with the precocious capacity for abstraction demonstrated in "House," would later serve well in the sciences as, for example, the concept of osmosis was mastered by imagining an ion, awash in an influx of cellular fluid), that was just dandy. Just dandy, especially since Mother Teresa, with Miranda gone, was now bound to issue the necessary ontological edicts. Yes, and so soon a person would be caught in whatever nominal net her mother chose to cast—although the preference was for a kitten. On little cat paws, therefore, the door was approached, the breath light and through the mouth, the body tensed to pitch itself at Teresa's feet, a quivering ball awaiting the command to "be."

At the threshold of the bedroom, a standstill was reached. Mother Teresa, seated on the chenille bedspread, her back to the hallway and the Titmouse in her arms, continued to sing: *Dormi ben, e mi bel fiol, dormi ben, e mi fiol.* The Titmouse, however, was not only resisting the imperative to sleep soundly—he was refusing to sleep at all. He stared over Teresa's shoulder, his blue eyes softly luminous in the shade-dimmed room and not unlike the glow-in-the-dark numerals of the Bakelite alarm clock that summoned Raymond each morning to another round of commerce at Ramee's Carpet Emporium. Clearly, however, that lambent gaze, unlike the alarm clock, drew upon no internally supplied energy source; clearly it was only a mirror playing back the solar rays that spilled through the window out in the hallway. Yes, undoubtedly the light emanating from his eyes was derived from outside and yet, nevertheless, it seemed to come from within. So that it felt strangely compelling, like a silent command. Yes, his gaze felt akin to a silent command, even though surely it must have been out of focus, the Titmouse in a lactose induced stupor after his recent feeding. Then again, it is conceivable that his gaze felt mutely mandatory precisely because it was out of focus, because it sidestepped rather than addressed a person, surrounding her in the diffuse net of the decentralized decree. But regardless of the source of the authority of that gaze, what is certain is that it compelled a person to do something...or be something...only what? Bathed in blue, RR stood in the doorway, brain churning out one image after another—a fuzzy wuzzy bear, warm milk, a bright red rattle—but nothing congealed and finally all that could be seen was blackness, a soft blackness that lapped lightly at the skin like a multitude of light slippery tongues, lapped lightly yet insistently, pulling the self down, pulling it under, until finally comprehension came: the Titmouse didn't want a person "to be," but "not to be."

Which was out of the question. Out of the question because it was outside the parameters of the imagination. Any*thing* was possible—but not nothing, without contours or coordinates. Despite a precocious capacity for abstraction, a person could not, finally, go to the place where there was no sight, no smell, no taste, no texture to seize, no form to inhabit. Anything was possible, absolutely. But not no thing at all. Therefore, urination ensued. Or to draw, for the sake of greater historical veracity, on the preliterate diction employed by the young RR—"peeing." Eyes squeezed shut, the young RR peed, the fulsome distillation of the two cups of cherry Kool-Aid consumed at lunch steaming down the inside of the pants, splattering the threshold. And there, hearing that autogenous splatter, feeling the warm leg-defining mold of wet corduroy, smelling the fruity ammonia of *her* tinkle, RR soaked up *her self*. Soaked up *her self* until the self spilled over the self, floating in a surplus of being. Yes, so that when the Titmouse began to whimper, it was as if a person was lying back in the bathtub down the hall, listening to the feeble puling of a kitten outside the door, only a person couldn't hold *her* breath forever. Soon she would have to come up for air and the kitten would become a cat, a big scabrous tom like Smokey. With claws which could dig into the flesh like the nails of Teresa, who was shaking the shoulder with one hand as the other balanced the blanket-wrapped Titmouse on her hip and her lips hissed, "Rosemarie, aren't you ashamed?" No attempt to explain was made as the Titmouse hid his face, burying it in the folds of soft wool. Because he was biding his time.

Yes, he was biding his time, like Smokey under the porch peering through the latticework at the robins in the flower-beds, calculating the exact moment to pounce. In contrast to Smokey, however, the Titmouse did not seem to be watching. No, he never looked at RR nor spoke to RR—directing his first primitive speech acts at Teresa, Raymond and the Admirable Miranda, who in an uncharacteristically analytical mode, spent hours helping him to identify and categorize his body parts (e.g. "Is that your nose? Yes, it's *your* nose! Is that your ear? Yes, it's *your* ear!"). Indeed, he directed his attention to all but RR, to other family members, friends, neighbors and even strangers, so that Teresa wrote in her yearly holiday missive, four years after the Titmouse's birth, "he captivates everyone." Everyone but RR, of whose existence he simulated total ignorance. Until one morning shortly after his fifth birthday he was discovered mutely screaming on his bed, swinging his leg, to which Smokey clung as if the leg were a tree limb and the floor below the bedrock of a canyon. Without premeditation, the tomcat was seized by the nape and as he retracted his claws, flung into the hallway. Afterwards in the bathroom, as the Titmouse's punc-tured calf was dabbed with hydrogen peroxide soaked gauze, he'd looked up, his blue eyes wide as tripped traps beneath the springy brown tendrils of his hair, and said, "Thanks RO, you're my heRO."

As evidenced above, following the Smokey incident the Titmouse's full attention was now had. Now, when RR entered a room his gaze would always envelop RR, a softly bright blue pod that held a person, probed a person with a frequency that could not be evaded. And as evasion was impossible, submission was complete. Yes, complete, however laughable that may seem. For while the humanist views the world through a wider, fuzzier lens than the scientist, it is possible that this is all too preposterous even for you, Ms. Wall. Admittedly, it strains belief to the breaking point first to propose that RR was not a monster or a sociopath, but a rational being with whom it is possible to empathize, and then to claim that RR was under the emotional control of the Titmouse. The Titmouse, who after the Smokey incident, which he claimed was precipitated by the cat's "hanky panky" with his "blankey," was now fondly called "Tom Tom." Further, this account of Tom Tom's uncanny influence over yours truly could also be seen as an attempt to establish a defense based on psychoanalytic theory. That is, to lay a foundation for the claim that these early experiences with a younger male sibling (whether fact or fantasy) rendered the subject susceptible later on to juvenile males of a similar type. Yes, a psychoanalytic defense could be seen as the subject's object here, even though as already indicated, there is little faith in psychoanalytic theory. For faith is what is required, given the lack of empirical evidence for said theory. In fact, scientific as well as personal misgivings were suppressed before divulging the above, as it stinks of the confidences released on the analyst's couch. At the same time, however, to leave that formative scene out would be to render the report less complete, and in the end, less scientific. Responsible science does not throw out the data that does not fit the paradigm; rather, if necessary, it seeks a new paradigm to fit the data.

Which is not to imply that a new paradigm will be sought—this is only a report. Only a report, reporting that RR once had a brother, Tom Tom, with whom what is called "a close relationship" was had. Indeed, in the words of Mother Teresa, RR and Tom Tom had become "partners in crime," an interesting phrase as it suggests a felonious strand in the admittedly intense sibling bond, some illicit filament in the socially ratified tie between brother and sister. For the record, there was not. There was not, although as Teresa correctly surmised, that socially ratified tie was secretly tightened by the siblings' new indifference toward her. An indifference that Teresa viewed as illegal in the sense that it violated so called "natural law." Didn't children instinctually and unconditionally adore their mothers, and vice versa? Adoration of one's mother, according to Teresa, was as simple and unassailable as the affinity of pasta for meat sauce, although as Tom Tom, a lacto-vegetarian since infancy, pointed out, he preferred his plain: "no red on my bed, Mom," he'd say, holding his hands over his bowl of linguine. Indeed, while Teresa Tomasino Ramee's meat sauce had many adherents (Raymond jested that he had married her for it), for a younger tongue with denser concentrations of protein receptors per taste bud, it was too much. As Teresa herself had become. Despite a full recovery (according to the GP) from the weeping depression that had followed the cessation of suckling, she remained emotionally incontinent. There were, for instance, inexplicable episodes of bliss, which though generally anchored in objective physical phenomena (unlike hallucinations), nevertheless seemed disproportionate to them (e.g. "See the dew drops trembling on the spider's web: it makes my heart ache with pleasure").

But this report is once again digressing. Questions as to whether RR and Tom Tom behaved feloniously, and if so, whether Teresa's emotional excesses justified their "crime," lie outside its scope. What is admissible is that the siblings now shared everything, with the exceptions of the favorite books, *The Chronicles of Narnia*, which Tom Tom rather precociously referred to as "The Chronicles of Narcolepsy," and of the Narnia-inspired practice of standing in the hall closet amongst Teresa's extensive coat collection, a practice Tom Tom simply called "nuts." Which it probably was, a form of self-medication as well as an imaginary journey into another world as the sensation of wool and fur brushing over the skin provided relief from scholastic pressure, that although self-imposed was nevertheless, at times, felt. Aside from C.S. Lewis and the closet, however, everything else was now shared, including the western saddle of the mechanical Appaloosa in front of the A&P, which when fed with a quarter in change would provide six stimulating minutes of cowboy-style transport.

Yes, everything was now shared, and not only positive experiences such as supermarket pony rides, but negative ones as well. Indeed, affiliation often served to make less positive experiences more positive. Less positive experiences that became more positive through mutual participation included the series of drawing lessons taken with Mrs. Parshikov, an elderly, half-blind Russian émigré who supplemented her exiguous income by offering full classical instruction to the Hudson half-pints. Full classical instruction, and more appealingly, according to the calligraphic advertisement on the community board at the A&P, the opportunity to "Discover Your Self." However, Mrs. Parshikov's ego-directed invitation (with which she had no doubt hoped to appeal to American individualism and the Me Generation) notwithstanding, the lessons turned out to be exercises in ego abnegation as they were dedicated to the penciled replication of flower pots and twelve-inch wooden mannequins reminiscent of the jointed block inserts used by Raymond to preserve the form of his dress shoes. The only deterrent to terminating the lessons was the desire to avoid maternal reproach ("I give you children everything and you just throw it away. When I was your age, I would have traded every hair on my head for such training"). Fortunately, just as said reproach was beginning to seem preferable to another week of Parshikov's "instruction," Tom Tom, claiming that he too would like to "doodle with the old poodle," attended a lesson, during which he proceeded to combine the flower pots and mannequins in unlikely and even unseemly arrangements (e.g. in one drawing the mannequins appeared to be using the pots to defecate; in another, two mannequins were inverted in a single pot, artistically embellished pelvises and lower limbs sprouting into the air). At the end of the hour, Mrs. Parshikov served black twizzlers and tea. Employing a strip of licorice as a pointer, she proceeded to evaluate Tom Tom's representations, commenting on the foreshortening where there was none, recommending straight lines instead of squiggly ones for what she took to be cross-hatching, but was in fact a patch of pubic hair, as in the meantime the giggling siblings tried not to asphyxiate on Earl Grey.

Yes, affiliation served to make less positive experiences more positive, another, perhaps stronger case in point being the episode of the head in the paper bag. This occurred in the twelfth year during a family excursion to a small ski area in the Catskills. For the record, it should be noted that this "family" excursion did not include Teresa, whose post-lacteal depression had been succeeded over the years by other depressions—post-educational, for example, when her attempt to earn a bachelors degree in art history from the state university ended in a screaming fight with a professor, and post-sartorial, when her career as a "couture" dressmaker to Hudson's smart set was terminated by a tremor in her hand. Subsequent medical evaluation of the tremor and other symptoms including a general feeling of malaise, joint pain, heart arrhythmia, swelling of the lymph nodes and protein in the urine (although not the famous "butterfly" rash across the cheekbones), had recently led to a diagnosis of systemic lupus erythematosus, a diagnosis that, given the association of SLE with CNS damage and psychosis, may also account for the screaming fight with the art history professor, in addition to other instances of emotional volatility.

Sans Mother Teresa, who had remained at home due to a lupus "flare-up," the incomplete family group arrived at the small, back-country ski area at midmorning. By midafternoon, after four continuous hours of skiing, Miranda and Raymond were still out on the slopes. RR and Tom Tom, however, having ascended and descended all four hills, from the "beginners" to the "expert," as well as examined the amusements in the lodge (a pinball machine and an air hockey table), had exchanged their ski boots for rubber soled mukluks and set off down the snow paved road toward a boarded-up farmhouse spotted earlier on the approach to the back-country ski area.

Although the windows were obstructed with gray splintered planks, the door of the boarded-up farmhouse was unencumbered and opened when force was applied. Inside, random chinks of light fell upon the white chipped paint of an iron bedstead, upon a rusted coil protruding from an imploded mattress, upon the broken spindles of a capsized rocking chair, upon the faded print of a stack of newspapers, upon the shredded lace paneling of a large elastic girdle, which lay on the floor beside the bed—suggesting years of desuetude. Yes, years of desuetude were implied, not only by these illuminations but also by the odors suspended in the cold, close air, the odors of dust and mildewed newsprint and the faint but unmistakable olfactory signature of urine. Who had lived here and where had they gone? Why hadn't they taken their furniture with them, or for that matter, their undergarment? Possibly someone had murdered someone, only no evidence of violence (e.g. rusty splatters of oxidized blood, bullet-sized holes) could be seen. No, more plausibly, some bucolic contagion had crawled forth from a pail of warm milk carried in one morning from the barn. Which would make a gastrointestinal tract infested with *Salmonella typhosa*, ensuing multiple trips to the outhouse, and finally a collapse in the snow on a subzero night, almost inevitable. Or maybe the infectious agent had been *Bacillus anthracis*, whose dormant spores surely remained, waiting to hatch in the lungs of the unwitting intruder (as described in Teresa's *Modern Family Health Guide*, which had been read from cover to cover). Just as a resolution was forming to exit the farmhouse, however, Tom Tom walked over to the girdle, stepped into it and pulled it up over his ski pants. As he held the undergarment up and out with one hand while using his incisors to pull the nylon mitten off the other, he demonstrated a circumference of fabric at least four times the circumference of his hips, a ludicrous ratio which served to instantly eliminate all septic imaginings.

"Wow, the lady must've been a cow," Tom Tom stated, as he shook off his second mitten.

This was concurred, although an equine figuration would do equally well, for of course she also could've been a horse.

Now holding out the girdle with both arms outstretched, Tom Tom nodded, the brown helixes of his curls bouncing, down at the expanse: "Why doncha get in and we'll go for a spin?"

Why not? Additional gloves were removed and tossed on the bed, for what harm could there be in two siblings finding amusement in a plus-sized woman's undergarment? Which they did, first stretching the girdle this way and then that way, as one leaned back and then the other, suspended by that serendipitous elastic, and then one reached for the other's bared hands and they started spinning each other round and round, splinters of light stippling faces faster and faster round and round like a centrifuge stirring the piss tainted air round and round so fast so fast that the head felt like a planet about to fly off its axis so fast so fast that mind seemed to be separating from matter because to spin like this together was surely impossible, yes impossible, and so finally one tilted or maybe it was the other toward the bed where they collapsed in a pile.

The siblings lay there, throbbing chest to throbbing chest, due to their clasped hands and the trajectory of their two bodies as they had fallen onto the mattress (fortunately avoiding the protruding spring). Yes, they lay there and it is possible that they lay there for some time, throbbing chest to throbbing chest, bound by a vertigo that made it not only difficult but unadvisable to suddenly sit up or even pull apart. Further, it is possible that both siblings fell asleep, with one sibling's warm moist breath ever so lightly rustling the hair surrounding the other's ear and even his or her saliva slicking the other's temple. For young bodies and brains require restoration after intense stimulation.

At any rate, clearly one sibling had fallen asleep, as evidenced by his shallow respiration and fluttering eyelids. What to do until he regained consciousness? The gaze fell upon the newspapers in the corner. They would be marked with dates that could in turn indicate when the farmhouse had been last inhabited—information that had no application, but nevertheless would be interesting to discover. Hence, the other sibling extricated herself from the girdle.

With numbed hands (the gloves remaining pinned beneath Tom Tom), several newspapers were gathered from the top of the stack, the capsized rocking chair righted. It turned out that all four of the newspapers from the top of the stack bore dates from the winter of 1965, coincidentally the season and year of Tom Tom's birth, and thus it could be inferred that the farmhouse had been occupied at this time. From the headlines— BACK ALLEY BARBECUE: WOMAN SEEKING ABORTION SOAKED IN GASOLINE AND BURNED ALIVE BY GANG. PASTOR'S SEX GUIDE FOR GIRLS BANNED. I CUT HER HEART OUT AND STOMPED ON IT. OLD GOAT CHASES KID SISTER. DEAD GIVEAWAY GETS MAN LIFE. MAN KILLS WIFE IN ROWHOUSE ROW. IT WAS IN THE BAG—additional inferences could be drawn about the tastes of the farmhouse's former tenants and their notions of newsworthiness. No conjectures were formed, however, critical distance having collapsed into pure curiosity. Said curiosity can be attributed in part to youthful naïveté: equating journalism with "just the facts," the immature RR assumed that the stories that followed from the headlines must be true. Further, residing in a household that subscribed to data based publications such as the *Albany Times Union* and *Newsweek*, RR was unacquainted with the form of empiricism that treats sensation as a source of knowledge and so was persuaded by the chill down the spine elicited, for instance, by the image of a woman in flames. Fortunately, this callow susceptibility to yellow journalism was eventually outgrown: no ocherous residue, so to speak, will be found on these pages.

At the time, however, titillation predominated: WHAT was in the bag? Beneath the headline was a grainy photo of an apparently soiled paper sack, but no text beneath. For this, it was necessary to turn to page eight, to a single column of print between advertisements for Four Star Roach Hotels and Ladies Knit Slacks at $2.00 a pair. In the dim light, a few lines of text were read, then read again. As it was ascertained that a head had been in the bag, the head of a Caucasian female in her late thirties, the stomach churned. Yes, and the stomach continued to churn as further perusal revealed that the head had been discovered by a twelve-year-old boy who had kicked the bag while walking home from school. A head in a paper bag as if it were a melon—a cantaloupe or a honeydew—only with eyes and a nose and a mouth and useless brains inside... And what had happened to the body? Where was it? Maybe in an abandoned house on a blood soaked mattress the shredded stump of neck still warm and oozing red fluid slippery as saliva. Slippery as saliva or upward-surging bile...

"Jeesum Crow, Ro, did you launch your lunch?"

Apparently roused by the racket of peristalsis, Tom Tom sat cross-legged on the bed. The newspaper, still folded to page eight and now splattered by gastric fluid, was delivered to him. He scanned the article, brown coils of hair flopping forward like antennae, then, having peered closely at the accompanying photo, set the paper down on the mattress. Blue eyes wide, he gazed up: "I don't get it. Maybe someone lost their head. So what? In the olden days it happened all the time."

Yes, so what? Maybe it was the absence of the usual word-play in Tom Tom's speech, surely a meaningful omission that expressed his sincerity, or maybe it was the manner in which he took the cold hands and pressed them between his own warm palms—at any rate, the lurid incident in the paper was no long-er important. What did it have to do with RR and Tom Tom, two siblings who were "partners in crime"—although there was nothing criminal in their relationship? No, there was nothing criminal in their relationship, only shared positive and negative experiences, the less positive ones such as the newspaper article about the severed head in the paper sack rendered more posi-tive through affiliation, so that afterward fraternal feeling was stronger than ever.

Therefore, RR and Tom Tom continued to be always to-gether, this close and constant association rendering positive ex-periences more so and negative ones less. Indeed as puberty was entered and social invitations, evoked by the copious growth of a head of lightly pigmented hair, as well as the more limited but nevertheless significant development of a pair of breasts, en-sued, fraternal affiliation eased the passage. For example, when the mass of bodies in the kitchen of a Hudson High classmate

whose parents had gone to Florida became too thick to penetrate, Tom Tom cleared the way to the keg by announcing that
some "kickass grass" was being "toked out back." Afterward, as
he had handed RR a foam-capped plastic cup of thin but highly
carbonated beer, the few remaining in the room had looked on
with admiration for both his ingenuity and its object: "Hey your
little brother's really cool and so are you."

Consequently, by the fourth year following menarche (which
had taken place in the thirteenth), RR and Tom Tom were
considered a permanent pairing, their combined presence the
necessary molecular ingredient, the requisite mojo, for the success of any underage social event or experiment. To be sure,
the term "permanent" should be understood in the context of
the adolescent sense of time as an infinite present (hence the
frequent appearance of the declaration "_____and_____4-
ever" in the metal stalls of public toilets). Then again, it was
reasonable to assume that the alliance with Tom Tom, given
its strength and utility, would endure. Yes it was reasonable to
assume that the alliance with Tom Tom would endure, unlike
the alliance with Laird Darlone, the heir of a chain of nursing
homes with whom RR had now been linked for six months.

Highly regarded for his familial assets, which in addition to
the aforementioned chain of nursing homes, included a Cadillac with a silver telephone, and excellent teeth (the whiteness of
which he accentuated with a perpetually sported strand of puka
shells), Laird Darlone had provided social status, as well as an
introduction to sexual intercourse. What he could not supply,
however, and would never supply, as corroborated by a recent
perusal of his score on the Stanford-Binet test while the staff in
the guidance counsel office was out to lunch, was intellectual

stimulation. When the score was related to Tom Tom, who had dubbed Laird "Lard," despite the latter's tightly muscled physique, he responded, "What did you expect? That puka-shelled palooka's got fat for brains."

Therefore, by the night of June 10th, 1979, a decision had been made to end the course (both "dis" and "inter") with Laird Darlone. College was approaching and despite four years of moderately high alcohol consumption combined with regular ingestion of illegal substances (procured by Laird, who maintained connections with illegal commerce not only in Hudson and Albany, but also in Manhattan and the four boroughs), scores in the hundredth percentile had been attained in all sections of the standard standardized tests—an achievement that had secured acceptance into the Life Sciences Program at Cornell University. Correction. Scores in the hundredth percentile had been attained in all sections but the math, where the total percentage achieved, although above average, was disappointingly low. Despite the tutelage of Tom Tom, whose comprehension of mathematical concepts, it must be admitted, exceeded RR's. Yes, because the former had tried to instill an understanding of infinity in the latter ("You just gotta go with the flow, Ro"), to no avail. So there—a deficiency has been acknowledged, in keeping with the strictly veridical nature of this report. To continue, given acceptance into the highly competitive Life Sciences Program at Cornell University, relatively low (although still above average) math score and all, the retention of a puka-shelled palooka for a boyfriend was no longer tenable. Tom Tom agreed. "Drop the prop," he'd said just two days before as they reclined in the grass behind the garage, sharing a handmade but cylindrical cigarette (fashioned by Tom Tom, who liked to keep his fingers dexterous for the rolling of "spliffs"). He then went on to pronounce Laird otiose: "we don't need his weed."

In fact, however, Tom Tom's pronouncement was premature, as Laird Darlone's assistance was required to fulfill a goal: to sample every controlled and uncontrolled substance available on the black market before college (for once at Cornell, academic success surely would require an unaltered consciousness). As of June 10th, 1979, in the basement recreation room of a Hudson High classmate, one item on the list of illegal substances remained uninvestigated, an item that that night Laird Darlone happened to possess: phencyclidine, the dissociative anesthetic known in popular idiom as Angel Dust.

If you were a medical doctor or researcher, and not a high school English teacher who implicitly condoned drug use (e.g., as you urged your students in AP English 12 to put works such as *On the Road* and *Naked Lunch* on their summer reading lists before college), you might ask why a person of high intelligence would ingest disabling psychotropic substances. Surely such a one would act in his or her own best interest, reason recognizing the need to maintain the integrity of the neurophysiology that supports reason. However, as demonstrated by the self-defeating decisions intelligent people make about money, as they blackjack away the family paycheck or squander their savings on investments touted by known swindlers, ratiocination is subject to and even subsumed by other mental phenomena. Yes, other mental phenomena come into play, variously referred to as caprice, whimsy, impulse, instinct and gut reaction, the last term suggesting the extracerebral regions from which these phenomena exert their influence, which is why, possibly, it is said that one who is under their sway has "lost his [or her] head."

To be sure, the aversion to acephalization was strong (as demonstrated above by the episode of the head in the bag); however the behavioral inheritance must also be taken in to account (as mentioned previously, Teresa was subject to irrational outbursts while Raymond had a little glue habit). Couple this behavioral inheritance with the fact that the incomplete development of the frontal lobes in the adolescent brain predisposes it to risk-taking behavior and the drug quest becomes plausible. Which is not, however, to excuse it. Nor for that matter, to condemn it. No, the objective here is simply to report the facts. While questions engendered by said facts may occasionally be explored, as at the beginning of this paragraph, no explicit powers of judgment have been given.

It is, however, admitted that scoring an additional hit of PCP that night from Laird Darlone for Tom Tom was a poor choice. Yes, a poor choice, but he was so insistent: "Ro, I lust for dust, just one hit." He was so insistent, his fingers locked around the wrist, his pupils dilated and brimming with exigency in the dim of the paneled basement recreation room. Thus, when Laird ascended the stairs and exited the kitchen door out to the street where his daddy's caddy was parked, he procured not just one powder pink tablet from the glove compartment but two. Yes, he procured not just one pink tablet, but two, although not three, as he still had a "delivery" to make on the other side of town. Sans Laird, the two tablets were ingested in the corner of the basement, the blue glow of a tropical fish aquarium washing over Tom Tom's face as he placed his on his tongue, washing in a fashion that could be described as prescient, only the pathetic fallacy is inconsistent with the strictly factual, non-sensationalistic nature of this story. Indeed, if this were not a strictly factual account, the course of events would be altered, imagination having free rein. Unfortunately, however, this is a factual account and therefore Tom Tom placed the pink pill on his tongue which he then withdrew into his mouth and then a few seconds later extended again so that the pill could now be seen half dissolved and reminiscent of the pink candy hearts children exchange on Valentine's Day. "Be mine," it might have said if it had not partially melted away and this was not a rigorously veridical record of events.

Twenty minutes were spent, crouched on the orange shag that carpeted the concrete floors of the recreation room from mahogany laminated wall to mahogany laminated wall, all sense receptors on the alert for the side effects of the phencyclidine. Just as Tom Tom pronounced "this dust is a bust," something began to unfurl in the lower back, as if a tangle of ganglia had suddenly unknotted, unknotted and dropped from the base of the spine onto the carpet, where it was now delicately probing the shag, readying to explore the world in all directions, via the vectors of its ever extending axons. In every direction, but the most compelling was towards Tom Tom, who was himself beginning to feel the drug, as evidenced by the fact that he now lay on his back, limbs radiating out from his torso like a starfish, reiterating the sentence "I'm afloat on a glass-bottom boat." Obviously his claim was false, being based on the hallucinatory sensations of floating and weightlessness that accompany the absorption of phencyclidine (sensations that he was no doubt trying to enhance when he later entered the pool).

At the time, however, his claim seemed truth based, as verified by personal experience. Yes, RR as well was afloat on a glass-bottom boat, afloat next to Tom Tom and hovering over the undulating fronds of a bed of orange kelp. Fingers slid flush between fingers then curved, pulling the pads of palms together to form a flesh cup which something, it must have been his thumb, explored like a minnow nuzzling a vacant bivalve. Hand in hand, two bodies drifted on the dark laminated waters and initially it didn't matter where—all that mattered was that soft probe and the undulating orange below—until someone cranked up the stereo and Joe Walsh was wailing "couldn't get much higher" and of course they could because there was the sky above them and beyond the sky was the universe and beyond the universe were other universes all flying away from each other radiating out from an inconceivable origin to an inconceivable terminus like wall-to-wall carpeting ex nihilo and ad infinitum. Ex nihilo and ad infinitum, because how could something arise out of nothing and once it did how could it possibly end? Despite the above mentioned capacity for abstraction, it was impossible to conceptualize a limit without outer limits without positing another space beyond space and then another space beyond that space and another and another and another… Etcetera, etcetera, as the self floated further and further out to sea on its glass-bottom boat, floated dangerously and irrevocably adrift. Clearly it was time, so to speak, to jump ship—before Tom Tom went over the edge.

At this point the neuronal record grows faint, most probably due to the depressive effect of phencyclidine on the prefrontal cortex. Given the faintness of memory, would it be irresponsible to end here? Frankly, it is tempting to cut this chronicle of Tom Tom short, to proceed no further with a recollection that despite its lack of clarity, is still acutely painful. Indeed, if the intensity of anguish is taken into account, surely the emotional expenditure outstrips any factual gain. However, a commitment to full disclosure was made at the beginning, and therefore that commitment must be honored, no matter how unsatisfactory the result. No matter how unsatisfactory the result, which is discontinuous with the events preceding it, as there is no memory of the journey from the recreation room to the patio beside the swimming pool, where consciousness was roused by the strong odor of the chemicals used to sanitize the water, most probably a solution of ammonium chloride as the odor was not dissimilar to urine. There is no memory before this rude olfactory awakening, although it is likely that the journey to the pool was executed on hands and knees, a mode of transportation that would be in line with the impaired motor function associated with phencyclidine; however, this is purely speculation as there were no witnesses to departure (the observational capabilities of the others present—fifteen to twenty other adolescents—having been likewise disabled by the disassociative anesthetic, alcohol, or both). As there were no witnesses to departure, there is also no way to know if a purpose was expressed beforehand. Again, there is only speculation to fall back on; presumably Tom Tom's absence from the recreation room was noticed and therefore, despite the drug-induced fear of affiliation experienced earlier, the intent was to reunite with him. The intent was to reunite with him, but unfortunately now this was forever impossible. Forever impossible because he was floating facedown like a starfish or an angel, the fumes rising off the surface above him in the early morning air releasing an odor of ammonia of irreversible and profoundly regretted excretion.

2.a. Additional Background Information

RR had a brother, a fact that may or may not be pertinent in regard to the problem of the monster. Through the fractured gaze of the monster, a perspective compounded by error, both too much can be seen and too little. It is therefore impossible to determine, Ms. Wall, whether the events recorded above will be useful background in the final analysis. In all likelihood they will not; however, the record shall be retained on the principle that more information is generally better than less. As more information is generally better than less, an additional circumstance predating the events that unfolded in Germany will be related: there was a sexual partner, Mick Mackie, with whom regular intercourse had ceased several months before departure. As Mick possessed (and presumably still possesses) a wife and a son, the sexual relationship had been clandestine, occurring at opportune after-hours moments in the Sleep Wake Center at Weil Cornell in Manhattan, where RR had been employed before a transatlantic relocation to the *Schlafzentrum* of Mick's old friend and collaborator, Nils Wenzel, in Kiel. Of course whether the sexual relationship was a secret or known by every doctor, nurse, technician and service person at the hospital is almost certainly irrelevant in regard to this report; nevertheless the fact that it was illicit could no doubt be seen by some as further evidence of depravity (obviously not by you, Ms. Wall, who urged your students to read *Anna Karenina* and *Madame Bovary*, but by others, so please keep in mind that these pages are for your eyes only). Then again, if this were a defense or an apology, which it is not, but if it were, the illicit relationship with Mick Mackie could be counted in favor of RR, in that Mick Mackie was by no means a boy, which would in turn support the claim made in the preceding section of this report: that the relationship that began in Kiel was strictly circumstantial. In other words, there was no proclivity toward immature males prior to that meeting in Northern Germany. On the contrary, it could be stated that RR, although only thirty-something, had frequently ranged beyond peer limits to the forty- to fifty-year-old bracket, where an abundance of ready-to-go, if past-their-prime, partners could be found.

Which is not to imply that Mick was over the hill. No Mick, a sometime marathoner and frequent flyer to Rocky Mountain and West Coast road races, habitually ran in the under forty category, although forty-three-years-old. In fact Mick, if a bit stringy in the hamstrings due to the natural attenuation of muscle tissue with age, had the body of a much younger man: with his narrow runner's torso, unusually smooth skin (inherited, he claimed, from his Irish immigrant grandfather, who had been a career houseboy to Boston Brahmins), and bouncing, Adidas-bolstered step, it would be possible to mistake him for the older of his two sons. Or vice versa. Indeed, the son was mistaken for the father the first time Mick's office was entered, an error then compounded by the assumption that the teenage, or at most college age older son, who had stopped by for a brief visit, would be intimidated by the sudden appearance of a slender, relatively tall, dirty blond in a white lab coat and rocket red lipstick. As a result, RR was overly pleasant and solicitous to the son, which somehow led to dinner and a subsequent sexual relationship with the father, although a decision had been made prior to accepting the position at the Weil Cornell's Sleep-Wake Disorders Center not to sleep with colleagues, or at least not to wake up with them.

Yes, a sexual relationship was initiated, one that involved both "sleeping" with Mick Mackie, and also, to be accurate, regularly rising with him, as Mick would often insist on continuing the amorous activities begun late at night in the lab at four and five star hotels in midtown Manhattan, where additional postcoital diversion could be found in the tiny toiletries and trampoline-firm mattresses. And in the spirit of full disclosure, great pleasure was taken in these diversions, Kai Mackie's importunate paging of her spouse in the midst of them notwithstanding. Even now, a smile is permitted, as an image of RR and MM leaping from one queen-sized bed to the other, crisscrossing back and forth, back and forth, like two crazy chromosomes in the metaphase of cell division, until finally each collapsed, side by side, in a fit of giggling exhaustion, is recalled.

If only it could have stopped there. If only the relationship could have remained suspended between the poles of separation and commitment, in an indefinitely protracted state of fun. Or, given the fact that biological processes, once initiated, tend to go forward unless terminated by disease or other means, if only the lemon lime flavored prophylactic had been lubricated with Nonoxyl 9, despite the unpleasant taste and numbing sensation the latter would have imparted, then the opportunity in Kiel might have appeared less attractive.

As you know, Ms. Wall, having accompanied more than one female student to the Clinic in downtown Albany, the procedure is an outpatient one, an in-and-out operation the duration of which generally lasts no more than ten minutes. A simple extraction of a cluster of cells, a dime-a-dozen aggregation of protoplasm such as can be produced by any one of us possessing a uterus. Thus it is a mystery why afterward a breakdown occurred in the beige and oxygen-deprived baby blue post-op recovery room. Surely the cause cannot have been dismay over the décor (poster of adiposal puppies mixed with yellow posies or no), though RR was more sensitive than most to aesthetic stimuli, due to the maternal inheritance. Nor can it have been due simply to the smooth muscle contractions that rippled the pelvis with waves of pain, for while these were more intense than anticipated, they were recognized as a purely physiological and transitory response to the procedure. The smooth muscle contractions, while more painful than anticipated, were to be expected and thus their cessation could be expected as well. What had not been expected was the concurrent surge of sorrow, which seemed to find its correlate in the oscillations of pain within the womb but must be treated as an entirely separate phenomenon.

The procedure was undergone voluntarily, a choice supported by Mick who was, in fact, pro-choice. However, when first informed of the pregnancy, he had immediately committed himself to paternity, and, following a divorce from Kai, matrimony as well. It was only when it was added that an appointment had been made that he had endorsed, again without delay, the decision to terminate gestation. He was a good sport who had endorsed, but certainly not forced, the decision—on the contrary. Therefore it was irrational to be filled not only with sorrow, but also with rage: a rage directed specifically at blameless Mick.

A rage directed specifically at Mick Mackie, even as it became apparent that he was simply a subset of a larger category. Men. Yes, because when an attempt was made to mentally envision Mick Mackie, his individual features could not be recalled.

Or even the color of his eyes. Were they blue, or green, or some indeterminate shade such as hazel? What was instead seen was his outline—the jug ears, the angular jaw, the square shoulders and tapering torso—an outline both completely anonymous and unmistakably adult male, like the shape of a target at a shooting gallery. Therefore it was men, not Mick, who would have been cursed if the mouth had not been full of wadded sheet, which had been stuffed there to prevent the nurse on the other side of the curtain from inferring pain. "Fuck Men!" the mouth would have screamed, although this ejaculation would have signified exactly the opposite feeling. For what was felt was the desire *not* to fuck men—not to fuck men, ever again.[4]

So there you have it, Ms. Wall—additional information that may or may not be relevant to the resolution of the problem of the monster.

---

[4] Please excuse the "French," which here is indicative of emotional duress. Indeed, "it is rare to meet scientists using slang or colorful profanity. For women, in particular, to violate this rule is to risk being perceived as crude and outlandish." Further, the use of such language belies the "many years of postsecondary education" required to become a scientist and is therefore generally frowned upon (Ilene J. Busch-Vishniac, "Climbing the Ladder," *Success Strategies for Women in Science: A Portable Mentor*, ed. Pritchard, P.A. [Burlington, MA: Elsevier Academic Press, 2006], p.74.)

3. An Artificial Fruit Flavor Whose Intensity Surpassed the Original

While the events recounted above may have had a hand in the cultivation of the monster, she did not emerge until Kiel. Indeed if there had been no Kiel, there may have been no monster: quite possibly that teratological potential would have remained untapped. A potential, Ms. Wall, which was in no way manifest, not even in the disguised form of a studied indifference. For always relations with preadolescents of both sexes were perfectly friendly and appropriate as queries were made about computer games and favored television series with an interest that was unfeigned, if not unfading. Yes, interactions with prepubescent individuals were perfectly kosher as anyone could observe when the wife and younger son of Mick would drop by the Weil Cornell's Sleep-Wake Disorders Center. Always young Malcolm was treated with a humorous decorum, as he was examined about what he kept stowed in his cheeks, or about when he planned to grow himself a neck. The fact of the matter is that no monster was evident, to the self or to others, nor would she have become so if had not been for the encounter with a certain kinky haired contingency, in Kiel.

Further, that encounter might not have occurred had the bulk of the wardrobe, packed in three large boxes and sent from a post office in upper Manhattan in late August (in order to reduce the load of baggage checked in on the flight from JFK to Hamburg three weeks later), not been lost in transit. Or stolen. For petty theft is frequent in the former Bundesrepublik, a phenomenon which perhaps can be traced to expectations cultivated by the welfare state and the subsequent disappointment of those expectations following reunification: i.e., having failed to receive what they consider their own, certain persons proceed to find commensurate substitutes. But of course that is pure speculation and thus out of place in this strictly factual account. What is certain is that RR arrived in Kiel via the airport shuttle from Hamburg with only a small suitcase of warm weather wear. And as the cold drizzly days typical of the Baltic fall went by, it became evident that heavier clothing would have to be purchased. Because RR enjoyed making sartorial selections, an activity that gratified the artistic side of the temperament, the task at first seemed a painless, even pleasant one. However, because RR, though 5'6 1/2" (almost tall enough to be a model), was smaller in stature than the average northern German woman (whose gargantuan proportions can perhaps be attributed to both the weight of history, Schleswig-Holstein having once belonged to the Great Danes, and a diet heavy in proteins and fat), finding attractive articles in suitable sizes proved difficult. The only solution was to buy the smallest possible examples of the extra large German clothing, and then to take these to the tailor shop, or *Schneiderei*, for alterations.

The *Schneiderei* is where RR was headed, having received the afternoon off from Wenzel and the *Schlafzentrum*, on Friday, November 5th, 1999. That date constitutes a fact. It is also a fact that it was a beautiful afternoon, the sky a supersaturated blue, as the descending sun deepened the tint of the red brick façades and kindled the leaves strewn over the cobbles into a conflagration of yellow. A beautiful, brilliantly lit afternoon soon to scatter into darkness but which was at present on the very verge of that dehiscence, bursting without yet having broken, swollen with a potential as yet unfulfilled. Strolling on this beautiful afternoon to the *Schneiderei*, which was on Holtenauerstrasse, the dress recently purchased during a weekend in Berlin to be altered for a cocktail party at Nils Wenzel's three weekends in the future stowed in a canvas bag slung over the shoulder, the aforementioned luminous effects of the late day sun (although it was not 4:00 p.m.), effects that have, alas, no equivalent in the United States or Northern Cyprus due to latitudinal restrictions, were enjoyed. Hence the blunder into the *Fahrradweg*, into the trajectory of an oncoming cyclist.

A bell rang and a voice barked "*VORSICHT!*"; however, only as a small, unidentified flying object struck the sternum did RR stagger back. Thus avoiding the collision that almost certainly would have occurred given the speed, weight and certitude of the cyclist, an enormous, trench coated brunette who shouted "*keine Fussgänger!*" over her shoulder as she pedaled past. Swaying, the object, which was no longer flying but stationary on the ground, was surveyed: a sodden looking brown paper wrapped package from which ascended a strong odor of onions and grilled lamb. Though a head injury had been prevented by the projection of the brown paper package, an observer might have concluded, from the stunned demeanor, that one had been sustained.

"*Sind Sie okay?*"

The gaze lifted from the sidewalk to a face just below eye level.

"*Fühlen Sie sich nicht wohl?*"

He was wearing mirrored sunglasses, two small blue-black discs in which the figure of a woman was reflected, twice. Twice, as all the German absorbed in high school and college, and finally employed during the last seven weeks in Kiel, seemed to have drained from the brain. To have drained from the brain, which was a partial rhyme, even as the words floating up from the boy's full lips were as empty as bubbles. Empty as bubbles, which allowed concentration on his face, a face that with its full lips, long high-bridged nose, and strong but rounded chin recalled ancient Greek or Roman statuary. Yes, his was a face that belonged to another epoch, a historical period long past and seemingly irretrievable, submerged in the depths of time; nevertheless, here it was—as positively viable as a rat crawling through a landfill, scanning the debris with a pair of shiny black and inscrutable eyes. As the lips of his long past yet positively viable face continued to move, his hand reached up and began to pull at the hair that framed it, as if to rake out even further the already extant brown aureole of frizz.[5]

"Sind Sie krank?"

What?

"Krankheit?"

Did someone come from France? Yes, it was possible, given a French Canadian paternal inheritance, that there was a Gallic cast to the features that, combined with the blond coloration derived from the Polish side of the maternal inheritance, re-called the young Catherine Deneuve. Unfortunately, however, the reality was as American as Doris Day.

"Ah, a Yank! Are you okay, miss?"

Suddenly he was speaking in a British accent—or, more spe-cifically, a lower class English or Cockney accent known from cinematic experience (e.g., *Sammy and Rosie Get Laid*), if not em-pirical. Yes, the accent was familiar, the language even more

---

[5] It takes anywhere from 6 to 60 seconds for one person to form a first im-pression of another. The most commonly cited time is 30 seconds.

so; therefore, this time the meaning of his words was clear. Yet now the situation was even more incomprehensible than before. For the sounds did not follow from the lips—they were as incongruous as a trophy for the World Cup emerging from the excavation of Pompeii. Finally, there was a fundamental expressive disjunction, a glaring tonal anachronism, although it is by no means certain the boy's classical good looks would have been better served by ancient Latin. But what would be a more appropriate vocal style? It was impossible to say. It was impossible to say and in the meantime the boy was waiting for an answer. And in truth, the answer was yes.

With his hands on his slim cargo pants-clad hips, he tilted his chin up so that his mirrored lenses reflected only the forehead against a background of bricks. Then he dropped it and they reflected only the breasts. "Are you sure, Miss?"

Well, it would not be unreasonable, given the circumstances, to claim a slight injury, or at the very least, discomposure and the need for an escort. But that would be erroneous. So once again, wellness was affirmed.

"Shiny and bright then."

Evidently the expression was some type of valediction as the boy then sauntered away, crossing the now deserted bike path to a bicycle propped against the front end of a car parked curbside. Slinging his leg over the crossbar, he looked back over the tops of his mirrored lenses—a sudden slash of green. "The Uncle Sam sarnie is yours, ducky. Set your pegs straight, it will."

The referent of "Uncle Sam sarnie" seemed to be the oily packet, which had been retained. Unwrapping the brown paper revealed a grilled lamb kebab, which was consumed on the remainder of the route to the tailor's, the last bit of grease licked from the fingers while standing beneath the yellow awning advertising "*Schneiderei*." It had been an episode of serendipitous nourishment (as a long morning at the *Schlafzentrum* and then an empty larder back at the rooms had precluded both breakfast and lunch). To be sure, skipping both meals altogether would have been feasible, given a well-developed ability to suppress the appetite. It may have even been healthy, as studies have shown that lab rats forced to fast every other day live 30 percent longer than those who are supplied with regular meals. Then again, the brain and other organs work best when provided with a steady supply of glucose, and certainly an optimum cerebral capacity would be required at the tailor shop.

Because the proprietor, Herr Mart, would attempt to decapacitate with a disorienting cloud of compliments mingled with the smoke of the little brown cigarillos he smoked as he performed the alterations. In fact, when RR had stopped the previous week to pick up a skirt he'd scaled down (a biaxial reduction being necessary in the case of all clothes purchased in Kiel, due to their elephantine proportions), his flattery had been almost overwhelming. Almost, as he'd attempted to overcome RR with compliments not only about the physical appearance, but about the professional accomplishments, which he claimed to have a grasp of, having acquired one year of medical education "before the war divided my country and drove my family into exile." No inquiry had been made about which war, or even which country, as this would have encouraged confidences and thus fostered familiarity. Nevertheless, there had been something appealing about the man, whose relatively small stature (for an adult male) had allowed for the level flow of his gaze (which was a buoyant blue-green that later would be recognized as akin to the color of the Mediterranean) as he claimed that "brains" were "beauty's best asset." It had not been effortless to pull away, and further the odor of the cigarillos, later discovered clinging to the altered skirt, was not unpleasant.

"Ah, it is the lovely Frau Doktor. Welcome."

Herr Mart had sprung up from behind the counter the moment the high pitched bell rigged to the door signaled entrance, and now he stepped around it, transferring the cigarillo between his fingers to his lips so that he could take the hand in both of his. Given that the late afternoon light shone through the display window directly into his eyes, it was not entirely certain, despite his greeting, that he recognized RR. Indeed, possibly he was confusing RR with someone else: this would explain the inappropriate degree of pressure applied by his palms. Yes, the pressure was inappropriate and further, his blue-green eyes were bloodshot and appeared less vivid than before. So that even if he was not confusing RR with someone else, clearly it had been a mistake to bring additional clothing in for alterations—there were other *Schneiderein* in Kiel. There were other tailor shops in the city but then a person was already at this one, and further, could continue on down Holtenauerstrasse to the gourmet market afterward, perhaps stopping on the way at that little café for a sliver of cake, since the kebab had not been overlarge. No, the kebab had not been filling and further, the café provided window seats with an excellent view of all passing pedestrians and bicyclists. Therefore, as Herr Mart inclined his head over the hand, presumably with the intention to kiss it, an angle that permitted the setting sun to highlight his all too visible scalp, a resolution was made to complete the transaction. Pronto. The fingers were retracted, the dress drawn from the canvas shopping bag. As the fabric, an attractive midnight blue merino wool threaded with silver, was gathered up before the torso, the dress was demonstrated to be both too wide and too long.

Herr Mart stepped back, the red tip of the cigarillo between his lips perceptibly growing. Just as the ember was about to drop to the carpet, he flicked it into a paper cup inscribed with the legend *"Kıbrıs Kebabs—Sind das Beste"* on the counter behind him. "Yes, that is because you possess a thin American physique. I can fix this but first you must try it."

The dress, although over-large and relatively elastic, could not simply be slipped over the head due to the fact that the waist was too narrow to accommodate the shoulders. To try it on, it was necessary to free from their loops the long row of small buttons extending from the neckline to the groin. Each button had to be pried from its tight circlet of fabric, and further, reinserted before it would be safe to step through the curtain of the changing room back into the shop since Herr Mart would probably interpret any uncommitted buttons in his favor. Given the size, number and symbolic value of the buttons, at least ten minutes elapsed before emergence was advisable.

Herr Mart had vanished. It appeared, however, that his return was imminent: a small table and two chairs had been placed in front of the counter, the blinds drawn and the *GE-SCHLOSSEN* sign hanging on the back of the glass-paned door reversed so that *GEÖFFNET* faced inside. On the table sat a metal espresso pot, from which arose the scent of strong, hot coffee, two miniature ceramic mugs, and a small metal tray of pink, pale yellow and apple green candies crowned with slivers of almond. The pastel colors of the candies were reminiscent of Easter Sunday, a holiday whose iconography had always seemed perplexing—how to reconcile the consumption of large amounts of refined sugar (which Teresa had on this occasion permitted) with the puncture wounds of the dying Christ? With the aid of hindsight, a person might also have asked how to reconcile this cloying scene of seduction in the tailor's shop with self-crucifixion on the cross of an irresistible desire. Unfortunately, however, hindsight was not available at the time. Lacking the benefit of retrospection and further, feeling a little shaky, RR took the chair that faced away from the door. Clearly, blood glucose had again dropped to a level where refreshment was appealing. Why not linger for a little elevation, because while large amounts of refined sugar are detrimental,[6] as well as unappealing, small amounts can provide a temporary lift with no long-term ill effects? Yes, for while Herr Mart's sea green eyes appeared less vivid than before, surely their buoyancy remained. Indeed, as he'd regarded the display of the dress their buoyancy had been evident, a lightsome sparkle which could now help to make up for a strange sense of letdown—a sense of letdown only recently recognized as such.

Yes, there was a sense of letdown, a feeling of deflation that caused a sagging in the chair despite the arousing aroma of the coffee. And further, this sensation had grown acute since the incident on the bicycle path. Possibly it stemmed from the kebab; if the mood was less upbeat than usual, maybe a mild case of food poisoning was to blame. Or the low mood could be symptomatic of insufficient sleep, for not only had the morning

---

[6] Although the body needs moderate amounts of sugar to metabolize for energy, cells can only handle so much. Excess sugar builds up outside cells where it reacts injuriously with the protein fiber network that gives skin its youthful resilience. The harmful waste products from that reaction, dubbed "Advanced Glycosylation End-products," live up to their acronym—AGE.

been spent assessing data, but half the night had been given to monitoring the instruments that gathered it, after the technician had failed to report for duty. No doubt a cup or two of strong coffee would prove uplifting. Just as the handle of the pot was grasped, however, Herr Mart stepped through the curtain that closed off the back of the shop, grasping a long necked bottle containing a clear liquid.

"Perhaps you do not drink," he said as he set the bottle on the table next to the espresso. "Although it is my observation that many American and also British women will take a glass, unlike Turkish and Cypriot ones who are afraid to behave as men. American women are not afraid to behave as men because they know they appear to be women, in whose presence a man is likely to find his tongue tied. Hence, even if you do not take a glass you must please allow me to take one, so that my tongue does not become tied."

As alcohol is a depressant and elevation was sought, "a glass" was declined and a cup of coffee requested instead.

"As I informed you last week, you must call me 'Samert,' spelled out S-A-M-E-R-T, but pronounced saMAHT. Or better yet, to make ease for your thin American lips, 'Sam.'" With the metal pot he filled the cup, the small capacity of which recalled the games of "House" played with the Admirable Miranda. Indeed, it is likely that the recollection of this early ludic pursuit and the role-playing it had required led to acquiescence. Within the parameters of the game, pet names such as "Honey" and "Pumpkin" had naturally displaced proper ones, and therefore the substitution of Sam for Samert was concurred with.

"Good, we are agreed. And I in turn shall call you 'Songül,' a lovely name that expresses the Turkish word for 'rose'—that is, 'gül.'"

Songül. More sensitive to the sounds of words than most, especially for a scientist, RR could not help but be put off. There was a glutinous quality to the name as a whole, reminiscent of overcooked vegetables, a flaccidness and also an adhesive cling to the second syllable that left a kind of glistening slime in the ear. RR could not help but be put off by the leguminous ring of Songül or by the languishing gaze of "Sam," who was now holding out the tray of pastel candy. Clearly it was time for extrication, coffee or no, because the situation was becoming sticky. On the other hand, the scent of the candy wafting from the tray—which was of almonds and oranges, as well as something flowery, perhaps rosewater, a term that just then popped into the head though no previous encounter with rosewater could be recalled—the scent of the candy wafting from the tray had activated the salivary glands.

The piece chosen was a pale pink, and upon ingestion, less flavorful than anticipated. The confection tasted predominately of sugar, a taste that in conjunction with the expression of inane anticipation on "Sam's" face was more than a little insipid. Returning to his establishment had been a mistake.

"You like it? This sweet comes from Paphos, the mythical birthplace of the goddess Aphrodite on the island of Cyprus, where our family resided for many centuries before the country was rent apart by the machinations of Greek priests. It is assembled by my mother and is said to have aphrodisiac properties for the reason that the recipe was created by Aphrodite herself. Obviously this is an unlikely story sustained by gullible peasants. Still you must admit the legend possesses, like an aging coquette, a certain faded charm."

As Samert undoubtedly supposed that he too possessed—although he probably did not view himself as faded. No, despite the bald spot capping his skull like the negation of a child's beanie, clearly visible as he bent to refill the small cup, which had been drained during his discourse on the candy, he did not view himself as past his sexual prime. No, "Sam" did not see himself as past his prime because although it is common knowledge that conception need not accompany coital pleasure and vice versa (knowledge that dates at least as far back as the Greeks), the perceived desirability of the senescent human male is clearly a function of his continued procreative capacity. Obviously Samert saw himself as a contender: this was evident not only in the arch tone in which he had uttered his speech, but also in the self-satisfied smile on his face when it was politely assented that the candy was palatable.

No mention was made, however, of the fact that the nearly unadulterated sucrose, together with the caffeine from the coffee, would expedite not only egress from Samert's shop but also ambulation to the bookstore five blocks away (the need to stop for a slice of cake having been obviated by the candy). The bookstore was an establishment there'd been no time to explore up until now, all leisure hours having been consumed in the procurement of a new wardrobe. Surely at least one shelf of work in English would be found, from which a fat novel could be plucked, for while work in the sleep lab was engaging, it was not, for the most part, transporting. Ideally that fat novel would be a translation of one of the nineteenth-century Russians, for whom a taste was first gained in your English 12 class. As you put it, "Why travel to other planets when you can visit other minds?" And indeed, in *Crime and Punishment*, foreign terrain had been visited and, further, returned from safely. That being the beauty of the bookish experience. To quote you again, "Literature allows us to know what it is like to give birth or to kill someone, without having to pay the price. After all, a life sentence cannot last beyond the final page." Yes, hopefully a work by Dostoevsky would be found, the Russian writer who demonstrates so beautifully the way emotional arousal frequently prevails over rational thought—a work to succumb to all evening and then put down when it was time to go to sleep. But if there was nothing by Dostoevsky, well then a tawdry psychodrama by Barbara Vine or Patricia Highsmith would do, in which entertainment, if not theoretical vindication, could be found while curled up for a few hours on the IKEA sofa in the spare but comfortable quarters provided by Wenzel's institute. And finally, lacking Vine or Highsmith, there were always the newspapers at the kiosk further down the street: the British *Guardian*, or better yet, the *International Herald Tribune*, which culled the most important stories from the *New York Times* and the *Washington Post*. Therefore, as Samert sat down opposite RR and proceeded to pour the clear liquor from the long-necked bottle into a narrow glass of ice, words were uttered to facilitate departure and the commencement of a temporary, fictional escape from Kiel.

The liquor had turned a cloudy white. Samert picked up one of the miniature coffee spoons and stirred it, the metal clinking against the glass. Although there was no ostensible evidence that he was staring, the eyes being fixed on the surface of the table, his gaze was felt.

"Alas—I had hoped for an enjoyable intercourse between us, on the topics of neurology and sleeping sicknesses. I had in particular thought that you might be interested in the case of my nephew…"

As he spoke, the tinkling of Samert's spoon grew louder, seeming to surround the table with a thicket of high pitched noise, a sonic bramble grown to hem RR in… only upon looking up it was seen that he had put the spoon down and was sipping from his drink, his blue-green eyes directed not at RR but at some point beyond.

He set down his glass: "Why are you not still working? Never mind. It is your good fortune to meet the Frau Doktor Professorin Rosemarie Ramee."

It was the boy from the *Fahrradweg*, the boy in the mirrored sunglasses who had averted collision with the oncoming cyclist by lobbing his oleaginous but nevertheless flavorful kebab. Yes, because not only the uncommonly symmetrical features but also the aureole of frizzy hair were recognized. The aureole of frizzy hair which now sparkled with drops of moisture. For while the boy continued to sport his pair of Polaroids, evidently the brilliant afternoon had broken into a drizzle: his damp cargo pants and t-shirt clung to his thin but well-muscled torso while his olive-skinned arms and face appeared as if sugar glazed.

In his own puzzling fashion, he seemed to experience recognition as well: "Yo ho, it's the lovely Widow Twankey." He slid the sunglasses down his straight nose, regarding RR with eyes that even in the dimness of the shop, now lit only by the last long rain filtered rays of the day, could be seen as similar in color to Samert's. Similar, but not the same. They were an even more vivid green that was the essence of the color of the other's, only strengthened and enhanced, like an artificial fruit flavor whose intensity surpasses the original, rendering the former not just insipid but even slightly sour in comparison. Indeed, the thought of such a flavor brings to mind the "farewell" apple martinis purchased by Mick at the Royalton Hotel on the eve of the departure for Kiel—the night it was speculated that "love," after the first throes of hormonal rapture, is probably a function of habit, whose appeal can be traced to the fundamental organismal urge toward homeostasis, which was why Mick should not leave his wife. But that recollection is clearly leading nowhere. To return to the report proper, the boy at last dropped his lustrous green eyes, which could also be compared, with less danger of digression, to the color of "apple" flavored Jolly Ranchers.

"Welcome," he said with a nod that bordered on an abbreviated bow. "My uncle is a lucky lemon squeezer." Then he addressed Samert. "What do you say guv'nor? Can I go to Suzi's flat?"

Samert stood up, removed a cigarillo from a tin inscribed *Café Creme* on the counter behind him, then sat back down. "I must offer two objections. First, I am not your 'governor.' Therefore you will use 'Uncle,' or possibly *'Dayı.'* Second, you are only eleven years old and already with a sweetheart. Soon you will be off to war, marching along in your military issue trousers. Therefore you may not go to see this Suzi. Instead you will stay to tell Frau Doktor Ramee of your condition."

"But she's not me girl, Uncle. Just me finger and thumb."

"What? She is your whore?"

The boy stepped round from behind RR, tearing at his own hair and thus demonstrating its tawny spirals were longer than they appeared. "No! I meant she's me chum—just a mate from school."

"Then why did you not simply state this? How many times must I tell you not to make use of this vulgar speech of the London streets of villains and vagabonds which is at best a collection of banal and meaningless phonetic coincidences. You must say what you mean in clear, precise, scientific words that are, as the Atatürk of the English language George Orwell said, clean and shiny windows to the world. Am I not correct, Frau Doktor?"

They were both waiting—Samert who had ended by drawing on his cigarillo, which he now held with the smoldering tip pointed at RR as if it were a microphone, and the boy, who almost certainly had just winked. Unfortunately, this "vulgar speech of the London streets" was unfamiliar.[7] However, wasn't there room in every language for both the standard form and the vernacular, and didn't the latter often serve as a source of vitality for the former, as languages were not static phenomena, but constantly evolving? Further, while yours truly was a neurologist, not a linguist, was it not a given in the field of linguistics that there is no such thing as a transparent window to reality? Indeed, this truth pertained not only to language, but more fundamentally, to perception: the most immediate seeming sensory impression is always a translation—the "message" of the sensory receptors transmitted via an extremely rapid series of chemical reactions to the relevant processing centers in the brain. In conclusion, to quote the eminent American neurologist

---

[7] Termed "rhyming slang," this specialized argot coined by lower class Londoners to conceal the meaning of their discourse from the establishment first teased the ears of the "ducks and geese" (police) in the early nineteenth-century. For a fascinating introduction to a highly inventive and playful lexicon, please refer to *Cassell's Rhyming Slang* by Jonathon Green (London: Cassell & Co., 2000)

Mick Mackey, there is no such thing as unmediated contact with the world.

As the disquisition ceased, the boy whistled. "Now that's what I call a real boffin with a first class ball and chain!" And then with a sidelong glance at his uncle, "Sorry, *Dayı*. I meant to say that the doctor is a very intelligent, as well as beautiful, woman."

Samert drew again on his little cigar, exhaling a fist of smoke. "You are too kind Frau Doktor Söngül. While all that you have said is of course highly interesting and no doubt theoretically correct, I am afraid that my nephew's unfortunate manner of speaking is beneath your notice. Please to accept apologies for his boorish behavior—he is the son of my dead sister and brother-in-law who allowed him to roam the streets of London like a specimen of wild swine."

On the contrary, the young man's behavior was commendable. Earlier he had prevented a crossing into the path of an oncoming cyclist, thus averting a collision that not only would have resulted in injury, quite possibly a head injury, but that surely would have prevented yours truly from continuing on to the *Schneiderei*. In other words, it was this model youth whom yours truly had to thank for her presence at "Sam's" establishment, and therefore an introduction would be appreciated.

Samert took another swallow of his milky drink, the fumes from his cigarillo coiling across the table, filling the nose with vanilla-scented airborne nicotine. Really, RR should have relocated, as the capillaries absorbed the molecular effluvium of the tiny cigar, enabling it to mingle with the blood and flow through the veins, to penetrate every cell of the body. Or even departed, given that numerous studies have demonstrated that second hand smoke is nearly as harmful, and just as addictive, as smoke that is directly inhaled. Instead, a kind of paralysis tied the limbs to the chair as the boy stepped behind his uncle, picked the *Kibris Kebabs—Sind das Beste* cup off the counter, and with a wink raised it in the direction of RR. Ignoring him, Samert dabbed his lips with a napkin and cleared his throat.

"It is true that behind every case history there is a human being, such as for example Sigmund Freud's Ratman whose actual name does not escape my lips yet who nevertheless once walked the streets of Vienna just like any other fin de siècle fellow. Nevertheless we did not expect the Frau Doktor to take more than a professional interest in the wretched child whose patronymic is "Hazar" and whose forename is unfortunately "Aslan."

The boy had set the cup back down on the counter and taken a cigarillo from the tin, which he now twiddled between his thumb and forefinger as he crossed his eyes over his uncle's shoulder.

How did one spell the forename?

"A-S-L-A-N," Samert replied, confirming that the name was one already known, for as mentioned previously, in youth the series by C.S. Lewis in which a lion named Aslan rules over the kingdom of Narnia had been read many times over.

But why did "Sam" consider "Aslan" an unfortunate designation? To be sure the novels by the Cambridge don C.S. Lewis were ultimately Christian propaganda (as first learned from you). Indeed, Aslan was a thinly veiled, or more accurately, furred Christ figure, as was evident in the "crucifixion" scene in *The Lion, the Witch and the Wardrobe*. Then again, the books were also considered classics of children's literature and had been translated into twenty different languages. Did "Sam," as a Muslim, oppose the name on religious grounds?

"Frau Doktor Songül with all due respect I am a man of science despite only one year of medical school and therefore an agnostic like the great J.B.S. Haldane who when asked what his study of biology had revealed to him about the mind of God replied, 'only that he has an inordinate fondness for beetles.' Further I was not aware of this C.S. Lewis, who though a Cambridge don, must have had some acquaintance with the Turkish language since *aslan* signifies "lion" in our mother tongue. I am opposed to the name for this reason alone—that it is ludicrous. Lion, who is named Lion? What is the boy to do with a name like that? Become the king of beasts? I am told by his teachers that he at least possesses intelligence. With some more dignified name such as Kemal he might be inspired to do something with it. Instead, like an animal, he runs around in the streets from dawn until dusk working for that damn kebab shop or lies home in his bed dreaming his life away."

It was not pointed out that from a neurological perspective Aslan was preferable to Songül in terms not just of sonance, but also significance given that the entity designated by the first term could be supposed to possess at least a modicum of consciousness. Further, it was not added that in truth the name Aslan had always been strangely appealing with its first vowel that began deep in the back of the throat swelling out and up raising the top of the mouth like the ceiling of a cathedral before closing down on that earthy "s" that ancient buzzing zed that opened the door leading out to a land stretched like a limb to an ever receding and infinitely alluring point of no return. Aslan Aslan Aslan...

Instead, the boy, who had just dropped the cigarillo into the pocket of his cargo pants, was asked what he thought of his name.

"Well me tin plates back in London town called me Oz or Ozzie on account of Aslan being clapped out. I mean those Captain Cooks aren't bad—I took a squiz at them when I was a teapot—but the fact is that next to J.K. Rowling old C.S. is a bit of a womble. Course now that I'm an old pot me pash is Neal Stephenson."

Samert slammed his fist down on the table, rattling the espresso pot, and to a small degree, the nerves. "Enough of this nonsense. Go to the flat of this Suzi, or go to the moon—I do not care where as long as you are beyond my eyes and ears."

But what about the interesting "case" of his nephew? Now that "Sam" had excited scientific curiosity there was an urge to investigate, and if a complete neurological exam was not possible at present the boy could at least be probed for a personal account of his condition. For as "Sam" surely knew, from his own medical training, the patient's subjective experience not only could not be discounted, but was the first step toward a sound diagnosis and, in fact, the very foundation of a responsible practice. Yes, because patients were not automobiles, or, for that matter, sewing machines, which when they malfunctioned could be examined without their own input. Therefore, it was vital to know what Ozzie, no Aslan (always Aslan), who, still behind his uncle's back, was now smiling and rolling his eyes back in his head (a trick which made him further resemble a piece of classical Greek statuary), had to say about his condition, whatever it was. Yes, whatever it was, as the olfactory sense once again registered the faintly floral aroma of the candies on the silver tray. This time a green one was chosen.

"Your point is well taken, Frau Doktor Professorin Songül. But as you yourself can hear at present, the boy is speaking gibberish and what use is that? No more I am afraid than the yowling of a cat or the hissing of a snake. It is better that you listen to him some other time perhaps next week when I will bring him to the *Schlafzentrum* where no doubt the presence of advanced technology will cow him into communicating clearly," Samert said, rising from his chair. Nostrils flaring, he dropped his smoldering cigarillo into the ashtray and gripped Aslan by the back of the neck. "Now, please take your leave of the distinguished Lady Scientist in whose presence you have so thoroughly disgraced yourself."

"Alligator!" Aslan cried, his frizzy coils jerking and swaying to the electronic jingle of the bell as his uncle thrust him out the door and onto the pavement. He lurched in the sulfurous glow of the streetlights and then he was gone, dissolved in the darkness beyond.

Could the boy be caught? Rising, a step was taken toward the door. A step was taken, two steps, and then all stepping stopped. For what reason, what rationale could justify pursuit, and further, if he was caught, what would be done with him? It was a dead end, a sociobiological cul-de-sac. Although there is a certain adaptive expedience in old men chasing after young girls (the susceptibility of the middle-aged male heart to myocardial infarction notwithstanding), given the economic resources of the former and the reproductive ones of the latter, no such advantage justifies the pseudonubile woman's tailing of the juvenile male. Even if she is an old money-bags, the fact of the matter is that she cannot support his jewels.

Yes, RR understood, having subjected desire to rapid but rigorous analysis, that from a sociobiological standpoint there was nothing to offer the boy. Then again, weren't there other perspectives besides the sociobiological one? For instance, there was the medical one, mentioned above, although the highly regulated environment of the clinic could present an obstacle to intimacy. Another possibility was the educational, the perspective you perhaps assumed, Ms. Wall, when you evaluated RR (who received "A"'s in every English class with the exception of the two she took with you) so harshly. According to a classmate confided in at the time, this was because you were a "lesbo." And while the confided-in classmate herself was a bimbo, it is possible she was correct, that your harsh evaluations were meant as an incentive to seek extracurricular aid from you, both academic and otherwise. Further, it is possible that benefit would have been gained.

Yes, perhaps Aslan could be taught, one on one, and in that instruction benefit would be gained for he seemed a willing pupil. But how to get the boy under tutelage? Palms open RR reached toward the street, the posture a supplication, a question that begged an answer, a blank to be filled.

Which Samert took it upon himself to complete.

Which "Sam" took it upon himself to complete as he encircled the hands with his own. His were warm, dry, and due (it would later be learned) to a dermatological condition induced by his work with fabric, slightly scaly as they coiled around the knuckles, then slid up around the wrists, two snug yet pliant bracelets spreading as they moved up the forearms softly rasping over the skin slithering up under the sleeves of the sweater dress cupping the elbows as he pulled a person toward him. His breath tasted like licorice. An old fashioned flavor, the taste of a forgotten Russian art lesson, the medicinal tincture of a discipline to be endured for the sake of future pedagogical certification.

Afterwards (for while the objective is to present as complete a record as possible, in the interest of economy, or as is said in the sciences, parsimony, perhaps every mistake, every failure need not be recounted in full), while lying on a narrow couch behind the curtains at the back of the shop, the smoke of "Sam's" cigarillo lazily pirouetting overhead, Aslan's malady was inquired about again.

"Ah, that is fascinating. Unlike the boy himself, although I love him dearly, the son of my deceased sister. First I will bring to your attention the Greek myth of Endymion, with which, as an American woman who lives in the moment, you are probably not acquainted."

Actually, yours truly was. Not only had all the Greek and Roman myths been read in childhood, but in college an elective in classical mythology had been taken.

"I meant no offense, sweet Songül. That is one of the charms of your people, that you are not burdened by history. You are dewy like a bud or a baby without the stink of grudge or the rancid taste of ancient defeat. Indeed I could lick your lovely skin all night long but for the moment I will desist. You say you know the myth of Endymion, the handsome shepherd who was condemned to eternal sleep by Zeus after gaining the nocturnal favors of Selene on the top of Mount Latmos—then perhaps you are acquainted with other such tales. With Epimenides the Cretan poet who fell asleep in a cave and awoke fifty years later to find himself the wisest man on the island; with the English King Arthur who fell asleep on Avalon and woke to face the Saxon invader; with Barbarossa who awoke from sleep only after his beard had thrice encircled a large table; with the Portugese hero Don Sebastian who awoke to fight the so-called Muslim infidel etcetera…"

More or less, it was indicated with a curt nod, the gesture of one "expert" indulging another, acknowledging the need to unload expertise even as the information thus received is already in stock. For while RR did not actually know each and every story on "Sam's" list, she recognized, from countless textbooks and pop science primers, the rhetorical move he was making. Yes, the trick was well known—how the writer lured the reader into science's hard domain with gauzy swatches of myth and spangles of legend. Further, it was obvious what Samert would reveal once there—a diagnosis of Kleine-Levin syndrome. Pulling the dress (which had lost several buttons in the precedings) from the floor and arranging it over the torso, RR allowed him to continue, certain he would recognize the indulgence as a professional courtesy and thus as a validation. A validation that would gain his cooperation. For as implied in Ray Ramee's old salesman's copy of *How to Win Friends and Influence People*, to get people to do what you want you must first affirm their self-image. Yes, and so "Dr. Sam" was allowed to continue.

"Well as it is so often the case there is truth in legend. While it is impossible to fall asleep for fifty years, it is possible to fall asleep for fifty days due to coma and other maladies such as Kleine-Levin Syndrome, a rare sleep disorder officially discovered in the nineteen thirties by the German neurologist Willi Kleine and the American Max Levin, but which the myth of Endymion advises us was already suffered in the ancient world. You are familiar with Kleine-Levin Syndrome, yes?"

The following information was withheld: that KLS is not only rare, but extremely rare (the official diagnostic statistic is one in twenty million) and therefore no clinical experience had been gathered. That as a neurologist specializing in sleep disorders RR was nevertheless familiar with KLS, for god's sake. That according to the literature, KLS patients did not sleep continuously for fifty days, but rather for five at most, and that often their episodes of hypersomnolence were mixed with a periodic trance-like state. Instead, another enabling nod was given. Taking this cue, "Dr. Sam" pushed a cushion behind his back and then, with his hands folded over his groin as if it were a podium, continued.

"While he has not been officially diagnosed, I am certain that it is due to Kleine-Levin that my nephew has twice in the six months since I have taken him in accordance with the wishes of my deceased sister and brother-in-law sunk into a deep sleep for three days from which nothing, not even the false fruit stench of these German gummis of which he is excessively fond, could wake him. I am certain because of two factors: the first being that his father, an unemployed academic from Istanbul who in London was good for nothing not even driving a taxi for he would fall asleep at the wheel, was diagnosed with this particular syndrome. The second being that the boy exhibits all the classic attendant symptoms in the advent of an attack including hypersensitivity to sound, so that the sound of my sewing machine drives him mad and something else which it embarrasses me to mention in your presence, Songül, despite your medical background."

Samert was most likely referring to the abnormally uninhibited sex drive that preceded a narcoleptic attack in KLS sufferers.

Could it be there had been a hint of this in Aslan's behavior earlier, in his compliments and nictitating glances, which then indicated no actual emotional bias toward RR but merely a compulsion initiated by abnormal activity in the hypothalamus? On the other hand, didn't the literature also state that a sleep attack could be precipitated by sexual arousal? That is, his amorous behavior was not necessarily compulsive, but indicative of genuine attraction. Then again, either way, whether voluntary or not, this behavior was likely to result in pathological somnolence, and as a physician, the duty, as stated explicitly in the modern version of the Hippocratic Oath, and implicitly in the classical, was to prevent disease. Either way, surely all thoughts of pellucid green eyes and sparkling frizz and glazed olive skin had to be suppressed right now—it would not be ethical to exacerbate the boy's condition. No, it would not be ethical to take advantage of the opportunity offered by pathology—it would be a breach of the doctor-patient relationship. Although Aslan was not a patient. No, he was not a patient, nor a student. There was no relation. Not yet.

4. The Connection Between Olfaction and Memory is Well Documented in the Literature

Most probably, Ms. Wall, you detected a burgeoning opportunism in those last sentences of the report. And it is possible this repulsed you. After all, while you were at times deficient in sensitivity toward your students, you never lacked in principles. Please keep in mind that this a record of past thoughts and feelings, rather than present ones, and remember as well that we are all, at times, under the sway of evolutionarily prior structures of the brain (which, in addition to the hypothalamus, include the anterior cingulate and the amygdala), structures which in the case of RR had begun to exert their pull on more recent ones by creating an overriding bias toward the boy. Which is not to discount free will or the possibility of rational decision making. No, for the progress of desire could more or less be tracked as it crept up from the deepest regions of the corpus into consciousness. Indeed, it could be dimly perceived, as if through a low grade security camera, crouched at the threshold between fantasy and action. All a person needed to do was press the button. Or not.

Yes, a choice was had and a choice was made on the following Saturday, November 13th, 1999, as RR stood outside Samert's door holding a bottle of wine: to press the button. And when no one answered, to press it again. Strange. Had the time or date of the invitation been misremembered? No, for Samert had unwittingly provided a mnemonic device when he had issued it, declaring that 13 would be his lucky number if "Songül" would join him for lunch at the 13th hour of the 13th day, at his home in Buchenholz, a new housing development just outside of Kiel. Then again, no car could be seen in the carport next to the entrance of Buchenholz 3, a lack unnoticed during the approach to Samert Mart's rowhouse, after parking on the gravel road leading into the development, but that now became apparent. Maybe it was the wrong house. Or maybe not. Maybe the Turkish tailor had changed his mind—a disappointment, in addition to an insult (who was he to stand up RR?), but possibly just as well. For as stated above, self-awareness was not lacking: the motivation behind acceptance of Samert's invitation was evident, and further, it was understood that there were moral as well as sociobiological and cultural obstacles to acting on that motivation. And then a click was heard.

"If it isn't me uncle's mother of pearl, the dishy doctor."

He was standing in the doorway, leaning against the frame. Once again, his springy hair was beaded with droplets of water and his skin was damp, so that his cotton t-shirt, which was navy blue with an embossed red arrow pointing toward his chin, clung to his torso. Below the ragged hems of a voluminous pair of blue jeans, which he'd cinched around his hips with a thick, faded green leather belt, his narrow bare feet were palely clean.

The luncheon invitation from Samert was revealed. A possible error in judgment: the revelation hung like a sheet of glass, through which Aslan gazed at yours truly as if regarding a zoo specimen of only mild interest. The chilled bottle of Riesling propped in the crook of the arm condensed on the leather of the jacket and seeped cold into the right upper arm and breast. But then he smiled and stepped to the side, soliciting ingress with a sweeping motion of his hand.

"I know, luv. Sorry about the door but the guv'nor's gone

to the grocer's and I was having meself a wash on account of what he said."

And what had Samert said?

"I rank like a dead donkey."

Well Aslan did not smell like a dead donkey now. This was certain as RR stepped past him into the narrow, tiled hallway of Samert Mart's rowhouse. No, the odor he emitted, while fundamentally mammalian, was not lifeless, evoking as it did the scent of Smokey's fur after a night out in the rain (the only time he permitted himself to be petted), as he lay sunning himself on the porch amongst Teresa's potted geraniums. But then Aslan was behind RR and other odors were met, almost equally compelling, as the kitchen opened up on the left. A tart was cooling on the counter that, extrapolating from its rich pungent steam, could be conjectured to be goat cheese and leek. Closer inspection, and perhaps a small peeling of the golden skin that had formed across the top, would surely confirm this hypothesis; however, there was no opportunity to linger as the boy led the way past the kitchen, through the dining area to a living room delimited at the far end by sliding glass doors.

"Take a load off, luv," he said as he indicated an overstuffed sofa upholstered with a nubbly red tweed, already familiar, in a sense, as Samert had couched his invitation in a proud inventory of his household possessions, all purchased from IKEA, "the home of the finest in modern design." Similarly familiar was the glass-topped coffee table in front of it, upon which the perspiring Riesling was set as a seat was taken on the overstuffed sofa. Aslan himself sat in a narrow red club chair (ditto) opposite RR, facing the glass doors, rather than next to her, as it had been supposed he would, although there was in fact no firm ground for this supposition. For while his behavior at times had seemed to indicate interest and even attraction, at others it seemed more ambiguous. Perhaps it would be wise not to make suppositions at present. Rather, the best bet might be to proceed as if Aslan were a juvenile male like any other, the son of a neighbor or colleague encountered exemptus parentis on an elevator or in a lobby (even though it was difficult not to see the workings of fate in the opportunity, given the tendency of the brain to look for patterns in chance events). Operating as if Aslan were a boy like any other, RR inquired about his interests.

"Oh sex and drugs and rock and roll."

Was this an invitation to continue with the conversation, or an attempt to foreclose it? As the next move was deliberated, a jingling sounded, at first taken to be the front door (in which case it seemed that Samert's return had obviated the question of a next move), but then apprehended as having issued from the bell-strung blue collar of a small black and white cat, which as Aslan swept it up into his arms and relocated to the sofa, now perched on the adjacent cushion, its back arching beneath Aslan's hands.

"You're a good kitty such a good kitty my little baby boy aren't you Elvis," the boy crooned as the cat rolled its spine under his palms, purring loudly.

What did they feel like, sliding over the cat's back? Could the cat appreciate the difference between Aslan's youthful hands, which more likely than not were smooth as silk, and his uncle's? Probably not. Or rather, it would prefer the rough texture of the latter, reminiscent of its mother's tongue. Aslan, however, appeared engrossed by the animal, and therefore a query was made regarding its name.

"The guv'nor came up with that one. Elvis's his cat you see, though he prefers me, don't you boy? Do you want to hold him?"

Why not? For then a connection could be engineered, via the cat. And indeed that seemed to be Aslan's intent, to use the cat as kind of social viaduct, as he now moved closer, sliding over the divide between the two thick cushions that padded the seat of the sofa. Yes, and as his knee actually touched the side of the calf, a boundary was crossed. At the same time, however, his approach was less than candid, and thus to be met with caution. Therefore, when Aslan placed the unusually docile cat in the lap (Smokey would never have stood for such a transfer), the hands were confined to its fine, slightly unctuous fur. Writhing with ecstasy, the animal rolled onto its back, exposing testicles the size of table grapes.

"Oh you love that you silly kitten. The doc knows how to make you feel good."

Given the dimensions of its gonads, the animal was clearly no kitten but a fully mature tom. This observation, however, was withheld—the following offered in its stead: if it weren't for the limited motility of the feline eye, Elvis's would surely be rolling back into their sockets.

"I can do that! Roll me eyes back in me head, that is. Look!"

While the human ability to roll the eyes back into the head is merely a matter of extraocular muscular coordination and control (specifically, of the four rectus muscles [medial, lateral, superior and inferior] and the two obliques [superior and inferior]), with the disappearance of the pupil and retina, the material nature of the eye comes eerily to the fore as, for instance, the

vitreous humor is recognized as simple substance, akin to limestone or the calcareous shell of a clam. Hence, it was as if Aslan
had suddenly transformed into a statue, the two white globes
that filled his orbits a marmoreal substitute for the living green
of before. Which was unsettling, in the sense of feeling unseat-
ed, as if a person no longer occupied his or her previous position. As if a person were in some new, cold space—a museum
without any other patrons or guards—free to walk right up to
any piece, to stare, to touch, to take... Then the gaze dropped,
and there it was. The form of his desire, this was certain, despite
the bunched fabric of his oversized pants. And it belonged to
RR. For you have to understand, Ms. Wall, that yours truly was
no thief, nor even an intruder. The line would never have been
crossed if he had not invited the first step. Yes, because couldn't
his ocular performance be construed as an invitation, an urgent
bid to proceed, in the way that the male frigate bird's inflation
of his crimson pouch signals to the female that their courtship
has begun?[8] If this new space was a museum, it was a museum
of natural history, and the exhibition on display was as ancient
as animal reproduction.

As ancient as animal reproduction, which is, fundamentally,
a replication followed by a division, a replication in which the
one becomes two followed by a division in which the doubled
one becomes none, for "who" remains when the fun is over?
And while, Ms. Wall, you might, if you had scientific training,
object to the preceding assertion on the grounds that nobody

---

[8] To be sure, eye rolling is generally not perceived as a courtship behavior.
On the contrary, quite often the motion indicates condescension, contempt,
boredom or exasperation. Hence the expression "rolling one's eyes to heav-
en," as if to signal a wish for divine rescue from boredom or frustration.

dies (at least not immediately) when two people, or for that matter, two drosophila, swap chromosomes, the truth that is made manifest in the postmitotic demise of the lowly amoeba still holds at the cellular level in every higher organism and finds expression in the phrase "the little death." To accept Aslan's invitation then, was to accept the possibility of self-annihilation, to stand swaying at the boundary, as if once again at the threshold of Mother Teresa's bedroom, between being and nonbeing. Yes, to accept was to decline to the point of nothing, of some one become no one.

And yet it was impossible to resist. Impossible to resist as the hand rose of its own accord and reached slowly stretching like a pseudopod sliding across the short space that separated his torso from another toward the faintly pilose surface of his cheek the fine blond hairs softly illuminated by the light slanting in through the sliding glass doors could anyone see no the view looked out onto the patio beyond there was nothing but a weedy bank thick hedges listing trees losing yellow leaves unless someone from one of the adjoining houses walked by but why would they visiting maybe but then the front door through which Samert might walk at any moment but in the meantime the stretching continued because it could not be stopped and therefore there was no transgression or rather if a boundary were to be crossed it would be because Aslan had permitted it Aslan Aslan Aslan had allowed it invited it initiated it and in the meantime the stretching continued trembling for contact though it was also delicious this liminal space between here and there this suspension like a taut hot pulsing rope running from groin to brain between here and there Aslan Aslan Aslan...

"Copped you!"

Yes, and so it was over, as the cat sprang from the lap and the boy's eyes snapped back into place. So it was over for though he was clearly aroused as indicated not only by the swelling in his pants (for surely there was a swelling, excess fabric notwithstanding), but now by the receptive black expanse of his pupils, these dilations could not counter the involuntary contraction that had followed his exclamation: the fingers had curved and dropped to the lap. Yes, it was over but then maybe not as Aslan added "but the game's not up—I've got more tricks in me bag!" tricks which he then proceeded to perform, and which included ear wriggling, tongue rolling, raising one eyebrow at a time (he could lift either, which is rare), index finger crooking and full hand "lobster clawing" (this last feat involved middle and ring finger abduction, or separation, concomitant with adduction of ring and pinky, and of middle, index and thumb). Indeed, as Aslan snapped his "claws," his hands darting in as if to snip at the hair and then out again, in a motion reminiscent of the zigzagging of the male stickleback fish as he attempts to induce the female to deposit her eggs, the situation once more began to appear promising. Especially when he suddenly leaned back and extending his narrow, bare feet out over the lap exclaimed, "Wait, I can do me dogs too!"

And then Samert returned.

Initially Samert's presence was not perceived. Only now, as he stood just a few meters away by the dining room table, was it registered. Only now did RR see Samert standing there, the cat coiling around his thickset, shoeless (though unlike the boy's, hosed), pedal members. Only now did RR see how one of Samert's hands gripped the back of a black lacquered dining chair, while the other bunched in the pocket of a pair of charcoal and cream tweed trousers. Thus it was not until this moment that the full size of the challenge was appreciated. For despite his boyish proportions, Samert was a grown man, with a man-sized sense of entitlement untempered in this case by paternal feeling. There was no possibility he would tolerate the youthful trickster's encroachment on what he perceived as his own turf, just as there is no way a silverback gorilla will voluntarily cede power or privilege to lesser males. Yes there was no possibility, no possibility at all, as the boy now knelt straight-backed and firmly in the center of the adjacent cushion, elbows pressed to his sides, hands clasped over the buckle of his weathered green belt, pale narrow feet tucked away beneath him. And then suddenly there was, as Samert, in a demonstration of the unpredictability of human as opposed to animal behavior, broke into a smile.

"Oh you silly boy, you silly fun fellow," Samert said as he stooped to pick up the cat. But his words were clearly directed at Aslan, upon whom he beamed his approval, his blue eyes both enhanced and softened by a slate blue V neck sweater that appeared to be knit of cashmere wool. "Your only failure as a host, Kemal, is that you have neglected to pour our dear guest a glass of the wine she has so thoughtfully procured for this occasion, or better yet, the Alsatian white burgundy now in refrigeration, which will be an ideal companion to the preliminary snack I have prepared. Therefore please to fetch this snack, and two glasses of white burgundy. You may also bring a glass for yourself, Kemal, to celebrate. By the way you have informed Dr. Songül that we will soon officially improve your forename to Kemal at the *Auslandsamt*? Because you are a man of my own blood, not a savannah animal. Or will be someday."

Aslan did not deny this new unsuitable, even untenable, designation (for what hold did "Kemal" have on the boy's fundamentally feral nature?). Nor did he protest as Samert, the cat still in his arms, directed him with a nod to vacate the couch. Apparently Aslan understood, as he rose (the front of his pants, it must be admitted, flat) from his seat, and then padded off toward the kitchen, that his best interest lay in seeming submission, in biding his time, like a beta wolf awaiting the alpha's demise.

Samert, rubbing Elvis under the chin with the knuckles of one hand and stroking his back from the nape of the neck to the tip of the tail with the other, had in the meantime continued to smile, though now expectantly, as if he were awaiting some favorable commentary. And it was true that he appeared attractive—beneath the slate blue sweater he wore a thick, white, high quality cotton t-shirt that along with the cashmere sweater and a pair of matching cashmere socks leant him a jaunty yet affluent air, as if he were standing, shoeless, on the deck of his own private yacht. Yes, it was conceded, he was looking very sharp.

"Thank you to Mr. Hugo Boss, who provides some of the finest ready-tailored men's clothing. I did not have time to make new clothes for the occasion and in addition could not knit a jumper, as I do not possess the hands of a woman. Do you knit, Dr. Songül?"

The reply was negative, although in keeping with the strictly truthful nature of this report it should be known that RR had been taught to knit by Mother Teresa, who had also taught Tom Tom, per his request. Tom Tom had in fact once knit yours truly a loose white acrylic poncho, a lovely purl stitched web, which in high school had provided a sense of arachnoid power.

This poncho is retained still (having been carried on the plane to Hamburg rather than trusted to the postal service) in the rarely opened suitcase behind the sliding doors of the closet, and would be worn for protection against the chill of Hassan's tower, only it is feared that at present the feeling would be more fly-like than spider.

"Ah, that is a shame." Samert extracted the cat from his chest, which had begun to work its claws in and out of the cashmere sweater, and placed it on the carpet. "Because I am sure that would be a beautiful sight," he added as he strode over to the sliding glass door, "your thin graceful fingers guiding the sharp tips of the needles, urging along the transformation of a mere skein of animal fiber into soft woolen garments to cover your thin physique." Having let the cat out, latching the screen but not the glass behind it, he took the position that moments before had been occupied by Aslan, or more accurately, one several centimeters closer. "Such as a pair of thick woolen socks. Then you would no longer need to wear outdoor footwear inside, an unsanitary as well as barbaric practice." He reached down and unzipping the ankle boots (Italian leather, recently purchased in Hamburg), drew them off. "Yes, you must knit soft woolen garments to warm your thin feet as well as to cover your thin physique."

It was that thin physique that Samert now proceeded to investigate, his fingers tracing a line from the nape of the neck over the vertebrae around the sacrum down to the coccyx. The investigation was not welcome. Indeed, it produced an unpleasant sensation in the spine, as if something had penetrated the cerebrospinal fluid and was now slithering down the length of the back, which in turn elicited an involuntary shudder (for there was no intent to inform Samert that the episode in the *Schneiderei* had been an importless deviation). Fortunately, however, he misinterpreted the shudder, taking it as a purely positive physiological response akin to the purring of Elvis.

"You like that my nervous rose, my high-strung lute? You see I understand you because I am a sensitive man, at times too sensitive hence a twenty-year addiction to nicotine which as a nerve specialist you know has a soothing narcotic effect. However this addiction causes you displeasure—do not think I have not noticed the way you wrinkle up your small thin nose in the presence of tobacco smoke—and therefore I am now attempting to cease the habit although I believe in English there is a better word…"

Beautiful. There was no other one. No other word for Aslan as he reentered the room bearing a tray, his slight but proportionately broad young shoulders straight, his frizzy head held high like some unobtainable prize. Which did not rule out success, not at all. However, given the proximity of Samert, it would be prudent to shift the gaze toward some other goal, in this case the refreshments on the tray, which in addition to the bottle of white burgundy included a plate of what appeared to be smoked trout.

"Excuse me, *Dayı*, here is the wine and the dirty dish… Sorry *Dayı*, I meant fish."

As Aslan set the tray down in front of Samert the scent of the fish wafted across the table, an acrid but cozy odor reminiscent of the autumnal bonfires of adolescence and the sexual tussles in the shadows beyond that accompanied them. The gastric juices gurgled forth in anticipation of digestion like the low growl of a feline throat, the sound of desire preparing to pounce, a ravenous need that would, however, be restrained given that social protocol did not permit immediate fulfillment. Yes, certainly a person would practice self-control despite the fact that the smoked fish, with its papery bronzed skin, with its pungent reek, provoked penetration. But hopefully Aslan would soon pick up the knife and fork that lay beside the fish, and with his slender, dexterous-appearing hands, cut RR a piece. A glance in his direction was stolen.

Aslan had sunk to his knees on the carpet on the other side of the coffee table, and was now looking expectantly up at his uncle, as if awaiting some long-anticipated treat or entertainment. While surely his interest in Samert was simulated, it could not be denied that all traces of his previous insubordination in the *Schneiderei* had disappeared. This was food for thought, if not the digestive tract, as the emergence of a bond between uncle and nephew had not been foreseen. A bond had not been foreseen, and would surely prove inhibitory, as the boy would now be hesitant to "steal" his dear Dayı's "Songül." What to do? Nothing at present, since creative problem solving sometimes requires that the problem per se be temporarily set aside.[9] Therefore the gaze was turned in the direction of Samert, who, sitting with hands palms up on his thighs, nostrils flaring and eyes rolling upward (though thankfully, not back into their sockets, as this would have seemed a grotesque parody of the younger

---

[9] E.g. as in the case of Friedrich August Kekulé von Stradonitz's discovery of the structure of benzene. It was only after Kekulé had thrown up his hands for the night that the molecule's ring structure came to him in a dream, in the form of a snake that seized its own tail and proceeded to whirl mockingly before his eyes. The iconography of Kekulé's dream draws from the ancient symbol of the self-consuming serpent or Ouroboros, although according to some accounts, his inspiration was actually the figure of a hexagon in a tavern sign in Germany.

male), began, once more, to speak. A side note: the intention, in reporting Samert Mart's frequent and lengthy discourse, is not to test your patience, Ms. Wall, but rather to create an accurate picture of the conditions that were endured.

"The shores of Lake Abant, lovely Lake Abant... The wonderful scent of this smoked trout, though it hails from the black heart of the Black Forest, returns to me my youthful summers on the shores of Lake Abant, where we would exchange the thick festering heat of *Kıbrıs*, or Cyprus, for the cool mountain air of the Black Sea region of mother *Türkiye*, our great house of whitewashed stone the largest in Paphos, now occupied by treacherous Greeks, for the simple wooden vacation cottage of my grandfather in which I would fall asleep each night to the waters sweetly slapping the rocks like a playful woman and then dream of giants and djinn and rocket ships and Kim Novak and all manner of fantastical things. In the mornings my grandmother, always the first to awaken, would light the oil lamp and a fire of cedar logs then she would pour water from a clay jug for grandfather to wash his face. From my mat by the fragrant hearth I would watch the shadows play over his features pooling in his deeply set eyes as he splashed his cheeks, patted them dry, and when he sat down at the table to a raw egg mixed with two fingers of cognac would see a sudden light leap forth from his sockets as he downed his glass, a light like a silvery trout breaking the placid morning surface of the lake beyond the rough hewn walls.

"He is dead for many years now, my grandfather, and grandmother too...But for a moment I see and feel and smell him—for instance the scratch of his woolen waistcoat on my face when he embraced me, the tang of tobacco that clung even to his cummerbund—and it was the fish that brought him forth which leads me to speculate that certain dishes are like sensational vehicles between the past and the present or shall we say a kind of molecular transport system like that employed by your Captain of the USS Enterprise who is perpetually reincarnated by the ARD broadcasting network, sensational vehicles which allow the ghosts of memory to materialize before us. Would you agree, my fair Dr. Songül?"

At this point, RR would have concurred with the most patent absurdity, which Samert's speculation was not (for if somewhat floridly phrased, it was supported by numerous studies as well as personal experience; indeed, the connection between olfaction and memory is well documented in the literature). No, Samert's speculation was not absurd; however, further theorizing was to be avoided, given the strategical problems that lay ahead. Stealing a glance at Aslan, who, incongruously and unintelligibly, was raising his right eyebrow while wiggling his left ear, assent was given. And then, politely, a request for a bit of fish was made.

Lips pursed, Samert picked up the utensils that had been placed next to the fish and excised a substantial piece of the dorsal side of the tail. He then turned this onto a small black stoneware plate, and handed it to RR: "Please."

For the sake of accuracy, it must be reported that no ghosts of memory materialized as RR took a bite, no musty grandfathers, nor even the autumnal bonfires of long ago adolescence: what was felt, as a vernal smoke like the taste of singed saplings flooded the mouth, was the overwhelming present, the sultry sweet flavor of the now burning in a haze that drifted up up up like the arrow on Aslan's t-shirt, an insignia which proclaimed the sky was the limit because why couldn't the day be seized? Why shouldn't the day that sat on the other side of the table be seized, the shifting sea green day that despite or because of its protean slipperiness was meant to belong to RR as surely as a snake possesses its own tail?

Of course, what this meant in practical terms remained to be seen—even as confidence in the ultimately satisfactory resolution of the situation surged, a surge no doubt abetted by the white burgundy that accompanied the trout, it was understood that a clear understanding of conditions (e.g., the precise nature of the relationship between uncle and nephew) was lacking. Consequently, a protocol could not be contrived. Yes, and so because the requirements for fulfillment were, in practical terms, currently unknown, it was determined to adjoin rather than seize the day, as the barnacle attaches to the sperm whale. No plans, choices or even objections would be made, no action taken of any kind. Instead, RR would, as popular idiom puts it, "go with the flow."

Which shortly thereafter led to the black lacquered table in the dining room, or more accurately, dining area, where Samert directed RR to the far end, sandwiching the torso between the edge of the table and the wall, a position that was less than ideal, given a tendency toward claustrophobia. Torso sandwiched, RR was, so to speak, served—served with a sliver of the goat cheese and leek tart spotted earlier in the kitchen, yes a sliver, a tiny sandbar in the sea of the black stoneware plate especially in comparison to the generous portions Samert set down at his own place at the opposite end of the table and Aslan's in between, explaining as he did so that, "I have given you only a small piece as I have noted that you ate heartily of the trout and so now I am sure like any American woman wish to restrain yourself in order to preserve your thin physique."

Suspended in the tide, RR made no mention of a high metabolism (which had perpetually been the envy of female peers, though biologically speaking such a metabolism is inefficient, and in times of famine, maladaptive). Instead, the fraction of pastry was accepted as if it were far greater than it was, declared in fact, to be "plenty." Even though it clearly was not, even though the size of the portion was unsatisfactory, each bite was treated as if it were an entire tart, as if there were no end to the food on the black stoneware plate and therefore the only course was to slowly and purposefully chew while in the meantime Samert continued to talk. Yes, he continued to talk (and here, Ms. Wall, you will be spared most of his actual words), about his youth in Cyprus and in Turkey, about the machinations of the Greek priests, about his interrupted medical education, about his unmarried status which was not due to "a lack of the fair sex," but rather to "highest standards," and so on, occasionally interrupting his own monologue with questions about upbringing and education (though curiously, not about amorous history) which were answered with one-word sentences and monosyllables, for despite the resolution to go with the so-called flow, it was concurrently feared, as Aslan sat silently and attentively watching his uncle, his fork resting on his plate by his untouched quiche, that a person was being carried further and further away from the objective.

Further and further away, when suddenly, the low distant growling which had all the while accompanied Samert's discourse, and which it had been assumed issued from a suppressed digestive system, wrenched into a high, piteous screeching.

"He's after him again!" Aslan cried, springing from his seat and running back to the sliding glass door.

"He" turned out to be an obese ginger-furred tom the size of a badger, who loomed over "him"—a tabby striped kitten cowering, belly to the bricks of the patio, tiny ears flat to the skull, mouth an open pink throb of panic. But the other tom, Elvis, was there too, crouched at the far border of the patio, its black tail weaving like a charmed snake against the backdrop of weeds and brambles. Was it simply mesmerized by the spectacle before it, or did it have an agenda all its own?

And what was Aslan thinking as he stood a moment later holding the kitten to his chest, having chased the ginger tom away, and gave RR a little smile through the screen? RR, who in the meantime had felt Samert's arm steal around the shoulder, and so now stood entwined by the Turkish tailor on the inside of the door out to the patio and the wild growth beyond, the wild growth into which, as Aslan drove away the big tom, the other, Elvis, had disappeared? What was he thinking as he gazed at RR with wide green eyes, the kitten distorting the line of the arrow on the front of his t-shirt with its clinging, kneading paws, although the direction was still, to be sure, up? Then again, did it matter what he was thinking, given that the body has, in a sense, a mind of its own, as evidenced earlier by the (almost definite) bulge in his pants? Yes, and given that the body has a mind of its own, maybe what was needed now was simply space for thought to roam. Yes, maybe leave should be taken because space was needed, because nothing more would happen in Samert's presence, because Aslan would eventually, with help, find his way (via instruction of some kind in the apartment in Kiel? English lessons? For while his English was fluent, it was not standard). Surely it was just a matter of time, of finding a proper space (and time), even as, in the next moment he went on to ask, "So *Dayı*, may I go to Suzi's sister's party now?"

Samert's arm dropped away and he moved toward the door. "For one week he behaves as a human being and not as a savannah animal, for one single week only and yet he thinks I will give him my trust?" He fumbled for a moment with the latching mechanism of the screen door, until Aslan walked over, and still cradling the kitten, released it with one hand. With his right fist aloft, index finger raised, Samert stepped outside: "Think again, boy!"

It was at that moment that the woman in the blond braids and baby blue terry robe appeared, from behind the fence that separated the neighboring patio from Samert's: "*Mein Liebling, warum rennst du immer weg?*"

She had lost her darling—this much was understood but not what followed, given the woman's thick provincial accent. Indeed, the guttural flow of invective she directed first at Aslan, as she snatched the kitten away from him and gathered it in the folds of her robe, and then at Samert, was incomprehensible (for while the German was admittedly not as strong as it could be, a demanding professional situation leaving no time for the kind of linguistic immersion that fluency requires, the woman, as Samert later confirmed, spoke dialect). On and on she cursed (for though the actual content of her speech was unavailable, her narrowed eyes and curled lip, as she clenched the now squirming kitten to her terry wrapped breast, indicated its maledictory nature), as Samert stood red faced, sputtering, over and over, "*Das ist falsch! Das ist falsch!*" Aslan simply smirked. On and on, until a deep voice summoned over the fence, "*Imke, Imke, komm hier,*" and the woman abruptly spun round, her blond pigtails flapping behind her as she vanished back around the corner.

A dog barked at the far end of the development, and somewhere a baby cried. Aslan's eyes rolled back white as the cumulus clouds scudding overhead, in full view of Samert, and yet Samert said nothing. Samert was silent but for a clicking noise now issuing from his pocket, a rolling clitter clatter, which as he reached in and then withdrew his hand, was revealed to be the sound of a string of amber glass beads. He rolled the string between his palms for a few moments, his nostrils fluttering in and out, then, his gaze directed at the pavement, finally said, "Kemal, you may go."

"Tom Hanks! I mean thank you, *Dayı.* And good bye, Dr. Ramee!" But, having exited through the sliding door, he thrust his frizzy head back out again: "You should stop by Doc. It's just around the corner from your building, on…"

"Begone boy, before I change my mind. I am sure the doctor does not care to attend your childish party—just go."

Which he did. Because at the time there was no way to retain him: the means to do so—a social relationship that would provide a claim on his person—was lacking. Yes, the means supplied, for instance, by the relationship between parent/guardian and child (or between husband and wife, or brother and sister, or employer and employee, or teacher and student, top and bottom) was missing, and while it would, theoretically, have been possible to bypass those means (RR could have, for example, abruptly departed Samert's house, intercepted Aslan at the bus stop to which he was presumably headed, and from there abducted him) to do so would mean taking another, socially condemned way, the path of the psychopath. Which was not acceptable. No the path of the psychopath was not acceptable. Was never acceptable, despite accusations of monstrosity. Indeed the deviation (if it was a deviation) from the norm occurred completely within the limits of the normal. More or less.

Without Aslan, from within the limits of the normal, Samert was regarded. He continued to play with his beads, scooping them up inside one fist, then the other, back and forth, back and forth, until finally they disappeared completely into his pocket. He cleared his throat.

"I am sorry for that little scene. That woman she has an ugly mind perhaps because she is the wife of a *Polizist* who brings home the filth of his profession. I am sure in fact that he beats her, she is not the only one who can hear through walls. However I assure you that what she said is not true not a word of it."

Not one word of what? Truth be told, the comprehension of the German language was less complete than it could be. Then again, surely the woman's manner of speaking had been inferior as well.

Samert slowly exhaled. "Yes. She speaks like a dog… And just as it does not matter what a dog has to say it does not matter what that wretched woman has to say. It is only barking. It is only barking…" With the back of his hand he wiped his eye, from which dripped a lachrymal secretion, then continued. "Please excuse me, this is most embarrassing. It is so hard, you understand…So hard to be all alone in a strange land with a child to raise up and no one, no lovely one… No wife."

5. A Closed Record

It was, as it is said in novels, a "marriage of convenience."
But that is a phrase that for you, Ms. Wall, probably holds no
more than superficial significance, despite all your literary acu-
men. Because according to recollection, you were a prime specimen of the liberated woman, that seventies efflorescence of
the second sex. No, terms such as "female eunuch" or "wife"
simply did not apply to Ms. Nikki Wall with her close-cropped
head, large silver hoop earrings and mammary-revealing knit
shirts. Indeed, evidently nothing (or no one) could detain you as
you slashed and burned, not only your bras, but your relationships, as you moved from barely mature male to barely mature
male (and the occasional female?), in a manner that some of the
more conservative members of the Hudson High faculty and
staff (had they subjected your private life to the same surveil-
lance allegedly practiced by the senior boys who wanted to get
into your pants) would have found shocking, although among
chimpanzees and other Pongidae such behavior is completely
acceptable. At any rate, because you never required the conve-
niences of the connubial situation, such as 24/7 access not just
to a husband, but also to his household (for if memory serves,
you already had a little out-of-wedlock pet to call your own.
Was the name "Dylan" for the poet, or for the folksinger? Or
both?), surely you have no idea how convenient a marriage of
convenience can be.

Having been conveniently cojoined (at the *Rathaus* in Hamburg), as well as expeditiously (on November 16th, three days
after the rowhouse luncheon; it was, as they say in both novels
and popular parlance, a "whirlwind courtship"), RR now sat

(on November 27th), thigh-to-thigh with Samert (a.k.a. "Sam") Mart on that type of abbreviated sofa known as a loveseat. The loveseat was located in a corner of one of the large central rooms of Dr. Nils Wenzel's large, fjord proximate apartment, a room that his Russian-American partner, Ludmilla Lipilina, an exophthalmic psychotherapist shirted in abdomen-baring muslin gauze, had referred to, with a toss of her black mane, as the "salon." The reason for the dismissive gesture was unclear, as the room did in fact possess the proportions and fixtures, including a large crystal chandelier, that film and fiction had led RR to expect of a space so termed. Possibly the Lipilina woman's motivation was to draw attention to her hair, which admittedly was thicker and more lustrous than most. At any rate, on the other side of the salon, a group of colleagues from the lab stood clustered around a baby grand piano, drinks in hand, gossiping (as evidenced by shaking heads and bits of phrasings such as *der arme Teufel, zu viel plastische Chirurgie* and also something about a person now being like a *Schüssel*. Apparently some poor devil had had her [or was it his?] appearance surgically altered, too many times, although how this person could have come to resemble a bowl or a basin was incomprehensible), while several of their offspring sat cross-legged on a shearling carpet, elbows propped on the low, leather inlaid table in the center, as they bleated at each other about a book that featured an either very clean or magical boy with no parents (*keine Eltern*) who apparently slept under the stairs (*unter der Treppe*), whatever that meant. But where was Aslan?

There were in fact a number of possibilities: hopefully these did not extend beyond the limits of Wenzel's apartment, which RR, Samert and Aslan had entered approximately thirty

minutes earlier as a family unit, despite Aslan's protests that he
needed to remain at home to work on his *Hausaufgaben* (a claim
Samert had refuted). One possibility was the room immediately
to the left, which appeared, given the glimpse of floor-to-ceiling
bookcases visible through the open door, to be a library or study,
and from which the odor of charring wood emanated. Another
was the balcony through the French doors at the northern end
of the "salon," which probably afforded a "majestic view" of
the mucous gray, freighter clogged waters of the fjord: several
guests had in fact just slipped out to consume cigarettes, as evidenced by one of the resident's heavily accented request for a
"flick of the Bic" as they had exited. Yet another was the kitchen,
most likely to be found through the door and down the hallway
on the right, given the fact that the two young caterers who had
been circulating just moments ago with trays of canapés had
disappeared in that direction, hopefully to replenish their supplies (in particular, the tiny sour cream and black caviar blintzes,
which had really *geschmeckt*). Yes, there were several possibilities,
the last of which seemed the most likely, so to speak, to bear
fruit. Aslan was, after all, an adolescent male, or pre-adolescent
male, and as such compelled to seek a variety of sexual produce, since the neural circuitry that releases chemicals that as-
sociate novel experiences with the motivation to repeat them
develops more quickly at this stage in life than the mechanisms
that inhibit urges and impulses. How could he not, therefore,
chase after the two nubile caterers with their identically dyed
strawberry-red hair and belly rings?

Extracting the hand from Samert's, RR professed need of
the "W.C.," a claim supported by the tall glass of *Hefeweizen* recently drained, and which now stood empty on the floor beside

the sofa, the lip ringed with yeasty scum. Yes, the bladder was filling, and although the organ had not distended to the point where urination was mandatory, surely the excuse was a legitimate one. Surely even a newlywed could "take a piss in private," phrasing RR did not employ but was tempted to as Samert caught hold of the fingers and drew them to his mouth, urgently osculating the tips as the hand pulled away. "Please to return swiftly on the wings of love," was heard, and then a clicking that had become increasingly familiar. No reason to verify its source: the worry beads, which presumably would fill the time sans "Songül," just as the rubber nub of the pacifier plugs up the absence of the mother. Because that is how it felt, like being a mother, one whose offspring did not play with others (the dampness of Samert's palm had clearly indicated social intimidation). Yes, the sensation was of motherhood, because even though actual motherhood had never been experienced, the harried appearance of mothers, both human and otherwise (note for instance, the exhausted glaze in the eyes of the nursing orangutan), matched that reflected each morning by the mirror over the sink in the second floor bathroom of Samert's rowhouse. Thank Science for the refuge provided by Wenzel's lab, or the assault on the self would have been unceasing (indeed, the round-the-clock togetherness of a honeymoon had so far been avoided with the claim that an important study was underway at the *Schlafzentrum*. Thus Wenzel's response to the news of the marriage—that a *Flitterwochen*, or honeymoon, could be taken at any time—remained undisclosed).

In the meantime, happily, the *Hefeweizen* had provided a pretext to separate from Samert and to find Aslan, that silly boy. The hallway did in fact lead to the kitchen, past doors on either side (one of which possibly opened onto a bathroom, but that investigation could be left until later). The cavernous kitchen however, was unoccupied, unless a fanciful exception were to be made for the two plaster figures perched on the windowsill— figures assumed, on the basis of their red conical hats and long gray beards, to represent garden gnomes. These gazed with black painted dots down upon a large, deep white porcelain sink, the rim balanced two crumb strewn silver trays. Indeed, following in the footsteps of fancy, it was possible to imagine that the two plaster gnomes were the two young women who earlier had been serving the canapes, masquerading as insentient matter, as nymphs do in classical mythology. In reality, however, RR was alone in the cavernous kitchen, which summoned the question, where had the two girls gone, if not back to the party? A question that knocked insistently at another—where the hell was Aslan? And now a vision arose, of three heads on a pillow, of frizzy brown ringlets flanked on either side by dyed strands of red, which although as much a purely mental construction as the conceit of the enchanted plaster figurines, was nevertheless persuasive. It might be worthwhile, therefore, to see where the other doors in the hallway led.

When suddenly a sound was heard, a sound somewhere between a wheeze and a whine. It issued from the corner, on the opposite side of the room from the sink, where there stood a jade-green, ceramic tile chimney-like structure with a metal hatch in the front, evidently some sort of stove or furnace, possibly dating from the days of coal heating, when carboniferous fumes peppered the moths of Manchester black.[10] What, or

---

[10] Of course only figuratively. The truth is that the so-called peppered form of *Biston betularia* gained an evolutionary advantage against the soot darkened

who, was inside the stove? And now a childhood game played with Tom Tom was recalled, a game reminiscent of Hansel and Gretel, though neither Tom Tom nor RR had made the connection at the time. It had been called "Little Person," eponymously after the focal role, which involved speaking in a high-pitched voice and walking on the knees, and proceeded with an invitation to the designated Little Person to "come over to my house for dinner." Thus accepted, the invitation led to Teresa Ramee's green leather reading chair in the living room ("Take a load off…"), which was, in "reality," an oven—at which point the dinner guest, with much shrieking and manufactured convulsions, became the main course. A sadistic game, Mick had said disapprovingly when RR had once shared a laughing reminiscence, a response that had led to the determination that childhood would from then on be a closed record.

"Whee, hee. Wheeee, hee hee hee. Whee, hee. Whee, hee. Wheeee, hee hee hee."

Circumventing a large, antique-looking trestle table, RR discovered a sensory error had been made—the sound emanated not from within the furnace, but from a basket on the floor beside it. An ovate wicker basket in which there lay, wrapped in a matted brown synthetic fiber blanket, a Pekingese dog. It gazed up through globular eyes, clouded over by cataracts, mandibulary malocclusion visible through the thin split of its lips as it drew its breath in, then out again: "Whee, hee. Wheeee, hee hee hee. Whee, hee. Whee, hee. Wheeee, hee hee hee."

Whee, hee, indeed: the dog was, so to speak, about to croak. The nubilous, mucous-clotted eyes, the thin white hair of the

---

trunks of industrial England. For more of this drab little illustration of natural selection, please refer to any General Biology college textbook.

foreshortened muzzle, the frail, brittle sound of the air conduct-
ed back and forth through the sclerotic ducts and tubules of
the failing respiratory system—all of this was indicative of advanced organic senescence. And yet, at the same time, there was
also something of the neonate about the animal. Yes, its facial
features—the high, bulging forehead, the oversized eyes and
small, bridgeless nose—were positively infantile, even embry-
onic, calling to mind images of fetuses in utero—features that
no doubt appeal to some (those who have been programmed
by evolution to respond to such features with nurturing behavior), but that to RR were repellent. Yes, the premature characteristics of the animal were repellent, as, of course, were the
manifestations of its superannuation. Representing both the ex-
treme of youth, the very threshold or entrance into being where
nothing suddenly, absurdly, becomes something, as well as the
exit where something, just as preposterously becomes nothing,
the Pekingese dog was doubly abductive, and thus RR began
to back away, stepping unheedingly rearwards, so that upon
reaching the area of the trestle table, about two meters away
from the ceramic furnace, the right heel presumably came into
contact with the lower rungs of a chair that stood with its cane
seat facing out from the table, a contact which led to the tipping
and consequent overturning of the chair, which in turn brought
about a kind of "domino effect" so that RR toppled with it, in
the process whacking the cranium against the solid wood edge
of the table (all of this "presumably" because consciousness was
lost, and thus the exact circumstances of the descent to the floor
cannot be recalled).

Consciousness was regained to the sound of voices. The
voices came from the other side of the table, which it can be

deduced blocked the view of RR sprawled upon the cold tile floor, and could not be distinguished clearly, either in terms of kind or in the content of their discourse. The experience recalled another, when a minor surgical procedure had been performed—a procedure for which general anesthesia nevertheless had been requested (the ob/gyn was a former medical school classmate) and received. Then, as now, RR had awakened in a cold room to the sound of human discourse that while perfectly audible, had been incomprehensible. It was only after several moments of focused listening that three distinct voices had been discerned—two female (one middle aged, the other young) and one male (also young), all of which employed the flat "a" of upstate New York—and after several more, the subject of their conversation—a medical technician who had grown his hair to his shoulders and consequently looked "like a girl." And now the sensation of lying stretched out in the post-op, prostrated by anesthesia, had been reproduced, although there'd been no surgical operation, at least none that could be recalled. Once again, focused listening was practiced.

"He's a wanker, a bloody wanker."

"Wanker?"

"You know, a chicken choker."

"OK, I'm guessing you mean masturbator. There's nothing wrong with masturbation. Nothing wrong at all with giving ourselves pleasure, as long as we do it privately, in a special private place where no one can bother us as we explore the special private parts of our body. But maybe you're really talking about something else? Maybe you're talking about his history of self-indulgence, the multimillion dollar playground, his 'Neverland' where he thought he could do whatever he wanted with boys like you, and never ever get caught? And that's very upsetting, isn't it? Very upsetting that somebody could do that to other people, touch the special private parts of their bodies without permission. But worse, maybe you know someone like him, someone who has touched your special private parts? Would you maybe like to talk about this person? Would you like to talk about this person here, right now? Should we make this kitchen a safe zone?"

One of the voices was surely Aslan's, though a stabbing sensation at the back of the skull, as a better view was attempted, prevented visual corroboration. But the other?

"A safe zone? You mean like a bomb shelter? Bombs away, baby."

"I think you're being defensive, Ozzie. With good reason. We don't like to admit when someone else has touched our special places, our lovely but hidden spots where we'd rather not be touched. We wonder if we somehow invited him, or her— because women as well as men can do bad things to children— to touch our special hidden spots, if we somehow 'asked for it.' If maybe something about us, some characteristic or quality to which we'd rather not own up, brought us to his, or her, attention. If instead of a sign that says 'no trespassing' we put out one that said 'come on in.'"

"First, I'll have you know I ain't me mother's joy any more. Second, I heard all that about special parts and safe zones and don't let anybody touch your G spot or your bubblegum at me ship of fools back in London and it's all a load of codswallop."

While the full semantic significance of Aslan's words, for surely it was Aslan speaking, was unavailable (what for instance, did he mean by not letting anybody touch "your bubblegum"?

Presumably the term was not to be taken literally), the tonal import was clear. A loud sigh of relief was emitted.

At which point what has been evident to you, Ms. Wall, became clear to the kitchen's other two inhabitants: "Hey, there's somebody in here!"

Assistance was received, providing an opportunity for observation from the once again upright cane-seated chair. One of the voices had indeed issued from Aslan, whose usually smooth brow was pleasingly marred by a slight crease, an effect that recalled a once disputed remark of Teresa Tomaszewski Tomasino Ramee's—that "the beauty of a work of art may be made more captivating by its flaws, as in the case of the Venus de Milo whom our eyes would not embrace so lovingly if she had arms." The same, however, could not be said for the source of the other voice. No, her large, exophthalmic eyes did not enhance her appearance, despite the contrary opinions of others (whose tastes, perhaps, had been conditioned by the outmoded forms of beauty displayed in the fashion magazines of the sixties, an era when buggy, black-ciliated eyes and insect thin limbs were all the rage), nor, as she moved in closer to probe the occipital contusion received during the fall, her black hair gliding over the cheekbones, did her exposed abdomen, its gibbous curve recalling the optic bulge above. In fact, one might speculate that the Lipilina woman (for the aforementioned consort of Dr. Nils Wenzel, it was) was twenty weeks enceinte, given the low, pronounced protrusion of her stomach in contrast to a body that was nowhere else corpulent; however, no evidence of parturition was observed over the course of a nearly nine-month acquaintance with the Lipilina, even as the latter's contours remained unchanged.

"We should consult a professional," the Lipilina declared as she withdrew her fingers, long, substantial appearing fingers with short acrylic-coated nails that had investigated the injury more forcefully than necessary. "Nils will know what to do."

Given that RR was herself a "professional," the suggestion was somewhat insulting. Then again, the imperative "doctor heal thyself" is generally disregarded in the medical community, as we know that the closer the physician to the case, the greater the potential for misjudgment (which is why doctors are discouraged from treating family members). So perhaps it was best to obtain a second, more objective opinion, especially given that the most telling symptom of concussion, asymmetrical pupils, could not be detected at that moment, as it is impossible for the self to observe the self without a mirror. Endearingly, however, Aslan did not agree:

"She don't need a Gamble and Proctor—she is one."

Yes, she is one. Was one. No, is one. A fully licensed medical doctor entrusted with great responsibilities as outlined in the ancient oath to Apollo, Asclepius, Hygieia, Panaceia et. al., responsibilities which include the following: "whatever houses I may visit, I will come for the benefit of the sick, remaining free of all intentional injustice, of all mischief and in particular of sexual relations with both female and male persons, be they free or slaves." Although the preceding mandate appears only in the classical version of the Oath, and not in the modern version written by Louis Lasagna in 1964 to which adherence was pledged upon graduation from medical school. Therefore, there was no binding agent to prevent what happened next, nothing to counter the process of dissolution.

To continue, RR was attired in a midcalf length dress of

silver shot midnight blue merino fastened along the axis from sternum to pubis with a long row of small, mother of pearl buttons—a garment which you may recall, Ms. Wall, from the incident in the tailor shop, or *Schneiderei*. Due to Samert's adept alteration, the dress now fitted like a fine woolen dermis, hugging every centimeter of the lean but very female form. With the physique revealing fit, however, came an accompanying tension, which in the descent described above had resulted in the popping of the four uppermost calcareous discs, ultimately leading to a greater revelation than originally intended. As you may also recall, a narcoleptic episode may be triggered in Kleine-Levin patients by sexual arousal. And as had gradually become evident, Aslan was staring fixedly at the chest, his pupils dilated, his cheeks suffused pink with capillary heat. Reflexively, the gap in the fabric was closed, a gesture of knee-jerk modesty, which was perhaps more effective than the most calculated striptease: the boy licked his full lips, and then, as his eyes slid upwards in their sockets, folded at the knees, crumpling to the floor.

Now once again, KLS is extremely rare. Though a specialist in sleep disorders, RR had never actually witnessed a KLS patient experiencing a narcoleptic fit, and was, therefore, unprepared for Aslan's cataplexis and the abrupt loss of consciousness that had accompanied it. One moment he was "here"— the next "there."[11] And it was, in some impossible to articulate sense, shocking. Though not, apparently, to the Lipilina, who

---

[11] To be sure, according to *Principles of Neurology* (Raymond D. Adams, Maurice Victor and Allan H. Ropper [New York: McGraw-Hill, 1997]), cataplexy (which refers to a "sudden loss of muscle tone brought on by strong emotion," causing "the patient's head to fall forward, the jaw to drop, the knees to buckle, even with sinking to the ground") generally follows rather than precedes the narcoleptic attack, sometimes by many years, and further, in such

having knelt and felt for his pulse, commented "when I was a child in Brooklyn, there was a dog in my neighborhood that used to keel over into sleep, tout d'un coup, just like this when he smelled a bitch in heat. Pardon my French."

But there was no need to request indulgence—"bitch" was in fact the proper term for a female dog.

"I know. I actually meant my French, which is rusty. However, I can see you're very upset about Kemal, who really should be examined by a qualified professional. And, again, so should you—I think we might have a little concussion."

As the Lipilina exited the kitchen to locate "a qualified professional," meaning Dr. Nils Wenzel, even though there was one right there in the room (cerebral impairment or no, a medical degree merited a measure of acknowledgment), RR determined that the term denoting a female dog was in this case *not* to be taken literally. Which is not to say that the Lipilina was allowed to kennel in the consciousness—no, there were more interesting subjects to think about, such as the way Aslan's lashes feathered the smooth curve of his cheekbone, like a tiny paused wing, as he lay fast asleep on the kitchen floor. Or the mousey darting beneath the lid that indicated the R.E.M. phase. What was he dreaming about, and what if it were possible to follow him, to burrow with him beneath the surface of consciousness? What if it were possible to join him in those warm neural warrens, down down down tunneling together through the kaleidescopic corridors of recalled images (as opposed to immediate sensory

---

cases, is accompanied by "the perfect preservation of consciousness" (397). However, given that every person is different, and life is filled with variation and contradiction, the credibility of this report is in no way compromised. Which is not to deny that Aslan's cataplexy and subsequent narcoleptic attack served yours truly well.

impressions, or perceptual images), exploring this concavity and that without ending up anywhere in particular, stuck in some ultimate den or cul-de-sac? A hot hard breath burst the bud of Aslan's lips, followed by a spasm of the pelvis, probably random motor events unlinked to whatever images played in his brain, but wouldn't it be pretty to think so? And then the Lipilina woman returned, ushering in Herr Doktor Wenzel, along with the two delinquent caterers.

Reeking of incinerated cannabis, the caterers recovered the trays from the sink and, appearing absorbed in the task, began to replenish them with additional hors d'oeuvres drawn from the refrigerator. However, their curious glances could be felt as Wenzel engaged with the two patients, beginning with the more juvenile one. It should be noted here that Wenzel had prior knowledge of Aslan's condition, acquired during a brief personal conversation at the *Schlafzentrum* re: RR's newly acquired marital bliss and the boy who'd come with it, a condition in which he had expressed considerable scientific interest, insisting Aslan be brought in for testing, "immediately."[12] Now stooping over Aslan's recumbent body, he exclaimed, "This is a rare treat, but unfortunately much as I would like to bring the boy to the lab at present I must play host rather than scientist. One moment please while I examine him, and also my colleague, and then we will carry him to a bed."

Having checked Aslan's pulse and thumbed back his lids, Wenzel stood up: "*Viel Spass in deiner Traumwelt, mein Kind.*" Then

---

[12] While "[t]here is a strong tendency in science to compartmentalize one's life and to hold personal matters as truly private, as things your colleagues may not know" (*Success Strategies for Women in Science*, ed. Peggy Pritchard, p.78), it was decided that disclosure of these matters would serve the best interests in the long run.

he turned to RR: "Tell me, Dr. Ramee, where are you?"

Knowledge of place, as well as time, was correct. Further, Wenzel's question had not been misunderstood. It is possible, however, that attention was elsewhere, as the answer "a dream world" was provided first, and then hastily replaced with a more accurate one.

"*Hmmm. Eine kleine Desorientiertheit...*" As his narrow face drew near, his deutschmark-sized lenses refracting the light fixture overhead, his breath bore the acrid odor of the older man, which can be compared to the smell of cured meat, and which perhaps signifies the body's losing battle to preserve its own tissues, although that is admittedly pure speculation without empirical support. At any rate, despite his senescent breath, the proximity of Wenzel was not unpleasing, as there was also a boyish quality about him, manifested on occasion, as now, by a bright and uncharacteristically German grin (indeed, the others at the lab referred to this dental display as an "American smile"). "But the eyes are fine. More than fine—the pupils are symmetric and the irises *so blau wie Gottes Himmel*, as my Grannie Semmelmeyer, from *Bayern*, used to say."

The Lipilina, who was standing to the side, leaning against the table, snorted. A cold glance could have been cast in her direction, only now Wenzel was holding up his index finger, commanding "follow me with your eyes, *bitte*." The digit arced through the air, tracing a curved arrow that in its descent pointed directly at Aslan. "*Gut.* Now hold your arms out straight, the palms up, as if holding a salver. *Gut.* Now walk straight ahead, heel to toe, in the direction of the washbasin. *Gut.*"

With the instructions above, Wenzel was, as you may have inferred, inspecting for brain injury. RR had assigned such exercises many times, but had never had to perform them, having always been on the other side of the diagnostic divide. The position now, as examinee, rather than examiner, was not made any easier by the two giggling red-haired caterers, one of whom had picked up her freshly loaded silver tray, and now carried it stiff armed, with rigid, robotic steps, toward the door. To discourage further parody, the seat was reclaimed, and Wenzel, colleague suddenly turned inquisitor, addressed. Well?

Draping his right forefinger over the bridge of his nose, his elbow resting on his left arm, which wrapped across his ribcage, Wenzel peered back. "Well. *Ja. Ja*, I think you are well. However, there is always the possibility of *eine Blutung*—a bleed. Therefore, I think you must stay here tonight. You must stay here tonight, and so should the boy, for observation." Then turning to the Lipilina, who for an unknown reason was smiling, he requested, "*Schatz*, please go to the *Türke* and tell him that Dr. Ramee and the boy will remain here tonight for observation."

"Of course."

Scooping Aslan up in his arms, Wenzel indicated with his chin for RR and the remaining red-headed caterer to follow. Out in the hallway, the caterer stepped past and opened the door on the far right, allowing Wenzel to enter the room beyond with his somnolent load (an image that called to mind the ancient matrimonial custom of "crossing the threshold," which two weeks earlier Samert had wished to practice, but RR had declined to perform the requisite feminine role). A current of air carried the odors of decaying deciduous foliage through the open casement window, along with the faint shouts of children: clearly this side of Wenzel's flat faced the park. Indeed, standing there in the darkness lifted only slightly by the lunar glow from without, it was easy to form a mental picture of blond pixies scuffing soccer balls along leaf littered paths, the numbers on their jerseys glowing in the sulfurous lamplight that filtered through the drooping boughs overhead—RR had seen them (on their way home from practice?) as she frequently crossed through the park in the evenings, to and from the *Schlafzentrum*. But then, suddenly, all mental images, and thinking in general, were suspended by the sight on the bed.

Wenzel had drawn back the duvet, and deposited the boy there, where he lay, his dusky form sunk in and yet set off by additional white cotton covered down, so that it seemed simultaneously both submerged and elevated, a contradiction that would not, could not, be resolved. No, because he simply was, his frizz a thick spray against the pillow, in the center of which rested his smooth, expressionless face, immobile but for the respiratory flutter of the nostrils. Aslan simply was, neither acting nor reacting, as if composed of insentient matter, devoid of force and thus inviting it (as a soccer ball calls to be kicked), and then the red-headed caterer pulled the chain on the bedside lamp, the sudden light causing his frontalis muscle to contract, so that he appeared to frown.

Of course the frown was a mere simulacrum of one, since a genuine frown signifies deep concentration or displeasure, whereas Aslan's expression expressed nothing—was merely a reflexive response to illumination, akin to avoidance behavior in paramecium. On the other hand, it was clear that at some level there was a wish to be left in the dark, even if the wish was unconscious and purely instinctual, and thus Wenzel directed the girl to turn off the lamp: "It is unnecessary. His clothing can be removed later, one way or another." Then, again hooking his finger over his nose, he considered RR: "I think we will put you in the adjoining room."

The adjoining room?

"*Ja ja*, we will put you, as they say, 'next door,'" Wenzel said, walking over to the right wall, in which there was indeed a means of egress (and ingress), previously unnoticed. "*Gut*, it is unlocked."

Ten minutes later (according to the Timex), RR was sitting in a small brocade armchair next to French doors that opened out onto a balcony, as if awaiting the serenade of a paramour. Wenzel had in fact suggested as much, before exiting the room: "*Eine kleine Nachtmusik?*" he'd asked, gesturing toward the open glass doors, through which the vocalizations of the prepubescent footballers beyond wafted. However, as the response had been negative, he'd pulled them closed, and further, promised there would be no intrusions, except for the purpose of neurological evaluation ("*Natürlich*, I will return every three hours to observe for symptoms"). Thus far he had remained true to his word, as on his departure from the bedroom he had denied entrance to a person identified as Samert (whose voice, when excited, had an adolescent tendency to fracture), overriding the latter's objections ("*aber dass ist meine Frau und mein Junge!*) with a firm, "*es tut mir leid—kein Eintritt!*" In fact, judging from the strained breathing and scuffling, followed by heavy, yet diminishing, footsteps, Wenzel, assisted by what sounded like one of the male residents, a young Austrian ("*Ist schon gut, Sam. Beruhige dich. Ich fahre dich heim.*") had not only forcibly led Samert away, but also dismissed him for the night: "*Bis morgen! Und danke, Oliver.*"

Yes, and so Samert would not return until tomorrow, and Wenzel had bolted the door between the first and second bedrooms on the side of the latter. Which meant it could be unbolted. Which meant that there was no reason to sit expectant, like a fairy tale princess or a first time gravida, waiting for deliverance. The doctor, after all, was already in, already in to do an inside job—it was criminally easy. Criminally easy as the bolt slid back with a smooth, German-engineered compliance and the well-oiled hinges silently yielded, as the soft, thick carpet absorbed each measured step. At the time, however, no sense of unlawfulness accompanied these actions, and even now it could be argued that because words have been used carefully, with due attention to connotation, denotation and etymology (as you always urged us to pay, Ms. Wall), all remains with the scope of the "law," as its roots—in the Old English *licgan*, which means "to lie" (as in "to recline") and the Latin *lectus*, which means "bed"—supplied permission "to lie" with Aslan. Yes, it could be argued that "to lie" with him was within the "law," but it won't be, as the argument would be a fallacious one, based on linguistic coincidence and the unpredictable mutability of words over time. Although that never stopped you, Ms. Wall; it is recalled that you frequently relied upon such spurious associations to "reason" for a deeper meaning in the story, as, for example, in your "analysis" of *The Portrait of Dorian Gray*, in senior AP English. Somehow, with the invalid aid of various etymons, one being the Old Slavic word for "to see," which you claimed was a forbear of "Gray," you concluded that the hero was willfully blind, not to his own physical decline, but to the decline of desire itself. Bullshit *n* [origin unknown] (1915). For what you elucidated was not *Dorian Gray* but the difference between those in the Arts and Humanities, and those in the sciences. The scientist, unlike the "artistic type," rejects the seemingly fateful connections between words and events. The permission to lie within the law, a box of lost clothing—there is no pattern, no "story," only the vagaries of chance. Then again, it is also the case that the scientist occasionally skirts the scientific method with intuition, as illustrated by the anecdote in the preceding installment of this report about Kekulé and his discovery of the structure of benzene. Therefore, while it was understood that the two adjoining bedrooms were the work of chance, a little bird, so to speak, indicated that Aslan would not be opposed to a visit.

No, Aslan would probably not be opposed to a visit, although to be sure, the problem at present was whether the softly respiring, but currently noncogitating body on the bed actually be considered Aslan. *Cogito, ergo sum*, said the philosopher. But what happens when "I" am comatose, psychotic or simply fast asleep? The dilemma in the bedroom that night is in fact one of the major problems of modern neuroscience; that is, where does body end and mind begin? Or where am "I" when "I" am not "there"? It could be conjectured, as was earlier in this installment of the report, that Aslan had retreated beneath the surface of awareness, to roam through the recalled image-lined corridors of subconscious sexual fantasy—but, it must be admitted, there was no way of joining him there, and thus of verifying whether any of those recalled images recalled RR. The upshot was that while it had been easy to enter the bedroom, it was less so to enter the bed. It was not, however, impossible—for three reasons:

1. Although there was no way of verifying whether Aslan currently dreamed of RR, his dream state

could be attributed to RR, or at least a portion of
RR. That is, it was almost certain that the partial
exposure of RR's breasts had aroused him, which
in turn had triggered his cataplectic descent into
REM. Therefore, it could be claimed that RR was
Aslan's "dream girl," in the sense that she had induced his dreams, just as, for instance, the sight of
a particular "dream car" in an automobile show-
room, or an advertisement in the newspaper for
a particular "dream vacation" will launch certain
persons into reverie.

2. Further, his waking behavior on numerous occasions had indicated possible sexual interest (e.g., the
"tricks" described previously, which could be viewed
as a form of courtship behavior). Of course, there
had been no definitive sign, such as the locked, lingering gaze exchanged between consensual adults
planning to leave a cocktail party together. Then
again, Aslan was not an adult, and therefore practiced a different sign system, the key to which was no
longer possessed, as said key is necessarily forfeited
upon entrance into the so-called prime of life.

3. Finally, the combined effect of the half-liter of *Hefeweizen* and the mild concussion was to lower inhibition. For while the consequences of consuming that
amount of alcohol in and of itself would have been
null or slight, in tandem with the cerebral swelling,
inebriation was marked. Not, of course, to the point
that coordination was decreased or that words, had

they been uttered, would have been slurred; however, it could be said that judgment was impaired and therefore, that barriers that might have otherwise seemed insurmountable, were not.

Yes, and because barriers that otherwise might have seemed insurmountable were not, it was possible to climb into the bed next to Aslan, to lay supine beside him in a warm white nest of cotton sateen and down. But to lay supine beside someone is not, in itself, much of an accomplishment. Really, as the word "supine" suggests, there is a degree of abjection in the posture, and in fact, lying there in the darkness, listening to the even intake and outtake of Aslan's breath and watching the drawing and undrawing of the tree limbs outside on the opposite wall, like an inconclusive Etch A Sketch (familiarity with the popular children's toy from the 1960s is a prerequisite to visualize this image), the hand advancing toward the adjacent, radiant body of Aslan, then retracting, advancing then retracting, RR was undeniably downcast. A move would never, at this rate, be made. A move would never be made because the necessary enterprise, the requisite chutzpah, was lacking. In short, balls. Because while it is true for humans that environmental factors are as important as genetic ones in the determination of gender, the influence of male hormones such as testosterone cannot be underestimated. Despite an analytical and incisive mind, a mind other, more conventional intellects would describe as masculine, RR was, in terms of sexual temperament, typically feminine and had always, in precoital rituals, been the one pursued, rather than the pursuer. What, or *how*, to do? When suddenly a tiny pffffft was heard, the sound followed by the odor of anaerobic decompostion—i.e., a fart had escaped the boy's buttocks. Yes a fart, which mainly signified, as had Wenzel's breath, that metabolism was operative. Unlike Wenzel's breath, however, the odor was young, indicative not of the decline of the organism, of the losing battle to maintain normal functioning in the face of tissular attrition and gradual systemic breakdown, but rather of its ascent, thus recalling the green tips of burgeoning bulbs poking through sun warmed, compost enriched soil, as seen in Mother Teresa's garden in the spring.

Osman has returned.

Yes, the low rumble of Osman's voice can be heard through the walls. His presence in the penthouse at this time of day, late morning, is unusual. On the other hand, in the past he has been known to return unexpectedly. He has also been known to enter this room, if not unannounced, then with no more than a rap or two on the door, which, given the sluggish nature of the Powerbook 100, is insufficient time to save and close the document. For instance, if he had entered with the completion of the last paragraph above, he might have glimpsed the last several sentences on the screen and asked, even though the answer would seem obvious, "who is RR?" And upon hearing the response, he would have laughed, as he did the first time, when he also commented, "that is the name of an American porn star, such as Linda Lovelace" and then went on to inquire "are you a porn star?" The response was of course negative, as the term "porn star" was (and is) not appropriate. Nor is "pornography." The intention is to present a report, a clear and objective account of what happened. However, given that in certain cases a clear and objective account can have a pornographic effect, as demonstrated by the many who were aroused by that much earlier and better-known report compiled by Dr. Kinsey, no additional details of the first encounter with Aslan will be provided. No further disclosure, not because of shame or embarrassment, although it is recognized inappropriate acts were committed, but to prevent others from using this report for erotic stimulation. In the future it will be, like the above-mentioned prandial games of youth, a closed record. For now, however, another subject must be found—at least until Osman leaves.

So to proceed from the plant image in the second to last paragraph above (a less than logical transition, but the best that can be devised at present), RR was a vegetarian in college, a nearly year-long commitment that had been initiated by participation in a failed experiment. The failed experiment had been directed by an untenured professor, whose research assistant RR was at the time, and had involved injecting twenty rats directly into the hypothalamus with various hormones, as well as saline solution, in order to observe the effect on eating and drinking behavior. Injection was performed via a cannula, that had been surgically introduced into the animal's brain and then secured with a cap of dental cement—an apparatus that looked not unlike a pink plastic beanie outfitted with a miniature stove pipe. Obviously, the professor had admitted, as all the rats had died within three weeks of being outfitted with their skullcaps, the procedure had compromised the animals' well-being, although he would not go so far as to acknowledge that the "sacrifice" had been in vain, and had asked RR to "save" the data by extending the results collected in the first week (which the animals had all survived) over six. When she had refused (and to this day the scientific integrity of yours truly remains intact) he had broken down, claiming that it was "publish or perish."

Whether it was disgust with the dog-eat-dog world of academia (the professor had not in fact received tenure and so association with him had been fruitless), or the lingering pocks and striations on the forearms (the rodents had resisted the cannular injections with tooth and claw), after this episode a resolution to become a complete vegetarian had been made, and kept for eleven months and ten days, until finally resolve was broken by a pastrami sandwich. While the commitment to a diet of vegetables had lasted, however, there had been an accompanying sensation of both purity and entitlement, as the fleshless, dairy-free regimen had not only cleansed the body of unsalubrious substances and byproducts, such as LDL cholesterol, but had provided a kind of existential mandate; because despite the cannibalistic role-playing of youth, yours truly has never felt at ease with the taste and sensation of meat in the mouth, of flesh entombed by flesh (an unease no doubt attributable to Tom Tom, who'd called Mother Teresa's beef brasciole "dead cow roll"). A cucumber, however, is a completely different story.

Yes, a cucumber, like a crisp drink of lake water encased in smooth waxy skin, can be consumed with impunity. Or a fresh plucked fig, a warm weight in the hand seeping the scent of its sweet inner heat…Or a glazed blue bowl of basmati rice lightly seasoned with soy… Or a paper cone of roasted chestnuts, with plump tanned kernels peaking from the splits of charred shells easily pried apart with two thumbs… Or a not quite ripe banana, its yellow peel still flushed with green and slightly adhesive when peeled back to reveal the dulcet horn infused with just a hint of tart, a microtang of kiwi. Or a dangled spoon of honey dripping amber tendrils on a creamy wedge of silken tofu…Yes a person can consume all these things because they lack any kind of consciousness whatsoever, can consume them without concern, either ecological or ethical…taste them, nibble them, lick them and suck them…taste them…nibble them… lick them…suck them…

The door. Yes, that was the door and the rumble of Osman's voice has ceased. Although he can return at any time it is probable, based on past observations, he will not return soon. Most likely he will not reenter the penthouse any time soon and in the meantime this ancient Macintosh is overheating, yes it is overheating its warmth bearing down through the pillow into the thighs the groin and will surely break down unless relief is provided. Relief.

6. A Family Outing

While different human societies prohibit different human behaviors, one practice is universally discouraged: sexual relations between relations. Exceptions to this cross-cultural constant are rare and notable (e.g. ancient Egypt, where intrafamilial intercourse was the exclusive privilege of sovereign siblings). Per usual, science supplies a plausible explanation: as relatives share large percentages of genetic material (50% of chromosomal alleles in the case of sister and brother or mother and son, 25% in the case of aunt and nephew), the possibility of homozygous pairing of harmful recessive genes increases significantly. Or to put the situation in laywoman's terms, a girl who diddles her daddy is more likely to bake a botched bun. Therefore, it is in the best biological interest of society to disallow copulation between individuals with overlapping genetic materials. Science does not explain, however, why the incest taboo extends in many cultures to interactions between individuals with less congruent chromosomes (e.g., to the interactions between stepsisters and stepbrothers, or between stepparents and their stepchildren). The truth is that many of the rules governing social behavior lack biological support, their roots sustained by the dubious nutrients of myth. Unfortunately, the absence of solid ground does not make the consequences of breaking such rules any less real.

Yes, because the absence of a rationale for the prohibition of carnal relations between nonrelations offers no reprieve: punishment is inevitable, whether society's ban against relations between adult and nonadult nonrelations is explicit (as in most American states, where they constitute an offense codified by law) or implicit (as it seems to be in the Turkish Republic of Northern Cyprus, where it remains unclear what statute has been broken). Indeed, punishment is inevitable minus explicit or implicit rules against relations between adult and nonadult nonrelations. The reason punishment is inevitable is that nonrelations between such nonrelations are inevitable: in other words, all relations between nonrelations come to an end, sooner or later. The end of relations between nonrelations can be observed by anyone, by anyone who has had relations with nonrelations (i.e. any person who has grown tired of a lover or had a lover grow tired of them), or anyone whose relations have had relations with nonblood relations (i.e., any person who has noted that their parents always went to bed at different times in different rooms, a case in point being Teresa and Ray Ramee, who after twelve years of marriage retreated to the bedroom and den respectively, the former often reading until the light of dawn commingled with the light of the lamp on the bedside table, the latter falling asleep to the opening witticisms of The Tonight Show with Johnny Carson). Further, this phenomenon (i.e., the cessation of relations between nonrelations) that can be observed by anyone occurs sooner rather than later when only one of the participating nonrelations is an adult. The reason for the premature cessation of relations between adult and nonadult nonrelations is this: sometime during puberty, the nonadult participant will succumb to ripening peers and rising hormonal levels, under whose influence he or she will suddenly recognize the adult participant as postnubile (i.e. as an old geezer or bag).

In any case, if not all cases, the cessation of relations between nonrelations commonly signals the end of emotional intimacy, and thus the loss is two-fold. The loss is two-fold in that it is both sexual and emotional, and as such, is unfair. Yes, unfair, though no doubt this assertion is meeting resistance. Hudson High rumors concerning hanky-panky with a senior ice hockey player or two aside, your view is probably that of most: that the two-fold privation is proportionate to the hubristic excess. In other words, who was RR to think she could have it all? The province of all, however, belongs to the aforementioned most, in that the majority of adults are parents (even you, Ms. Wall, had a small son to call your own), and parenthood is socially sanctioned incest. That parenthood is socially sanctioned incest is obvious: note, for instance, the prolonged coital glow of the mother-to-be, which is provided by the sensation of the fetus nestled deep within her reproductive tract. Further, the fact that parenthood is culturally condoned incest is common knowledge, but common knowledge that commonly goes unacknowledged, thus accounting for why Christian doctrine claims Jesus Christ was not "of woman born." Indeed, the one (and only) achievement of Sigmund Freud (whose theories rack up in silliness what they lack in empirical support) consists in the normalization of the parent's desire for the child via its perversion. Yes, because it is Dr. Freud who skillfully twists Daddy's wish to screw his little girl into her wish to screw *him*, and then declares this a crucial turn (of the screw) in the direction of her transformation into a total woman, as likewise he manufactures Junior's motherlust and then makes this the boy's magnetic North for real manhood. Thanks to Dr. Joy, it is via the course of deviation that children become straight, so that all the parents need to do is assume their posts along the way. The lucky stiffs.

The lucky stiffs who could be seen all around, standing

proud with the mitted hands of their pink-cheeked offspring encircled in their own, or bending down to zip or unzip a Gore-Tex ski jacket or to resecure the Velcro tab of a nylon trainer. But hold on—control has been lost: as evident from the preceding sentences, an unauthorized movement was made from an expository mode to a narrative one. Or more succinctly, no scene was set. To remedy that deficiency, as well as to steer this report "back on track," time and place will now be provided. The time: December 24th, less than one month after the party hosted by Dr. Nils Wenzel. The place: the *Fussgängerzone*, or pedestrian mall, which is located not far from the waterfront in downtown Kiel. Both, it should be noted, had been chosen by Samert—for the purpose of a "family outing."

More specifically, Samert had chosen for this family outing the *Fussgängerzone* during *Weihnachtszeit*, or Christmastime, which means that in the car-free cobblestone street between the glass-fronted shops a *Weihnachtsweg* (if memory serves, this was the correct term) had been built. The "Christmas way" consisted of two long rows of rough log stalls from which ruddy faced vendors purveyed seasonal merchandise. A raised wooden walk ran between, the walk extending out at each end to form two platforms, railed with additional wood. Above, boughs of pine and colored lights spanned a lattice that bridged the two sides of the walk, creating the effect of an arcade, or perhaps of two tall rows of conifers, their branches braiding over the gauntlet of their trunks. The Narnia novels also came to mind, in particular, the experience in *The Lion, the Witch and the Wardrobe* of the children as they walk through the fantastical wardrobe before emerging into the thick forest of another world, although the physical resemblance of the experience of passing through the

Weihnachtsweg to that of passing through the wardrobe is, admittedly, weak. Then again, a link may be found in the common sensation of both magic and peril.

But to return to the task at hand, the establishment of setting, further details must be supplied. As mentioned above, seasonal merchandise was sold within this arcade-like structure, but no examples were given. Here are several: candles infused with chemical approximations of the aromas of Oma's country kitchen; heaps of gray, brown and off-white woolen socks, mittens, sweaters and caps tacky with lanolin and *handgefertigt* by Peruvian peasants; wooden trains and animal figures stamped with minute gold foil ovals inscribed "Made in China"; mugs of hot, alcoholic grog topped with floating plaques of powdered cinnamon (again evoking, possibly with greater accuracy, the scent of Oma's country kitchen). Past the two lines of counters displaying these items (as well as others not listed) pushed tight packs of consumers—parents, children, couples, singles and triples—who examined and frequently purchased said items (and others), most often the grog (the mug, emblazoned *Weihnachten 1999*, included in the price).

At the time at which this narrative resumes, a quest for two portions of that last popular item had pulled Samert from the side of RR, into the dim mill of the retail tunnel. It could safely be assumed that he would be gone for quite some time, given the high ratio of consumers to both retail space and product (indeed, chances were that when he finally pushed his way through the Gore-Texed corps up to the counter, the drink would have run out, leading to further delay). Unfortunately, Samert's pursuit of grog was predicated upon his eventual return to RR, who stood on the platform at the end of the *Weihnachtsweg* (i.e., it had been his intention that he and RR should share together, out in the open, "the season's cheer").

In the meantime, however, Samert's absence provided freedom. Freedom to gaze out over the railing at Aslan playing Hacky Sack with a trio of somewhat older-appearing blond haired youths under a streetlight. Yet, in freely observing Aslan play under the streetlight with his near peers, RR felt somehow debarred. For beneath the diffuse yellow dome of illumination his face appeared pinched and wan, like the face of a changeling, if changelings existed, or of a child reared on a spaceship. Yes, his appearance was otherworldly, remote, unattainable. And yet he had been had, not just once, on the night of Wenzel's party, but twice more, as the sleep attack had lasted several days—the second time as he lay in the *Schlafzentrum*, sweetly tethered by the tendrils of dozens of silver electrodes, the third, after forty-eight hours of observation in Wenzel's lab, at home beneath the soft phosphorescence of the plastic stars studding his bedroom ceiling. He had been had three times, but at the same time, he had not been had, as even as he was there, breathing slowly, then breathing fast, with quick little gasps, he was also elsewhere, far far away, a rock-a-bye boy swaying in the tree tops.

It was a game, of course. Not the Hacky Sack, although that too was a game, a game at which Aslan did not excel—as evidenced by the way the sack, when in his vicinity, flopped onto the paving stones. The game in question, however, was not one at which he clearly did not excel, but one at which he did—that being the game of seduction. A game in which, as well known from personal experience, absence is a principle strategy, as "absence makes the heart grow fonder." Yes, absence is a principal and most effective strategy in the game of seduction, as evidenced by former lovers such as Mick Mackie, who, though initially hesitant to engage in extra-marital sex (claiming he just wanted to be "very good friends"), became progressively less so each time the answering machine picked up. And now Aslan was employing this familiar strategy, by continually exiting the scene. Almost always he was out, peddling kebabs or chumming with chums and even when he was in, he was out, chasing through cyberspace (in the novels stacked by his bed, and in the video games he played at the arcade on the *Fussgängerzone*) or, to make use of a term employed by the deceased Tom Tom, "catching Zs." To be sure, the last pursuit was not a conscious one, and thus could not properly be termed a strategy. Then again, the term "strategy" is quite often used to describe the behavior of organisms whose central nervous systems lack structures associated with consciousness (e.g. frontal lobes), a well-known example being the cuttlefish, whose sepia ruse throws off the most determined predators.

Indeed, Aslan's evasions were probably instinctual. If so, then in seeking to elude RR, he did not rely on reason. Which, after all, can be a crutch, and in some cases even a handicap. For if a person wishes to escape another person, or to flip the coin, to pursue another person, excessive ratiocination may impede flight, or conversely, capture. Consider, for instance, our ancestors, the brow-ridged but not beaten Cro-Magnons who supplanted the even more cranially robust Neanderthals. While the Cro-Magnons' evolutionary success may be attributed in part to frontal lobe expansion and the increased cogitative capacity attending such expansion, it can also be assumed, given the eye-blink speed of talon, tusk and saber tooth, that they were able to leap, so to speak, before looking. And now, like modern humans' not always forbearing forebears, as well as the delight-fully intuitive, naturally elusive pre-teen, RR too would leap. Like early man who rashly sprang for his supper into the midst of the wooly mammoth herd, into the musky churning swirl of pachydermal heat where one misstep would leave him bleeding in the slush, embossed by a throng of ice age feet, RR would jump, without accessing risk, into the pack of Hacky Sackers. Like early man, or one of the boys, she would join in their game, flipping the small bean filled bag up into the air with knees, hips and perhaps even forehead, but always without forethought, as she would rely on fast twitch muscle and reflex alone.

Yes, RR would join in their game, a game that might, it suddenly seemed possible, have been initiated to entertain RR. For the amusement, surely, of his attractive, young or relative-ly young step-aunt,[13] Aslan had gathered the group of blond sporting youths, having politely declined Samert's invitation to retraverse the length of the *Weihnachtsweg* (for they had already pushed their way through once) like a "happy holiday family or yule-tide trio."

"You old yokes don't need me—I'm just in the way," he had replied, and then vaulted over the railing, landing neatly on the cobbles below. (It should be noted, by the way, that there is no inconsistency here in the depiction of Aslan. His lackluster per-formance in Hacky Sack, or indeed in any game involving a flying object [which could be a ball, disc or birdie, as well as a sack] was *not* concomitant with an overall lack of athletic ability

---

[13] "Relatively" young, given that if yours truly were actually a relative of Aslan (e.g. his mother), she would probably be older, given the tendency of highly educated professional women to delay childbirth until their thirties or even early forties.

or grace. In short, he was a joy to observe.) Therefore, as Aslan had sauntered away to a cluster of boys loitering beneath a lamppost, RR professed that she would like to stand a while longer on the platform, breathing in the damp, bracing air blowing in from the fjord. Yes, because as Aslan pulled a small beanbag from the pocket of his cargo pants, tossed it up into the halogen glow, and cried "let the game begin!" what could be more pleasant than to remain outdoors? Of course, this last argument was not aired. Instead, RR had suggested to Samert that the Christmas crush inside the "*Weg*" would be less crushing and possibly even welcome following a stint in the cold. Further, in the meantime a mug of grog could provide warmth. Maybe Samert could obtain one. Or two. Yes, a mug for both himself and RR, so that they could share together a cup of the season's cheer (okay, a correction is in order: the idea for side-by-side seasonal quaffing, al fresco, was not Samert's. Samert, however, had readily agreed to procure drink for the occasion).

And now, given the Christmas crush inside, it would be, as noted above, some time before Samert returned with the requisite mugs of grog. Which gave a rationale for joining the boys (there were four, including Aslan) playing Hacky Sack (to keep warm)—though of course no rationale was needed. RR was free to join, free in the sense that there was no obligation to entertain the tailor in his absence (which anyway, without the aid of a closed circuit TV, would be impossible). Given the freedom to join, and also a high level of fitness (due to daily aerobic and anaerobic conditioning), it was easy to hop over the railing and drop to the street below. Indeed, the ease of the maneuver seemed to be an endorsement of it, and thus of the intention to join the game, whatever bystanders might think. For while the age difference between RR and the Hacky Sackers was admittedly large, the physical difference (leaving aside the chromosomal discrepancy) was not: with hair tucked under a knit cap, and breasts muffled by a down feather-filled parka or bound by a stiff denim jacket, RR looked like a boy. Many had said so, including Mick Mackie, who had also viewed RR unbound numerous times, and opined that from the back, from the waist up, she might be mistaken for a he, specifically a young he. As she strolled toward the Hacky Sackers, RR pursed the lips and blew, to heighten the boyish effect, although she also did not want to push it. No, for when an imitation goes too far, it becomes parody or burlesque. And the intention was not to ridicule, nor to make a theatrical spectacle of the self or of the boys, who had in the meantime stopped playing and now stood, Aslan included, staring at RR as if at a juggling clown or snake charmer. Therefore, halting in the shadows just beyond the perimeter of the lamp's halo, she ceased to whistle.

Good things, as oft noted by Mother Teresa, come to those who wait. As restraint was exercised, Aslan in the meantime drew the other boys together in a huddle, and murmured what can be assumed were inspiring words to each. For soon afterwards the game resumed, and within moments, the sack approached, propelled by a collapsed knot of kicking boys who now screamed, in a friendly way, for RR to hit it (as indicated by their use of *schlag!* the informal imperative of the German verb for "to hit, whack or beat"). This was done, with a roll of the shoulder and a flap of the attached, crooked arm (a gesture similar to the upper body movement performed in the popular wedding dance called the "chicken"), which sent the sack back into the fray. A trajectory which it was natural to follow, so that now young thermodynamic bodies surrounded on all sides, their heat unlocking the axillary malodors of youth—the fuzzy funk of bacteria feasting on nascent underarm secretions, the fust of semen-sprinkled underwear billowing forth out of the loose folds of oversized t-shirts and low-slung jeans. Yes, young bodies, including Aslan's, surrounded on all sides, spinning a dizzying vortex of protoadolescent stinks. Oh yes. Consequently, when the sack approached again, RR failed to make contact.

Consequently, the sack now lay on the ground, like a bird stunned in its flight by a windowpane. Aslan stood gazing down, helixes of hair like thick strands of yarn drooping over his forehead, his unzipped parka revealing his heaving chest, which strained against an unusually small athletic jersey (unusually small in that his shirts were usually over-sized) inscribed with the legend "RED DEVILS 97." What was he thinking? Would he continue the game, or would he initiate some new one? Would he stay or would he go? With his thumb and forefingers, he pulled at the cusps of his upturned collar. Then he lifted his eyes, his pellucid green eyes which, however, in the artificial illumination of the streetlamp could have been blue, or hazel, the eyes of some other boy, indeed any of the other three, the three lightly pigmented, as well as slightly piggish looking older boys who now looked to Aslan for the signal to resume. Suddenly, before any could protest, he scooped up the bag with his right foot, transferred it to his left, and flipped it up into his right hand. Stashing it in his capacious cargo pocket, he announced, "This game was me bastard child and now I've killed it." Funny boy.

As he walked away, back to the *Weihnachtsweg*, a decision was made to follow him. A decision was made to follow him, but not to catch up with him, as he had not indicated that he wished for a companion. Indeed, to be honest, he had not formally acknowledged RR's presence during or after the game, let alone his desire for it. Perhaps this was part of the game, which then could not be considered over but ongoing. Yes, perhaps this was part of the ongoing game, the larger game, which was not Hacky Sack but seduction. The larger game being seduction, the proper course was to follow, up the short set of creaking stairs to the wooden platform at the near end of the Christmas arcade, and then into the crowd inside, where Aslan had just disappeared, like a penny into a so-called wishing well.

Inside, as RR pressed through the carousing phenotypes of the North German gene pool (where the allele for blondness was as thick as pond scum), good cheer was maintained by imagining the fresh open air awaiting respiration at the opposite end, where at last Aslan would be joined, beneath a dark night sky whose remote astral bodies would seem as near and dear as the plastic glow-in-the-dark stars of a boy's bedroom ceiling. Yes, a positive attitude was kept up, like a chalice borne safely through a throng of foes (an inspiring image borrowed from a well-known work studied in AP English), even as the sour vapors of spilled wassail, not to mention the stearic reek of wurst breath (which seemed to emanate from all—from infants snuggly bound at their mothers' breasts to wobbling octogenarians), assailed. Yes, RR pushed on, ramming against solid-packed family units (for blood, not to mention flesh and bones, truly is thicker than water), enduring jabs of elbows and stomps of feet, slipping and nearly falling in front of a *Pfannkuchen* stall on a mucosal mat of regurgitated fried cake—pushed on, guided by the vision of the magical meeting that would surely ensue outside, beyond the end of the Christmas arcade.

Then again, the vision of success was not enough to insure success: quite possibly, Aslan would become weary of waiting in the gelid outdoors and would seek to warm himself in a shop or restaurant somewhere along the pedestrian zone, or through additional sport. A success-insuring measure would have to be taken, because otherwise by the time RR had made her way through the mobbed arcade, the boy might be gone.

Thus a guise was borrowed as well. In German, RR communicated her wish to find her lost *Kind* (or child) while adopting the appearance of a distraught mother. Instantly, the crowd parted. Indeed, the response to this guise of maternal desperation (a guise complete with rolling eyes and wringing hands) was more immediate than anticipated: it was as if an innuendo or mild proposition had been answered with the unzipping of a zipper.

"I'm afraid no one understands you. You want to 'make up' a child? Are you trying to say that you wish to conceive?" It was the Lipilina woman. The Lipilina, who had appeared as if spontaneously generated by the kin-thick mob, as sudden as a maggot in a parcel of decaying meat or a rodent in a bin of moist grain. Both of which she called to mind, her larval white face framed by a nylon hood trimmed with an oval of ratty fur.

What? RR explained that she did not wish to have a child, but to find one, specifically the boy Aslan, in relation to whom, as the spouse of his legal guardian, Samert Mart, she stood as a surrogate mother. The reason for the Lipilina woman's miscomprehension was not explored at the time, though in retrospect the verb *erfinden* may not have been the best choice, as according to *Cassell's German English Dictionary*, it has the figurative sense of to "invent" or "make up" as well as, surely, the more literal meaning of "to find."

"Yes, but surrogate motherhood is simply that—a way of satisfying emotional cravings but not the deeper physical ones, especially when the child is on the cusp of puberty. Is it possible that we're starting to hear the tick tock, tick tock of our biological clock?" the Lipilina woman asked, the scent of her breath, pickled onion, all too discernable as she invaded the two-foot buffer zone conventionally maintained between American speakers.

At this point a mistake was made—to dispute with rather than simply to disengage from the Lipilina. RR countered that while the basis of human personality was fifty percent genetic, it was also fifty percent environmental, as evidenced by numerous studies demonstrating divergent psychogenetic development in monozygotic twins over time. In other words, we are what we eat, both literally and figuratively—the twin predisposed to leanness and introversion but raised on a diet heavy on fatty foods and light on books will surely turn out differently than his or her identical sibling predisposed to same but raised on rice cakes and classics. Further, one of the defining characteristics of Homo sapiens, as opposed to other, more "hard-wired" species, is behavioral plasticity. Without delving into the neurophysiological basis of "behavioral plasticity," which would in fact be beyond the scope of the laywoman's understanding, it could safely be said that said plasticity would enable those brought up by shitty mothers to reflect on their upbringings and decide that they did not want to become shitty mothers themselves. Which was not to condone the post-Freudian practice of blaming everything on the mother, but simply to illustrate the point. The point being that the desire to reproduce was not a constant among women (even among women who in terms of sexual temperament could be considered "typically feminine"). Or in layperson's terms, being a broad was not the same as being a breeder.

"Although I'm not, it's true, trained like you and Nils in the hard sciences, I am a licensed psychotherapist whose many years of clinical experience have provided the ability to distinguish, with great accuracy, sincere utterances from insincere ones. In 'layperson's terms,' it's called a bullshit detector. Which right now indicates someone is full of shit. Is that possible? Is someone being a little disingenuous? Or could it be that someone doesn't even realize she's being disingenuous? Could it be that she's hiding her deepest desire, even from herself, by making inappropriate object choices?"

Without overreacting, it could be said that the Lipilina was outrageous. Yes, she was outrageous in her ratty, seventies polar explorer-style parka, which as she pushed back the faux fur trimmed hood to reveal her long, sleek black hair, was seen to be lined with orange nylon the exact shade of hazard cones on the highway—outrageous with her evasive "someones," and with her nevertheless all too obvious insinuations. However, at the time recorded by this report, it was thought best to appear unruffled. Therefore RR asked, without discernible ridges, what was meant by "inappropriate object choices"?

The Lipilina drew back, out of the crowd, back into a narrow space between a stall selling cinnamon and vanilla scented candles, and another vending fresh baked breads. At least, in following her lead, RR had the outside. Meaning there was no danger of being trapped between the wall and the Lipilina. No, there was no danger of being trapped, as long as there was an exit, or a direction in which to back away. Because there was no proof.

"Mmmm, I love the smell of fresh-baked bread, don't you? Even better when it's still in the oven, baking..." The Lipilina stroked the nylon wrapped bulge of her abdomen, just inches away. No reply was made, as the question was assumed to be a rhetorical one. And indeed this turned out to be the case as the Lipilina continued, her pickled onion breath combining with the odors of bread and cinnamon and vanilla candles wafting in from either side to compose a scent that might be found in a kitchen where a woman was perspiring freely, having done unpaid domestic labor since dawn (or as the maternal progenitor used to put it, "being a slave to you all").

"Yes, I love the smell of fresh, hot bread. And I also love to eat it—crusty French, stone-ground wheat, rye, and especially dark moist pumpernickel like my nana used to make. But if I eat as much as I like, I blow up like a balloon. So I try to exercise moderation... It's hard, growing up in a family where heavy, fattening foods are constantly on hand." The Lipilina's hands, palms pressed together, aligned with the zipper of her parka, partitioning her breasts. Her voice dropped to a whisper: "Always a struggle, always a struggle..."

Then her voice rose: "But not for my sister Irina. She hit puberty and all those years of subliminal and not so subliminal subjection to American beauty standards kicked in. Suddenly she hated Russian food, she claimed. Potato pancakes made her stomach flop, she claimed, borsht made her gag, pumpernickel bread made her puke. Now she said she loved the taste of iceberg lettuce—so delicate. That she adored cottage cheese. And the pounds fell away. But I knew she was lying."

"Obviously it was sublimation," the Lipilina continued, lacing her fingers beneath her chin. "What she loved was her taut stomach, her firm, well-divided thighs, her slim hips and little ass. The slender Barbie who'd stepped out of the round babushka shell. What she loved was absence, the absence of chafing flesh and dimpled skin, an absence processed out of presence, as flavorless as saltine crackers. Which she could not admit— could not acknowledge—was her sacrifice. Because it's hard in American society to admit privation. We're constantly told we can have it all—a family and a career, a Caribbean vacation and a Mercedes-Benz, just enter the sweepstakes, a cigarette and the stamina to climb to the top of a mountain to smoke it, cake and ice cream, the whole enchilada and a cherry on top. We're told we can have it all, especially we women, and when we can't, we validate our failure by embracing our failure, thus negating our bodies and ourselves."

Kudos to the Lipilina, for her theory was partially supported by personal empirical experience. That is, it was true that less than "all" had been procured (as already noted above in the discussion of parenthood as socially sanctioned incest), and that in the process self, and to a lesser extent body, had been denied. Then again, the bit about how "we validate our failure by embracing our failure" seemed off the mark, as well as quasi-mystical in tone. Neither praise nor criticism were proffered, however, as these would only prolong an exchange from which RR needed, like a motorist delayed by the orange cone constriction of a road repair zone, extrication. Before departure could be taken, however, a disturbing term remained to be clarified: so, again, what had been meant by "inappropriate object choice"?

The steady fringed gaze of the Lipilina was met, and returned. The Lipilina blinked, her mascara-thickened lashes sticking together for a second, then pulling apart. She may have cleared her throat as well, although the surrounding noise level was such as to obscure the sound. "Sometimes, when we want something very badly, yet feel we can't have it—maybe because we don't think we're good enough to have that thing, because we think we don't deserve it—we make it impossible. Sometimes we make a completely wrong, self-defeating choice just to assure ourselves that we have a choice. Or to put it another way, in making the possible impossible you've become the master, at least, of him."

She knew—the Lipilina knew. Through intuition, or some other nonmaterial means, she knew that service had been rendered, volitionally or not. Yet, again, there was no physical evidence, no ruptured membrane to be examined, no identifying semen to be collected. There was nothing to see, nor for that matter, to hear. The boy could say nothing because he remembered nothing. Therefore, all there was to remember was that there was nothing to remember. Therefore the best defense was none—that is, the best defense was to behave as if no offense had been committed. That is, to play dumb. How then, RR asked, was she Aslan's "master"? Surely the role, as the partner of his legal guardian, was more a caretaking than a subjugating one.

"I said 'im,' not 'him.' Master of 'im' or 'in,' in the sense of the Latin prefix for 'not.' As we make our only choice the choice not to have the thing, our only power is the power of negation. But maybe there is a 'him' in the sense that there is a person who makes your possible, impossible. How well did you know Samert Mart before you married him? How well do you know 'him' now?"

Suddenly, it became evident that the Lipilina was in the dark. Without a lumen in regard to the affair with the boy, she instead was groping pruriently for information about the relationship with the Turkish tailor. And indeed, the alliance had aroused curiosity in the Lab, as indicated by covert questions about Samert's educational, political and socioeconomic status (would he automatically be conferred American citizenship?), as well as more overt ones about his sexual abilities (e.g. could he, "like most *Türken*," maintain an erection all night?). No doubt the Lipilina had fed, through Wenzel, upon gossip and speculation, and now sought more substantial nutriment.

In recognition of the Lipilina's dietary needs, a bone was tossed. That is, RR told the Lipilina that she would in the future provide the "skinny" on Samert, over coffee and a plate of fresh, hot currant-studded *Brötchen*, but in the meantime, it was necessary to "skedaddle." Then, to insure that the *Brötchen* invitation would not be perceived as sincere, a common but effective brush-off phrase was employed ("call me") combined with a dismissive gesture (fingers wriggling weakly over a retreating shoulder).

"I will. I'd also like to hear…" What, however, the Lipilina would also like to hear could not be heard—for a quick departure followed the osteological tossing.

By now, much time had been lost, or at least appeared to have been lost, since time is experienced as linear and irretrievable. Fortunately, spatial gain could offset the temporal loss—prior to the encounter with the Lipilina, RR, in the guise of a distraught mother, had nearly reached the end of the *Weihnachtsweg*, as corroborated by the cold currents of air gliding through a crowd that in the meantime had grown considerably less dense. Within moments, RR was stepping out onto the terminal platform, experiencing a sensation not unlike stepping out into a winter woodland clearing, as the sky seemed to open up while at the same time there was a pungent smell of pine, suddenly evident now that the masking odors of food, drink, digestive effluvia and artificially scented candle wax no longer prevailed. Yes, the sensation was of a clearing in the midst of a forest, a forest filled with forest animals, with dark, furtive bright-eyed beings who, caught in the necromantic bath of lunar light, might reveal improbable, chimerical combinations—tree women with manes of cellulose hair and pliant, sapling limbs, for instance. Or goat boys with soft, smooth chests and hard, calciferous hooves. Or both, dancing together over packed shadow-dimpled snow like a vast rumpled bed sheet.

Opposed, however, to the sensation of a clearing in the midst of a magic imbued wood was the reality of the pedestrian mall. Therefore, reverie ceded to reconnaissance. On a bench, two senescent women in bone-toggled coats and feather trimmed felt hats leaned into each other, hands clasped, vapors of coalescing breath muddling their two faces into one. Clustered about an empty concrete planter, leather-clad, chain-festooned, skin-headed youths convulsed, smoking and spitting, dogs with steel studded collars and radically abridged muzzles snuffling at their feet. Beneath a sulfur streetlamp, identical to the one at the opposite end of the Christmas arcade under which the game of Hacky Sack had been played, a very lightly pigmented person, possibly an albino, in a short skirt and striped stockings pivoted, her right hand sliding around the iron pole like a cat around an ankle. From a yellow telephone booth, a pair of booted legs extended stiffly over the cobblestones, the slumped form within obscured by murky plexiglass. Otherwise, the mall was empty.

No doubt he had grown weary of waiting. Yes, he must have grown tired, or bored, or both. The possible albino's hand suddenly dropped, and she sauntered away, swaying in tall shiny pumps, into the shadows. Suddenly, a question came to mind: what if he'd never waited at all? What if there had been no game? Or what if the game had been one sided, as when RR was a child and would hit tennis balls alone against the garage (Tom Tom having no interest; it was a pastime, he said, for past times, for old goats and geeks)? And now an unbidden memory arose, of an afternoon when the ball had bounced off the garage door into the privet hedge. As RR had possessed only one ball, its loss had necessitated its immediate retrieval. On parting the hedge, however, RR discovered not the expected fuzzy green ball, but instead an animal whose waxen pink skin showed through its coarse gray fur like an old man's scalp through the strands of his comb-over. Hissing, the animal had gazed up at RR, the pupils in its yellow eyes contracted to pinholes through which RR's consciousness nevertheless seemed to drain so that as the moments passed there seemed to be nothing but it, nothing but the hissing, pulsing protoplasm of existence, which, when considered objectively, is simply matter and energy. Which, in turn, are ineluctably disposed toward degradation and dispersal. Or entropy. And then consciousness had, literally, drained away, as the vision grew dim and RR sank, slowly to the driveway in an eddy of syncope. Later, when consciousness was regained, the animal (most probably, in retrospect, a possum), had vanished, compressed leaves and broken twigs the only evidence of its one time presence, hissing in the privet. But in the meantime, the ball had reappeared, lying on the gravel just a few feet away as if it had been there the whole time. As had Aslan. Yes, for suddenly he was leaning against the lamppost abandoned just moments before by the albino.

Aslan's reappearance, like the long ago tennis ball's, had not been perceived, and yet he was there. He was there, leaning back against the iron pole, jacket still unzipped despite the cold, his balled hands in his pockets pulling the loose fabric of his pants down and out from under the hem of the unusually small, possibly shrunken RED DEVILS 97 jersey to display several centimeters of fly as well as the elasticized waistband of his white boxer shorts, above which could be glimpsed a silvery sliver of skin. What could not be glimpsed was the pilose texture of that skin, the scant blond down that in the median between navel and groin darkened ever so slightly, curling and merging into a faint soft bisecting line, a tracing by which to split one boy into two. Nor, for that matter, was it possible to read the expression on his face, turned and tilted toward the platform from which he was observed. His posture, however, seemed to indicate expectancy—to invite, at the very least, approach.

A bray of laughter erupted from the cluster of skin-headed youth, followed by "*Genau! Genau!*" as the cobblestones between the platform and the lamppost were crossed. Most likely this eruption bore no relation to RR—indeed, it would be paranoid to think so. Nevertheless, an unusual degree of self-consciousness was felt, concurrent with a flurry of tachycardia. Yes, the heartbeat quickened as RR stepped toward Aslan, who now had turned his face away, a gesture that could literally be taken to signify aversion, and which called to mind how Tom Tom had referred to all adult women as BAGs (for Big Ass Gals), a term which from the narrow-hipped standpoint of preadolescence had been perfectly fitting. Therefore, when the remaining distance had closed to about two meters, no further steps were taken.

"Hey," he said, slowly moving his face back into view. There was a sheen on his cheekbones.

RR nodded, actual words deemed hazardous until the appropriate tone for the occasion could be determined.

"So, am I going to get the push?"

The push?

"Like in shove. You know, the boot."

But why did Aslan...Ozzie, think that he was going to be sent away? A small step forward, what is termed a "baby step" in the children's game "Mother May I," seemed permissible.

"Cuz Uncle Sam said he found me a new ship of fools, run by Captain Kirks somewhere in Anatolia."

What was wrong with Ozzie's school here in Kiel? Wasn't the German academic system renowned for its rigor? Another baby step was ventured. And then another.

"Nantwas—absolutely nothing. But he thinks I'll carve up his plans. You know, ruin his chances with you..."

Apparently Samert had intuited that RR's interest in the boy exceeded the boundaries of simple goodwill or coguardianship. Yes somehow, without rational thought or evidence (for surely there was no evidence), he had sensed that the cathexis, as Dr. Joy would say, was in Aslan, not in him. And now, on the basis of this irrationally arrived at yet nevertheless completely correct conclusion, Samert was providing for the removal of his rival. Likewise, it appeared that Aslan, though he had not explicitly said so, had guessed that he was an obstacle to his uncle's matrimonial happiness—which was intriguing. Intriguing, but for the present not to be investigated. No, for the present, Aslan's awareness of the desire he elicited would remain unprobed, until his own feelings for RR were better understood. In the meantime, the problem of the Turkish boarding school had to be solved, but how? RR took a baby step back. Then, recalling the phrase that the best defense is a good offense, she reversed course: Samert's fears were denounced, in a firm tone, as totally ridiculous.

"I know," Aslan said, stretching the hem of his abbreviated jersey to wipe his cheekbones, and thus providing a view of the flutes of his rib cage and the small, tight stomach tucked below, a view which summoned associations of whale bones, wasp waists and dainty, poison-tipped stilettos. A view the memory of which even now signals a pause for an instant of reverie. There. RR cleared the throat and took another small step back.

Aslan released the jersey; however, due to improper sizing it remained bunched around his chest, necessitating adjustment. Having thus tugged the shirt down over his winsome abdomen, he paused and studied the front it. "This was a prezzie from me Mum. We used to kick it around together, me and her. She was a brainbox, like you."

Please consider, Ms. Wall, the problem. Important new data had been received—that Aslan identified yours truly with his mother—but what to do with it? On the one hand this maternal identification indicated the potential for a deep emotional attachment and, therefore, for the trust that typically accompanies such an attachment. On the other, it could also be an obstacle to intimacy (e.g., the phrase "you remind me of my mother" is not typically employed for the purpose of seduction). Then again, "We used to kick it around together" implied frequent shared activity, which in turn implied a pair bond, a connection usually only found between lovers or very dear friends. In which case, the maternal identification could serve as a platform for a mutually fulfilling relationship. Suddenly a question came to mind—a question subsequently asked: had Aslan terminated the Hacky Sack game because it had called forth painful memories of "kick[ing] it around" with his mother?

He stared at the ground, hands now in his pockets, tracing a circle with his toe. His tongue shifted from one cheek to the other. At last he looked up, his green gaze, as always, unfathomable, and nodded.

Mother may I? Yes you may.

7. The Clinical Method

As evidenced by Aslan's disclosure concerning the abrupt termination of the Hacky Sack game, a conflation had occurred. Specifically, Aslan had conflated the figure of the prematurely deceased mother with an extant, non-consanguineous adult female (i.e., RR). But what did this conflation indicate, libidinally? Had it served to increase or decrease Aslan's desire for RR—was it or was it not a turn on? While the boy's actual feelings had no coital import, as his autonomic response to stimulation could be counted on, they nevertheless were of value. Otherwise, there was no difference between a singular boy and an elaborately engineered doll or imaginary construct. That is, the game would remain hopelessly one-sided, like a tennis match played against the garage door.

In the weeks that followed the *Weihnachten* festival, the question of Aslan's actual feelings remained, like an unopened package beneath a yuletide tree, although they had, at Samert's insistence, opened all on the 25th, "in keeping with Songül's Christian and American tradition." Yes it remained, as neither the motorcycle jacket and Game Boy given to Aslan nor the Manchester United mug received from him revealed anything— during both exchanges he had maintained a neutral smile, even as a well-tied bow. Meanwhile, the day of the boy's departure for the Atatürk Academy in central Turkey (February 23rd, one week before the beginning of the spring term) drew nearer, the human experience of time being what it is, unidirectional and irreversible. His departure drew closer, while at the same time, he did not, as he worked long, seemingly continual, hours at the kebab shop in order to amass pocket money for boarding school (and to thus avoid, as he put it, being "pink lint" with the "Captain Kirks").

Coterminously, Samert was spending longer periods in his shop than usual, his hours expanded, he claimed, per the necessity to accommodate the "fat Germans who, becoming fatter the last year, now need their clothing increased in size for this new year." Indeed, frequently Samert did not arrive back at the development until the early morning. If Aslan had been more often at home, Samert's long absences would have provided intervals for observation and assessment. As the situation stood, however, these absences were a source of additional frustration, in that it is difficult to argue with a person who is not present. Surely, for instance, recent reports in the *International Herald Tribune* concerning the rise of fundamentalism in formerly secular Turkish institutions would have interested the atheistic tailor. But because he was, except for a few brief, flurried moments each morning before he left for work, not present, opportunities for well-supported objections to schooling Aslan in Turkey were, accordingly, unavailable. With the exception of Christmas day, now more than six weeks past. And on that day Samert had effectively buffered his presence with presents. That is, each time RR had broached the subject he had given her another: an exquisitely tailored Shantung suit, an embroidered vest of Anatolian origin, an oilskin rain poncho modeled on WWII stormtrooper designs, Bundeswehr-inspired velvet cargo-style hiphuggers, a "Blue Angel" silk camisole, knee-high patent leather boots, a green jade "Teiki" pendant from New Zealand ("because you are a warrior princess"), etc. Due to an admitted weakness for material goods, particularly for clothing, the degree of distracted pleasure had been such that the boarding school issue was pushed aside until the following morning, at which point Samert had escaped to his shop.

The problem, therefore, was twofold. First, how to assess Aslan's feelings re: RR when he was never about, and second, how to prevent his physical removal to the Atatürk Academy? Or rather, to prioritize, first: how to retain him, bodily, and second: how to assess his feelings re: RR? (For without their somatic substratum, the boy's emotions were immaterial.) While complex problems often can be solved by following a series of orderly steps, as demonstrated by the success of the modern clinical method, to follow said steps requires time. Thus how to obtain time? Yes, that was what it all boiled down to: how to obtain time?

Then, late one night at the Lab, a synapse fired, so to speak. RR had driven to the *Schlafzentrum* to recover the handbag, which had been left behind earlier in the evening and which contained the key to the as usual empty rowhouse. Rather than returning directly home, she'd lingered to look in on a middle-aged sleep apnea patient assigned by Wenzel to one of the residents, a young Austrian who earlier in the day had been summoned back to Vienna by a family emergency. Sitting in an overstuffed armchair (for there was no rush to return to the empty rowhouse), RR regarded the sleek beechwood headboard that rose up behind the prone, wire-twined bulk of the middle-aged sleep apnea patient. The bed was reminiscent of something, but what? And then it came: the bed was not only familiar, but in a sense familial, its style recalling the one in the connubial quarters of Teresa and Ray Ramee. Indeed, the sleep observation room with its midcentury modern décor of plush carpeted floors and geometric print papered walls (a décor meant, according to

Wenzel, to facilitate sleep by evoking the stream-lined comfort and security of the *Bundesrepublik* during the postwar economic boom), could have been the Ramees' bedroom.

Further, as one association so often triggers another, it became evident that the 44-year-old (according to his chart), mildly obese patient, who lay on his side snoring into a drool-darkened pillow, was in turn reminiscent of Ray Ramee. Yes, the patient could have been Ray Ramee, who having complied with Teresa's nightly imperative to *eat, eat, eat* would stagger off to his den, and fall to the couch in an ursine stupor. Yet, as the patient was reminiscent of the dopey, bear-like spouse of Teresa, he was also typical, one of many such overweight middle-aged men, who were married to or living with middle-aged women. Middle-aged women. The EEG machine began bleeping—respiration had, as is typical in apnea cases, momentarily ceased. 38, 39, 40. The bleeping stopped, but no record of the number of seconds of suspended breathing was made in the patient's chart. For 38 was only two years away from 40. Middle age loomed and the boy would be lost, his bloom blown off in the windswept plains of central Turkey. The patient wheezed, choked, sat up, then sank back again beneath a tangle of silver wire, just as Ray Ramee, after claiming he couldn't take another bite of Teresa's linguine, would succumb to a fresh plate because... *because I'm your better half and I say it's better if you eat; otherwise you're gonna be hungry later. So eat, eat, eat.*

Eureka, for at this last associative juncture, a revelation hatched: from the command post of the better half, orders could be issued. RR could, for instance, decree that the previously avoided honeymoon be taken, and Samert would have to obey, as the marriage vow mandated. Further, as Wenzel had said back in November that the honeymoon, or as he, with a twinkle in his eye, had termed it, *Flitterwochen*, could begin at any time, it would begin the following week, and would include Aslan, since true marriage entails complete acceptance of the other and his lot. Hence a little R & R would be compulsory for both males, to provide the elder with a respite from round the clock sewing (which was surely exacerbating the contact dermatitis on his hands), and the younger with a break between the kebabs and the mullahs. But where? Over on the bed, the patient gurgled then growled, again bringing to mind the bear-like bulk of Ray asleep in his den, a bulk consistently bathed in the cathode glow of some late-night oldie such as *Grand Hotel*. And once more free association delivered an excellent (if not free of charge) answer, as now another recent article in the *International Herald Tribune* was recalled. According to the travel section article, the luxury hotel featured in the classic film was in Berlin, and although completely rebuilt from the ground up in the mid-1990s (having been destroyed in WWII), belonged to another, more glamorous era—an anachronistic affiliation that was exactly what the doctor ordered. For surely the best way to forestall the future was to dwell in the past.

Initially, Samert had objected to the now mandatory postnuptial getaway (presumably because it was no longer his idea). Indeed, when informed at his shop the day after the Lab epiphany that their vacation at the famous Adlon Hotel in Berlin would commence on the following Monday, Samert had replied, like a typical husband, "Songül, it is impossible. I have not a spare minute for the next two weeks, not one." Twenty-four hours later, however, he phoned the Lab to comply—he had, evidently, located a temporal reserve. Aslan, assured in the meantime that his weekly earnings at the kebab shop would be matched (a pittance totaling less than one night's accommodation at the luxury hotel), and further, that Elvis could accompany them (the Adlon being *hunde- und katzfreundlich*), had packed a black nylon rolling suitcase, the handle tied with a personalizing red ribbon or pennant embossed with the words "Man United," and set it by the front door.

Thus less than a week later, on February 12th, the two males in the life of RR could be found in the classical Greek-style spa area of the Adlon Hotel in Berlin. The elder was completing lap after lap in the swimming pool, perseverating in a manner that would have been annoying had there not been the happy distraction of the younger, who over the two hours had been alternating between the frothy whip of the jetted bath and the white terrycloth of the oversized robe supplied by the hotel. Most absorbing, of course, was the short stretch in between, when his long black surfer shorts (purchased three days before at the famous Berlin department store, *KaDeWe*) plastered his buttocks and thighs as his feet slapped slapped over the tiles back to a chaise lounge shaded by a potted palm.

At present, the boy sprawled, reading, on the chaise lounge, his body concealed by the oversized robe, an excess of Egyptian cotton that deprived the eyes, yet also, admittedly, supplied the imagination well. Very well, indeed. For beneath the swathes of fabric, physiological processes were occurring, processes that could be envisioned, and further, elaborated upon. Blood, for instance, was flowing, propelled by the contractions of a specialized muscle, the heart, through a closed circuit of continuous vessels known from cadavers as well as anatomy textbooks; therefore the process could be envisioned. Yes, this ongoing, unceasing (until death) closed-circuit flow could be envisioned, and further, elaborated upon, to include dependent occasional functions such as the erectile one, which is caused by a dilation of arterial vessels and coterminous compression of venous vessels. All this could be envisioned and further, elaborated upon, as Aslan lay supine in his chair, his face hidden behind a copy of *Match* magazine, to the degree that the actual sight of it, and even the touch, smell and taste, was, in a sense, unnecessary. In fact, concealment was, in a sense, preferable to exposure, despite the aforementioned pleasure provided by the sight of glistening skin and glutei hugged by wet board shorts. Concealment was, in a sense, preferable for the reason indicated above: the imagination fed very well upon it. Because, to be honest, the imagination was eating for two: despite three sixteen hour days of rigorous attention (minus the eight the boy spent each night in his room on the floor below the room shared with Samert), not a nibble of interest had been felt.

"How about we go kick it around together, just you and me?"

From the cover of *Match*, two young men in red track jackets stared, posed one behind the other. The left forearm of the young man in the background was wrapped around the other's chest, while his right clenched fist was raised. Both bared white teeth. As Aslan's magazine remained aloft, obscuring his expression, a rhythmic splashing over in the swimming pool could be heard, chlorine vapors smelt. Probably, "it" could be understood as a ball, which Aslan wanted, literally, to kick, in imitation of the figures depicted inside his sports magazine. Probably, what Aslan had in mind was an hour or so of good, clean fun in the park not far from the hotel, nothing more. Nothing more,

as evidenced by the lack of evidence—evidence, that is, of interest. For even as he enjoyed all the spatiotemporal amenities
and services offered by the five star hotel, including the daily
wake-up call, he seemed to vacation elsewhere, absorbed in a
two-dimensional world of sports magazines, science fiction novels and video games. Probably, after three days at the hotel (both
males, after the excursion to *Ka De We*, had resisted additional
tourism), he only wanted open air and exercise. Which was
understandable. Indeed, after nearly ninety, mostly sedentary,
hours indoors (it was now two in the afternoon of the fourth
day), aerobic activity outdoors would be revitalizing. Further,
"just you and me" offered new conditions in which to apply
empirical methodology.

Yes, new conditions. Because when the cat is away, the mice
will play. For it would be erroneous to assume that just because
Samert's steady, skimming crawl possessed the regularity of an
autonomic process, of a bodily function that continues during
sleep, that his crawl was in fact an autonomic process. Oh sure,
it was pleasant, if unrealistic, to postulate that Samert in his
buoyant, seeming oblivion actually was asleep, or at least half
asleep, like a feline afloat in a pool of sun or certain aquatic
mammals such as the dolphin, which rest only one hemisphere
of their brains at a time. But even then he could become fully
conscious at any moment, as the very concept of sleep relies on
the concept of "not sleep." Of this possibility for sudden awareness Aslan was himself surely aware, and as such, deterred.
Under new, "cat free" conditions, however, Aslan could express
himself without inhibition—meaning a more complete set of
data could be gathered.

"Well, come on. If we bog off now, he won't know." The

boy had lowered his magazine slightly, revealing his thickly lashed green eyes, one of which he slowly closed, then opened again. Yes, it was an optimum time to go.

Fifteen minutes later, RR, athletically attired in a Hudson High fleece-lined nylon sport jacket and running shoes, waited outside the door of Aslan's room, only one floor down from the room shared with his uncle. The recessed lights in the ceiling diffused the hallway with an amber glow that called to mind a summer evening, when darkness had not yet fallen and familial attention was elsewhere. On such an evening it had been possible to share long, carcinogenic moments with Tom Tom behind the privet, as Teresa puttered in the garden, Ray sprawled in the den, and Miranda chatted on the phone with her friends, and then sprawl afterward on the grass, dizzy with nicotine as bats reeled above. Likewise, the clean scent of lemon and leather that pervaded the corridors of the luxury hotel recalled the act of patting Tom Tom's smooth face with an olfactory mask of filched paternal aftershave and vice versa, before responding to the maternal summons to return indoors for the obligatory before bed peck. "You smell like your father," had been the only comment. Life was so easy then.

Life was so easy then and so complicated now as Aslan at last swung open the door, stepping forward, but then stopping at the threshold. There, he occupied a liminal position that, depending on his next gesture, could either invite or rebuff entrance. Behind him, a parquet floor led to the inner doorway beyond. A mew sounded from within. He had only to retreat or advance, drawing his palm behind him or raising it up, to usher his visitor in, or out. The floor gleamed, another mew sounded. Aslan stepped out.

"Buck up, Elvis. I'll bring you back a treat," he called over his shoulder, as he pulled the door closed.

He was wearing his motorcycle jacket and scuffed, thick-soled green boots of the type affected by disaffected youth. Indeed, the boots appeared more suitable for denting garbage cans than for performing the swift, deft movements required to "kick it around."

"I know—I changed me mind." He pulled a folded brochure from the pocket of his oversized jeans: "A bunter in the lobby gave me this—don't it look brill?"

Brill?

"Here."

Beneath a black and white photograph of a leather gloved hand clasping a pair of metal pliers, tips darkened with what appeared to be blood, but was possibly oil, a caption read "Topography of Terrors" in Fraktur font. The terrors in question, as indicated by the short, somewhat sensationalistic text that followed, were the interrogations on the site of the former German Chancellery during the Nazi era. An open-air exhibit about these interrogations could be viewed free of charge until dusk each day. To be honest, the exhibit held little appeal for RR, who although never formally diagnosed, had exhibited symptoms of ADD in all courses dealing with AD historical periods (the ancient Greeks and Romans were another story). But given that the exhibit was gratis, and further, located relatively near by, in the center of the city, there was no reasonable objection. Also, at the one-time headquarters of the SS, RR could pursue the boy without having to simultaneously chase about after a ball. Aslan's proposal was, therefore, finally agreeable. Too bad, however, that he had not made it earlier: different, more sophisticated clothing would have been chosen. While thermally adequate for the excursion, sartorially the fleece-lined nylon jacket was a bit Rah Rah.

Once, many years ago, RR and Tom Tom sent away for "sea monkey" eggs. The advertisement at the back of the Marvel comic book had depicted four of the half-simian, half-piscine creatures: a family that included a "mother" and "father," "daughter" and "son," all with fish tails, and all wearing, for some reason, crowns on their smiling monkey heads. What actually hatched were two miniscule jerking bits of almost transparent protoplasm, to the naked eye scarcely more interesting than shredded cellophane, although even a low powered microscope would have revealed some degree of organizational complexity. From an anthropomorphic standpoint, however, a brine shrimp possesses no expressive capacity. The "sea monkeys" were, as Tom Tom phrased it, "a bust."

Likewise with the "Topography of Terrors," as could be determined from the sudden lack of animation in Aslan's face upon reaching the exhibit. As an educator, or former educator, you know this sudden lack, the moment when a student's face goes blank with disinterest. Or as you would put it, cleverly punning on your own name, "OK, I can see you're all just staring at the wall." Which was, more or less, all there was to see at the "Topography of Terrors"—the tiled wall of one side of the basement of the former Gestapo headquarters. The remainder of the building had been removed, and even most of the basement, it seemed, had been filled in: the extant stretch of wall lined one side of a long dirt channel, sheltered by a sunken, colonnade-like structure built of wooden planks. To be sure, there was something to look at on this wall—a series of posters with black and white images of various men in uniform and wartime scenes of Berlin, accompanied by explanatory text, in German. Then again, these images and texts easily could have been reproduced in a book. As Aslan demanded: "Why would I want to *read* about the Nazis and the Jews down in this chalky ditch?"

Up beyond the edge of the wooden roof of the colonnade-like structure, a yellow hydraulic shovel thrummed, dipper bucket raised against a cloudless blue winter sky. The raised fist of the exultant young man on the cover of the soccer magazine came to mind. Success depended on keeping Aslan *out*, and keeping him out depended on keeping him entertained, which clearly he was not. Clearly Aslan was not entertained, as he stood slumped before one of the posters, fists in his pockets, like a stubborn student kept after school. Any moment now he would ask to leave. What then? A return to the earlier plan, kicking it around in the park, first would require a return to the hotel, since the boy was not dressed for sport. And a return to the hotel entailed the risk of running into Samert, who could be out of the pool by now, sipping Pernod as he clicked his beads and methodically scanned the lobby from the dais of the bar (another daily form of perseveration since the arrival in Berlin). To remain in the text-lined ditch, however, was to hazard a disinterest that, given the brain's tendency to link unrelated but contiguous objects and phenomena, could prove fatal for future fun: i.e. via an illogical but nevertheless inevitable process of association, the boy's mind would dust RR with the same pedagogical powder that had turned the terrors "chalky."

Indeed, this certainly had been the case in RR's own youth—that a potentially interesting subject or person could be rendered dull by an unfavorable context. Ergo, Latin, a favorite area of study in high school, had at first seemed as dry and torpid as Mr. Kline, or "De-Kline," the hypothyroidic old coot who taught it. Then one day, Mr. De-Kline reached the point of no return. Fortunately, his replacement was pretty Ms. Pullulare, whose blackboard teemed with jokes and puns such as *semper ubi sub ubi*, and whose lessons were derived from the pages she handed out each week of her in Latin work-in-progress, *Carpe Diem*, an ante-Vesuvian potboiler about high-living Pompeiians. Suddenly, recollection tripped the light, as it so often does: what was required to make the terrors terrible again was simply a lumen of imagination. Ergo, RR turned to the poster, a chart of some kind on the wall directly before her; with a bit of application, surely there was amusement to be found. And when it had been located, Aslan, who was drifting toward the end of the ditch, perilously close to the exiting stairs, could be recalled with an enthused summons.

Konzentrationslager, the headline on the poster read. Below were horizontal rows of single inverted equilateral triangles interspersed with an occasional pair of equilateral triangles, superimposed upon one another to form a hexagram. Apparently, the equilateral triangles, which were differently colored, had been used to sort and designate political prisoners: indeed, one such pair of yellow superimposed triangles formed that icon known since the mid-twentieth century to all (RR and Tom Tom had in fact utilized said icon, fashioned from yellow construction paper, in a furtively played captivity game—furtively played because Mother Teresa expressly forbade it). Less familiar, however, were the red triangle overlaying the yellow that designated *Juden* who were also *politische Schutzhäftlinge*, the single purple triangle for *Bibelforscher*, the green for *Kriminelle*, blue for *Emigranten*, pink for *Homosexuelle*, etc. Jackpot. For here there was not just one, but three, six, twelve, fifteen, yes eighteen identifying equilateral triangles and hexagrams, almost twenty in all, to play with—potentially hours of role playing games as first one label could be acted out, then another. Probably Aslan, in his thick-soled green punk's boots, would want to begin with *Kriminelle*. If so, what role should be assumed in turn? Should RR play his fellow delinquent or his persecutor (the role of partner in crime would establish greater trust. The other, however, surely would supply more frisson)? When suddenly, a dorsal poke was felt.

"Excuse me, you're in my way."

RR swiveled round. A boy with straight blond hair, cut in the style known as a "pageboy," his jabbing digit still outstretched, was encountered. A boy, who, judging by the orthodontic wire glinting between his thin lips and the navy L.L. Bean jacket encasing his thick torso, as well as by his accent, was American. He peered up with pale eyes, his upturned nose lending him an appearance of porcine expectancy: "Well?"

Well, indeed. Due to distracting thoughts of future games, contact with present reality had been lost. The rude jab of the blond boy could therefore be viewed as a kind of summons or paging. A paging that had come just in time, as Aslan was spotted far down the wooden walkway, near the exiting stairs, wrapped in conversation with a man wearing an overcoat and brown fedora. Therefore the swinish but also serendipitous blond pager remained unrebuked as RR turned away and sped toward the end of the exhibit.

But then from behind came the thump thump of feet on wooden planks, and another dorsal poke. Pivoting, a premature decision was made to chastise the blond boy—premature, as the resultant slap did not strike the smooth firm cheek of a pre-adolescent male but rather the spongiform breast of an adult female. And not just any adult female, to whom apologies could swiftly be given and from whom departure could swiftly be taken, but the Lipilina.

Somewhere in the aboveground background, though it was no longer visible against the blank, deepening blue sky, the hydraulic shovel groaned. What were the odds? There was no choice, however, but to deal with the hand that had been dealt, with the Lipilina, who was rubbing her mammary gland. "Ouch," she said.

Responsibility was therefore taken, regret expressed. An offer of assistance was made, even, in the form of financial remuneration for the cold pack Ludmilla should now, immediately, run to the *Apotheke* to purchase. Indeed, an *Apotheke* had been spotted on the way to the exhibition, just two blocks away. But she should hurry, as the hours of operation were unknown, and the pharmacy shop might soon close. Yes, she should hurry, as the man talking to Aslan touched the brim of his brown fedora, as if to signal departure, but then actually moved closer to him.

"I'm OK," Ludmilla Lipilina replied. Which she probably was—her padded seventies Arctic explorer style parka had most likely muffled the sting of the slap. "And don't worry about your nephew—that's just Oliver from the lab."

Oliver from the lab? The young Austrian resident whose patient RR had observed the previous week? Wasn't he in Vienna, attending a funeral?

"He was. We ran into each other at the train station."

A smile was suppressed. They had "run into each other" at the *Bahnhof*, eh? And what had brought Ludmilla Lipilina to Berlin?

"I don't know about you, but I'm a city girl. Every once in a while I need a little good shopping and culture with a cosmopolitan 'c,' not a 'k,' which Kiel, charming as it is, lacks."

Sure, culture with a "c," not a "k." No further questions were asked, although the word that came to mind began not with a "c" or a "k" but with an "s": the same in German as in English, it was ubiquitous on posters and marquees on select little side streets all over the city. Yes, the word began with an "s," and it was not "subterfuge," although this surely applied to the situation as well. Again, a smile was suppressed, as no comment was made. No comment was made because the situation served RR. That is, as the Lipilina strove to hide her own affair with the Austrian resident, she would be less likely to uncover the affairs of others.

Without commentary, RR walked with the Lipilina toward the exit, where the Austrian resident, a smooth skinned, slender specimen of a type sometimes selected in the past as a sexual partner, stood making an inaudible speech to Aslan. Aslan, in the meantime, stood, apparently silent, slouched against one of the posts that supported the sheltering colonnade-like structure. Because only the Austrian resident spoke while Aslan remained apparently silent, his posture expressing indifference, the interaction appeared one sided—as if the former was attempting to convince the latter to do something, to provide, perhaps, some favor. This impression strengthened upon arrival, as arrival coincided with the Austrian resident handing a colorful cellophane packet to Aslan—a packet filled with the gelatin-based candy that Aslan favored. In short, it appeared that the Austrian resident was proffering the standard bait of the pedophile. A reminder, therefore, was in order—a reminder never to accept candy from strangers.

"But he's no Uncle Lester—this is the chappie I met in the lobby. Anyhow, he says he knows you." Aslan zipped the cellophane packet inside his leather motorcycle jacket.

RR acknowledged a professional acquaintance with the Austrian resident, who in response, tipped his brown felt fedora, briefly revealing pale, infant-fine hair. Although his body type—smooth skinned, ectomorphic—had appealed in the past (as evidenced by Mick Mackie), the blond fuzz was a turn-off. Wenzel, with his sleek silver Caesar, was surely preferable. The Lipilina's affair was, however, the Lipilina's affair. Just as the affair of RR was the affair of RR. Hence RR proceeded to explain, casting a pointed look at the Austrian resident, that an acquaintance with one person did not automatically presuppose an acquaintance with another. Indeed, when it came to interactions with unknown older males, too much caution could not be exercised.

The Austrian resident had removed another cellophane packet from the pocket of his overcoat, and torn it open with his teeth. Peering into the bag, he spoke: "Well, no damage has been done. Further, can two fellows who share a passion for gummis truly be considered strangers? I tell you, Frau Doktor Ramee, we each immediately recognized the other as a gummi man this morning in the lobby, although my preference is for worms, while his is for bears. Ozzie was the only one with Haribo candy in hand, yet he was so kind as to share his with me. Having replenished my stock along the Unter dem Linden, I wanted only to repay your...nephew for his generosity."

"Rosemarie has a very important point, Oliver," the Lipilina inserted, while reaching over to pat Aslan's arm. Aslan
drew himself up and away from his post, moving two steps
back toward the stairs. Good boy. "We live in a world where
sexual predators of the young, taking advantage of the dissolution of traditional family structures, as well as the opportunities
for contact provided by the internet, have become increasingly
bold. In America this is a huge problem—Michael Jackson is
only the poster child, no pun intended."

Having at last selected a piece of candy (a bear, not one
of the worms he claimed he preferred), the Austrian resident
popped it into his mouth. His characteristic Germanic self-
absorption was noted, as he offered the open package only
to Aslan, who declined. Masticating, he eyed the boy: "That
is truly perverse, given the complete lack of sexual appeal of
the American youth, who is like the American fast food, the
McChild of children. With his small even teeth like kernels of
corn, his 'couch potato body,' he is bland and uninteresting, the
over-protected under-exercised mass product of the American
so-called democratic masses. Any person who would chase after one of these boys is clearly ruined, his taste corrupted by a
country that has managed to convince itself that yellow painted
arches signal culinary excellence."

The Austrian resident now shifted his light blue eyes to RR:
"Don't you agree, Doktor Ramee? I saw you approached back
there by the American youth, and also saw that you quickly dis-
engaged yourself. I was approached earlier as well—the brat
wanted one of my gummis. I told him that he was a typical
American, in that he had overestimated his charm."

Although, as stated previously, no attraction to immature males had been felt before Kiel, the Austrian resident's blanket dismissal of the American type could not be concurred with. While specific, individual examples did not come to mind, lithe, young and appealing American males had been observed—skateboarders, for instance, whose flat, almost concave bellies twisted in cradles of jutting pelvic bones in the midst of their aerial rotations. Surely American boys of this type could hold their own against the European type, or types (as the Mediterranean variety could, for instance, be distinguished from, and found superior to the Germanic). Then again, at present, types—whether American or European—held no interest. There was only Aslan. The inimitable Aslan, who had just moved to the first step of the metal exit stairs, and who, with lifted chin (and a jaw line as sharp and ruthless as desire), was indicating departure. Therefore, although the Austrian resident's blanket dismissal could not be concurred with, the above argument remained under the covers. Instead, an excuse was offered—that Samert, husband and uncle, was expecting wife and nephew back at the hotel at five, and it was now almost a quarter of the hour before. So, ta ta.

For no apparent reason the Austrian resident smiled, which was strange; however, at the time his oddly meaningless smile seemed meaningless. RR lightly shook his hand and the hand of the Lipilina, respectively, then followed Aslan, who already had ascended the metal stairs halfway.

"Oh Frau Doktor, have you ever wished that you could be invisible?"

What? With one hand gripping the hem of Aslan's jacket, RR turned. The Austrian resident, blue eyes shadowed by the brim of his fedora, peered up.

"Invisible. That is, have you ever wanted not to be seen, wished for a respite from the gaze? I know I have. At thirty-two years of age, I am well aware that ultraviolet rays and airborne pollutants, not to mention gravity, have each taken their due. Anyhow, if you have wanted the same, perhaps you might be interested in *unsicht-Bar*. As you may or may not know, the name of this totally dark restaurant and musical café in Mitte is a pun on the German word for invisibility. And indeed, as all the waiters are blind, the experience of being draped in a magical cloak of blackness is complete. The delectable Frau Lipilina and I have reserved a table for this evening, at twenty hours. Perhaps you and…your family would like to join us."

Obviously the invitation was itself a kind of camouflage. The Austrian resident and the Lipilina hoped to hide their relationship from RR, who enjoyed an unusual degree of collegiality with the Lipilina's partner, Nils Wenzel. Yes, by inviting RR along they hoped to demonstrate that they had nothing to conceal. With everything out in the open, and yet in the dark, an illusion of candor could be maintained. What the duplicitous pair failed to realize was that the stratagem was unnecessary— RR could not care less. Then again, while about the affair between the Austrian resident and the Lipilina she could not care less, about the affair, or potential affair, with Aslan she could not care more. To react indifferently to the invitation to the so-called invisible restaurant (the pun was, by the way, obvious) would betray preoccupation, which could in turn elicit inquisition (i.e., *why* didn't RR give a fuck?). Therefore, while the duplicitous pair's stratagem was not necessary, perhaps playing along with it was. Yes, to play along might be best, and not only to prevent inquisition, but also to keep an eye on the Austrian resident. For despite his obvious affair with the "delectable" Lipilina, the Austrian resident's sexual taste was, quite possibly, omnivorous. Further, to expressly forbid contact between the "gummi" friends would be to make the not unattractive Austrian resident only more attractive to Aslan. Best then to allow the candy connection to continue, only under strict supervision. Thus in the end a noncommittal query was made re: the address of the totally dark dining establishment.

Samert was indeed at the bar dais in the lobby of the hotel. Spotting him, Aslan requested permission to retreat upstairs and order room service for his pet, in lieu of the "treat" he had promised it earlier. Permission was granted, with the extraction of a promise that he would return in twenty minutes. In this interim, RR rejoined Samert alone. As Samert greeted RR with a curt nod, the truth was confronted: no progress had been made. No progress—and, in fact, regress. For after three expensive days at the famous five star hotel, RR not only was back to where she had begun four months previously, sitting alone at a small table with the Turkish tailor, but the latter was no longer congenial. In fact, he was the very opposite of congenial: sullen and morose. Sullen and morose, he scanned the lobby of the famous Berlin luxury hotel as if it were a poorly stocked, third world grocery. He scanned, and he clicked, rolling his beads in the fist of his right hand, while on the low marble-topped table before him sat a half empty glass of Pernod, clouded and sallow. Occasionally he lifted this clouded and sallow drink to his lips, but he did not speak, maintaining the sullen and morose demeanor. As long as he maintained this demeanor, there was no hope of conversation. And as there was no hope of conversation, not only would dinner in the hotel restaurant be, as it had been each of the preceding nights, silent and uncomfortable, but the subject of the Turkish boarding school would remain unbroachable. The clinical method had failed. Or rather, the clinical method could not even be implemented. There was no way to solve the problem of Aslan's feelings re: RR via a series of orderly steps when the path was so totally obscured. In truth, RR all along had been taking stabs in the dark. And now, what to do but to continue to stumble along? Hence the encounter with the Lipilina and the Austrian resident was mentioned, along with the invitation to join the pair at the totally dark, equivocally named *unsicht-Bar*. For surely there was nothing to lose but the sight of Samert's morose visage.

Contrary to expectation, Samert not only acquiesced to the invitation, but displayed avidity: "My dear Songül, that is a fine, an excellent idea." Samert's hyperenthusiasm was surprising. Then again, Homo sapiens are an unpredictable species. This unpredictability can be attributed to the proliferation of neuronal connections that came with the evolutionary expansion of the frontal lobes, leading to a vast array of behavioral possibilities. Therefore the Turkish tailor's gung ho response went unquestioned and was even encouraged, as "Songül" suggested manicures and pedicures in the Adlon Salon beforehand (for the reservation was not until eight), and, in general, whooping it up.

Two hours later, the three family members, uniformly well-groomed and less uniformly well-dressed (Samert was dressed up in his Boss trousers and a matching jacket, while Aslan was dressed down, in a pair of nylon track pants. Yours truly had chosen the golden mean—luxurious but casual in a cashmere "hoodie" and the *Bundeswehr*-inspired velvet cargo style hiphuggers) stood before a wooden door set in a brick wall. On the other side of this, as indicated by a black and yellow sign printed with the caption "*unsicht-Bar*," as well as a stylized illustration of a dinner plate flanked by cutlery, lay the totally dark restaurant. Suddenly, apprehension was felt, an apprehension that was founded in a childish fear of the absence of light, but that was nevertheless arresting. It was Samert who stepped forward, pushing open the heavy wooden door and leading the way through an arched portico lined overhead with a strip of blue neon that seemed to radiate unpropitiousness (while obviously there is no causal connection between colors and events, even intelligent people sometimes make irrational associations). Yet Samert appeared anxiety-free: there was a bounce in his gait and he hummed a tune reminiscent of the nursery song "Three Blind Mice." Evidently he was in a buoyant mood, a mood that, juxtaposed with his previous depression, suggested a bipolar disorder. Nevertheless, apprehension began to give way to optimism: for in the throes of mania, Samert would perhaps take a more expansive view and allow Aslan, who was currently whistling in tune with Samert's humming, to remain at home, in Kiel. Indeed, suddenly the blue neon strip overhead no longer seemed ominous, but favorable—a litmus test indicative of the desired outcome.

The door to the restaurant proper lay on the other side of a small courtyard, opposite the portico. Behind long, darkened glass windows, lights flickered, like emanations of methane gas playing over a wetland area. As entry was gained, these were seen to be votive candles set on low tables, around which were clustered black leather chairs occupied by other patrons, study-ing menus. Samert's humming ceased, and with it, Aslan's whis-tling. At the end of the long, corridor-like space, on one side of which ran the windows and on the other a bar, two figures rose and approached. The Lipilina was clad, more or less, in her usual explorer style parka, low slung cords and abdomen baring top. The Austrian resident, however, had not only shed the aforementioned overcoat and brown fedora—he now wore a sleek, collarless suit expertly tailored from a dark, lustrous ma-terial that was clearly both high tech and high end. Together, the narrow, slimming cut and expensive, futuristic fabric wicked away years: no longer did the Austrian resident appear some-what past his prime, but rather as if brilliant prospects lay be-fore him. A jocular query, accompanied by a pointed look at the Lipilina, was made: had someone's mommy taken him school shopping on the K-Damm?

"Ha ha Frau Doktor Ramee, but I assure you I can afford to pay my own way, even with only a lowly resident's stipend. And someday soon, of course, I will be making much more."

"A brain box is a cash box, me mum always said. Oliver's going to be dripping with honey!"

"Enough, you impudent goat!" As Samert moved toward Aslan, his purpose, indicated by both his open, raised right hand and past precedent, to smack the boy's ear, the Lipilina in-tervened, seizing Samert's hand with both of her own. Having thus subdued the volatile tailor, she kissed him first on one cheek and then the other: "Great to see you again, Sam."

Samert smiled and drew back. His smile, it was noted, uti-lized the zygomatic muscle but not the orbicularis oculi (i.e., he smiled with his mouth, but not with his eyes). Ditto with the

Lipilina, who had donned a mask of congeniality, as if she were a contestant in a beauty pageant.

"Sam, this is Dr. Oliver Rauch. He works in the *Schlafzentrum* with your…wife and Dr. Wenzel."

"Actually, we have met," said the Austrian resident. With his hands clasped behind him, a posture that emphasized his prominent pectorals and combined with the streamlined cut of the suit conferred him with a new, military air, and one eyebrow lifted, he regarded Samert. "We me at the party hosted by Herr Doktor Wenzel last November."

"You were with that dirty mac brigade?" asked Aslan, performing a dismissive dorsiflexion of the wrist. No doubt his recollection of the party was tainted by the mild depression that had followed his sleep attack.

The Austrian resident ignored him, and continued to gaze with one eyebrow raised at Samert, who in turn stared fixedly at some point beyond the Austrian resident's shoulder. Samert no longer employed either orbicularis or zygomatic muscles. Indeed, his facial expression was one of stiff discomfort. "Yes, we had a conversation about the field of neurology."

Evidently, Samert had somehow embarrassed himself, possibly by claiming to possess a medical background and then proceeding to display his exiguous knowledge of the discipline. Yes, for in the past (as recorded in an earlier section of this report), in his insistence on sharing his "knowledge" (acquired during the alleged one year of medical education), through "stimulating exchange," he had exhibited that he had almost nothing to share. His lack, however, had not been pointed out, as lack is the agar upon which insecurity feeds, and insecurity in turn is the favored nutrient of hostility. The Austrian resident, however, had no need to cultivate Samert's trust and goodwill. Feeling no such need, he would state the obvious—that there was nothing beneath Samert's lab coat, so to speak.

But here speculation ended, or rather, a new speculation began, as Aslan exhibited unexpected behavior: suddenly he slid under the left arm of RR, grasping said arm and wrapping it around his chest. Out of the blue, the boy, the warm, solid, animated boy, had put himself, voluntarily, within the corporeal compass of RR. Of his own volition he'd initiated this absorbing contact, and now he gazed up, employing both zygomatic and orbicularis oculi muscles. While the small, lean dense mass of his body, the sweet and sour candy-scented tickle of his breath had been felt before, never had such sensation been accompanied by the certainty that he, too, was feeling (e.g., the tightening cinch of an arm around his thin, firm torso)—feeling and responding (e.g., as his snuggling, accordingly, intensified). And if Aslan was feeling and responding, didn't that take things to a whole new level? To be sure, his snuggling did not necessarily indicate that he wanted to do anything more than that— i.e., snuggle. On the other hand, his snuggling had established the preconditions for more, and further, he had established the preconditions for more at an interesting, perhaps even strategic, time. For in the darkness of the dining room beyond, a new level could be reached. In that darkness, it would be impossible to detect whether, as Mother Teresa used to say, all four feet had remained upon the ground. Or not.

In the meantime, however, the lights were still on: "You look good together. Sometimes life gives us what we need, right kiddo?" the Lipilina inquired, although her question was obviously not a question.

"If you're talking about me mum, she didn't look nothing like the doc. Nantwas." Aslan slipped out from beneath RR's arm, but his retreat was not taken personally. No doubt the Lipilina's attention had made him uncomfortable. No doubt and no matter: the lost ground could be regained, soon enough.

Soon enough, as a peroxide-blond woman appeared and handed out menus with black lacquer-tipped fingernails (black lacquer incidentally a choice Aslan had been disallowed by Samert at the hotel salon, on the grounds that Aslan would then be taken for a "houri"). "*Wilkommen in die unsicht-Bar.*" She then proceeded to explain the menu, that there were only two choices, two three-course dinners for 42.50 and 40.50 marks, designated as *Kalb* and *Mediterranean* respectively. When each had made his or her choice, the assigned waiter, "Hercules," would serve as a guide down into the dining room.

"Who better than a heroic Greek to lead us into the Stygian dark below?" the Austrian resident inquired.

"Just about anybody besides a sneaky bubble and squeak, I should think."

"Well don't, boy," Samert reprimanded, although he also occasionally maligned the Greek people. But tonight he was allowing Aslan even less latitude than usual, as if to display to the Austrian resident that he possessed a tutelary, if not disciplinary, authority. Hopefully, once he was in the dining room and without a light source to illuminate his performance, he would cease to put on this show.

In the meantime, the sentences on the menu beneath the *Kalb*, or veal, were studied. Although, as stated earlier in this report, RR's absorbing career as a research scientist did not allow for full immersion in the study of the German language, a level of proficiency had been attained. At present, however, proficiency did not seem to be enough. The sentences made no sense: "*Umgeformtes Federvieh schwingt nach winterlichen Klängen auf grünem Tanzboden. Es badet ein Männlein mit braunem Hut eisiger Luft. Junger Wiederkauer beobachtet Vögel als Nussknacker und liegt warm und sanft im Winterkleid...*"

A query was made to the Austrian resident, who as a native German speaker would perhaps be able to glean linguistic nuances that were, admittedly, imperceptible to RR.

"Of course. It says, 'Transformed poultry with wintry accents on a green dance floor. It bathes a little man with a brown hat of icy air. Young ruminant observes birds as nutcrackers and lies warm and tenderly in winter dress.'"

Yes, but the sentences still did not signify what, exactly, would be received if the selection *Kalb* were ordered.

"Surely you are familiar with the Futurists, the early twentieth century avant-garde group. One of their projects was the 'tactile dinner party,' during which guests might feast in the dark on Polyrhythmic Salad or on Magic Food—the latter consisting of small bowls filled with balls of caramel-coated items such as candied fruits, bits of raw meat, mashed banana, chocolate or pepper. The purpose was to forego preconceived notions of experience and to give in to the now. This is in keeping, of course, with what we now know about the brain: that it filters current interactions with the environment through the lenses of mental models created from patterns of experiences in the past. In this case, the surrealistic menu and the absence of light serve, more or less, to obscure the lenses. Not knowing what I'm going to get, I can form no preconceptions about it. I am free, to touch, to smell, to taste the new..."

To touch, to smell, to taste the new. Yes. For while the unintelligible menu (which by the way recalled the equally unintelligible *Tough Buttons* briefly studied in your AP English class), denied access to meaning, at the same time perhaps it opened the way to a new, experimental space in which unanticipated data could be gathered. At any rate, having been led single file, hands linked, by "Hercules" (whose short stature, proportionally overlarge cranium, and evident optic atrophy contradicted his heroic name), down a hallway and flight of stairs and seated at a table, adjacent to Aslan, who as indicated by the rustle of his nylon pants seemed to be only a foot or two away, certainly it now seemed that anything could happen.

Anything could happen even as the sounds of other diners filled the room—the steady drone of German, regularly broken by brays of laughter, the clink of silverware on dinner plates, scraping of chair legs, the slurping of what was most probably soup—were predictable. Because nothing was heard that hadn't been heard before. Nor was nothing smelt. Indeed, the smells were all too familiar—the greasy pall of overcooked meat, the flabby middle rank of cabbage spiked with vinegar, the grounding murk of curdled cream and egg noodles—smells that could be found in any *Gaststätte* in Kiel. Anything could happen and probably nothing would as nothing had happened so often before.

As evident from the two preceding short paragraphs, the mood had shifted within a very brief period of time from one of elated anticipation to one of hopeless despondency. The shift did not go unobserved: notice was taken of this emotional lability, a symptom of the bipolar disorder exhibited by Samert, as well as brain diseases of various types, but more likely an indicator of stress. Yes, stress was the most probable explanation for this newly volatile condition, the stress of the preceding four days at the hotel, which was in turn the distillation of over four months of uncertainty and frustration. And then, suddenly, a gastrointestinal toot sounded, announcing the noxious fumes of anaerobic bacterial decomposition.

"Is that a broken heart I smell?"

"Do not think that because I cannot see you, I cannot strike you down, boy."

"No one doubts your ability to do so, Herr Mart, but perhaps we can make better use of this unique opportunity to experience the world without the aid of visual perception," suggested the Austrian resident, whose voice came from the other side of the table, proximal to Samert's.

"I agree." The Lipilina was at the end of the table, to the left of RR. "Instead of beating each other up, we should use this time in the darkness to dissolve our differences and get in touch with our essential relatedness."

"Actually, I had something else in mind…a kind of *Gedankenexperiment*. As we are reminded by the lingering odor of recent flatulence, we all have bodies. What if, however, we did not? What if it were possible to remove my brain from my cranium and to suspend it in a solution of glucose and other essential nutrients, where its dangling nerves would be stimulated by electrical impulses in precisely the way they are now? In other words, what if I were a brain in a vat of nutrient broth?"

"*Ich habe die Suppe gebracht.*"

"Very good. *Danke.*"

As dishes were set on the table, by literally invisible hands, the Austrian resident was silent. Someone, presumably Hercules, explained that spoons were at "*drei Uhre*," but that there were also handles on the sides of the soup bowls if the spoons proved too difficult to use. From the end of the table came the clink of teeth on metal; apparently the Lipilina was one of those who bite their utensils when they eat. "Yummy," she said.

The Austrian resident resumed: "Yes, what if I were a brain in a vat, an image that you, Samert, may recognize from an episode of the original Star Trek television series."

Samert grunted.

"The brain in a vat is in fact the basis of a famous thought experiment—being otherwise impossible to perform. If I were such a brain, without a body, would I still be I? The commonly reached conclusion is 'yes.' But my answer is 'no.'"

Steam rose up from the bowl. The prevailing scent was of dairy lipids turning rancid—an overpowering, butyric reek that seemed to question the possibility not only of fresh butter, but of boys. But wasn't Aslan right there, his young presence confirmed by the delicate rustle of his nylon pants as he shifted in his seat? Couldn't a hand simply creep along the edge of the table to find his?

"No?" echoed Aslan.

"My answer is 'no,' because my literally disembodied brain would lack the necessary feedback loop experience that constitutes 'self.' Normally, as my brain is receiving sensory input from my body, it is in turn generating output. As my body is then modified by this output, new information is communicated back to my brain—input that alters the next output, respectively. Therefore, even if we were able to stimulate the dangling nerve endings of a hypothetical floating brain, so as to create a facsimile of sensory input, without a body to communicate back the effect of the output elicited by stimulation, that brain's sense of self is necessarily incomplete. Therefore, brain and body are inseparably intertwined: no self, no I, can have one without the other. Therefore, a certain person should have no fear that I am only interested in him for his body. I am very glad just to talk."

Suspicion was felt. Not in regard to the idea that consciousness is as much a product of the body as of the brain,[14] but in regard to the idea that someone was afraid that the Austrian resident was only interested in him for his body. If that fearful someone was the Lipilina, the Austrian resident surely would have used the feminine pronoun. Clearly, as suspected earlier, the Austrian resident was pursuing Aslan, and probably not in addition to the Lipilina, but in lieu of her. Yes, and with the help of the time-worn but frequently effective "just talking" strategy of the older male, the Austrian resident hoped to capture the boy by first gaining his trust. So what to do? The Austrian resident's pursuit of Aslan was an added complication in an already complex situation. As is frequently the case when one is faced with complex, seemingly insoluble problems, a sense of paralysis, of static, ineffectual suspension emerged—as if RR were, indeed, a brain bobbing in a vat of nutrient broth.

Rolling and clicking sounds rose up from across the table—Samert's worry beads. A throat cleared—Samert's, but also, possibly, the Austrian resident's. Without the aid of sight, it was impossible to tell. Indeed, as the sound of the beads seemed to emanate from the same location as the Austrian resident's voice moments before, the two men could be sitting one in the other's lap, although presumably they were, in their separate chairs, at

---

[14] The theory that consciousness is as much a product of the body as of the brain is not, by the way, the Austrian resident's own. Please refer to the writings of Antonio Damasio, among others.

least a foot apart. In the dark, without the delimiting function of vision, boundaries dissolved, so that now the beads seemed to grow louder, to encroach over the table, pressing closer and closer—an audial distortion, no doubt, resulting from the lack of input from other sensory modalities, but despite its hallucinatory character, nonetheless compelling. Nonetheless compelling, in that a fight or flight response was elicited (as indicated by a sudden increase in heart rate). Only who to fight? Samert? The Austrian resident? Both? Or if the better option were to flee, where? And how to get the boy to go? Despite the adrenaline surge, paralysis prevailed.

Suddenly, at this juncture of inaction, a woman's voice began to sing, accompanied by a piano and saxophone, in a jazzy manner familiar from old phonographic records owned by Ray Ramee: *I went to the party, just to have a little fun. Yes I went to the party, just to have a little fun. Well the joint started jumpin', that's when the fight begun...*

As the mid-twentieth-century style music, which judging by the clarity and depth of both the vocal and instrumental sounds, was an imitative live performance rather than an original recording, filled the room, the Austrian resident, the Lipilina, and even Samert began to argue excitedly about the musical merit of the saxophone. Apparently the Austrian resident had an aversion to the sound effects produced by this type of horn, while the Lipilina and Samert were, on the contrary, "saxophiles." The Lipilina even went so far as to claim that only a single vowel separated the experience of the "sax" from her most enjoyable bedroom experiences. The conversation was tuned out.

Now some were drinkin' whiskey, some were drinkin' rum. They had some sneaky pete but they wouldn't give me none ...

No, not a drop, as once again deprivation prevailed. Not a drop not a drop not a drop. When, contrary to all expectation, a light touch was felt. Yes a light touch light as a blade of grass light as the tip of a reeling wing grazed the back of the hand and then soft sweet and sour lemon breath breathed into the ear: "I think I know the way out of this hock hole."

They were talkin' in the kitchen, boogyin' in the hall, nobody payin' any mind to me at all…

Was Aslan suggesting that a surreptitious exit be made?

"Just belt up and clap me hand."

Yes they raided the joint, took everybody down but me. Yes they raided the joint, took everybody down but me. So let's talk some trash, spend some cash this mornin'. Let's all get high, don't go home til dawnin'…

Students and residents coming to the neurology ward or clinic for the first time are easily discouraged by what they see. Having had only brief contact with neuroanatomy, neurophysiology, and neuropathology, they are already somewhat intimidated by the complexity of the nervous system. Confronted with a patient exhibiting an array of disturbingly disparate symptoms, they are likely to find themselves stymied. Through instruction in the clinical method, however, they learn that complex problems can be broken down and solved, step by step. The case described above is not meant to discount this valuable diagnostic tool, which always in the past had provided a reliable, if slow and arduous, course through the darkness of the body (for somatic organization, contrary to the schematizing illustrations and diagrams in anatomy and physiology texts, is not as clear or systematic as one would like. Indeed, to make use of such illustrations and diagrams is akin to relying on maps describing lands whose contours and topographies shift with each new journey). No, the case described above is not by any means intended to discount the clinical method, which provides a kind of compass with which to negotiate the often bewildering terrain of biological existence; however, waking up in Aslan's hotel bed the following morning, with the warm, vibrating weight of Elvis pressing into her sternum, RR could not claim that she had arrived there via a sequence of orderly steps.

8. A Biological Hypothesis is Favored

It is early summer on Cyprus. It is early summer on Cyprus and in the late afternoon when the sun is low a walk to the beach is authorized. A walk to the beach is authorized with the older woman Sibel, who offers her arm, strong from scrubbing the ceramic tiles and polishing the plate glass windows of Osman's tower, in assistance. Yesterday, the jasmine bush outside the entrance to the tower was in bloom, the small white star-shaped florets shamelessly releasing their mellifluous musk. A movement was made to pluck one, a gesture that Sibel intercepted. Because apparently it is not allowed here to pick the flowers. Yes, it seems that picking the flowers here is not approved, that not even the tiniest blossom is permitted. And yet, even now, as the fingers are lifted to the nose, a faint, sweet odor remains.

But to return to the report. Obviously, an explanation for the serendipitous success that followed the failure of the clinical method is owed, and therefore an effort will be made to provide one. While the origins of homosexuality are still obscure, a biological hypothesis is favored. First, morphologic studies of the hypothalamus indicate such a tack. As shown by LeVay, an aggregate of neurons in the interstitial nucleus of the hypothalamus is two to three times larger in heterosexual than in homosexual men. Second, genetic studies point in the same direction: pooled data from five studies in men have shown that about 57 percent of identical twins (and 13 percent of brothers) of homosexual men fish, so to speak, in the same waters. Further, the inheritance pattern of male homosexuality comes, as with Judaism, from the maternal side, implicating a gene on the X chromosome. All in all, homosexuality seems to arise from a deep-seated predisposition, probably biological in origin and as ingrained as heterosexuality. Then again, the status of bisexuality, to which, as confirmed by personal experience, Samert was disposed as well, is undetermined.

At any rate, whatever the origins of Samert's attraction to the Austrian resident, whether biological, psychological or anti-logical, the affair (which evidently had been going on for months, ever since the latter had given the former a ride home from Wenzel's party) was a crucial factor in the accidental Adlon conquest of Aslan. A conquest that was, by the way, to all appearances mutual. Yes, for following the return to the hotel from the totally dark restaurant, *unsicht-Bar*, Aslan had requested company in his room, in order to chase off the "glooms." There, insisting that unlike his uncle and that "trimmer" Oliver, he did not go "Howard's way," he had placed his head in the lap of RR, then reached up and performed a gesture indicating desire (in keeping with the nontitillating nature of this report no description of that gesture will be offered, although a hint in regard to its object may be found nuzzled in one of the syllables of the preceding clause). Simply, let it be said that the remainder of the scene unfolded in such a way that joint fulfillment was found. Yes, and even now, as the fingers are lifted to the nose, a faint, sweet odor remains.

There remains a faint sweet odor thanks to Samert's attraction to the Austrian resident, an attraction that led to his dulcetly empowering departure. For Samert did not return to the Adlon hotel that night. Or rather, he only returned to check out. An inspection of the room upstairs the following morning revealed his absence: his luggage, every trace of him including the milky dregs of a glass of Pernod that had been standing for two days on the bedside table, was gone. Suddenly, without a trace, Samert had disappeared, and he did not reappear during the remaining two days in Berlin,[15] nor in the ten weeks that followed back in Kiel, nor in the time thereafter. Suddenly, Samert had vanished completely, and although vague rumors circulated at the Lab that he had gone to Vienna with the Austrian resident (who had apparently relinquished his residency), no forwarding address materialized. Indeed, as Samert had vanished completely, leaving no forwarding address nor means of contact, it was as if he had died. It was as if he had died, as if he had been stricken by a fast-acting, fatal disease such as pancreatic cancer or run down by a speeding car while crossing the street to drop a letter in a mailbox, but without the usual, emotionalistic final scene—deathbed or otherwise. Hence, gratitude was felt—to Samert and to what was (and still is) regarded as fate, although technically there is no such thing as the latter. Fate is simply a fictionalization of chance, chance in this case possibly being a random, maternally heritable mutation that had precipitated Samert into the arms of the Austrian resident.

It is hoped that Samert is happy.

---

[15] Which, excluding two additional sessions between the sheets, were spent enjoying the city of Berlin, both the eastern and western sectors. For although Aslan claimed each day to be satisfied with a "long lie," a feeling of claustrophobia or captivity is to be avoided: a prisoner of love is still a prisoner. Hence sights were seen and souvenirs purchased, the latter including a Stasi summer uniform acquired from a hawker inside the Brandenburg Gate, which was also a birthday present (the 24th of February being Aslan's 12th birthday).

II.

1. Once a Child is Procured, He Must be Cared For

At a latitude of nearly 55 degrees, the German city of Kiel is practically in Denmark (Kiel was in fact once part of Denmark's territories). Practically in Denmark, Kiel is very far north, and the days around the time of the winter solstice, no more than 6.7 hours long, are correspondingly short and dark. In Kiel, during the short, dark days of winter, a feeling of hopelessness is not uncommon. As the North Pole tilts closer and closer to the sun, however, the number of daylight hours between sunrise and sunset rapidly increases, reaching a total of over 17 hours by the time of the summer solstice. While the difference in length between a day in December and in June in Kiel is less dramatic than the difference between a day in December and in June in Lapland, it is more dramatic than the difference between two such days in New York or in Denver. Relatively rapid and dramatic, this shift toward increasingly longer days (days which by early May are close to 15 hours long) can instill in the denizen of Kiel relatively positive expectations.

By early May, therefore, the outlook re: the affair with Aslan was relatively positive. As indicated above, intercourse had finally, since that watershed night at the Hotel Adlon, become consensual, and had remained so for over two months. In fact, when the boy suffered another sleep attack ten days after the return from Berlin, his condition was not exploited. Having experienced the gratification provided by the boy's waking participation, of his wide glistening young eyes, who could settle again for a merely autonomic response? Who could settle for insensate distension without comprehension when a little patience, a brief coital hiatus, would surely be rewarded by a carnal collaboration all the more fulfilling for the wait? Which, indeed, it was. Yes, the outlook re: the affair with Aslan was relatively positive, as it had been and remained consensual. To be sure, his interest was not to be counted on indefinitely. No, eventually his interest would diminish and even disappear, as normal reproductive urges would drive him to seek a more nubile and potentially fecund mate. For, to be honest, the end of RR's childbearing season was rapidly approaching, as signaled by increasingly heavy menstrual bleeding, due to the rampant growth of uterine fibroids (recently diagnosed by a gynecologist in Kiel). Indeed, this increasingly heavy menstrual bleeding had already led RR to declare two additional coital hiatuses—for probably the hematological excess would have horrified and repulsed the boy. While the cessation of intercourse was hard to bear (as the clock of the December-June relationship was ticking), some compensation followed each period of prohibition, in that after Aslan participated with greater fervor than ever.

By early May, therefore, the hopelessness of winter had given way to a controlled ecstasy. On the one hand, the affair with Aslan exceeded RR's wildest dreams. On the other, boundaries were nevertheless observed. Or more precisely, boundaries were anticipated, in that although at present it seemed there were no limits, at some now indefinite but in the future conclusive moment, everything would be finished. Everything someday would be over between RR and the boy, due to the inevitable, inexorable constraints of biology (which, since brains grow more myelinated and neuronally integrated, or complex, with age, and RR's brain was already nearly three decades more complex than Aslan's, included the possibility that the former could eventually grow tired of the latter. Sure, because sex is, after all, not everything). Currently, however, complete gratification was found on a nightly (and sometimes daily) basis. Therefore, while the end could be anticipated, and thus in some sense circumscribed existent gratification, when, on the twelfth of May, Aslan's paternal uncle, Osman, called the Lab in the middle of the afternoon, a profound shock was felt.

Yes, because although the end of the affair had been expected, it had not been expected any time soon. It was as if moderation had been exercised at a wild party that was now, suddenly, over. Thanks, apparently, to an e-mail that Aslan had written to one of his cousins (for having failed to consider the possibility of extended family contact, RR had failed to prohibit it), the cops, so to speak, had come. For the uncle, Osman Mart, was demanding that the boy be returned to Cyprus. Obviously, said Osman, in a British public school accent, Samert, alone for years in "a highly-sexed, alien culture," had succumbed to "libidinal forces" that in a more supportive environment would have been "less avalanchine." Thus, obviously, the boy had to be returned at once, to the guardianship of his extended family, which would provide, Osman claimed, "the guardrails of love." Unfortunately, a consultation with a German *Rechtsanwalt*, or attorney, the next day indicated that Osman was right about the guardianship if not the guardrails—sans the missing Samert (who had in fact never formally adopted Aslan) or legal residence in Germany, the boy had to be returned to his nearest blood relatives in Turkish Cyprus.

The sense of profound shock gave way to a sense of profound loss. Because there had been no time to prepare, no time even to stockpile the small irritations that come with daily intimacy (e.g. the soiled socks and underwear discarded on the bedroom floor; the trails of potato chip crumbs leading from the kitchen to the living room; the gummi candies nestled between the sofa cushions, etc.), that when tallied up surely provide some compensation. Yes, compensation was completely lacking. So, too, was comfort. For most people, when their intimate relationships come to an abrupt end, can count on the sympathy of others. In this case, however, societal disapprobation precluded the possibility of commiseration (i.e., since RR could not say what she had had, she could not say when she had it no longer). Both compensation and comfort were completely lacking. Which was completely unfair. Life, however, as Mother Teresa, used to say, is not fair. Nor, for that matter, unfair, since life in itself has no agency. Further, from the perspective of rationalism, the guiding perspective of this report, some responsibility for the loss had to be assumed.

For it was only reasonable to expect, given the characteristic candor of youth, that Aslan would feel the need to communicate Samert's disappearance to another family member. Yes, for it is very hard for children to keep secrets, due to their underdeveloped frontal lobes. Therefore, the boy's indiscretion should have been anticipated. At the same time, maybe gratitude should now be felt. Maybe gratitude should be felt because Aslan's indiscretion was no greater. Because apparently he had not mentioned the relationship with RR. Otherwise, Osman would not have asked RR to return Aslan. No, Osman would have asked someone else to return the boy, rather than entrusting the boy to RR. Instead, he had entrusted Aslan to RR by asking RR to return Aslan. Which meant that the boy would be in RR's hands at least a little while longer. To be sure, RR was legally obligated to return him to his family. Eventually. Yes, eventually she would return Aslan to his blood relations in Cyprus, because an impeccable reputation for integrity is essential, particularly in the sciences.[16] In the meantime, however, if RR was obligated to return the boy, she was not obligated to return him anytime soon. For Osman had not stipulated a return date. In the end, the sense of profound loss therefore yielded to thankfulness. Thankfulness for what could be seen, if life were actually fair or unfair, as one of its small reprieves.

The sense of profound loss yielded to thankfulness, as RR, who was sitting in the living room in one of Samert's red leather chairs with the *International Herald Tribune*, consumed the last portion of the last of Samert's raki. The newspaper fell to the floor. They would leave in the morning, a.s.a.p. That way, if Osman suddenly decided to issue a return date, no one would be at home to receive his call. There was only one drawback: leaving in the morning, a.s.a.p., left no time to inform Wenzel beforehand that an indefinite leave had been taken. This information would instead have to be communicated on the road, after the journey was well underway. Unfortunately, however, no alternative could be seen. Unfortunately, because no doubt the abrupt departure would be detrimental, in terms of the reputation for reliability that is essential for success in a scientific career.[17] However, sometimes it is impossible to juggle a personal life with a professional one—a ball must be dropped. Further,

---

[16] This is particularly essential in the sciences, because success rests on the perception that a person and her data are honest, reliable and completely kosher. Otherwise, grant opportunities quickly dry up and the respected journals close their pages.

[17] See fn. 16 above.

it would surely be possible to pick that ball up again. At least two cases of female research scientists who had taken extended maternity leaves and then returned to full time lab work were known.

So, it was settled. They would leave in the morning, at the instant when the leading edge of the sun's disk meets the horizon, if not before (since due to atmospheric refraction, the sun's disk is visible for several minutes before its geometric edge actually reaches the horizon). RR climbed the stairs to inform Aslan, who had retreated, as was his habit, to his room for the two to three hours between dinner and bedtime (this habit was, by the way, encouraged. For unrelieved association hastens disassociation).

A knock on the boy's door received no reply. Possibly he was asleep. Or he had courteously placed headphones over his ears because he knew his taste for rap and ska was not shared. Or, possessing an ability for sustained, focused concentration, he was simply absorbed in a science fiction novel or video game (an ability also possessed by yours truly, who as a child, curled up with a book on the couch, had been able to tune out the roar of maternal vacuuming. Indeed, this common capacity for sustained concentration seemed as strong an authorization of the relationship as any mere blood affiliation. Yes, it seemed there was a sanctioning dispositional connection, despite the differences in age, sex, culture, country of origin and musical taste. But tell that to the judge). RR knocked harder. Still no reply. A dilemma. For while it was important for the survival of the relationship to respect the boy's privacy, it was also important for the survival of the relationship (if only for the short term) that he be ready to leave very early in the morning, at the instant when the leading edge of the sun's disk meets the horizon. And then a yowl sounded from within.

As the door handle was pushed down, the latch lifted: entry was possible and ergo desired by Aslan. Therefore, the correct choice had been made. The correct choice had been made, although as the door swung open, RR wished that the door had remained closed. For one thing that is hard to stomach is the ill treatment of animals—even cats. Yes, the ill treatment of animals is hard to stomach, even when the ends justify the means, as when important scientific discoveries result. Even when lives are being compromised or terminated in order to save lives (hence the commonly used laboratory euphemism, "sacrifice"), a visceral objection is often felt, as in the case of the cannulated rats described in a previous section of this report. That visceral objection, though autonomic and uncontrollable, goes hand in hand, or neuron to neuron, with higher brain development and the capacity for empathy associated with the right hemisphere. Because while empathy is irrational, it is also very healthy and human. Indeed, the lack of empathy, toward both other humans and animals, is strongly connected in the literature with sociopathology.

Then again, it was only a game. It was only a game as Aslan stood over Elvis's small steel travel crate wearing the Stasi summer uniform purchased in Berlin as a birthday present.[18] It was only a game, like the games that had been imagined while viewing the triangle patches exhibited at the site of

---

[18] See fn. 15 above. The information that a Stasi uniform was purchased in Berlin was originally presented in a footnote in order not to disrupt the flow of the narrative. While this is ultimately a true report, not a fiction, the hope is, nonetheless, to engage the reader.

the former German Chancellery. Yes, and the uniform and the patches were merely symbols that, as bygones were bygones and restitution had been made (most recently, according to the *International Herald Tribune*, by Swiss banks), could be manipulated for mutual fun. Only the cat did not look like it was having any, as it huddled against the metal bars, fur wet and plastered to its still immature form, pink lined mouth and yellow eyes wide with what, based on the continuity of expression between humans and other mammals,[19] appeared to be terror.

Then again, the animal was merely wet, ice cubes melting in the sheet of water that covered the metal floor of its crate. No incisions had been made, no prussic acid spilled. However, unlike Schrödinger's cat, invisible inside its black box, this one could clearly be seen, as in the meantime Aslan stood looking on, his arms folded over the sage green, silver-buttoned front of his uniform, apparently unmoved by its distress. Apparently unmoved, he was, possibly, considering dousing the animal again, as suggested by the still half-full tan rubber basin of ice water on the floor beside him. Intervention was necessary.

"He pissed my bed."

While Aslan's anger was justified (for the odor of feline urine is very displeasing), his response was not. Especially given the fact that the animal's prune-sized brain was incapable of connecting the pissing to the dousing. Indeed, incapable of connecting the pissing to the dousing, the cat's brain was experiencing cognitive dissonance, and hence additional instances of misbehavior were likely to ensue.

---

[19] For an early but still worthwhile discussion of this subject, please refer to Charles Darwin's classic, *The Expression of the Emotions in Man and Animals*.

"Oh? He's all ballsed up is he? That's what they all say. I don't buy it for a bloody minute." The boy lifted the basin and heaved the remaining ice water up over the crate.

The cat howled again, or rather, was howling as sound continued to emerge from its throat. Swiftly, the door of the crate was unlatched, permitting egress. Which the animal took, streaking out of the bedroom down the stairs, probably to cower under the couch.

A seat was taken on the unmade, unclean bed, at a distance from the urine stain, beneath a poster of Arnold Schwarzenegger in *The Terminator*, a film that Aslan had once said, in passing, reminded him of his "mum." Because the room was fully illuminated by both wall and floor lamps, the phosphorescent glow of the plastic stars affixed to the ceiling overhead could not be seen. The glow of the stars could not be seen in the fully illuminated room while at the same time a pallor was newly perceptible in Aslan's face. Suddenly, he looked as if he had not been outside for months, as if he had been confined within an institutional setting such as a hospital or prison, although this was not the case, as should be evident from the proceedings recorded above. Nevertheless, the pallor indicated a failure to thrive: despite Aslan's repeated claims over the past months that he was completely "chuffed," some crucial factor was missing. Some factor essential to the boy's well-being was missing, as indicated by his pallor and also, come to think of it, his mistreatment of the cat (for such behavior, as noted above, is strongly associated in the literature with psychic disturbance). But what? For in his Stasi summer uniform, which fit surprisingly well (as the average height in Europe during the early to mid-twentieth century was considerably less, due to nutritional deficiencies, than now), he did not appear incomplete.[20] On the contrary, he appeared fully finished, consummate and self-contained, like a small man.

The unopened case of a recently purchased video game lay on the floor at his feet—Super Mario Brothers. He kicked it. He kicked it, as if a small man, impatient with puerile pursuits. But he was not a man, even a small one. To be sure, with his broad shoulders and consummate demeanor, he emanated maturity; however, other indicators—scant axillary hair, knobby carpi, and disproportionately large feet—signaled that adulthood lay in the temporal distance. No, developmentally, Aslan had advanced only as far as early adolescence, if adolescence can be considered an advance over childhood. Developmentally he was only a young adolescent, even if he appeared, at times, to be a small man. Now the failure of an organism to thrive at a particular stage in its life cycle can often be attributed to a missing necessary environmental requirement or condition. Take, for instance, the well-established link between folate deficiency and certain congenital birth defects. As we know, fetal growth and development are characterized by widespread cell division. Because folate plays a role in DNA and RNA synthesis, it is critical to normal cell growth. A deficiency in folate can cause abnormal cell division and growth, leading to devastating and sometimes fatal neural tube defects such as anencephaly or

---

[20] A person's height is determined by the span of the vertebral trunk and the length of the bones of the lower limbs. Children's growth in height is influenced by climate, including weather and sunlight, by diet, exercise and posture, and particularly by glandular action. So while the failure to achieve full height can be attributed to environmental deprivations, such as those commonly seen during wartime, inherent biochemical deficiencies, for which no blame can be assigned, must be taken into account.

spina bifida, not to mention an increased instance of cleft palate or 'hare-lip," which while not life-threatening, can seriously limit romantic success later on. Therefore, some hard questions were in order. Had Aslan's needs, developmentally, truly been considered? What were his needs?

Well, what were the needs of children in general? Rapidly, an internal review was performed of pediatrics and the prescribed needs of childhood and also of early adolescence (since Aslan, though nominally still a child, had entered the early stages of puberty). Surely nutritional requirements were being met, as the refrigerator was well-stocked and multivitamins were supplied. Good nutrition, check. So too, were intellectual and physical requirements, as a recent visit to Aslan's school on *Elternabend* (or parent's night) had provided assurance that both the academic and athletic facilities were top-notch. Regular, structured opportunities for mental and physical stimulation and advancement, check. Naturally, the nascent adolescent accrued a sleep deficit during the week; so far, however, the budget was balanced every weekend by a "long lie" on both Saturday and Sunday mornings. Adequate sleep, check. So what was missing from the prescribed list of requirements for optimal growth? Internship engrams were pulled up, then quickly discarded, the files of medical school memory ransacked, when suddenly a maternal adage repeated ad nauseum was recalled: "all work and no play makes Rosie a dull girl." Yes, that was it. Yes, although Teresa had used the adage, repeatedly, to suggest that academic success was impeding matrimony, she was, in a sense, correct. To be sure, experts in child development regard unstructured play, which can be defined as any joyful activity that has no clear-cut goal and is done for its own sake, as the "work" of children; however, unstructured play is work that strengthens the capacity for imaginative thinking. Numerous studies have shown that most of the very highly creative and successful people in the long run are adults who can still adopt a playful attitude toward ideas. Of course, no illusions were held about maintaining a relationship with Aslan over the "long run." Still, success was wished for him. For while RR was not, and never would be, Aslan's mother, two months of domestic service (for clearly no one had ever taught the kid to pick up after himself) had evoked quasi-maternal feelings.

So. Play. It was recalled that RR and Tom Tom had played frequently—probably at least 40 percent more than children today.[21] They had played all kinds of games, some singular and spontaneous (like the girdle game), others ongoing and almost ritualistic (such as the furtively performed yellow star game). Playing frequently, RR and Tom Tom had thrived, or at least RR had thrived, and most probably Tom Tom would have as well, if he had not died, accidentally and prematurely. Therefore, regular playtime needed to be incorporated into Aslan's routine, so that he too could achieve optimal growth. Granted, it is difficult to incorporate playtime into travel, as the quotidian tasks of procuring meals and lodging, not to mention the simple need to cover the distance from point A to point B or from point B to point C, can be temporally consuming. Nevertheless, it is possible, especially if playtime is combined with sightseeing. Yes, because sightseeing is a reasonable activity to include in any

---

[21] Since the late 1970s, American children have lost more than 12 hours of playtime per week, which means they play 25 percent less than their parents did. As the author of this report played more than average, even for the era (roughly 15 percent more), a difference of 40 percent seems plausible.

travel schedule, especially a relatively flexible and open-ended one (idem: while eventually the boy had to be returned, he did not have to be returned any time soon). But what "sights" could be mixed with playtime? Well, a recent article in the *International Herald Tribune* travel section had featured a famous concentration camp, located near Prague. Indeed this famous camp was the one the maternal progenitor had claimed she would visit if she ever "returned to the old country," because Jews had not only died there, but had produced works of art, thus attesting to "the triumph of the imagination." Of course the "triumph" of the imagination held little interest, as there is no goal to unstructured play; the camp's reputation for inspiring creativity, however, was a distinct draw.

So, the famous concentration camp for artists was one possibility for combining sightseeing with healthy, unstructured play. Another was an American Wild West style theme park in eastern Bavaria, also recently written up in the *Tribune*. Featuring, like the camp, a genocidal opposition (sure kindling for any kid's imagination, the world over), the Cowboy and Indian theme park would, like the camp, be conducive to hours of robust pretending. Further, although the theme park was a reproduction of the Wild West rather than an actual historical site like the camp, it included a "Main Street" equipped with three licensed saloons, a cluster of authentic teepees, certified pony express rides and live bison—thereby providing a genuine glimpse into the past. Now, how to choose between the camp and the park? How to choose between these two compelling recreational and educational options, because a choice needed to be made? A choice needed to be made so that an itinerary, or at least the beginning of an itinerary, could be presented along with the announcement of tomorrow's sunrise departure. Because while children require unstructured play, they also require a reliable routine into which unstructured play can be scheduled. Because it would not do for Aslan to think RR had no definite plan.

No, it would not do for Aslan, who now sat at the desk in the corner, pale-faced and hunched over the yellow, paperback sized form of his Game Boy, to think RR was making it all up as they went along. As he tapped at the tiny control panel, eliciting small creaking, whirring and whinnying noises, followed by a jingling tune that evoked the mechanical lurching of a super-market pony ridden long ago by the young RR and Tom Tom, Aslan needed to believe, like all children, that an adult with a definite plan was in charge. Therefore a decision was made to git along (little doggie) to the American Wild West style theme park, at sunrise, if not before.

Although RR owned a newer model, fuel-efficient Renault (purchased upon arriving in Germany from a departing fellow American), and although European driving presents no great challenge, since the right side of the road is utilized, RR and Aslan (sans cat, which had been deposited in its crate on the Polizistin neighbors' doorstep) traveled by rail. RR and the boy traveled by rail because the transcontinental trip was undertaken in Europe, where train service is more frequent, efficient and economical (particularly with a four week InterRail Pass), than in America. Further, RR, although a capable and competent driv-er, did not really like to drive. Finally, travel by rail in Europe is highly enjoyable, often combining state-of-the-art technology (as on the German I.C.E. trains, with their memory foam seats and world wide web access) with old-fashioned ceremony and service (e.g. an order of champagne in the first-class car comes complete with a silver ice bucket, fluted glasses and a white towel-wielding attendant to pop the cork). The one drawback of travel by rail is that it is sometimes more time consuming to reach a particular destination.

A case in point would be the trip to Pullman City, the American Wild West style theme park situated in eastern Bavaria. To be sure, the initial delay could not be attributed to the mode of travel: no, the fact that the first day's destination was overshot by two hundred miles had to be blamed on the bubbly. As is well known, alcohol is a CNS depressant. The depressant effect of the alcohol in tandem with the giddy sensation induced by the carbon dioxide bubbles served to create confusion, so that when the conductor announced disembarkation for Regensburg (which according to the *Tribune* article was the closest major stop to Pullman City), something else was heard. Something else was heard by both RR and Aslan (in the case of the latter, who was wearing headphones, probably rap or ska; in the case of the former, who knows), so that Regensburg was passed by and Austria was entered. As Austria had been entered, and Vienna was only two hours away, a decision was made to continue on to the nidus of psychoanalysis for the night.

Now Sigmund Freud, whatever one thinks of his controversial and largely discredited theories, began his career as a neurologist. In fact, not many students and clinicians in the neurosciences, let alone lay people, are aware that the Viennese cocaine addict made significant contributions to knowledge of the brain. For instance, his innovative staining technique with gold chloride provided a method to view the microscopic world of the neuron and to trace the interconnectivity of different areas of the nervous system. Indeed, although it was H.W.G. von Waldeyer who would coin the term "neuron," the groundwork for what we call "neural doctrine" was done by "Coco" Freud, who, by the way, appears on his birth certificate as "Sigismund." If this were not a completely factual report, with no room for untethered ideation, one might ask if the loss of that ballasting extra syllable, that existential "is," symbolically allowed for the flight into what "is not" (e.g., penis envy). But setting the trained neurologist's later intellectual follies aside, credit should be given where credit is due, and therefore the next day a visit to the Freud Museum was made, where the aforementioned birth certificate (which also revealed a middle name, "Schlomo"), as well as the famous couch were seen.

Having no interest in either psychoanalysis or neuroscience, Aslan did not enjoy the excursion to the Freud Museum (which he termed "king dick hydraulics"). Consequently, RR let him eat cake. He was allowed to eat cake in a café off the Ringstrasse, even though he could have been more forbearing at the Freud Museum (after all, the long, expensive and career-risking journey to Cyprus was for him). Even though he could have been more forbearing, he was allowed to eat not just one but two large pieces of overpriced *Sachertorte*, served with sizable dollops of *Schlagobers*. Served with *Schlagobers*, or freshly beaten cream, the apricot jam-filled, semisweet chocolate-encased cake was apparently too rich to consume, or more specifically, too rich to digest, as afterward Aslan regurgitated it onto the cobblestones outside.

That evening, therefore, RR spent alone while Aslan, who was still feeling queasy and further, smelled of vomit, recuperated in a modestly priced (as a budget had to be adhered to) pension. Alone, RR walked back to the Innere Stadt and entered a small cocktail lounge located off the Kärntnerstrasse, taking a seat in a green leather booth with a fine view of a mahogany bar and the art deco design of the black marble and mirror inlaid wall beyond.

In between the art deco wall and the bar stood a thirtyish female bartender, blond hair cinched atop her cranium to form a cascade of curls, attending to an older male accompanied by a very young one. Indeed, the very young male appeared to be no more than five and as the bartender bent down, presumably to procure a garnish for the whiskey sour she had just replaced for the older male, the very young one, kneeling on his stool, leaned over the counter and reached for the bartender's blond cascade. Rising up with a fruited toothpick in one hand, the bartender laughingly caught the boy's wrist with the other, uttering a phrase that contained the term *Vati* (daddy), and something beginning with *neben* (next to), which caused the older male, presumably the father, to laugh as well. As a Gibson martini was ordered from a circulating waiter, the antics at the bar continued—the boy vying for the bartender's attention, as she mixed and poured drinks for the various patrons scattered around the bar, the father consuming whiskey sours at a relatively rapid rate.

Observing the somewhat weathered-looking but attractive father, sympathy was felt. Evidently he had no one to help him care for the boy, and thus could not even go out for a drink without his so-called precious cargo in tow. So burdened, the man might just as well have remained at home: how, for instance, could he appreciate the bold hard outlines and geometric patterns of the lounge's art deco interior, when he had to keep an eye on the squirming, wriggling brat beside him? It is hard, having sole responsibility for another, underage person—this had become apparent over the course of the unplanned afternoon in the adult-oriented, fin-de-siècle city, in the struggle to keep Aslan entertained and happy. Gazing at the weathered but attractive man across the room, for the first time RR wondered if it might have been best to put Aslan on a plane.

As if he had somehow picked up on RR's kindred, so to speak, feelings of encumbrance, perhaps through pheromonal channels, the weathered but attractive man at last swiveled around in his seat. Smiles were exchanged. Smiles were exchanged and the trade was more than satisfactory, as his, subtle yet playful, was of a favored sort. But what next? With the lips, a pearl onion was plucked from the plastic spear that had been resting in the well of the Gibson martini. As the pearl onion was rolled about in the mouth, the man was regarded. His eyes were blue. Not green, but an attractive, mature blue. The pearl broke between the teeth, bathing the mucous membranes with the strong, briny flavor of pickled organosulfur compounds. Mixed with gin, the flavor was strong, briny, harsh, but also bracing, like the first night alone in a foreign city, without family, friends or even an acquaintance. The weathered but attractive man raised his glass to his lips and drained it, mature blue eyes smiling over the rim. Anything could happen.

Anything could happen and then the boy, who had been standing on his stool, fell. The boy fell to the ground, and although no head trauma occurred (otherwise assistance would have been offered, in accordance with the Hippocratic Oath), began to scream. As the boy screamed, the father was all solicitude, crouched on the tiled floor and cradling him in his arms.

And now it was certain that the promise of the preceding exchange would remain untasted, just like the fresh whiskey sour
the bartender had placed moments before on the bar.

Further, while returning to the pension a realization came:
there was no going back. There was no going back, as the
weathered but attractive man had demonstrated, cradling his
son in his arms. Once a child is procured, he must be cared for,
no matter how inconvenient and constraining the responsibility.
The footloose days before the boy were over, and as Aslan was
later viewed sleeping in his bed, the red glow of a neon sign
across the street spilling through the window and washing over
the smooth planes of his face, a second realization came: sometimes it is pleasant to be tied down.

As once a child is procured, he must be cared for, the next
day the trip to Pullman City was resumed. The trip was resumed, but unfortunately not completed. For the information
that the American Wild West style theme park was near Regensburg turned out to be erroneous, as a query at the train station
there confirmed. Located just outside a village called Eging am
See, which was in turn outside the town of Passau, near the
Austrian border, the theme park had once again been overshot.
It would be necessary, therefore, to catch an eastbound train
back in the direction of Vienna. Since RR and Aslan had arrived in Regensburg relatively late on a Sunday, however (having
had a "long lie" back at the pension, after Aslan had brushed
his teeth), the last opportunity for travel by rail to Passau had
passed. Thus the night was spent in Regensburg, an inconvenience mitigated by the comfort and charm of a four-star hotel
tucked behind the cathedral in the old city center (for after two

two-star nights at the Viennese pension, a decision was made to splurge). Its creamy stucco and timber façade ornamented with geranium-filled flowerboxes overlooking a cobblestoned court-yard complete with plashing fountain, the hotel lent a pleasing old world ambience to the new, child-centered world that had been entered in taking on responsibility for Aslan. Indeed, the next morning, sitting alone in the courtyard with an espresso and buttery rich croissant, observing a smiling blond woman humor her toddler (as first the mother, then the child, would run behind the fountain, calling "*fort*," and around again, an-nouncing "*da*"), RR realized that self-sacrifice does not preclude self-indulgence.[22]

Again a late start was made, as Aslan did not arise until ten minutes before checkout time. Consequently, although Passau is only an hour by rail from Regensburg, arrival in Passau was delayed until after two in the afternoon. Further, by the time RR and Aslan, rolling suitcases in tow (thank god the boy had agreed to leave his cat behind) reached the local *Verkehrsamt,* or tourist information office, it was learned that the last bus for Eg-ing am See had left for the day. When incredulity was expressed, for surely there were additional daily buses to the vicinity of

---

[22] The "Fort/Da Game" (a.k.a. "the Pomo Hokey Pokey") was first described by Freud in *Beyond the Pleasure Principle,* after he observed his 18-month-old nephew playing with a wooden spool tied to a length of string. Having thrown the spool over the side of his crib while holding onto the string, the little boy would announce "*fort*" (gone), then, as he pulled it back up into view, "*da*" (here).

According to Freud, what the game enacted was the child's "great cul-tural achievement—the instinctual renunciation (that is, the renunciation of instinctual satisfaction) which he had made in allowing his mother to go away without protesting. He compensated himself for this, as it were, by himself, staging the disappearance and return of the objects within his reach" (*SE,* v.18, 14-15).

the famous American Wild West style theme park, the woman behind the desk cast a blank stare and returned to her computer screen.

Because self-sacrifice does not preclude self-indulgence, and because the sojourn in Passau would after all only be for a night or two, a room was reserved in another stucco and timber four-star hotel, this one perched on a low promontory over the confluence of the Inn and Ilz rivers. The next morning, however, having been lured into surplus somnolence by the lapping of the water below, RR, too, woke late. Fortunately, time remained to catch the last bus to Eging am See, which after reserving the river-side room for another night and securing a taxi cab across town, was boarded less than an hour later.

In terms of physical and sexual development, females are a bit more precocious than males. Certainly this was true of the youths who filled the early afternoon bus to Eging am See, apparently returning from school to homes in the countryside outside Passau. [23] While the youngest of the boys appeared less physically mature than Aslan, every single girl on the bus appeared noticeably more so. One specimen of the latter in particular caught the eye: a voluptuous pygmy (for she could not have been much over a meter in height) in a snug orange tank

---

[23] Given the early hour of dismissal from school, it can be assumed that the start time had been early as well, possibly as early as 7am. Studies have shown, however, that as children enter adolescence, they develop a "phase delay": naturally they stay up later (in fact, often Aslan was alert and ready to go as late as 4:00am), as melatonin enters the brain later, and therefore they need to sleep later. As tiredness impairs cognitive performance, educators could better serve adolescent students by instituting more reasonable start times. Indeed, a plan had been formulated to present the officials at Aslan's school with research findings in support of more reasonable start times, but now there was no longer a need.

top, black capris secured by a steel grommeted leather belt and high top Converse sneakers. The pistil at the center of a cluster of like-attired young females across the aisle, she appeared, as she shook her plastic bangled arms in the air, apparently grooving to the sounds piping through the headphones of her Walkman, to be self-fertilizing. Appearing autonomous, but also clearly integral to her group, she drew the covert attention of every other youth on the bus, including, it could be seen, Aslan. Yes, Aslan was watching her, even as he appeared not to be, flocculent coils obscuring the upper half of his face as he bent over one of his portable video games. He appeared not to be looking but the sinistral flash of his eyes could be seen through the tendrils of his hair, as they darted every now and then to the left side of the bus, even as the yellow box of his Game Boy chirruped and buzzed, the sounds blurring with the humid greens and golds of the rolling hills and fields of the passing countryside, a completely rural prospect which offered no possibility for an exit any time soon. What if they started talking? What if the autonomous appearing but at the same time integral to the group girl were to suddenly lean across the aisle and ask what game Aslan was playing? Wouldn't Aslan—responding not just to nascent reproductive urges elicited by the girl's parthenogenic appeal, but also to the wish to belong, as it is in the nature of the adolescent (which he nearly was) to seek status and acceptance among young people of his own age—wouldn't he all too readily answer? A conversation would ensue, and in the course of the half hour or so that remained of the ride to Eging am See, possibly an invitation to the American Wild West style theme park as well. Which is not to imply that Aslan was not allowed to have friends—of course he was allowed to have friends and even, at some future date, girlfriends. However, given that the visit to the theme park could not last more than a few hours, as the day was already half over, and further, that tomorrow the journey to North Cyprus would necessarily be resumed, quality time together was limited. Yes, quality time—during which RR would happily stoop to Aslan's childish interests (for admittedly the Freud museum had been over his head), and through that stooping perhaps get just a little closer to him—quality time was limited. Therefore, Aslan was made to switch places, to the window seat, for the remainder of the ride.

Although the date was only the 17th of May, and although the springtime climate in Germany is on average rainy and cool, the sky was cloudless and the air was warm. Indeed, outdoors, in the sun, it felt like mid-July. This comparison came to mind following disembarkation in the village of Eging am See, since according to the woman at the tourist information office in Passau, there was no direct bus to Pullman City. Originally, the plan had been to walk the remaining three kilometers to the Western theme park: this plan, however, was abandoned after a perusal of the sun-bleached schedule posted at the bus stop in central Eging am See. For as indicated by the schedule, the last bus back to Passau departed in an hour and twenty minutes— insufficient time to walk to the theme park, disport there, and walk back. To be sure, according to the *Tribune* article, Pullman City offered overnight lodgings (in both log cabins and teepees for six, as well as in an Old West style hotel on Main Street); however, suitcases and toiletries (including prophylactics since conception, theoretically, was possible) had been left behind in Passau. So now there was no option but to wait in Eging am See for the bus back to Passau, where the shadow cast by a closed cleaning supply store provided only partial shelter from the sun.

A poster of a blond smiling *Hausfrau* with a mop in her hand floating in the expanse of window glass behind him, Aslan once more sat hunched over his Game Boy. Now, however, he cast no sideways glances, neither sinistral nor dextral. Hunched over his Game Boy, looking neither left nor right, he appeared closed in upon himself, like an embryo in utero, mute and secret. Which was fine, for no urge was felt to draw him out: he was not the only one disappointed by the aborted trip to Pullman City. He was not the only one sitting in front of a cleaning supply store only partially sheltered from the sun in a seemingly deserted village in eastern Bavaria. Because not a single person could be seen out walking along the smooth, uniformly surfaced street (no cobblestones here), or even peering through the lace-curtained windows of the tan stucco, clay tile roofed houses. Not a single person could be seen and yet behind the mute, cemented surfaces, someone stirred, as evidenced by the odor of grilled lamb emanating from what appeared to be a Greek restaurant, the legend "Poseidon" painted in peeling blue letters on a wooden sign over the entrance. If Aslan refused to come out of his shell, that was fine. In time, he would emerge.

In time, but in the meantime the sun was hot and boredom prevailed (unfortunately a most interesting article by E. T. Rolls on the neural basis of emotion had been left behind at the hotel, in order to more fully attend to Aslan). Perhaps distraction, as well as UV protection, could eventually be found at the Greek restaurant across the street. At present, however, it was closed— as indicated by the sign on the door. And in truth, a plate of oily steaming souvlaki would not improve the situation, which included dryness of the mouth, as well as ennui. Given the both overheated and dull situation, something like a cold bottle of water seemed more remedial—perhaps there was a grocer down the street, around the bend. Having asked Aslan to wait (a request that he acknowledged with an almost imperceptible nod. Screw him), RR set off in search of hydration.

Because once a child is procured he must be cared for, not much thought had been given earlier to clothing. As a result, on this particular occasion, RR, like many who play a caretaking role, was poorly dressed in running shoes, black denim jeans and a black nylon polo shirt purchased in Berlin because Aslan had said it was "hot." Which indeed it was—the dark shade absorbing rather than reflecting radiation, the synthetic fabric countering the cooling effect of perspiration by trapping moisture and heat energy. Consequently, when at last an empty but open minimart was reached, about a kilometer down the road, where two bottles of mineral water and then a plastic basket of ripe red strawberries were purchased from a young attendant who despite the "Superwoman" emblazoned t-shirt stretched across her oversized mammaries, seemed mentally deficient, twice making incorrect change, sunstroke already could have been a problem. Yes, sunstroke, the early symptoms of which include dizziness and confusion, as well as dryness of the mouth, already could have been a problem—hence the young attendant's insistence that she was not the one who was a *Dummkopf.*

Certainly by the time Aslan was rejoined, all the symptoms of sunstroke—dryness of the mouth, dizziness and confusion, distended blood vessels, tachycardia and nausea—were present. Further, the odor of grilling meat emanating from the Greek restaurant across the street had acquired a strong, almost rancid tang—as if the supply of lamb had run out and only mutton remained. Therefore when Aslan ignored both the mineral water and the strawberries, instead remaining sullenly fixed on his Game Boy, maintaining composure was no picnic. Suddenly a long-forgotten and previously dismissed adage of Mother Teresa's came to mind: that children were vipers who inevitably bit the breast that suckled them.

"Oh boo hoo. You know what I think? I think this is all about you."

What?

"Yeah, that's right—all about you and some home on the range idea you have of fun."

No reply was made. It was as if the neural pathways crucial for speech and communication had suddenly disappeared, leaving nothing but an impenetrable tangle. An impenetrable tangle, as Aslan, who had swept back his springy tendrils with one fisted forearm as he spoke, regarding RR with a glare, yes a glare, dropped his gaze back to the Game Boy. As it was impossible, seemingly, to speak, there was nothing to do but eat— one strawberry, and then another, and another, the warm seedy pulp filling the mouth with the unmitigated acids of unripeness. Because the berries beneath the top layer were all a glaucous green, and yet these too were consumed, the entire basket consumed, as the sun beat down and the mutton stank and the stomach churned in a racket of peristalsis, until in the end the whole, moments before the last bus back to Passau arrived, was disgorged, splattering the pavement with a glistening greenish, red daubed mess of macerated pericarp and seed.

As learned in AP English, irony in literature occurs when there is an incongruity between expectation or belief and actuality. If this report were a literary fiction, an example of irony could be found, since, contrary to expectation, the bus did in fact make a stop at Pullman City. The incongruity between expectation and actuality became apparent about ten minutes after the departure from Eging am See, as first a ragged row of American, German and British flags flopping in the breeze and then, topped in gold with *"Die Lehende Western Stadt—Pullman City,"* a tall log gate through which a man in a Stetson was leading a lurching quarter horse, drew into view. A group of laughing Germans boarded: an adult male in black western wear, complete with a ten gallon hat, spurred boots and a long braided bullwhip which he carried in one hand, the strap twined about his waist; an adult female girdled in rhinestone-studded denim; and two small children in feathered headdresses, their cheeks striped with red and white greasepaint. Apparently a biological family, as evidenced by the combination in the two children of the woman's widow's peak and the man's close-set blue eyes, the four took seats near the front of the bus, the denim girdled putative mother drawing the smaller of the children, a male, onto her lap. Positioned sideways on his mother's lap, the boy peered over her shoulder, the red and white lines of grease paint fanned like cat's whiskers over his cheeks. With small, close-set blue eyes, he regarded Aslan, who, having pocketed the Game Boy in his cargo pants, now sat listening to his Walkman, his face turned away toward the window. Suddenly the boy's gaze shifted and his tongue shot out.

Now as also learned in AP English, irony in literature often serves to demonstrate the limits of human understanding.

Because this account of the trip to Pullman City is not, however, literature, its ironic conclusion does not, technically, demonstrate the limits of human understanding—only the limits of
RR's German. Nevertheless, as the boy continued to thrust out
his tongue, as Aslan remained turned away, the tinny, muted yet
nevertheless impenitent voice of gangster rap escaping from his
headphones, and as once again RR was overcome by the waves
of peristalsis, understanding seemed very puny indeed.

Usually, it is better to admit quickly to errors and failures,
rather than to try to hedge or deny. Therefore, while lying alone
that night listening to the confluence of the Inn and Ilz rivers,
it was acknowledged that a mistake had been made. Aslan had
never once expressed interest in the American West, cowboys
or even in Native Americans. And why should he? Raised in exile, his playground had been the mean streets of East London,
not the wooded hills and dales of upstate New York, or even
the high plains of Colorado. To be sure the German children
in the feathered headdresses had seemed to be enjoying themselves; however, as indicated by the yippee ki-yay couture of
their parents, theirs was a household that embraced Western
culture.[24] So, while listening to the confluence of the Inn and Ilz
rivers, it was acknowledged that a mistake had been made: spec.
Aslan had been conflated with Tom Tom. Yes, Aslan had been
conflated with Tom Tom, who had enjoyed playing Cowboys
and Indians more than anything, even the Yellow Star game.

---

[24] In fact, every German schoolchild is familiar with the novels of James
Fenimore Cooper, as well as those of Karl May, a German who, although he
never set foot in America, in the late nineteenth and early twentieth centuries
painted a vivid, entertaining and not entirely inaccurate account of the Far
West. His full-blooded fantasies have sold more than 100 million copies in
German and have engendered successful films, summer festivals and other
popular spin-offs.

But Aslan was not Tom Tom. No, for even given that 99.9 percent of every strand of human DNA is indistinguishable from every other, the remaining portion (three million out of three billion base pairs) is unique, and thus no person is quite like another, especially when environmental influences are factored in (as demonstrated by the minute but nevertheless very real differences between identical twins). Not Tom Tom, Aslan was, irreplaceably, himself, and therefore when he at last returned early in the morning to the hotel, after having stolen away hours before, no comment was made for fear that in the future he might not come back, at all.

If this were a literary fiction, one final irony would remain. That irony would emerge the morning after the trip to the American Wild West style theme park, as Aslan, whose mood was once again bright and sociable, pointed out a "yank tank" parked not far from the hotel. Closer inspection revealed an old Cadillac, its dark red paint stenciled in script under the driver's side window with the legend *"Pullman City."* And within, strung from the rearview mirror, dangled a pair of dice, cat's eyes aligned, and a tiny beaded moccasin.

2. Self-Support is Increasingly Untenable

Although the adjective "kittenish," more commonly refers to young females, it sometimes pertains to young males as well. Certainly it was relevant in the case of Aslan, who was sitting on a low stone ledge outside the Colosseum making tiny smacking sounds with his tongue as he consumed a lemon gelato. If produced by an adult, the sounds would have been annoying. As made by Aslan, however, they worked in tandem with the sensual warmth of the late afternoon sun to trigger a kind of let-down reflex, a vague but potent urge to give him all. Yes, a vague but potent urge to give him all, even though he'd already received a great deal, as evidenced by the large Strada shopping bag resting beside him (from an excursion earlier in the day to the Via Condotti shopping district at the foot of the Spanish Steps) and also by the much smaller bags beneath the eyes of yours truly (as frequent nocturnal intercourse had disturbed the sleep-wake cycle: afterwards, often two hours or more were spent staring up at the hotel bedroom ceiling). Indeed, the provision of a great deal had taken a toll, both on finances and sleep. However, thus far the expenditure had been completely worthwhile, and hence at present no need to hold back was felt. On the contrary.

This vague but potent urge to give Aslan not just a great deal, but all, was experienced on the first of June, in the eternal city of Rome (as hinted above by references to the Colosseum and Spanish Steps), two weeks after departure from Passau. It should be noted here that a new style of making travel arrangements had been adopted, one that included maximal input from Aslan: for as demonstrated by the Pullman City debacle, pleasure would be minimal unless the boy was on board. Accordingly, the preceding fourteen days *had not* included culturally enriching excursions to world capitals such as Paris ("No kermits for me, thank you") or Barcelona ("They say the rain in Spain is mainly a pain"). The preceding fourteen days *had* included, however, minus transit time, a one day jaunt to Graz, the hometown of Arnold Schwarzenegger, to view the vast Arnold Schwarzenegger Stadium and attached petite museum devoted to the Austrian actor's iron pumping juvenescence; a week long sojourn in Romania on a packaged tour encompassing a visit to Sighisoara, the birthplace of Prince Vlad the Impaler a.k.a. Count Dracula, a day long horseback ride through the dark Transylvanian woods where allegedly the Count once roamed, topped off with a traditional Romanian sunset barbecue, and six nights' accommodation in a small grim garlic suffused hotel in Moecin; and finally, two days in Ljubljana, the capital of Slovenia, on the recommendation of a British boy on the Transylvanian tour who had somehow convinced the usually incredulous Aslan that a dragon-like species inhabited the caves located one hour outside the city center.[25]

It should also be noted that the vague but potent urge to give Aslan "all" was probably exacerbated by the immediate setting

---

[25] Only when he was able to see for himself that there was nothing to see in the limestone caves of Karst, besides colossal caverns traversed by roaring rivers and other such humdrum spelunker's wonders, did Aslan relinquish his stubborn belief that mammoth flying reptiles resided there. Given the boy's obvious intelligence, his resistance beforehand to logical refutation (which had included a detailed explanation of the principles of evolution and radiocarbon dating methods) came as a surprise. On the other hand, it was sometimes easy to forget that he was only twelve years old and that myelination of the fibers connecting the corpus callosum to the parietal cortex (the part of the brain linked to logic) was still incomplete.

and cultural context. The setting and cultural context being that of the capital of Catholicism and thus the heart of Mariolatry. Churches, basilicas, chapels, sacred grottos and holy niches were, of course, ubiquitous, bursting with representations of the Cristo and his Santa Maria Madre, which no doubt worked upon the collective consciousness to produce an inordinate respect for the maternal bond, the bond between mother and son in particular. Because Aslan was, admittedly, young enough to be the son of RR, and further, shared in common the trait of light curly hair (which when lit by the oblique rays of the late afternoon sun resembled an aureole), everywhere shopkeepers, vendors and waiters assumed that he was, endorsing the presumed kinship with complimentary limonate, cappuccini, gelati, pizze and panini. This constant, erroneous assumption was allowed to stand, as free drinks and snacks were welcome, while speculation and query were not. And fortunately it prevailed, remaining unchallenged by Aslan, who so far had been dissuaded from divulgence (e.g. "she's not me mum") by ever greater indulgence. Clearly, however, there was a connection between the urge to give all and the possibility that the boy, irritated by the Romans' unremitting presumption of his filiation with RR, would tell all.

And now, as Aslan had expressed a desire to see the Colosseum ("where Spartacus and his lads went at it"), the greater part of an afternoon had been spent waiting in a long, snaking line of shorts clad, video camera carrying compatriots, first outside the ancient sporting arena, and then inside, in a perimetric, arcade-like structure which at least provided respite from solar radiation, if not from the automotive combustion products of the city beyond. When at last admittance was gained into

the roofless interior, however, the sun's heat struck full force—
necessitating immediate restoration of body fluid levels and
also the reapplication of UV protection. To this end, a leather
backpack, the underside slick with sweat, was removed from the
shoulders, and a bottle of water and tube of sunscreen extracted, while the boy stared about the rubble strewn, weed choked
crater as if he were in a surround sound multiplex, waiting for
the show to begin.[26] Because his childish capacity for wonder
was part of his charm, no withering comments were made as
first H_2O was drunk and then SPF 45 lotion was applied to
the face. Indeed, the back was briefly turned as the contents
of the pack were restored, allowing him to gaze uninhibited at
the dustbin of history. A mistake, because upon looking round
again, it was discovered he had disappeared. Hence the forty
minutes that followed in the antiquated arena (which by the

---

[26] Perhaps he was envisioning a "naumachia," a bit of apocrypha provided by
a middle-aged American male in cargo shorts and a yachting cap, who had
been standing uncomfortably close in the line to enter the Colosseum. Having failed to initiate a conversation with yours truly ("I have a kid back home
about his age. Don't see him as much as I'd like—lives with his mother."), the
Skipper had turned to Aslan and claimed that in ancient times the arena had
been flooded, and historical naval battles, complete with full-size replicas of
the boats involved, re-staged. Skepticism was then expressed: while the near
sea level area of the Colosseum and of the adjoining Forum (where evidence
of human activity has been found as low as 3.6 meters above sea level) was
well-watered in ancient times by the Cloaca Brook and its tributaries, so that
the Forum was always among the first places inundated in the wet season, the
engineering feat required to channel these water resources into the Colosseum
and then to fill the structure to a sufficient depth for sailing (presumably at
least two meters—which if the dimensions of the arena were, as stated in the
man's guidebook, 76 by 44 by 55 meters, would mean pumping in 186,670
cubic meters of water; unfortunately, the mathematical knowledge to convert
this figure into liters is lacking), not to mention draining it again after, surely
surpassed the technological capacity of the period. At which point Aslan had
interjected, "Congratters, you win the crasher of the year award."

way elicited a retroactive appreciation for the "state-of-the-art" concrete and steel sporting facility viewed previously in Graz) were spent attempting to locate the boy, who, although recently provided with a small and costly Nokia cell phone, either would not answer it, or could not (for reception was not always assured). He was at last spotted outside, sitting on a low stone ledge, swinging his cracked green leather combat boots as he tongued the above-mentioned lemon gelato.

As the delinquent gelato licker was approached, he slowly turned his head, each of the mirrored discs of his sunglasses displaying a tiny quivering woman clad in a diaphanous peaches and cream print dress and cream straw topee. For the sake of temporal as a well as emotional exactitude, it should be noted that the first thought following reunification was not "to give him all." Instead the first thought was, as Mother Teresa used to say, "to give it to him": specifically, to rip off those sunglasses and then to belt him, perhaps first obtaining a cat-o'-nine-tails from one of the men strolling by in gladiator costume, although that would mean involving others, who then might discover the relation between nonrelations. Further, "to give it to him" would no doubt mean to get it back, as castigation would be met with rancor. Not just rancor, but prepubescent rancor, which is only a few degrees less noxious than full blown adolescent rancor, as it employs the same arsenal,[27] albeit less intensely and consistently. Therefore, no words of reproof were offered re:

---

[27] Said arsenal consisting of sulking, sniping and snarking, and even sabotage: e.g. the previous week someone had tossed out someone else's last pair of contact lenses, just because she had ventured that it was blind stupidity, given the mass of scientific evidence to the contrary, to insist that giant reptiles existed coterminous with Homo sapiens.

Aslan's inconsiderate disappearance. No words of reproof were offered as instead the late spring air was respired—the humid, thick spring air spiked with the sharp odor of some unidentified pollinating plant, perhaps the yellow, paintbrush-like flower, that along with bright red poppies, stippled the grounds both within and outside the Colosseum. This sharp scented plant elicited an allergic reaction—sneezing and also itching of the mucous membranes of the eyes and throat—which would have rendered contact lenses unwearable.[28] Fortunately, prescription photograys had been worn instead.[29] However, these too, as a person undergoing an allergic reaction experiences an overall over sensitivity and irritability, can become suddenly uncomfortable, due to the pressure of the earpieces on the ears. It was only after the photograys were removed, the loss of visual acuity augmenting aural reception (so that the sound of Aslan's lapping came to the fore), that the urge to give all welled up.

In order to act on this feeling, however, first it was necessary to pin down the nature of "all," which at present was indeterminate. At present indeterminate, the nature of all could be existential (in the sense of giving up one's life, either literally or figuratively, as in some cases giving up one's life means giving up career or family, and not an actual forfeiture of somatic

---

[28] An emotional factor as well as an allergenic one may have come into play. While the idea that diseases such as hay fever, asthma and hives are psychosomatic is countered by experience and the observations of medical professionals, to ignore emotional stresses is unrealistic. Persons with allergic disease may become disturbed, anxious or apprehensive, just like those with other illnesses. And as with other persons with other illnesses, their symptoms may become more severe under or even be precipitated by conditions of emotional stress (e.g. anxiety, displeasure, frustration and insecurity).

[29] See fn. 27.

existence), emotional (in the Freudian sense of the overestimation of the object) or simply economic (in the sense of signing over all income and assets, to be established, for example, as a trust). Or it could be some combination of the three (as the overestimation of the object often leads to both existential and economic overexpenditures). The fact was that "all" could be any number of things, which made it difficult to give "all." After "all," the transitive verb "to give" requires a direct object, a requirement that "all" satisfies grammatically but not semantically—for finally what does to give "all" mean? Yes the urge to give all needed to better defined before it could be acted upon, no matter how insistent the boy's licking, which now had become more cat-like than ever.

More cat-like than ever, the sound of the boy's licking was small but pointed, with a kind of raspy vigor that penetrated the ears like two invasive pinky fingers so that finally the analysis of the nature of "all" gave way to the immediate perception of the "one." Only the one was not the same one as before. Where Aslan and his Strada bag had been there was now a cat, a young orange tabby industriously lapping from a flattened and tattered paper cup the last traces of lemon gelato.

Yes, there was now a cat with a tattered paper cup where the boy and his shopping bag had been—as if the molecules composing the former had somehow diminished in number and then redisposed themselves as the latter. In actuality, of course, the boy had simply run off again. Therefore, no fantastic suspension of the laws of physics could be blamed for his disappearance—just a plain lapse in attention. Just a plain lapse in attention, a momentary shift in focus, and now he was missing, again. Obviously, more awareness was needed, a more constant

and heedful application to Aslan's presence—otherwise like a
tricky equation, he would continue to elude. Yes, and perhaps
this, finally, was what giving "all" entailed—a full, unwavering
regard for the boy.

With some difficulty, the scrap of paper cup was retrieved
from the cat (the animal having attempted to secure said scrap
with its claws) and deposited in a nearby trash receptacle. For
it is important to set a good example at all times. Even though
the boy was nowhere in sight, he might out of nowhere appear
and witness his trash being deposited in the trash receptacle,
where it belonged. Yes, he might suddenly appear and therefore
it was important to behave as if he was always there, even if he
was not. Indeed, if giving "all" entailed an unwavering regard
for the boy, then acting as if he was there even when he was not
was surely part of the program. That is, even when he was not
there, he would be there, at the center of consciousness, the idea
of him indexing the way back to him. In the meantime, however, he had yet to be located, and as his cell phone remained,
for whatever reason, unreachable, a decision was made to proceed in the direction of the Forum and of Palantine, where the
palaces of the ancient city had stood, since earlier, Aslan had
expressed an interest in the architectural remains of the "drool-
ing class."

According to the map obtained with admission to the Colosseum, the way to the Forum and to Palantine lay beyond the
Arch of Constantine, which loomed to the left. When suddenly
a hard clasp was felt, and turning, a gleaming brass cuirass was
seen. Above rose a broad coriaceous face, the expression of
which could be termed implacable, as a speech, along with a
spray of saliva, issued from the thick, rufous lips. Because the

speech was in contemporary Italian, little sense could be derived from it, although a few Latin-derived terms could be made out (e.g.: *scusi* and *attenzione*), as well as the now familiar *ragazzo*. Was the boy in trouble? An attempt was made to break free of the man's hold, but it seemed, in keeping with his gladiatorial apparel, to be a death grip. Further, in the meantime, several of his loin cloth and cuirass clad compatriots had gathered round, as if to prevent escape. A request to use English was made.

"Of course. Of course you do not understand that by right it was his."

What?

"Signora, I am guessing you are from America where maybe nothing is honored, not even human life. Who knows, I have never been there. But this I can tell, here catti are considered citizens as well as a symbol of the Eternal City."

He had relinquished his hold. The bicep was massaged: citizens?

"Yes, they are citizens and so the Colosseo and whatever spoils it brings belong to them just as to all citizens. *Per favore*, what belongs to the *ragazzo* by right of citizenship must be returned to him."

The cardiac function quickened, the rate of respiration increased. Who was he talking about? A cat? Or the boy?

"To the *piccolo gatto*." As the other "gladiators" gazed on, nodding, the man unsheathed a plastic sword from a scabbard at his hip and pointed it first at the trash receptacle where the gelato cup had been deposited and then at the cat, supine on the ledge, waving its limbs at the sun. "*Capisce?*"

The lungs inflated slowly and fully: his referent was the animal, not Aslan. Still, in order to avoid additional harassment, an attitude of compliance was adopted, the paper cup retrieved. This stratagem succeeded, as the ersatz gladiator then strolled away—over to a group of tourists clothed in yellow polo shirts emblazoned with the legend "Sheboygan Bible Club." Touching the tip of his sword to the distended abdomen of a corpulent young adult male, he proclaimed "too much spaghetti." As departure was taken, harsh laughter broke forth from the ersatz gladiator's brothers-in-arms.

Harsh laughter chased RR across the piazza, harsh laughter that seemed to commingle with the plant irritant in the air to form a new, potent psychotropic allergen, one that inflamed the imagination as well as the mucous membranes. For what if the ersatz gladiator really had meant the boy? As the pedestrian street into the Forum—the Via Sacra—was entered, a wave of paranoia washed over the mind. And then, countered by rationality, it receded: for how could he know anything about Aslan? He couldn't. More likely, the ersatz gladiator habitually and indiscriminately persecuted tourists, as, for instance, Smokey had once chased and even injured all backyard intruders, including human ones (having more than once striped the calves of neighborhood children). Yes, that was it: clearly he habitually and indiscriminately persecuted tourists, as evidenced by the fact that he had then moved on to the Sheboygan Bible boy. That was it and nothing personal—to believe otherwise was to succumb to the deleterious effect of sleep deprivation on rationality. Tonight, therefore, Ambien would be used—regardless of Aslan's desires.

Yes, regardless of Aslan's desires, tonight Ambien would be used and soundness of mind restored. At present, however, there was no choice but to hobble on, hamstrung by sleep deprivation.

Crippled by sleep deprivation, or more specifically by the delete-rious psychic side effects of sleep deprivation, which frequently include paranoia as well as a heightened emotional lability, RR would press on, nevertheless—for Aslan had to be found. Oth-erwise, to whom would "all" be given? Indeed, if the boy were lost, "all," in a sense, would be lost as well. Therefore, onward ho. Onward ho, only now vertigo, yet another deleterious side effect of sleep deprivation, took hold, and as derailment was imminent, a tall, wrought iron fence along the edge of the Via Sacra was grasped. Then, as dimming vision indicated the onset of syncope, a deliberate descent, the leather backpack rasping down the iron bars, was made, in order to place the head be-tween the knees and restore blood flow to the brain.

Within moments, equilibrium returned, but then, rais-ing the head, a new challenge was faced: a phalanx of Asian, probably Japanese sightseers (as inferred from their high, broad cheekbones as well as worldwide tourism trends and distri-butions), cameras aimed as if at some natural, or unnatural, wonder. And while an obscene gesture easily discouraged the photo opportunists, dignity required further delay. Only when they were out of sight was an attempt made to stand. In ris-ing, the gaze fell on the other side of the fence: there a dozen or more feral cats of various sizes, exhibiting various patterns and hues, sunned themselves, nesting in the clumps of vegeta-tion that tufted the stony ground, or sprawling across the tops of broken marble pedestals and columns, including a few ap-pended with squirming kittens. One of these appended cats, a calico, lay just beyond the iron bars in a patch of red poppy spattered grass, spine bolstered by a pillow sized half moon of marble as it nursed. Raising its head, the animal blinked in the sun, and suddenly Aslan's words back in Eging am See came to mind: "Boo hoo…it's all about you." Because obviously it was not. Obviously the Japanese amateur photographers had had no interest re: RR—it was the picturesque pride of felines beyond they'd hoped to capture, in particular the nursing feral cat, which as it lay collapsed on the patch of poppy spattered grass, as if sucked nearly flat by its young, appeared the epitome of maternal self-sacrifice. The truth being that a single perimenopausal female is of little interest to anyone.

A single perimenopausal female is of little interest to anyone, unlike, for instance, a single middle-aged male. Which, as the feral cat dropped its head back to the ground, apparently depleted, could be seen as an advantage. For the single middle-aged male is invariably an object of matrimonial speculation (whether the risk is assumed or not), whereas the single middle-aged female, because she is not seen as in the market, can steal out of it, undetected. Indeed, without a husband, or children, or other significant others, a woman of a certain age is more or less invisible and thus free to freely indulge herself, within the market or without. Free to freely indulge herself, a single woman of a certain age could sit for as long as she liked, or even, if she wished, leave the Forum and return to her hotel for a late afternoon siesta behind drawn shutters, alone. Because even though the dizziness had passed, upon rising a sense of exhaustion remained. A sense of exhaustion remained that was both systemic, as the entire body dragged, and localized, as the legs, afflicted by a distinct dull ache, felt as if congested with lead. How pleasant it would be to extend those dully aching legs out flat, over cool bleached sheets on a mattress of unlooked for firmness (at least in a three-star hotel). Yes, and let the brat make his way back alone.

When suddenly the feral calico cat, which had appeared bolstered by the marble chunk, as fixed in position as a statue in a niche, rose, the nursing kittens falling away. Its offspring milling and mewling beneath it, the cat stood for a moment, tail twitching as it stared back in the direction of the Colosseum, then dashed off. For the maternal instinct is strong, but not absolute. Occasionally other instincts prevail—such as the hunting instinct, which in this case led to the capture of a lizard, at least ten centimeters long, colored the same dun as the stony soil. The feral calico leapt with its prey upon a broken pedestal, and as indicated by the convulsive motions of its turned back, proceeded to consume it. Abandoned, the kittens cried.

Yes, the feral cat, which just moments before had seemed the epitome of maternal sacrifice, now sated itself on saurian flesh, oblivious to its puling offspring feebly crawling and falling one over the other, like a rippling patchwork of ill-matched furs, breaking apart at the seams. Unbidden, a vision came of Aslan stumbling about the Forum or up Palantine Hill, lost, for he had no map, no guide. Without guidance, the boy was likely to land on the wrong, or even worse, the right side of the law, having nothing to rely on but whatever scraps of counsel he'd accumulated in the course of his spotty education—e.g., "don't accept rides from strangers," "avoid deserted places," "ask a policeman," etc. Then, all plans for the future (since after a restorative nap surely mutually fulfilling relations between non-relations could be resumed) would be in tatters. Because, for instance, if he were to "ask a policeman," questions would lead to more questions, and inevitably, a rending call to Cyprus from the central *Commissariato*. Clearly, to prevent Aslan from asking

for directions, constant direction was needed: that is, it was necessary always to be there for him. Which was, in the existential
sense outlined above, "all." Because it is a logical impossibility
to be in two places at once, to be both always there for the boy
and there for the self—therefore one existence would have to be
forfeited for the other (although maybe always being there for
him did not necessarily mean being "all there"?). At any rate,
the brat could not be allowed to find his way back to the hotel
alone.

With aching legs, the smoothly eroded but nevertheless un-
even cobblestones of the Via Sacra were once again traversed.
According to the map, the tall, freestanding stone gateway
straddling the path up ahead was the Arch of Titus. Beyond
this, a choice would have to be made, to hike up to Palantine or
to penetrate further into the Forum. While Aslan had, as stated
above, expressed an interest in the remains of the residences of
the aristocracy, he could not, mapless, be assumed to know that
these stood on the hillside off to the left (even though it is the
custom of the economically empowered everywhere to build
their houses on elevated ground). Beyond the Arch of Titus,
therefore, a survey would be made, concomitant with an effort
to stand in the boy's combat boots (which surely would abrade
heat-swollen ankles) and to see the ruined landscape through his
young green eyes.

Beneath the Arch of Titus, however, a delay occurred. A
delay that eventually became a setback. A setback that in no
way could have been anticipated as a cluster of children approached. A cluster of children approached who as they came
nearer could be differentiated by sex—at the fore, two soiled-
faced girls with long dark hair, between eight and ten years of

age and at the rear, three boys, somewhat younger and of the same unhygienic ilk. Differentiated by sex, the children were of little interest—the boys were not only rather young and dirty, but unattractive—and would have been passed by with no further regard. Only, as if out of nowhere, the girls then pulled two rolled newspapers and snapping open the pages, began waving them in the face. Dancing swiftly and silently around, they waved and swatted, filling the ears with rattling paper, the nose with the smells of wood pulp and ink, around and around so that it was impossible afterward to determine at exactly what moment the boys had darted in.

In fact, it was only after, standing beneath the dank stone curve of the arch, pages of newspaper strewn over the ground, that the dangling nylon flap of the backpack was discovered. The pack was unshouldered, an investigation made—confirming, as suspected, that the contents were gone. Fortunately, however, the wallet and passport had not been among these contents, which had included an old Kodak Instamatic camera (overdue to be supplanted, as the boy had expressed a strong desire for a more technologically advanced model with a video function), a cell phone,[30] a toiletry kit, sunscreen, two liter bottles of water (one almost fully consumed), three power bars (originally four, but Aslan had eaten one while waiting in line at the Colosseum) and two paperbacks (*The Idiot* and *Snow Crash*). Yes, fortunately the wallet and passport were zipped inside a money belt, worn strapped around the hips beneath the

---

[30] Which at the time would seem no great loss, the cell phone having proved more or less worthless as a means to communicate with the boy. Later, however, a large bill could be received, incurred by the pick-pocketing urchins or maybe a black market customer. And it would be painful to pay such a bill, months later, at home in some place like Colorado.

clothes, despite the disfiguring effect.[31] Therefore, initially the theft seemed merely a minor and irritating inconvenience—a delay, as the loss was inventoried, but not a setback since all the items were either unimportant or easily replaceable, including the series of snapshots taken earlier in the day of Aslan on the Spanish Steps, which simply could be taken again.

Indeed, at first it seemed there might even be profit in the loss—that a colorful cautionary tale of Roman chicanery had been netted for Aslan.[32] In the evening, after the restorative nap, followed by coitus and a shower, this cautionary tale could be related to the unrelated but nevertheless dear boy over a candlelit dinner in Trastevere. It was simply a matter of locating him. Only then, where the Via Sacra split, leading on the left side to the hill up to Palantine and on the right deeper into the Forum, the uterus contracted.

The uterus contracted and pain ensued, buckling the knees. Contraindicating a hike up the hill. Because while both the contraction and the accompanying pain then passed, another contraction was sure to come. Further, as the contraction signaled the onset of menstruation, blood would soon begin to flow. A premature event that a hike up the hill, by increasing blood

---

[31] A disfiguring effect alleviated somewhat by a long, loose cotton gauze dress printed with ripe peaches. This gauzy gown had been purchased the preceding afternoon on the Via del Corso, as the more fitted clothes normally worn had proved chafing in the heat. Accessorized with the cream straw topee, it surely evoked a garden party ease combined with a certain bushwacking adventurism (and did not seem just a pathetic attempt to disguise both the money belt and the flaws of a middle-aged physique).

[32] Because injudicious interactions had been witnessed. The day before, for instance, as seen through the window of the dress shop on the Via del Corso, he had been standing with a local juvenile, stroking the gas tank of the latter's bright red motorized scooter.

pressure, would only expedite. Yes, blood would soon begin to flow, a premature event that had not been anticipated, although, unlike the theft, it had not been unanticipated either: for the stolen toiletry kit had contained sanitary products, just in case. Because the body, although regulated by endogenous rhythms, circadian and so on, is not entirely predictable.[33] Just in case, because the body is not entirely predictable, sanitary products had been packed. Which in fact showed some foresight. But as the toiletry kit was now gone, foresight was useless. Or rather, of limited application—right now, it was impossible to think beyond the nearest public bathroom. Which unfortunately could not be located on the map. No bathrooms whatsoever could be located on the map that seemed to be of poor quality overall, the paper fibers already beginning to break down at the folds. A "WC" sign, however, had been seen back at the Colosseum. The only choice, it seemed, was to turn back.

Voices drew near. Quavering voices, which signaled not only the advance of others, but of advancing old age. Turning, two senescent women were seen. Two senescent women in identical dresses printed with animal figures resembling Cro-Magnon cave paintings, their poppy red painted mouths working beneath white tennis visors. Speaking an incomprehensible language, possibly Hungarian, they passed with surprising briskness. As they swiveled in the direction of the Forum, a gynecological fact

---

[33] Thus, for instance, a woman whose menstrual cycles ran, from age 13 on, like clockwork, suddenly finds that her periods come a few days to a week early or late, and sometimes not at all, with no discernable pattern. In truth, sometimes the body is incomprehensible. Oh sure, fluctuations in the menstrual cycle after age 40 can be attributed to age related declines in estrogen and progesterone. But what about the sudden, deeply visceral desire for a child at age 45, a point when ovarian reserves have hit bottom? This is a wake-up call that biologically (given that it is impossibly overdue) makes no sense at all.

was recalled: following menopause, the lining of the urethra becomes thinner, the muscles controlling the outflow of urine weaker, leading to a more frequent urge to urinate and even incontinence.[34] Possibly, if not certainly, the two elderly women were speeding to a bathroom. A decision was made to follow.

Quavering in their incomprehensible language, leaning in one toward the other, their arms linked, the women nevertheless moved briskly, forcefully over the cobblestones as if they were following some definitive guideline, or series of arrows stenciled down the center of the path. As the last contraction had been succeeded by another, and strength and resolve were at an ebb, this illusion of guided focus helped, just a little. Yes, it helped just a little to imagine that there was no other way. If only it were possible to grab the long gray braid that bisected the back of each woman, and so be pulled effortlessly, certainly along. If only a certain, kinky haired contingency had never been encountered, in Kiel.

At present, however, there was only the present. The present of the two senescent women with their long gray pigtails

---

[34] The need, or urge, to urinate frequently in an older woman can also result from a pelvic floor disorder. Essentially, the pelvic floor is a network of muscles, ligaments, and tissues that act like a hammock to support the organs of the pelvis, which include the rectum, uterus and bladder. Being pregnant and having a vaginal delivery may weaken or stretch some of the supporting structures of the pelvis, so that, for instance, the bladder drops down and protrudes into the front wall of the vagina. Because prolapse of the bladder can lead to nerve damage in both the bladder and urethra, some women may develop urge incontinence (an intense, irrepressible urge to urinate, resulting in passage of urine). The wish to avoid pelvic floor disorder is one good reason not to give birth, particularly at an older age, when a decrease in collagen and elastin (fibrous proteins which serve to make tissues strong), are already weakening the "hammock," so to speak. Indeed, it is an especially bad idea to bear a child at an older age, as the relentless loss of mental and physical vigor makes even self-support increasingly untenable.

out of reach but nevertheless in sight as a steady, if painful, pace was maintained. A steady pace was maintained, despite the convulsive waves of uterine pain experienced in the wake of the senescent yet smooth sailing women who continued to chatter without stopping for rest beneath the shading trees to the right, without stopping to view the sulfate streaked and pocked church or basilica or bank or whatever up ahead, but turned sharply left on a straight course past piles of atmospherically decayed marble or travertine or who knows bone, strewn across the near sea level floor of the ancient city. Yes, a steady passage was maintained over the near sea level floor of the ancient city past the architectural wreckage of centuries past as the two smooth sailing senescent women swung left again past broken façades toppled columns and scattered plinth stones even as the waves of uterine pain crested with nausea and the chest and wrists began to tingle as if the blood were churning and frothing in the veins so that when the two women suddenly stopped before what appeared to be the remains of a small temple, a three-columned crowned ruin, RR sank, so to speak.

Yours truly sank, on a block of ottoman-sized marble beneath a densely foliose tree, unable, hopefully only temporarily, to advance another step. Hopefully only temporarily as the first bit of warm moisture, spotting the crotch fabric of the panties, could be felt, while in the meantime the two senescent woman moved on, their incomprehensible language dying in the distance. Because otherwise yours truly was now stranded, so to speak, in the dank, urine-scented shade of the densely foliose tree, staring at the stony ground littered with dirt powdered cuspidate leaves and cigarette butts, willing the impossible, since blood flow, like all autonomic processes, is not under conscious control.

"Too hot? Why don't we step over here for a minute under these nice shady laurel trees. Laurel trees had special significance in the ancient world. Do you know why?"

The eyes were raised. Two flush-faced, black banged, Japanese appearing schoolgirls, wearing matching black t-shirts embossed with pink cartoon kittens, and a pale-skinned woman whose features were obscured by dark "cat-eye" sunglasses and a huge straw sombrero, stood just a meter or two away. The girls mutely shook their heads as the woman adjusted a white gauze shawl around her bare shoulders—an accessory that together with the sombrero and the "cat-eye" sunglasses, a red wicker purse and a tight-bodiced, bouffant-skirted, white and red polka dot dress conveyed a camp, *Roman Holiday* effect, circa 1955.

"There. Have you ever been in a situation where somebody liked you more than you liked them? A situation where maybe they liked you a lot and maybe you didn't like them at all? No? Well imagine you had some pest after you who just wouldn't leave you alone. That's what happened to poor Daphne, a nymph who was being stalked by the sun god, Apollo. Poor Daphne, Apollo was always after her, and then one day chasing her through the woods Apollo got closer and closer his panting breath blowing upon her hair, his hands just about to grab her when with a little help from her father the river god, Peneus, she turned into a laurel. So what do you think Apollo did then? He decided that if he couldn't have Daphne as his girlfriend, he'd have her as his tree: 'I will wear you for my crown,' Apollo proclaimed. 'I will decorate with you my harp and my quiver. And when the great Roman conquerors lead up the triumphal pomp to the Capitol, you shall be woven into wreaths for their brows.

And, finally, as eternal youth is mine, you also shall always be green, and your leaf know no decay.' You look skeptical, Yoshiko. Why?"

It was the Lipilina. Although camouflaged in fifties camp apparel, which not only served to hide her identity, but also, with the aid of the bouffant skirt, her protruding abdomen, it was nevertheless the Lipilina, accompanied, for some reason, by two Japanese schoolgirls whose small dark eyes gleamed up at the Lipilina from beneath their shiny black bangs. Yes, it was the Lipilina, who thankfully had not yet spotted yours truly. The head was lowered, hope invested in the narrow but shadowing brim of the cream straw topee. For the Lipilina had not yet spotted RR—otherwise she would say something. She would say something and then something would have to be said back, while in the meantime remaining planted on the block of marble. Because if a stand were to be taken, blood would flow. Or rather, given that blood was already flowing, the hematological excess seeping through the thin fabric of the panties no doubt suffusing the even thinner fabric of the floral print dress, the flow of blood would be revealed.

"Could she walk?"

"What a silly question, Yoshiko, of course she could not walk. She was a tree."

"Is it a 'silly question,' Sadako? Or is Yoshiko maybe getting at something deeper? What if we think of walking as not just the ability to physically go from one place to another, as we just did from Palantine Hill to here, but as the ability to go somewhere in life? In Daphne's day, or more generally, classical times, both Greek and Roman, girls had very few opportunities. Very few opportunities and so they couldn't go to school like you two do and if they worked outside the home it was for their fathers, brothers or husbands—in the family butcher shop, the taverna, etcetera. If a girl wanted to get away from her family, her only choice was to become a prostitute, or if her family was rich, a vestal virgin. Would anyone like a snack? I've got some delicious and healthy Fruit Roll-Ups in my purse."

"Oh yes, please!"

"Thanks, these are my favorite!"

A beetle was scuttling over the ground, thorax gleaming bronze in the shadow of the laurel. Behind the insect a fine yet discernible track lengthened, a chronicle of minute locomotion through the powdery dirt. Chewing could be heard as they all gnawed on their strips of dried fruit, and the trickle of blood could be felt, dribbling down and around towards the back of the left upper thigh. At least the cramps had ceased.

"What was a vestal virgin?"

"A vestal virgin was a girl chosen between the ages of six to ten from a patrician, which means wealthy and upper class, family to tend the shrine that held the Palladium, which was a statue of Minerva, the goddess of wisdom. The shrine, which you can see the remains of over there—it's the roundish building with the three freestanding columns and two pilasters—also held the sacred fire of the city, which had to be kept burning, no matter what. In return for thirty years of service during which she had to remain a virgin, the vestal enjoyed special privileges, including a box seat at the Colosseum."

"Could Yoshiko and I have been vestal virgins?"

"Yes, if you came from a patrician family. You can just drop that fruit wrapper on the ground, Sadako. It's biodegradable. Do you remember what patrician means? Good. But would you want to be a vestal virgin? Sure there were perks but you had to live in the House of the Vestal Virgins and you couldn't go anywhere but to the shrine and once in a while to your box seat at the Colosseum. Have you girls ever heard the term 'bird in a gilded cage?' No? That's what a vestal virgin was—a special pet of the city of Rome."

"What did they eat?"

And then a male voice was heard: "We had *keine Idee, Jungen*, no idea at all."

"Not a dickeybird? What about the night of the knees-up and knickers-down at your flat?"

"Great God, Ludmilla, that hat could shade a village."

It couldn't be. But lifting the head, it was. That is, it was Nils Wenzel, Nils Wenzel with Aslan.

Nils Wenzel in white linen, dark green clip-ons and a khaki Legionnaires' cap, and at his side, Aslan, swinging his Strada shopping bag, eyes hidden by the twin mirrored discs of his sunglasses, smirking. As Wenzel in turn sighted yours truly, he lifted the Legionnaires' cap off his head and tipped it, flipping the neck-screening flap. "Greetings, Dr. Ramee."

Replacing the cap on his head, Wenzel returned to the Lipilina woman: "So, I see that you have found her."

"Not exactly. Hello Rosemarie—I never would've spotted you. Very tea on the verandah in the twilight of the Empire. Where on earth did you get that hat?"

The question was ignored although the same could have been posed in turn to the Lipilina, and also to Wenzel. Instead, the empty knapsack, which had been on the ground at the base of the block of marble, was pulled up onto the lap as queries were made re: the boy. Where had they found him and what had he told them, for as Wenzel at least knew, the Kleine-Levin patient's grasp of waking reality is sometimes less than firm.

"Maybe on occasion I kip down longer than most but that don't mean I'm a dimmo!" Aslan glared at the two girls, who behind small hands were tittering.

"No one thinks you're a dimmo, Ozzie. No one thinks you're a dimmo at all. It's hard though, isn't it, being all on your own in a world of adults who do things for reasons that aren't always clear. Who knows why Rosemarie abandoned you, leaving you to wander around, completely alone surrounded by strangers. If I hadn't spotted you up on Palantine Hill..." The Lipilina slowly swiveled her sombrero-topped head from the boy to Wenzel to yours truly. An image once seen in a film of an alien spaceship performing reconnaissance came to mind.

"*Ja ja,*" said Wenzel. "But we do all have our reasons, each and every one of us. We all do have our reasons, even though they are not always clear to us, let alone to others. For example, I look at one woman and she is not sexually attractive to me and then I look at another and she is and I do not know why. I am a neuroscientist and yet I do not know why, for instance, I am instantly attracted to you, Ludmilla, when the first time I look in your eyes, all I see is a half-bored interest in food. All I know is this: that my sexual attraction to you is as much a natural law as the downward growth of a rootlet toward the earth, or the migration of bacteria to the oxygen at the edge of a microscopic cover glass."

Blood could be smelt. Wet, meaty, acrid, the odor of blood ascended into the nostrils of RR and possibly, as a breeze had started up, into the nostrils of others as well. Did they know? It seemed likely they did, the still tittering girls included. It seemed likely they did; however, it also seemed likely they were not going to say. They were not going to say and no stand could be taken, literally, because then the blood truly would begin to flow.

"Enough, therefore, of reasons," Wenzel concluded, clapping his hands. "As Niels Bohr has put it, 'You are not thinking, you are just being logical.'" Taking hold of the hands of the two black-banged girls, he moved on: "Girls, please allow me to introduce you to my elusive colleague Dr. Rosemarie Ramee—her research in sleep disorders has taken her far and wide. And Dr. Ramee, please meet Sadako and Yoshiko, daughters of Dr. Ken Fujiwara, whose name I am sure you recognize for his highly regarded work on narcolepsy in Japan."

The smaller of the two girls took a step forward, holding her free hand out, palm skyward, as she peered up through the canopy of the tree: "I think it is going to rain," she said.

"Yes I think for once you are right, Yoshiko," said the larger, breaking away from Wenzel. She pointed south, in the direction of Palantine Hill, over which slate blue cumulonimbus formations hung: "Look, it is very dark. Let's go, before we get wet."

"Good idea. Besides I'd like something in my belly before tonight—otherwise the alcohol will go straight to my head," the Lipilina said as she removed the cellophane wrapper from another strip of dried processed fruit.

"Will they have a bowl full of jelly at this knees-up? I need to find out how me man Becks played today."

Was Aslan planning to attend a party? To attend a party with the Lipilina? A breeze kicked up, stirring and thickening the odor of urine that emanated from the trunk of the laurel tree. The padded straps of the lap concealing pack were clutched, as the Lipilina turned to Wenzel, and Wenzel turned to the Lipilina.

The Lipilina looked away, gnawing on her fruit strip. And then the second, smaller of the two girls broke from Wenzel, freeing his hands. With the left, he reached in the pocket of his linen trousers, and having withdrawn something, cupped it inside his palms and shook. A rattling sound emerged, reminiscent of Samert's beads. Finally Wenzel spoke:

"We are all attending, and you must attend as well, Dr. Ramee. Indeed, you surely have an invitation, resting on your desk back at the *Schlafzentrum* in Kiel. You will not regret it— the Annual Sleeping Syndromes and Disorders All-Night Gala is hosted by a very wealthy and so far very lucky member of a family afflicted for generations by FFI.[35] Each year this man opens up his seventeenth-century Appian Way villa to neurologists and geneticists from all over the world. So far he has never managed to stay awake the entire night, a failure that always calls for extravagant celebration and culminates in a dawn toast on the man's manicured lawn, with flutes of the finest champagne provided by his large and attentive staff. I tell you the ASSDANG is an event not to be missed—one of the few opportunities for sober, world class men and women of science to,

---

[35] Fatal Familial Insomnia. Attributable to a heritable autosomal mutation that causes a normal brain protein to fold into a shape like deformed origami, called a prion, FFI generally strikes between ages 40 and 60. The patient's fatal decline occurs over a period of twelve to eighteen months, in four stages. The disease begins, like so many, with a feeling of unease—progressively worsening insomnia coincides with a sense of panic. This first stage lasts about four months, before giving way to stage two, during which the patient experiences hallucinations, panic attacks, excessive sweating and tearing, as well as insomnia over a period of about five months. Stage three, in which insomnia becomes total and is accompanied by weight loss and a drastically aged appearance, lasts two to three months. Finally, in stage four, after a six month period of continued total insomnia, dementia, and in the last days, muteness, sudden death occurs.

in the American idiom, 'go wild.'"

"Nils, I'm going to go wild if I don't have something to eat. Soon." The Lipilina let her empty wrapper fall.

A decision had to be made. A decision had to be made as the sky over Palantine threatened rain, as the uterus, suddenly seizing, threatened to disgorge another several grams of blood, as Aslan, crouching over the laurel littered ground, poked at something with the tip of the Swiss Army knife purchased for him the previous day from a vendor on the Via Del Corso.[36]

"A nice big plate of paper thin, ruby red carpaccio, drizzled with olive oil and garnished with arugula and thick shavings of parmesan, maybe. Oh I can't wait a minute longer."

"Yoshiko and I are hungry, too! We would like some gelato."

"Et tu, Tutti Frutti!" Aslan held up his jackknife: a beetle wriggled at its tip, all six legs extending, then contracting, as its neurons fired a final salute.

A decision had to be made, to stay or to accompany Wenzel, the Lipilina, et al. Because it was evident that Aslan would go

---

Phenotypically identical to FFI is Sporadic Fatal Insomnia. In the case of SFI, no genetic cause has been determined. For instance, a previously healthy 44-year-old California man with no family background of insomnia, fatal or otherwise, suddenly developed increasing trouble falling asleep. His doctor initially dismissed his trouble, stating that it "was all in his head." Eighteen months later, severely delusional, weeping and finally mute, the man died.

Much less dramatic (being non-fatal) while at the same time much more common is Mid-Life Insomnia, which like FFI and SFI typically strikes between ages 40 and 60. In women, the onset of MLI has been linked to the fluctuating hormonal levels accompanying perimenopause, although no doubt other, less concrete and physiological factors come into play such as existential angst, bad faith and bad conscience. Or as Macbeth believes, in murdering Duncan he has "murder'd sleep." Which is not to suggest that any murder has occurred, or will occur.

[36] See notes 31 and 32, above. Chronologically, the purchase of the Swiss Army knife came after.

with them. Yes, it was evident that Aslan would go, and in addition, that there was no means to retain him. For although "all"
been given—there was always more. Which he surely knew, and
so calculated that he could come back whenever he wanted. To
open arms. Yes, the brat would go, and if RR went as well, the
bloodied peach print dress would be revealed.

Therefore, an excuse was offered: the Forum had not been
fully explored. The Forum had not been fully explored, and further there was also Palantine, renowned not only for its palatial
ruins, but also for its cypress flanked flower gardens. Even as
an excuse was offered, however, an address was requested: for
there was no reason why the party could not be reached by taxi,
later on.

"*Ja ja*, why not? Do you have a pen and paper?" Again,
Wenzel shook his hands, rattling whatever was cupped inside.

No, a pen and paper were not on hand. Perhaps Ludmilla
had one in her purse? The Lipilina shook her head, tucking
the red wicker purse beneath her arm. A miniature beaded
moccasin was clipped to the strap, which at the time did not
signify.

"A pity. You will just have to remember." Returning the
rattling object or objects to his pants pocket, Wenzel pulled a
billfold out of the lining of his linen jacket, from which he withdrew a card. He read: "Number 199, on the Appia Antica,"
then replaced the card in the billfold, and the billfold inside the
jacket. "I would give you the card but I am afraid that my own
memory is not what it once was."

And then they left. They left, all five together like a family or
the five fingers of one thieving hand, Aslan alongside Wenzel,
whose arm was draped over his shoulder. He did not look back.

He did not look back, even when the Lipilina turned and called, brandishing her red wicker purse, "Don't get soaked!"

Long ago, the advice column of the agony aunt Ann Landers, which appeared in the *Albany Times Union*, was read regularly. Now, as large drops of water splattered the ground just beyond the perimeter of the laurel tree, a decades old reader's query came to mind: does a person actually become just as wet running through a rainstorm as he or she does walking, even though less exposure occurs? Ann's answer could not be recalled, but surely in both cases there is a point of saturation, where it does not matter, either way. Let the little prick go. When, once again, the two senescent women came into view, returning from wherever they had gone, sailing smoothly past in the ever harder rain. They turned left at the Via Sacra, presumably heading for the exit at the western end. Aslan and his new companions, however, had turned the opposite way, back toward the Colosseum. Still, it would have been so easy just to follow the two smooth sailing women, to simply go forth in the downpour, which would have rapidly drenched the peach print dress, leaving nothing but a faint pink stain.

Instead, the rain was waited out, and then, holding the leather back pack like an apron over the groin, as blood congealed between the thighs, yours truly hobbled off in the direction of the Colosseum, back though the entrance to the Forum, and finally, to the hotel.

2.a. Only Words

Health is freedom from pain, weakness and disability and possession of vim, vigor and vitality. Free of pain, weakness and disability and in possession of vim, vigor and vitality, a person may feel capable of almost anything, whether it is climbing a mountain or writing a book. When a person is unwell, however, bodily functions that under normal circumstances are performed unthinkingly now occupy the mind, while small tasks, such as writing to the end of the page, loom large. Thus the inflation and deflation of the lungs with damp sea air or the swallowing of a bit of dry pide bread, not to mention the completion of a sentence, can become a struggle, and even hardly worth the trouble. Nevertheless, a commitment has been made: to complete this report. Therefore, the body must be disregarded.[37] The body must be disregarded, as if there are only words.

As if there are only words, then, this report shall proceed. Upon returning to the hotel, 600 milligrams of ibuprofen and a cleansing shower were taken, and two PowerBars eaten. Then,

---

[37] The body must be disregarded, even as the state of the body affects the mind. A woman recovering from a surgical procedure, for instance, may experience not only pain and weakness, but also a sense of paralyzing isolation (even in the presence of visitors). For any breach of the body serves to delimit the boundaries of the body, from which there is no escape. Further, even after the stitches have dissolved, leaving the nearly invisible seam of the "bikini" incision (which anyway becomes overgrown with pubic hair), a feeling of futility may linger. If the body has healed, become "whole" again, more or less, the fact is that any tissue repair is only temporary—all cells cease to divide, eventually, their telomeres spent. And while some may assert that eternal life can be achieved through the replication of DNA or of words (such as the novelist James Joyce, who claimed that by writing books that would keep scholars puzzling for centuries, he had assured his "immortality"), the question is what lives on—other than DNA, other than words? James Joyce is dead.

to prepare for the evening ahead, an "ultra" tampon was inserted and snug spandex-reinforced panties fitted with a "heavy days" sanitary pad pulled on, over which a silver silk knit Diane von Furstenberg, a dress suitable for a range of occasions from a pajama party to a black-tie gala, was wrapped. Also, in anticipation of the need for rapid motion, fashionable but flexible silver "mica" finished leather pumps with aerosoles were placed on the feet. Finally, a Swatch "fun watch," purchased recently at Aslan's insistence (because Timexes were for "crowies"), which utilized three silver droplet shapes to mark the hour, half hour and the first of the two quarter hours, instead of numbers (presumably to express the fluidity of what the boy called "party time"), was strapped on the wrist. Thus ready, surely, for any contingency (additional sanitary supplies, as well as ibuprofen, had been stashed in a silver mesh evening bag with a chain link strap), RR stepped, shortly after 7:30 p.m. (or was it 8:30?), from the curb in front of the hotel into a taxicab. While unessential as background, one additional detail will be permitted here: as the taxi was entered and the address of the party provided, the driver, a thick-lashed, cologne-splashed twenty-something male, turned in his seat and wolf whistled. And an admission will be made: in the aftermath of Aslan's rejection, gratification was felt.

When the taxi reached the Appian Way, on the outskirts of the city, the sun was sinking fast. The sun was sinking fast, so that as the road grew rougher, pavement turning to cobbles, it also seemed to grow darker, grassy banks converging into night. Dim visions of vegetal life registered—dusk leeched patches of poppies, black stands of cypress—and also animal, as, for instance, on the other side of a length of stone wall two white horses stirred the gloom. Here and there tall iron gates rose up, past which long tree-lined driveways could be seen, presumably stretching to distant villas. But what if the gate was locked? The driver rolled down his window and scents of grass and pine resin penetrated the car, interlacing with the musk of his cologne into one big stink. Or if there was a gatekeeper who wanted to see an invitation? Finally the tires rumbled to a stop—not, as anticipated, before one of the gated driveways, but instead in front of a modestly-sized stone house enclosed by ivy smothered stone walls, set close to the road.

"*Cento novanta nove*, Via Appia Antica. Hundreds ninety-nine," the driver announced.

And indeed, with squinting, "199 Appia Antica," along with the phrase "*Beata Solitudo*" inscribed in a plaque of marble set into the ivy smothered stonework, to the right of a tall, solid wood gate, could be seen. But no light, no sound, emerged from the modestly-sized house, which could even be termed a cottage, certainly not a villa, beyond. The driver was instructed to wait, and a small metal button, gleaming in the ivy just below the plaque, was pushed. All around cicadas hummed. But from within—*silenzio*.

As only the clay-tiled roof and dark upper story of the house could be seen over the gated ivy smothered stone wall, and it was possible that light emanated from a window in the lower level, the road was crossed and an elevated view gained from the bank on the opposite side. A courtyard garden was revealed—filled with masses of yellow roses somehow still vivid in the dimness, dwarf palm trees, interlinking graveled paths—but otherwise, empty. Further, the windows of the lower story, flanked by wooden shutters cut with Xs that clearly did not mark the spot, were, like those of the upper, unlit. The address had been recalled incorrectly—somehow mangled or transmogrified. If only a pen and paper had been available back at the Forum, to counter memory's tricks. When suddenly a small, black wrapped figure exited the house and began hobbling across the courtyard. RR scrambled down the bank, back over the cobbled street to the closed gate, where a pose of hopeful inquiry was struck.

The gate creaked and a black lace cowled head poked out, bright eyes pooled in shadow. Unexpectedly, a juvenile sounding voice emerged: *"Che?"* An Italian phrase recalled from the Cadogan Guide to Rome was employed—apparently immediately indicating nationality, as the small, cowled woman switched to English: "What you want?"

A party was sought. A party for scientists who studied sleep. The small woman shook her head. What was the Latin word for sleep, as that might provide the Italian? Then, serendipitously, a long forgotten phrase sparked into consciousness: *"Dormi ben,"* sleep well…[38] *Dormi*, it was something like *dormi*. The word was pronounced, along with the term "scientist," which given that it was Latin derived, could be assumed to be close to the Italian. Then, for additional clarification, a gesture was made by resting the head on the hands, palms pressed together, and momentarily closing the eyes.

"You want to go to a party, or to go to sleep?" the woman inquired in her stilted, strangely puerile voice.

---

[38] Utilized near the beginning of the report, this phrase is from a lullaby sung by "Mother Teresa." As any writer knows, it is a principle of good composition to refer back to and redeploy concepts and images from earlier on. Through such means, an illusion of cohesion can be maintained, even if, ultimately, the work does not hold water.

Both. The sleep gesture was made again, as well as a dancing motion with the feet, and a drinking one with the hand and mouth.

"You are crazy. You should go where all the crazy people are: one kilometer that way." Gathering her arm in the folds of her shawl, as if to disguise a skin condition, she pointed back in the direction just traveled. "It is on the left, and you will see two stone lions."

Back in the taxicab, a sense of optimism arose. From the simple, peasant perspective of the small woman, no doubt a housekeeper or domestic of some kind, the attendees of an event such as the one Nils Wenzel had described would indeed appear eccentric and possibly imbalanced. Yes, there was reason to think, even though now, at 8:30 (or was it 9:30?), when solar illumination was at an absolute minimum, the countryside barely intelligible, that the taxi was heading in the right direction. And in fact a floodlit stone gate, barred with wrought iron and attended on each side by two stone lions, couchant, materialized soon after.

The driver braked and turned his head toward the back seat, his white teeth floating in the darkness: "*Qui, Signora?*"

Yes, for although the entrance was barred by iron grillwork and barbed wire ran across the top of the stone wall that extended from each side of the gate, where else could the ASS-DANG be? Indeed, the two couchant lions seemed to confirm this new address, whatever it was (no number could be seen): the head of each rested on its paws, eyes closed as if in sleep. Besides, the meter was running. Therefore, the fare was paid, along with a ten percent gratuity, and the driver's card accepted, in case additional service was required later on. The taxicab pulled away, tailpipe scraping over a cobble.

A small metal panel, keyed with numbered buttons, was set into the wall alongside the gate. Apparently, a code was required. Cicadas hummed. On the other side of the grillwork, the floodlights displayed a stretch of gravel drive striated by tire marks, bordered on each side by the dark trunks of some species of deciduous tree. Overhead, foliage rustled. And then, coming out of the darkness beyond the floodlight's pool, a voice was heard, a young female voice laughing. A deep, much older sounding male voice joined in.

A request for assistance was made. And when no response came, or only disembodied, mixed-sex laughter, another request, employing greater volume, followed. More laughter. Maybe they couldn't understand. Therefore, the Cadogan Guide to Rome's term for help—*aiuto*—was used. Again, only laughter. Well, perhaps pronunciation was the problem. Vowel sounds were lengthened, abbreviated, added, deleted and even recombined—all to no advantage. To no advantage, and even disadvantage, as mockery ensued. Yes, mockery ensued as the laughter became howling—a long, loud animalistic ululation that clearly parodied the effort to pronounce the word *aiuto*. Or so it seemed. And this is why it is important to keep an open mind and to never interpret the data before it is complete. For then, out of the darkness and into the floodlight, three howling Irish wolfhounds trotted. As they halted at the gate, their vocalization ceased: they stood, rib cages heaving, eyes and teeth gleaming, saliva dripping, splattering on the gravel. Momentarily, gratitude was felt for the locked gate, for the barbed wire strung along the top of the stone wall.

Gratitude, however, again gave way to frustration, as after a few minutes of sharing the meaty stench of their breath, the dogs turned tail, leaving no sound but the rustle of leaves over-head, the hum of cicadas all around. A glance at the watch: 9:00, or maybe 10:00. At any rate, it was not yet very late and surely there were others who had yet to arrive at the ASSDANG. When they did, entrance could be gained. To the right of the gate, a careful seat was taken on the grassy bank: the silk knit of the Dianne von Furstenberg was delicate and easily snagged. And indeed, at last the twin white glow of headlights appeared, slowly and steadily brightening as a car drew nearer and nearer over the rock paved road. When, inexplicably, a third, flashing blue light joined the white.

As the car parked before the gate, the blue light atop its cab continued to pulse. Blue block letters along the side spelled "POLIZIA MUNICIPALE." The doors swung open and two persons in white caps with black visors and dark blue or black uniforms stepped out—the driver a middle-aged male with the typical android or "apple-shaped" fat distribution associ-ated with increased risk of cardiovascular disease, his partner a younger female with a healthier, if no more tempting gynecoid or "pear-shape." The apple spoke, beginning "*Signora*," but then following with a rapid, incomprehensible string of Italian.

A blank look was cast, while remaining seated on the bank.

The apple turned to the pear, his hands turned palms up, as if to indicate exasperation, although surely the failure was his (English being the modern day lingua franca).

With her right hand resting on her holstered truncheon, the pear approached. She spoke, and again the words were incom-prehensible with the exception of something that sounded like "prosciutto." Perhaps a sandwich would be offered (judging by her hips, it appeared she had more than she needed). Instead, she raised her hand from the truncheon, extending it. Given that the grass was coarse but comfortable, and further, the dress delicate (snagging a constant danger), the hand was refused.

If the hand had been taken, the dress could have been saved. The dress could have been saved, if not face (for there is no dignity in police custody). As for the boy, it seemed he was lost altogether. Yes, for following two hours at the Roman *Commissariato* (where, it was learned, an unidentified resident of the Via Appia Antica had called to complain about a soliciting prostitute), and a sleepless night at the hotel, an attempt was made the next morning to return by taxi to the gate with the slumbering stone lions—but it could not be found. It could not be found, although the cottage with the plaque inscribed *Beata Solitudo* still stood at 199 Via Appia Antica. Repeatedly, the bell of the cottage was rung, but no one came to the door. And yet, there it stood, surrounded by thick stone walls, as all around cicadas hummed. A solid foundation surely, a basis in fact, for the rest of the night. It was, however, as if the rest of the night had transpired in some other dimension, some alternate space and time. Or as if it were all an invention or fabrication. But whose? And what next?

After the second visit to the cottage on the Appian Way, the hotel room was searched. Searched for anything, for a ticket stub, a toenail clipping, any small clue or even a momento that would serve to make the boy real again. Because all that remained was the black nylon rolling suitcase, emptied and stripped even of the personalizing red sports pennant. A black nylon rolling suitcase of the kind that could be found in the luggage compartment of any train, or in the baggage claim area of any airport, anywhere. The kind of suitcase that could belong to anyone. And then, in a side pocket previously overlooked, a brochure was discovered: a brochure for the "Pyloros Hotel of Mytilene," a "small luxury hotel" located on the island of Lesvos. In Greece. It made no sense—no sense at all. For, as already indicated in previous installments of this report, Aslan despised Greeks. However, now there was no other choice—no other choice but to travel to Lesvos. Otherwise, the report would have to end here.

3. Mithymna

In the waning light of the early summer Mediterranean evening, the pale yellow stucco façade of the Pyloros Hotel of Mytilene, plastered ad nauseam with white garlands, braids, wreaths and bouquets, presented a romantic atmosphere that according to the brochure, took a person "back in time to the nostalgic nineteenth century." Presenting such an atmosphere, the turreted, "second empire style" mansion was an unlikely place to find Aslan. A Henry James character, perhaps, or even an early twenty-first century American woman of a certain age and literary type, but not the Game Boy playing boy. Inside the hotel, amidst additional elements of period opulence—striped silk upholstery, velvet drapes, gilded wood, parquet floors, Persian carpets and three tear-drop chandeliers, one suspended in the deserted lobby, one in the deserted parlor, and one in the deserted dining room—the chances of discovering Aslan seemed even less likely than outside the hotel. It would be akin to opening a satin-lined music box and being blasted with rap music. Indeed, an inquiry seemed almost unnecessary—a formality only, for the sake of harmony of action with motivation (because otherwise there was no real reason for yours truly to check in).

Therefore, when the mature man in a bellboy's jacket and height-enhancing black pompadour who'd finally come skipping down the staircase and slipped behind the reception desk replied, in a strong Australian accent, that yes, a limey lad fitting that description, along with a Yank sheila claiming to be his auntie, had stayed for two nights, and then bailed out, wonder was felt. Wonder was felt because truth be told, the flight from

Rome to Athens and then from Athens to Lesvos had seemed more one of fancy than anything, unlikely to touch down in fact. And now, amazingly, there was something to go on, an actual boy who fit the description of Aslan. Something to go on, and even more auspiciously, somewhere to go to: according to the receptionist, the Yank sheila (surely the Lipilina) had indicated that their next destination was Mithymna, a town on the other side of the island. Of course, when the receptionist pulled out his record book, the names, as anticipated, did not conform— the woman's American passport, according to the receptionist's record book, had yielded "Silvia Silverman," the boy's British passport, "Adam Silverman." These, however, were presumably aliases, fabricated, along with the phony passports, in the back of some backstreet cell phone shop in Athens, perhaps, or even before, in Rome.

So yes, there was someplace to go to, but not tonight. For, advised the receptionist, "you'll need a car luv—buses here are scarce as swim tops on titties." And the car rental agencies were, as to be expected given the hour (eight or nine?), closed until the next morning. However, as it was still too early to re-tire and further, a state of excitation ruled, milk was ordered for its soporific effect (RR's supply of RX having been depleted the last night in Rome). Then, following egress through the French doors of the deserted dining room out onto an equally deserted balcony, an alfresco seat affording a view of the dark, oleaginous sheen of Mytilene harbor was taken. A sheen rep-licated moments later by the play of the porch light over the receptionist's pompadoured hair as he set down the glass of milk·and with it, a large oozing piece of baklava, even though no request for pastry, or indeed for food of any kind, had been made. "No worries luv—it's on the house."

Sitting in a viscous amber pool of bee exudate, the stack of phyllo at first did not appeal. At first it did not appeal, but then at last, it did. At last it did, as the odor of the honey was absorbed and the digestive system was activated, triggering salivation. Consumption thus proceeded. Yes, even though sugary, rich foods, when ingested close to bedtime, provoke pancreatic activity nonconducive to restful sleep (not to mention their aging effect on skin tissue, as stated earlier), consumption proceeded. Because the flavor, intensely sweet and nutty, as if the taste buds themselves were molecularly blooming, multiplying, summoned forth a lost mellifluousity, a distant dulcet tune that surely became a little clearer with each bite. When exactly, where exactly had such sweetness sung before? And then it was gone. Then it was gone, and all that remained were a few cloying flakes on the lips, a sticky film on the teeth. So that what was recalled, in the end, was that there was nothing exactly to recall—the intensely sweet dessert had supplied nothing more than a sensory souvenir of the time when all desserts had tasted thus—that is, childhood, when there actually are more taste receptors on the tongue.

Which left RR with nothing but a racing heart. Nothing but a sucrose-revved heart, as a probably unnecessary wake-up call was requested, and the stairs to the second floor were climbed. Yes, a wake-up call was probably unnecessary as moments later RR lay in bed, in an air-conditioned turret room located on the street side of the hotel. For the hexagonal array of windows, though closed and draped with thick green velvet curtains, nevertheless provided ingress for the constant sound of mopeds rocketing up and down the road. Surely, between the racing heart and rocketing mopeds no sleep would be had. But then it was. As is sometimes the case, especially when a person is exhausted by travel.

Sleep was had and with it, a dream. A dream that something was imprisoned underneath the earth, something invisible rocking the tower with its exertions. As if on a monitor, this something appeared: horned, with black, bovine features and soft-looking, scampering human feet, it was breaking bars, smashing bolts and chains, caving walls. A minotaur. A minotaur, which could be seen as if on a monitor, literally destroying the foundation. So that there was no choice but to watch and to wait. No choice but to watch and to wait, for the imminent, inevitable collapse of the structure as a whole. When suddenly thunder split the ears and the image of the rampaging minotaur broke up and dispersed in the storm raging outside the turret bedroom. An external atmospheric disturbance that had no doubt contributed to the internal psychic disturbance of the dream.[39]

Yes, the high decibel, windowpane-vibrating storm outside had merged with the hallucinatory rampage of the minotaur within, amplifying the emotional affect of the latter. Hence the

---

[39] This, however, is not to suggest that the storm hatched the subterranean minotaur. Indeed, the theory that external stimuli infiltrate the sleeping brain and initiate dreams has been discredited by modern neuroscience. While certainly thunderstorms, train whistles and spouses coming home late can influence dream content, they also often don't. But then what is the source of the dream? And why does one person dream about a raging minotaur and another of a beautiful girl in a kingdom by the sea? According to Freud, the source of the dream is an unacceptable wish that lives, snug as an anaerobic bug in a buried rug, in the unconscious. Because the wish is unacceptable, it must remain hidden, permitted to broach consciousness only if secured within the obscurely inscribed capsule of the dream symbol. While Freud's dream

dread that was now felt, as deep breaths of the air-conditioned dank were gulped, the green velvet counterpane gripped. But it was, finally, only a dream. Only a dream, the dread simply an emotional emission of a limbic system in sleep-induced over-drive. Therefore there was no reason not to continue, no reason not to resume the search for the boy in the morning. No reason no reason as the sound of the rain drumming against the win-dowglass mingled with the thumping of the heart no reason no reason no reason.

Fortunately, sleep at last overcame dread (as it generally does, sooner or later, in healthy persons). In fact, the morning wake-up call proved necessary after all. However, although fi-nally rest had been achieved, it must be admitted that a feeling of unrest remained. The brochure in the suitcase, which could have been placed there by some previous owner (for who was to

---

theory still, believe it or not, has supporters within the scientific community (see, for instance, recent articles by I.C. Dicks and P. Nuss-Covitz in *Neurop-sychologia*), most researchers now believe that aspects of dreaming previously thought to be meaningful and psychologically significant are the simple reflec-tion of sleep-related changes in brain state. That is, there has been a shift from the study of dream content to the study of dream form and the physiological events underpinning dream form. Thus, as there is in dreams a loss of logic and of constancies of time, place and person, concomitant with a heightened capacity for vivid, autogenous imagery and an increased susceptibility to emo-tions such as fear and lust, so too there is deactivation of the prefrontal cortex (the "executive 'I'") and memory systems of the brain concomitant with acti-vation of visual and auditory centers, the amygdala and the white matter at the base of the forebrain. Which is not to say that dreams are without meaning—however, meaning is always discovered after the fact, by our cause-and-effect-seeking brains. As the eminent J. Allan Hobson, M.D. has put it, "we are all engaged in a kind of dream interpretation all the time. Why did so and so say such and such? Why do I feel anxious when I pick up the phone?" (*Dreaming: An Introduction to the Science of Sleep* [New York: Oxford University Press, 2003], 156). Or when I turn on my computer? Or why am I writing this story?

say the suitcase wasn't secondhand?), had been shaky ground, at best, for the journey to Lesvos. And while surely the limey lad and his Yank auntie were Aslan and the Lipilina, traveling under assumed identities, it was also possible that they were not. Sometimes a name is just a name. As a rose is a rose is a rose. Which in the meantime, as indicated by the sudatory stink rising up from the pits, "Rosemarie" was not. A shower was needed— to both wash away sebaceous secretions and to dispel the night's unease. And indeed, beneath the hot, restorative spray, a sense of equilibrium returned. Because if he was not here, he was nevertheless somewhere. Because Aslan wasn't just a name, an abstraction, but an actual concrete boy, who could be found. Who could be found. Hence there was a solid premise for the search. Then by mistake, while groping for the soap dispenser, the "Emergency Assistance" button set in the wall of the shower stall was pushed. Moments later came a loud knock, and then a bellowed query: "Fall on our bum, did we?"

As no assistance was needed, annoyance was felt. Annoyance was felt as water ran down the limbs, pooling on the bathroom tiles. An apology was projected through the door, however, along with an order for a continental breakfast.

Downstairs, a breeze blew through the again deserted rooms, vaguely stirring velvet curtains and dispensing the harbor scents of petroleum and fish. Evidently the other guests had either already departed for the day or had not yet risen. If there were any other guests—the fact that only one of the six tables on the balcony was set, with a single place setting of silverware, a white linen napkin, and a wire mesh basket of assorted seedy looking breads in the center, seemed to indicate that there were not. Not that it mattered: in a short time the Pyloros Hotel, born (so to speak) from a brochure, would disappear forever in a rental car's rearview mirror. A seat was taken, a sesame stick selected and clamped between the teeth as a map of Lesvos, procured earlier from the reception desk, was unfolded and spread out over the white tablecloth. While the road appeared to be exceptionally winding, circuitous and even, at points, digressive, the island was nevertheless small: surely it would be possible to reach Mithymna by noon, which would leave the rest of the day to search the hotels. When suddenly the pompadoured receptionist appeared, bearing a linen-draped tray on which rested various containers of beverages—a silver pot of coffee, a glass pitcher of orange juice, a carafe of water—and a bowl of honey laced yoghurt (which after the previous night's unsweet dreams elicited instant distaste).

"I see you're planning your route. Bet you expect to reach Mithymna by midday—ay?" He set the tray down on top of the map.

The sesame stick was removed from the mouth and twirled with the thumb, fore and index fingers, like a tiny baton or pencil. Yes, why not? The expectation seemed reasonable, despite the rather dauntingly indirect roads, which were presumably so due to the mountainous topography of the island, and not to whimsy or caprice.

"I wouldn't plan or expect or presume anything, luv. You can't. Not here. For instance, I came to this island for the first time in February eighteen years ago, expecting to attend university. I get a flat, get the electricity going, pay my fees. First day—no class. Second day—no class. Third day—no class. I say 'what the hell' and they tell me it's festival time and there won't be class for three more weeks. So I say 'what the hell' again. And that was it." He picked up the carafe: "Care for some ouzo?"

The sesame stick snapped. Ouzo? It was only seven thirty in the morning. Or maybe eight thirty.

"The best time to drink, luv. You might find it inspiring."

The offer of alcohol was of course declined. After all, the problem was not a lack of inspiration, but of information— information concerning the boy and his exact location. Further, alcohol, as it interferes with both motor and intellectual functions, would not serve the negotiation of winding, digressive mountain roads. No, yours truly would be sure to get lost, or worse.

Probably the decision not to drink was a good one. Because not only was the way winding and digressive, but unforeseen dangers were encountered. On a curve just beyond the village of Mantamados, for instance, a flock of gray sheep the same color as the pavement suddenly foamed up, appearing even to unimpaired vision as a kind of hallucinatory froth or fog that could be driven right through. Luckily, since the animals were real while the rental car, a very small, poorly constructed red Opel reminiscent of a matchbox toy, perhaps was not, the level of cognitive lucidity was sufficiently high to discount the optical illusion. And then on the short but precipitous stretch just before Mithymna, a pickup truck disgorged a mattress, which bounced once and then fortunately flew over the cliff to the rocks below, for if it had hit the windshield of the toylike rental car, most likely the latter would have gone over the edge as well. Yes, the decision not to drink was probably a good one, for even though in the second case, if the mattress had in fact hit the windshield it surely would have been impossible to maintain control of the car, whether driving under the influence or not, in the end a sober note is best, even in a farce.

Besides, as already stated above, the problem was not a lack of inspiration but of information. With so little information, it was impossible to know where in Mithymna to begin. Indeed, it was not even certain that the search for the boy should begin in the village of Mithymna, per se. Therefore, as the tiny, toy-like rental car rattled in neutral, windows open (for the a/c was kaput), at a conveniently empty junction on the outskirts of the village (reached more or less by midday, thus refuting the pompadoured receptionist's claim that a person could not "plan or expect or presume anything"), the terrain was surveyed. To be sure, in comparison to the view on the right of the small but populous-appearing hillside town with its crowning medieval castle and red clay roofed houses lavishly crusting the slope down to the topaz blue sea, the view on the left, which more or less collapsed in upon itself, the road disappearing around a bend as if sucked up by the dark groves of olive beyond, did not look promising. How could someone, i.e. Aslan, be found where there seemed to be no one—in that apparent vegetal void? And yet, according to a white wooden sign planted amongst the rustling purple-tipped shrubs across the road, "Premier Accommodations" were available, at the "Delphis Hotel & Bungalows," just one kilometer away, to the left, as indicated by the pointing snout of a delicately painted dolphin. The scent of some sun steeped herb filled the open car as the engine idled, a scent that was both cozy, recalling long ago linen closets and the orderly comfort of youth, and incommensurably austere, while from beyond the sign came a faint metallic tinkling. And then the faint metallic tinkling began to swell, the sharp, rather astringent herbal scent to thicken and deepen into something more substantial and even a bit rank... Suddenly out of the rustling purple-tipped shrubbery burst a small brown goat, stumbling on the roadside as if its momentum were not its own, but had been provided by some external propelling force (e.g., a shoving cane or big, heavy boot). Collar bell jangling, legs buckling, steps weaving, it staggered on the verge of collapse, but then somehow swiftly and simply pulled itself together, so that a moment later it was standing silent on the side of the road in front of the "Delphis" sign as if it had always stood there, steadfast as myth, regarding the toylike rental car with black-slotted yellow eyes. As a sign is surely a sign and further there hadn't been just one sign, but two, a left hand turn was made.

If it had been right to take that left hand turn, however, this was not immediately apparent. According to the receptionist at the Delphis, an unsmiling menopausal-appearing Greek woman who nevertheless spoke English like an American girl (a proficiency acquired, she claimed, long ago in Westport, Connecticut, in a Rotary exchange program), no one who'd like fit those descriptions had like registered, either under their actual names or under like an alias. Fortunately, such a response had been anticipated, as deep down there was a sense that from hereafter it was going to be a struggle every step of the way. Yes, deep down there was a sense, a sense that the previous night's dream had only served to quicken, that although the boy had not yet been lost entirely (for who else could the limey lad be?), it was going to be a real fight to find him, and further, that that fight might in the end be lost (for although the pompadoured receptionist's tip was something to go on, it was not much). In which case, why not start the fight to find the boy at the Delphis Hotel, which at least would provide a very pleasant base of operations? Yes, why not start at the premier resort hotel that in addition to its own private beach and a seaside saltwater swimming pool, offered a lavish Greek breakfast buffet, price included, to launch the day?

And since breakfast was over, why not launch this first day with lunch, which according to the unsmiling older Greek woman could be eaten, like, by the pool, as there was like a taverna right there? Yes, because the boy would not be found on an empty stomach, the morning's breadstick being long digested. Therefore, after depositing the luggage in a second floor room (after the spinster fuss of the Pyloros, a simple but sensual affair with light modern furniture, soft white cotton bedding redolent of cloves, and a balcony that looked out over the dark slope of olive trees to the brilliant sea beyond), and pulling on a rather flattering flesh-colored Wonderbra incorporating one-piece by the designer Stella McCartney that Aslan had nevertheless failed to appreciate, asserting that its wearer looked like a "boiled rag," the verdant, rhododendron-lined path down to the pool was taken. Yes, the verdant, rhododendron-lined path down to the pool was taken as the sun sifted through the low canopy of olive trees softly flattering the crinkled pink flowers like rouged skin in candlelight. Because as the skin becomes less elastic softer lighting is best.

Which is not to say that when yours truly reached the pool and stood fully revealed in the brightness of midday, there was anything to hide. No. There was nothing to hide as the way was picked through a field of well-oiled, well-done middle-aged bodies sprawled out over the slats of white plastic chaise lounges like a vast, tasteless barbecue. For in contrast to that great display of both over- and undersupplied bodily tissue manifested as beer bellies, pork backs, love handles, turkey wattles and atrophied hamstrings, RR surely presented, Wonderbra notwithstanding, a model of mature fitness. And possibly even appeared to be a model, or a model turned actress as the following query was heard in passing: *"Ist das Nicole Kidman?"*

Yes, yours truly may have even appeared to be a model, or a model turned actress, sauntering into the wisteria-shrouded, cabana-like taverna that stood at the far end of the pool and then dropping, with leggy grace, into a white plastic deck chair. Indeed, when a not unattractive thirty-something waiter took an order moments later for unsweetened iced tea and *kalamaria*, the way his gaze lingered over the firm plump mounds cresting the top of the flesh-colored, Wonderbra-incorporating one-piece suggested as much. At which point ouzo was substituted for the unsweetened ice tea. Ouzo was substituted for the unsweetened iced tea because every model should indulge herself, now and then. Otherwise people will think she is not a real person. Otherwise she will think she is not a real person. Because too much denial of the self is detrimental to the self. Which in turn is detrimental to any project or pursuit: for can a boy be chased if there is no one there to chase him?

Therefore, while earlier the decision not to drink was a good one, this was no longer so. It was time to take a break, to loosen up, like all the overweight, overaged and underclad Germans and Brits at the surrounding tables with their scum-ringed glasses of beer and ash strewn plates of *patates*, who appeared to have been taking a break, loosening up for years. Indeed, amongst this crapulous crowd yours truly surely had an edge, in addition to visible ribs and a waistline. So that if the twenty-something young man sitting at the next table, who was not only younger than but even more attractive than the not unattractive waiter, was in need of a sexual partner, the choice was obvious. Because while there was no intention to drop the pursuit of Aslan, which of course would be seen through to the finish, successful or not, it would be nice to have something to fall back on. Yes, it would be nice to have something to fall back on and someone to fall back with, into the cool white clove scented bed up in the hotel. A bed that was not only richly scented but queen-sized, as opposed to the two single or at best two double beds that had been the only socially acceptable choice while traveling with the boy. Because the possibility of censure or worse is constant when traveling with a twelve-year-old male whereas a twenty-something (or on closer inspection, older adolescent) collects raised eyebrows at most, especially in Europe. Because in Europe the woman who is of a certain age and the man who is not are a cultural institution, and it is much easier to work within a cultural institution than without (as it is no doubt easier to rob a house when a copy of the key is possessed than when one is not). As the not unattractive but thirty-something waiter set down a basket of bread, a glass of ouzo and a glass of water with ice, the probable nineteen-year-old at the next table was studied.

With an aquiline nose, curving lips, olive toned skin and tightly curled hair the maybe closer to seventeen-year-old was a Mediterranean type. A Mediterranean type who truth be told resembled Aslan. Yes the seventeen-year-old (at least) resembled Aslan who in turn resembled not just a Mediterranean type, but a particular Mediterranean type—the type of classical statuary and of ancient coins, an image of Graeco-Roman symmetry buried deep but nevertheless genetically accessible in modern populations, now and then.[40] Resembling Aslan, the seventeen-year-old man (sixteen being the age of consent in most European countries) therefore resembled not just a Mediterranean type, but also a particular Mediterranean type: which meant, perhaps, that Aslan's rare appeal was his as well. So the relationship would not only be easier to sustain (much easier), but in addition could be (theoretically) as rewarding. Because maybe there was no real difference, finally, between the two, except for age, just as there is no real difference between the Turks' raki and the Greeks' ouzo, other than the somewhat higher alcohol content of the latter. For both are anise flavored drinks, variations of which can be found everywhere.[41] Variations of anise flavored drinks can be found everywhere, but in Greece the variation is ouzo, which even outside of Greece, in Europe and in North America, is, due to stronger cultural and commercial ties, easier to obtain than raki.

Of course, the fifty-something-year-old couple sitting with the young man could present an obstacle. For most would assume that the fifty-something-year-old woman (at least: it was obvious that her uniformly dark hair was dyed), as she licked

---

[40] Yes, it is a type that is genetically accessible, now and then. And not just amongst Mediterranean or Levantine populations, as evidenced by the adjacent childhood photograph of a man whose surname and known ancestry are entirely northern European. It is a source of disappointment to his daughter that she did not inherit his classical Graeco-Roman features, in addition to his swarthy complexion.

[41] The French, for instance, have their Pernod, the Germans their Jagermeister, the Hungarians their Unicum. And that is why finally everything tastes like licorice.

the corner of her white napkin and then reached over with it
and rubbed an invisible spot off the young man's cheek, was
the mother, and that the fifty-something-year-old man (in whom
the aquiline nose had become a beak), as he grimly chewed his
mezedes, eyes narrowed on some objective beyond the pool,
perhaps the medieval castle of Mithymna just down the coast,
was the father. As such, the fifty-something-year-old putative
parents could also be assumed to be overly protective, particularly the putative mother. They could be assumed to be overly
protective, although who better to introduce a young man to
coital pleasure than a mature woman, who could be counted on
to exchange thoughts and ideas and not just bodily fluids with
their son, as the true meaning of intercourse is not simply
sexual? Who better than yours truly, who although committed
to the search for Aslan (at least until the trail was as cold as a
plate of untouched food, for the arrival of the order of
kalamaria had gone unnoticed), also had a life to live. The plate
of small rubbery rings of mollusk torso and twisted clumps of
tiny mollusk legs was therefore pushed away and a swallow of
ouzo taken instead. A swallow which filled the mouth like an
anise flavored swell of possibility as the young man suddenly
looked over and lifting just the left hand corner of his mouth,
smiled.

And then, unfortunately, the surge subsided as it became
clear that the half smile was for another—another being an
adolescent female who had been down at the beach, as sub-
stantiated by her sand dusted orange board shorts and black
bikini top and a blue plastic bucket filled with some sort of dark
wet seaside debris. Solemnly she presented the bucket to the
fifty-something-year-old man, and as she did so it was evident

that her nasal profile, like the young man's, matched his. Which meant that the young man's half smile probably had been only filial—so there was hope still.[42] For the time being, however, the moment was past. Yes, the moment was past as a little family scene unfolded in which the girl followed her father with wide bright eyes, while the latter, having procured a sharp knife from the waiter, plucked a dark spiny ping-pong-sized ball from the blue plastic bucket and proceeded to bisect it. A family scene that became a family romance as the father, now holding one spiny hemisphere of sea urchin (for what else could it be?) in a napkin, spooned up a bit of the pudding like viscera therein, while the girl watched, intent as any rose supplying swain. He chewed, eyes distant, lips smacking slightly at the end of each bite until both spiny hemispheres of sea urchin were scooped clean, at which point he went on to bisect another as all the time the girl looked closely on, hands clasped together over the crotch of her orange board shorts. When the father had finished off the second sea urchin, however, he did not go on to bisect and eviscerate a third. Rather, without a smile, without a word, he returned to his *mezedes*, commencing work on an orange langoustine perhaps as bright as his daughter's board shorts, only

---

[42] For the statistical probability of a sexual relationship between siblings is extremely low. Indeed the Freudian viewpoint that sisters and brothers innately desire to commit incest has, despite its cultural and historical popularity, very little empirical support. Studies of nonsiblings raised as siblings (e.g. children raised on kibbutzim) in fact demonstrate the opposite, as they later on manifest an aversion toward each other as sexual partners. However, if sibling incest is rather uncommon, intense sibling bonds are not, and such bonds can even be compared to little marriages, as, for instance, sisters and brothers are often extremely possessive of one another. A similarity that was the basis for imagining the relationship with Tom Tom, because although there never was a brother, there is a husband. And sisters (three. In fact, the joke while growing up was "we had a brother, but we killed him").

the latter, as the girl had slumped into a seat and then more or less slid under the table, were no longer available for comparison. So much for the family romance.

So much for the family romance and so much for the young man, who really only slightly resembled Aslan as he worked away at his own langoustine, studying his father between maneuvers, as if for guidance. For studying his father as if for guidance, he was clearly in his father's thrall, they were all clearly in the father's thrall—the sea urchin-bearing daughter, the hair dyeing mother, and the langoustine-eating son a charmed circle in which there was no chink. But who would want a part in it anyway, a part in a round of parts that had been played again and again, a ring around the rosies a pocket full of posies we all fall down? Which yours truly would soon do if she drank any more ouzo on an empty stomach. And then it might not be all that easy to get back up again, to resume the hunt for Aslan. Because finally that, detours and distractions notwithstanding, was the priority, the only game worth pursuing, little brown goat or no. No more drinking, no more stalling. Therefore, yours truly settled her bill (while simultaneously masticating bites of rubbery but protein rich mollusk) and then, after a pit stop up at the room (where a sundress was slipped on over the Stella McCartney swimsuit and the straw topee donned), departed for town in the toy-like red Opel.

Medieval castle ruins dank with urine at its apex, beaches littered with the wreckage of the body's losing war against gravity at its base, shops full of pension-priced detritus (e.g. plastic beach thongs, poly blend t-shirts, crudely daubed pottery and dessicated leather goods) lining the narrow, cobblestone streets in between, Mithymna is less impressive experienced close up than when viewed from afar. Further, the frankly moldering, middle class and aged resort village seemed an even more unlikely place to find Aslan than the Pyloros back in Mytilene. To be sure, there were fleeting glimpses of youth—adolescent boys gunning mopeds along the main road that split the beach front and harbor from the winding streets of commerce above, small children darting in and out of darkened doorways, half-grown cats scooting down fishbone scattered alleys—but for the most part, the town seemed targeted toward tourists of advanced age and limited means. So that all in all, the situation appeared unpromising. Very. Nevertheless queries were systematically made on foot (for the labyrinthine streets were steep and the Opel's clutch was slippery), starting with the barracks-like but budget-priced, bare sandstone hotels and boarding houses flanking the beach, all the way up to the whitewashed, lace curtained cottages offering cheap single rooms and a modicum of charm (if not easy sea access) just below the ramparts of the castle.

By 5:30 in the afternoon (or was it 6:30?), the majority of the village hoteliers had been interrogated, as indicated by a crossed-off list of village accommodations (said list picked up early on in the afternoon at a tourist information kiosk down below). Of course, in the case of one or two with limited English, the question asked may not have been the question immediately understood. However, as reasonable likenesses of both Aslan and the Lipilina were reproduced (thanks to those long ago Russian art lessons) on the back of the accommodations list with a borrowed pen, it was certain that understanding was achieved in the end. Therefore at 6:30 (or was it only 5:30?) only a few establishments, on the fringes of the village, remained to be investigated. Just a few, but in the aftermath of an afternoon of disappointment (not to mention excessive perspiration and lactic acid accumulation, for again, the streets were steep), a few was too many. Rejuvenation was needed before investigating the fringes, which as the dusty twisted streets of Mithymna were descended, quadriceps screeching, seemed sure to be found in the sun gilded waters of the harbor below.

Suspended in the buoying salt solution of the Mediterranean, a person may feel as if all tangles have become unknotted, as if all troubles have floated off. This was the sensation experienced by yours truly, as she lay in the cool silk of the sea, a wisp of cirrus cloud wafting overhead like a feather of escaped eiderdown. In the cool silk of the sea it was again a childhood Saturday morning, when animated fantasies flitted endlessly across the television screen, and Monday seemed an unreachable horizon. Of course this sensation of carefree, limitless space was only temporary, as a person can lie in the sea for only so long, lacking the necessary adaptations (fins, scales, a water resistant hide, etc.) for aquatic life. Eventually the suspension ceases to seem effortless, the skin starts to shrivel, eventually solid ground must be regained. Solid ground must be regained, concrete pursuits resumed—because otherwise a person is at loose ends, drifting through life. Which would be the condition of yours truly if the fringe establishments of Mithymna yielded no definite information—she might as well chase after the wisp of cirrus cloud overhead. Or sink. Yes why not sink, as if into sleep? Why not sink now, as if into sleep, but actually into the silky translucent sea, a yielding that would be an ending, a laying to rest, at last. Yes at last, to rest. Yes. But then something flitted along the back of the leg. Something flitted, no slithered, along the back of the leg, which next begged the question, a laying to rest on what? Because as investigation revealed, the bottom could not be seen. Through the translucent water, the view below was both as glossy as a photograph and unintelligible, fractured patches of vivid green and black that were, it is admitted, frighteningly obscure. No, the bottom could not be seen, and therefore was not an option.

No choice then but to return to shore, where, dripping, blinking, stumbling the way was made back to a rented canvas chaise lounge and towel. Only the chaise was occupied. Recumbent, abdomen bulging over the upper border of her bright pink bikini bottom, face hidden beneath a straw topee, another woman had taken yours truly's place (as well as her hat). Another woman, who as the topee was retrieved was disclosed not just as another woman but *the* other woman. Slowly, stickily, her lashes pulled apart: utilizing her hand as a visor, the Lipilina sat up. "Oh, it's you."

Oh, it's you, she said, her voice bored, familiar, as if she were a napping housewife hearing her husband's key turn in the lock. Yes, her tone suggested long term cohabitation, a complacent intimacy that went back years, perhaps to the era of her bright pink bikini, which was cut in the high, pubic stubble revealing style of the nineteen eighties. Which was outrageous. The tone, that is (the bikini was simply hideous). Outrageous because it suggested a decades-old domestic familiarity, even a partnership—as if there were no struggle, no drama between the Lipilina and yours truly, but rather only the dull drone of presumed alliance.

"But I think we are on the same side, Rosemarie," the Lipilina asserted, adjusting the two pink triangles of her top over her breasts. "Oh I'm not saying we're not also very different—

for example, I love being a woman, an adult woman. I love not just my breasts but my hips, my belly, my ovaries, my menses, my moods, my yeasty beasty fecundity. Still I believe in the end we share certain common values and beliefs and in the end want similar things." She groped in the sand beside the chaise, located a cloth sack from which she pulled out a pair of sunglasses. The lenses were perfectly round, and darkened on her face: photograys. "Don't you agree?"

Yes, it seemed that similar things were wanted, particularly one thing, which she now had. Where was Aslan?

The Lipilina's lenses were now two black portholes: "Ozzie? He's not with you?"

Mixed in with the stones strewn over the sand were bits of bright green and white kelp that looked exactly like plastic. Maybe they were plastic. Indeed maybe suddenly nothing was real, maybe the whole situation was completely fictitious. Yes, it had to be. For surely the Lipilina's response did not fit with the previously established facts: the last time Aslan had been seen, after all, he had been seen in her company.

"Actually, that's not true—he went off with the Fujiwaras. Ken said they'd drop him off back at your hotel when they were done with him."

When who was what with him?

The Lipilina picked up a tube of sunscreen, squirted a dollop on her abdomen, and proceeded, with slow, circular motions, to rub the lotion into her skin. "The girls. Playing with him. Peer companionship is extremely important for older children and adolescents. With their peers, both same and opposite sex, they can be both connected and independent, as they break away from their parents' images of them and develop identities of their own. Of course Sadako and Yoshiko, who are home schooled by Carol Fujiwara, wanted to spend time with Ozzie, and vice versa—it was only natural."

The boy was being played with by the two Japanese schoolgirls?

"All I'm saying is that he was at their place the last time I saw him, at their vacation cottage on the Appian Way, just down the road from the ASSDANG. But the Fujiwaras were about to head back to Japan. That's it—all I've got." The Lipilina smirked.

Because she surely had more. Yes, she surely had more, as she lay back in the chaise that was not hers to lie in, smirking and slowly rubbing her bulging abdomen like an expectant mother or a cat cleaning its fur of feathers and blood. She had more.

"You think I'm against you, Rosemarie, don't you? I wonder why? Maybe someone is projecting? Because when we lose a child, deep down we blame ourselves: if only I'd been more attentive, if only I'd been more present. Deep down, we blame ourselves, but we don't want to admit we blame ourselves, so we blame others. I'm not against you, Rosie, I'm really not. I could help you. But you don't want my help—you just want to fight. You want me to be against you. So I'll be against you. Do you know how to play backgammon?"

Backgammon?

"Yes, backgammon, a family favorite whose roots can be traced back to the ancient Mesopotamian game 'tabula.' A simple game, with deep strategic elements. I think we both know what I'm talking about." She reached again into her beach bag, pulled out a yard or three of pink Shantung silk the same shade as her bikini, and standing up, wrapped it around her breasts and hips.

A simple game with deep strategic elements, she'd said. Obviously the Lipilina, as she secured her Shantung silk sarong, had more in mind than a board game. The question then was whether to play along. To be sure she knew where the boy was, as indicated by her smirk and also her insinuating self-massage. However, given the "closed-off" nature of consciousness, there was no way to access what she knew without her consent, except through force, which was not an option. Because beating it out of her would require more strength and mass than yours truly possessed. So the answer was yes, to play along—a simple game with deep strategic elements. For finally, it was obvious what the Lipilina was talking about—there was no other way to win back the boy.

Consequently, one hour (or maybe two) later yours truly could be found sitting over an open backgammon box at a café on the main road, downing yet another *café freddo* (two had been consumed already). At present, red plastic checkers lay strewn over three quadrants, in contrast to the pineapple yellow checkers, which had already assembled in their home square and now were swiftly exiting the board. Indeed, as streamers of smoke from the surrounding tables swirled through the air, melding into billowing clouds that hovered before the deep barred windows and open door of the café as if to block egress while outside mopeds roared relentlessly over the cobblestones, the truth was inescapable: the Lipilina was ahead, two games to zero, and would soon be three. The Lipilina was ahead and would probably stay ahead because backgammon is a game of skill as well as luck and the Lipilina seemed to possess excessive amounts of both. Not only did she roll doubles almost every other move, but she knew exactly how to deploy her doubles, doubling her luck, so to speak, so that her pineapple yellow checkers seemed almost to skip together around the board and into her well. The only way to win back the boy was to continue to play. Yet to continue to play was almost certainly to lose.

Yes, to continue to play was almost certainly to lose, for while yours truly rolled the right to start the next game, with a four to the Lipilina's cat's eye, a four-one is arguably the worst possible opening roll. To make the best of it, a strawberry red checker was removed from each of the heavy points—with luck each lone red blot would acquire reinforcement, to form a future blockade. Unfortunately all luck belonged to the Lipilina, who went on to roll a pair of fours with her next move, enabling her to take out the two blots. So that to continue the game, yours truly would first have to get back into it. Which she did, to be sure, on the next move, with a two and a three, but only to be knocked out once again as once again the Lipilina rolled doubles. Just cat's eyes this time, but two ones were just enough to take out the first red blot, and then the second. Cat's eyes. It was all beginning to seem preordained, like a rigged game in which to continue to play was almost certainly to lose. A plot.[43]

---

[43] Or is that just wishful thinking? What is plot but a retroactive attempt to impose a cause and effect order upon events? You take your story, or you take your life, and you play certain events up or down, look for patterns and even fabricate them in order to create an illusion of unity and coherence. Where there is none. For who, even, are "you"? As Slavoj Žižek remarks, "if we penetrate the surface of an organism, and look deeper and deeper into it, we never encounter some central controlling element that would be its Self, secretly pulling the strings of its organs"(*The Parallax View* [Cambridge, Mass: MIT Press, 2006], 204). Then again, I am sure I saw your eyes shining in the darkness of your shell.

"We really are on the same side, you know." The Lipilina marshalled the pink silk of her sarong to conceal her bikini bound breasts, which had lunged forth as she'd borne the last of her checkers off the board: "There." Then, rooting in her beach bag, she pulled out a Fruit Roll-Up: "Want one? No?" Peeling back the cellophane, she nibbled the loose end of the strip of dried fruit with her incisors.

A glance at the board, with its teams of pineapple yellow checkers already poised for victory, indicated otherwise. Indeed, just then the waiter walked by and set down the bill for the *café freddos*, pinning it with a painted stone weight, as if to confirm the game was over—yours truly had been slaughtered.

"That's just a game. I'm talking about life." She unrolled her Roll-Up, folded it in half vertically, then bit into it. Masticating, she continued: "You've been chasing after a dream, Rosemarie, when the possibility for the real thing was right here, all along." She dangled the strip of dried fruit over her abdomen.

The real thing?

"A genuine opportunity to escape the cell of solipsism, or as my nana used to say, 'get over yourself.' To get over yourself and find the other, to follow the spiral not inward but outward spinning the web of attachment the tapestry of connections with others that is the essence of living a vital life and remaining open to all layers of our own emerging experience. I'm not saying men don't have a chance, but I am saying that we women have unique access to dyadic states of resonance as we are literally, through the medium of the umbilical cord, attached to the other for thirty-eight weeks." The Lipilina tore off another bit of fruit strip with her teeth.

Hold on. Was the suggestion then to manufacture a boy from chromosomal scratch? To incubate fetal cytoplasm for the purpose of future affiliation?

"More or less. Of course there's a just under fifty percent chance you'd end up with a girl, and obviously, you like boys. But at this point it really doesn't look like it's going to work out with Ozzie. You just didn't get him. When's the last time you spoke to a boy? What do you really know about boys? Maybe if you had a boy of your own, a real boy to observe on a daily basis, you would know something."

The stone that secured the bill was painted with a nautilus design, a thin white whorl executed with great precision. Yes, with great precision someone had painted the gyrating line starting at the center of the stone around and around in ever expanding circles until at last they'd arrived at the edge. Or had it been the other way around? Had they started at the edge and then gyred inward? At any rate, either way, whether one started at the center or not, there was a periphery, an area beyond the strict limits of the precisely executed design, and now, in that periphery a small grubby finger appeared. The small finger of a child. A girl.

Yes, it was a girl, maybe five or six, who had materialized as if out of a cloud of cigarette smoke alongside the table, and who now began to trace the design on the stone with one tiny dirt-rimmed fingernail, starting from the edge, around and around until she reached the center and then around and around back out again. Through sun bleached brown tangles she peered, black eyes gleaming, as she coyly traced the stone with her tiny dirt-rimmed nail. Coyly tracing the stone with her tiny dirty nail, she was clearly asking for coin, clearly, yet not clearly as her request was indirect: she was not directly asking for money but rather relying on her audience to follow a train of association from finger to stone to check to currency. How rewarding. Yes, how rewarding as the girl's meaning could, with a little effort, be understood. Because the Lipilina was right: yours truly hadn't "got" the boy, and probably never would. No, yours truly would probably never get the boy, even as she had, in a sense, already got the girl. So if the statistical probability of having a girl was more than fifty percent, perhaps that wasn't such a bad thing. Maybe it was even possible to have this little girl, for, as a quick survey of the surrounding tables indicated, no parent was in sight. A 1000 drachma coin was therefore extracted from the wallet and tucked into her dirty, soft little hand. When the match was over, the little girl would be transported back to the Delphis, and from there, to a life of greater opportunity.

Because here, clearly, she had less, as evidenced not only by her mendicancy, but also by her clothing: a soiled yellow Ralph Lauren Polo shirt that looked as if it had once just covered the torso of a middle-aged golf enthusiast, and that now hung to the girl's scabrous knees. Indigent as well as female, she could be presumed to be at the rock bottom of society in a country where, according to a recent article on travel bargains in the *International Herald Tribune*, the annual household income still fell short of the European Union average. And without aid, she would remain there, as firmly fixed as the cobblestones over which the mostly male-driven mopeds raced through the seaside town. In a more prosperous and liberal society, however, with abundant, vitamin enriched food and a No Child Left Behind educational policy (a move could be made, if necessary, to a better school district), she would ascend, increasing not only her ultimate height and

IQ, but also her earning potential. Further, she would be better dressed, as one of the first tasks would be to take her to the Gap, where, it had been heard, high-quality, attractive children's wear could be found for a reasonable price. The girl would thrive, and so would yours truly. Yes, yours truly would thrive, with a girl to nurture and even empower. Because full potential as a woman is achieved through helping others to reach theirs (e.g. Take Your Daughter To Work Day would facilitate networking with child rearing colleagues with whom small talk, so important for career success, was nearly impossible).

"She's not a stray dog—you can't just take her," the Lipilina said as she let her cellophane fruit wrapper waft to the floor. "Or even buy her. International adoption is very complex, and not only legally or procedurally, but also ethically. Do we have the right to tear these children away from the only culture they have ever known? Oh without a doubt from our first world feminist standpoint this little girl's life as a second class citizen is not ideal. On the other hand, it is real. It is real, at least for her. Could you offer her that in America? Think about it. Does softer toilet paper make for a finer quality of life? Can a dishwasher set you free? Is the pursuit of happiness facilitated by an off-road vehicle? Besides, she's not alone. Watch."

Clutching the 1000 drachma coin, the girl had in fact slipped away and now was heading toward the door, to the right of which slouched an older boy, perhaps ten, with a grayish white canvas fisherman's hat shading his small grim face. As the girl came near he straightened, and grabbing her arm, pried the coin from her hand. Then he smacked her on the side of the head. He smacked her on the side of the head, and she did not smack him back, but rather laughed and tucking back her tangles, cupped her already purple ear with her hand, as if to display a prize. Yes, as if to display a prize, or maybe a plum, as the boy, his hand now flat between her shoulder blades, shoved her out the door.

And then the game was lost as the Lipilina rolled double sixes and bore her remaining four pineapple yellow checkers off the board. The game was lost and truthfully, the match too because the Lipilina had won four games out of five. Then again the match had been lost for some time, even before the appearance of the girl. The match had been lost the moment the Lipilina had triumphed in the third game, and yet yours truly had continued with the hope of winning the next two, as if it was possible to be less of a loser, as if there weren't always already only two possible outcomes: success or failure. For the Lipilina was right: even if the girl had stayed, finally she was no more attainable than Aslan. In her own way, she was equally elusive, the cryptic whorl of her attachment to the boy in the fisherman's hat impossible, in the end, to delineate. Thus as the plunk of plastic on wood was heard (the Lipilina had begun to set up the board for another game), the match was, at last, formally conceded.

"You know, Rosemarie, I think we're finally getting somewhere. But it's tough, isn't it, to face up to our fictions, these auto-stitched flimflams that we use to hide ourselves from our selves but that actually don't cover anything, least of all our asses." The Lipilina again adjusted the voluminous silk of her sarong, which seemed to have grown even more voluminous, so that the swathes of stiff, light fabric wrapped her torso in a kind shimmering pink cocoon, over which her talking head, piled high with her shiny black hair, seemed to float.

"Yes it's tough when we've worked so long and so hard, tough to give up, to throw in the towel, especially when the towel is all we have left, the terrycloth tatters, so to speak, of our illusions. I assure you, however, that you'll be happier with the real thing, if it works out, which it should—assuming you're still under forty. You'll be happier, much happier, with the real thing because there was never anything there with Ozzie, no substance, not even the faintest trace or powdery dusting of life. It was laughable, your idea of a boy, completely laughable. You know that, don't you?"

A stab in the gut was felt. Yet upon inspection, no evidence of a wound could be seen. No evidence of a wound could be seen, or felt, as the forearms were pressed against the abdominal wall in a futile attempt to forestall the next thrust. Which meant that the cause of the lancinating pain must be internal. Yes, the cause must be internal, a disease or growth of some kind, e.g. a malignant tumor. Which would be devastating, and yet in some sense a relief. For then there would be something to grapple with other than the Lipilina, a tangible if sometimes all too lethal foe, depending on the tumor's metastastic capacity. Cancer, even terminal, would in some sense be a relief, for then a genuine struggle, a fight for life (if only to the death) could unfold. Then again, in certain cases pain cannot be traced to any visceral abnormality.[44] In certain cases, pain arises spontaneously, for no apparent reason, which does not make it any less painful,

---

[44] According to the authors of *Principles of Neurology*, intractable pain of indeterminate cause is in fact a strong indicator of hysteria. "Every experienced physician is familiar with the 'battle-scarred abdomen' of the woman with hysteria (so-called Briquet disease) who has yielded to one surgical procedure after another, losing appendix, ovaries, fallopian tubes, uterus, gallbladder, etc., in the process ('diagnosis by evisceration')" (Raymond D. Adams, Maurice

and perhaps even more so. For there is comfort in knowing. Because knowing implies that there is something to be known. As opposed to nothing. Yes, pain with a determinate cause, no matter how painful, is perhaps less so than pain without one. So that the next thrust seemed even harder, doubling the torso over the table. The surface of which was wet. Because the last *freddo* had spilled a little as the waiter slammed it down. Eureka: the *freddos*. Because the corrosive effect of caffeine on an empty stomach is well known. Therefore the source of the lancinating abdominal pain was now well known as well: the three *café freddos*. Likewise, when the eyes began to sting, this too was completely understandable. Just as the gut writhed due to an internal irritant, the eyes stung due to an external one: i.e., the smoke filling the room, smoke that seemed to have suddenly grown thicker— as if the incineration of some meatier matter than shredded plant fiber in paper was occurring. Thicker, denser, even mordant, so that the eyes not only stung but watered, watered and overflowed as the gut writhed, writhed and then heaved.

Disgorging its contents. Which, disgorged, glistened in the right side of the backgammon box. Which, truth be told, were

---

Victor and Allan H. Ropper, [New York: McGraw Hill, 1997], 141). Did you notice, by the way, the flippant tone of the preceding sentence, a tone secured by the unnecessary but apparently irresistible inclusion of the medical bon mot "diagnosis by evisceration" (a tidbit of wit student readers of *Principles of Neurology* no doubt eagerly lap up, anticipating future banquets of collegial banter). And yet the hysteric (who is identified as almost always female in her own special section of the textbook later on; it is a "chronic illness…mainly in girls and women"[1517]) and the neurologist would seem to have much in common—both, ultimately, are reductionists, operating on the notion that there is finally something *there*, some root thing or cause to be located and excised. Because it all starts somewhere. Then again, maybe not. Maybe what drives the hysteric's diagnostic quest (i.e., what makes her hysterical) is her deepseated fear that somewhere might finally be nowhere.

meager: a thin viscous brown puddle in which sat a few slippery looking, amorphous nuggets. But the stomach had been empty but for the *café freddos*, which, it could be inferred, had been reduced to the thin viscous brown puddle. So then what were the slippery looking, amorphous nuggets? What were they as the sour odor of bile swelled the air and as the stomach, twice empty now, continued to wrack in peristalsis, as if to insist there was more to come. Continued to wrack in peristalsis, as if to insist that more could come, ex nihilo, for surely there was nothing there—not a bite had been eaten for hours. For hours, so that the contractions were probably pangs of hunger. Pangs of hunger, which could be assuaged back at the Delphis, perhaps through room service. Followed by a warm, restorative bath. Because a sense of depletion was felt. Because there was nothing there, nothing at all left to come out. And then it did, this time into the left side of the backgammon box. Another nugget, still trembling from its expulsion, centimeters away from the Lipilina's well of invincible yellow checkers. Slippery looking, but this time not amorphous, at least not completely, as tiny protrusions, like little legs, could be discerned. Little legs. Which twisted together in a rubbery clump that was also like a very small fist. Eureka: the calamari. Yes it was the calamari, which meant that there had been something there. Yes there had been something there. Not much, to be sure. A few rubbery scraps, shreds, remnants of once squirming flesh, but still. But still, that was something more than nothing. Something had been there, however limited the attention, however minimal the feeling. It hadn't all been the imagination, a doll blown firm with midlife fears and fantasies. Something had been there, taken in, felt and absorbed, however poorly. It had been there, inside, something real, and maybe was still. Yes, maybe.

"You can't be serious." Outside in the darkening street, a man shouted in Greek and someone else shouted back, a woman or maybe a boy. Turning, the eyes of the Lipilina, glittering in tangles of mascara, were met. Mares' nests. Whatever that meant. "You can't be serious," she repeated and then she said something else, something that could not be heard, as if she were receding, her mares' nests, her moving lips, her shimmering cloud of pink shantung all the floating bits of her withdrawing as if borne away by some waterless tide. Or soundless blast. And then she was gone. Along with yours truly, who, weak from caloric deprivation, sank, once again, into syncope.

Consciousness was regained to the sensation of wetness beneath the cheek. Wetness, and as the cheek was lifted from the tabletop, stickiness. Presumably the filmy residue of the freddos, and not the vomit, which hopefully had not splattered outside the perimeter of the backgammon box. Which was gone—cleared away by the Lipilina, or perhaps by the proprietor of the café. All that remained was the bill, pinned beneath the painted stone, the loose edge fluttering in the damp breeze blowing in from the darkness beyond. Yes, all that remained was the bill, the reckoning, which presumably would include a rental charge for the game and which the Lipilina nevertheless had left entirely to yours truly, for there was not a drachma to be seen. Only it wasn't a bill:

He'll be at Skala Eressos. The north end of the beach. June 16th. Because you are incorrigible.

4. It was Just Too Great a Leap from Here to There

Like other humans, yours truly has a penchant for changing appearance. Now an alteration in appearance can be celeritously effected through the application of cosmetics or hair dye, or by assuming uncustomary apparel. Such quick and easy methods have been used by humans to alter their appearances for millennia, going back to the first Cro-Magnon who plastered her face with alluvial mud and consequently went unrecognized by her own family. In more recent times, it has become possible to alter the appearance, often radically, through reconstructive surgeries and the like. Undoubtedly, surgeries and the like can provide a more complete, as well as more permanent change that is also more convincing to the viewer (for no sooner had the Cro-Magnon's muck facade dried than it began to crack). On the morning of June 16th, however, there was no time for them—an immediate makeover was needed.

Yes, given that the boy had escaped yours truly, and further, that this, possibly, was the last chance to recapture him, an immediate makeover was needed.[45] Therefore, millennia-old methods—the application of hair dye and cosmetics, the assumption of uncustomary apparel—were employed. To this

---

[45] Because as soon as the boy recognized yours truly, he was likely, having run away once, to run away again. Unless he suffered from *prosopagnosia* or, more informally, face blindness. If the boy suffered from *prosopagnosia* he would not attempt to escape yours truly because he would not recognize yours truly. But it is too late now—the fiction is too far gone. Furthermore, *prosopagnosia* is a condition a person would not wish on anyone. Life is hard enough as it is. Life is hard enough as it is because we can only know each other approximately, through external signs—a soft gaze, slightly parted lips, a catching of the breath. To be unable to attach those external signs to any particular face— mother, lover, a suddenly sympathetic acquaintance or even a reader—would be to exist in even greater isolation than ever.

end, as soon as the shops of Skala Eressos opened (which frustratingly, was not until nearly 10:00 a.m.), the following items were purchased: one box of Clairol Herbal Essences "Sapphire Black"; one tube of Coppertone self-tanning lotion; a pair of Ray-Ban "classics"; a leopard print baseball cap; an oversized purple nylon jumpsuit with the legend "Lesvos is for Livers" (presumably a production malapropism) embroidered over the right chest pocket; and finally, a pair of gold platform tennis shoes. With the appearance temporarily altered by the above products and items, yours truly would seem as if cast in someone else's psychodrama, in the role, perhaps, of an overweight middle-aged housewife from Athens, clomping her way toward a new, lavender identity, or maybe of a recently betrayed brodie, scouting in touristic incognito for a fresh prime set. And seemingly cast in someone else's psychodrama, a person might find another, more successful way to approach the boy. Because the story was getting old.

By 11:30 a.m. (the Timex had been restored to the wrist), the transformation, which took place in a hotel room procured upon arrival at Skala Eressos at 10:00 the previous evening, was complete and a post had been taken, at the north end of the beach, in the bright, hot sun. A post had been taken in the bright, hot sun, at the north end of the beach on an orange nylon webbed aluminum chaise lounge rented from a stand, an action consistent with someone else's psychodrama, but also conducive to descrying the boy. In the meantime, the transformation could be enjoyed. Yes, enjoyed. Because ironically, it is extremely tiresome to be confined to one body, and with it, one sequence of experiences, a whole life long. Ironically, given how loathe a person is to leave that body, to abandon that sequence of experiences, at the end of life (as well as before). For admittedly, yours truly has always evidenced a strong attachment to this specific existence, to this singular body, to this singular head. Which, also admittedly, may have been the problem with the boy—it was just too great a leap from here to there.

Just too great a leap from here to there, but not, perhaps from here to the corpus of a forty-seven-year-old Athenian housewife with mild insomnia and a weight problem. No, because such an existence could be inferred, an existence which, though very different from that of yours truly, would be marked by certain common conditions and limitations. To give an easy and obvious example, perception and consequently behavior in each case would be shaped by the physical fact that the muscle mass of the average human female is often significantly less than that of the average human male, and further, that the pelvic width is often significantly greater (which renders her less aerodynamic and therefore less capable of evading those possessing greater muscle mass): i.e. in each case a tendency to avoid the shortcut provided by a dark and/or deserted alley could be assumed. A tendency that on a daily basis would be manifested, say, in a perpetual furrowing of the brow or in an intoning of statements as questions? Yes, the existence of the forty-seven-year-old Athenian housewife could be extrapolated from a common, sex-based oppression, despite the greater freedoms life had granted to yours truly. But the boy, surely, with his cocky walk, his always already broad shoulders, was another case entirely.

Yes, surely the boy was another case entirely, despite the greater biological fragility of the male. Which must be acknowledged. For while at conception there are more male than female embryos (as the spermatozoa carrying the Y chromosome swim faster than those carrying the X, again due to aerodynamics), because the male embryo is more vulnerable to environmental insult than the female, an immediate reduction in the male to female sex ratio ensues. Indeed, from here it is, in the words of the British researcher and physician, Sebastian Kraemer, "downhill all the way."[46] But notice the phrasing, "downhill all the way," as if life were a luge. Or the Tour de France. A bungee plunge at breakneck speed, an acephalous pitch for the finish line, for accolades, free Gatorade and fresh cold beer.

Because for Sebastian et al being alive is, from conception on, fraught with peril, but also fun. Perched from the get-go in a more rickety, but also vaster framework, the human male in developed countries is sixty-one percent less likely to survive life's ride beyond age seventy than the female, but oh what a thrill, surely, to be a boy say age sixteen bounding from one car to the next or even flying off the tracks entirely.[47]

Yes what a thrill to be a boy age sixteen, or possibly younger, though no younger than eleven or twelve, to be the opposite,

---

[46] Kraemer S. "The Fragile Male." *Br Med J* 2000; 321:1609-12.

[47] Like Rory, Rory R—, or to protect privacy, RR, the first boyfriend, with whom yours truly was deeply intimate, emotionally and physically, between the ages of 16 and 18. RR, with his long-limbed, rangy frame (already 6'1" at 16-years-old), springing step, dirty blond center-parted mane and asymmetrical yet conventionally "cute" face, as if the profiles of two different *Tiger Beat* idols had been fused together into one slightly irregular but blandly pleasing and even erotic whole. A small defect that, combined with moderate to severe dyslexia, was probably indicative of genetic and/or gestational damage, the prenatal burden that so many males carry with them throughout life. Which was a drag for him but not for yours truly. If anything, his slightly irregular appearance and skewed understanding, combined with a greater than average adolescent male recklessness, served to make association with him all the more alluringly novel. Indeed, during those two years yours truly largely gave up the novel. Because for a while, RR was so much more engrossing than books.

So much more engrossing than books, at least for a while, because RR dared what yours truly had only approached in imagination (if even there)— from the perilous but still socially and/or legally permissible physical stunt, to actually flying in the face of the law. An example of the former being the time RR borrowed yours truly's bicycle, a gleaming black Raleigh five speed complete with a wicker basket which had been purchased partially with babysitting earnings and partially with paternal aid, and which RR called "the granny wheels." Having borrowed it, he proceeded to ride it off a triple-tiered embankment in Washington Park, like a plastic groom escaping from the top of a wedding cake. As the gleaming black Raleigh hit the top of the bottom tier, it bounced once, then sailed through the air, hitting the road below with a frame-torquing thud (afterward, the suspension was never the same), but never, de facto, crashing, as RR managed to wrench the cycle upright before it could topple to the ground, kickstanding it with his banana yellow Frye boots.

In addition to performing perilous but still socially and/or legally permissible physical stunts RR, as mentioned above, also at times flew in the face of the law, and persuaded yours truly to do so as well as, for instance, speed limits were exceeded, illegal substances bought and sold, and statutes regulating public sexual conduct broken (a more specific instance of the last being the time coitus was had on a municipal water tower in Altamont, New York, in full view of the two, maybe even three, airplanes that passed over head).

RR's most memorable legal infraction, however, may not, technically, have been a legal infraction. The question of legality hinges on whether or not there was a "No Trespassing" or "Do Not Enter" sign posted outside the double swinging wooden doors. Frankly, yours truly was too nervous at the time to notice. Yours truly was too nervous to notice even though she did not know, at the time, specifically where RR was leading her, only that they had entered, as they stepped off the elevator, a floor of the Albany Medical Center that seemed to be for medical staff and personnel only (judging by the absence of patient rooms, gurneys, etc), though fortunately no staff or personnel appeared. Here, presumably, RR would show yours truly what he had promised as they had first entered the teaching hospital below: "something really cool."

"Something really cool" was revealed to be a roomful of long narrow metal tables covered with stiff, tarp-like white sheets. Or more specifically, as RR lifted back the corner of a sheet to expose a waxy brown foot, calf, knee and portion of cellulite dimpled thigh (which resembled, with its hard, embalmed surface, tooled leather), a roomful of dead bodies. Yes, a roomful of dead bodies emanating a sweetish, smothering miasma that yours truly would later learn in pre-med courses (as at one time she planned to become a medical doctor, like William Carlos Williams) was formaldehyde. Dead bodies, not "cadavers," because at the time the appropriate term, contextually, was unknown. Or as RR described them, "stiffs." Though a "stiff" can also mean a person, a living person. Hence parents were described earlier on as "lucky stiffs"(see 131). "Stiffs" who are "lucky," or more precisely, fortunate, not just because as parents they enjoy unlimited access to juvenescence, but because they may feel that for the first time in life, they are not just advancing toward death. Because as a parent, breathing in the warm, light scent of newborn skin, a person may feel, for the first time, that the air has cleared, the miasma lifted, at least temporarily.

Or more precisely, a person may feel that for the first time since adolescence her constant awareness of her own mortality ceases, temporarily, to oppress. For the first time since adolescence, because during adolescence, death was given little credence. Death was given little credence, especially in the company of RR. In the company of RR, death, or even mutilation, as a consequence of risk taking behavior seemed no more or less real than Miss Havisham or Mr. Rochester, no more or less real than any other element of the entertainment, of the page-turning discovery of sex and drugs, if not rock and roll (which, being a ubiquitous component of American culture, was already known). Especially death as it pertained to others—others such as the once living beings in the anatomy lab who were now insensate forms, or "stiffs." Plugged, like most adolescents, into the moment, yours truly could not seriously imagine a time beyond the moment, a time when the sound track, so to speak, would stop. The visit to the anatomy lab was, therefore, no memento mori. And yet, for some reason, the visit to the anatomy lab made a deep impression, and remains imprinted still, like the words of a song listened to over and over, during the seemingly endless but now forever posterior days of youth.

As does RR himself. Yes, at midlife as gradually all is effaced but the flatline looming to the fore, he remains imprinted still. Still, even though yours truly broke off the relationship decades ago during the first semester at SUNY Purchase, after receiving the second of the two letters below.

1.
Hello [top of page instructs to "smoke…read." There is no date.]

What time are you coming home on thursday. When you get to the bus station call me I see if I can pick you up. The nest is still here but I broke out saturday to party at boytons. Jim has wierd friends. Burt had the party he told us it would be a big one. I should not have broken out of that nest. How was your weekend hope it was better then a party at Boyton I sure there not to many place like the boyton.

It was so beat that I played Monophily with Jim and Beth I was winning then they quit. How the social life. How Kenney and Genney and there car. My body is in much pain since I tried to play football.

It wierd everytime I see you

I found hair growing down from my belly button I not sure wether I like this

I think it will look like a zipper or maybey I like it

I wrote that because I just found it dose that matter or make sence

There's a haunted house in town think you want to go

Pot couldn't get pound to smoke so bought smaller amount

Not a lot to write about Okay Louse wrote me

She living with Harlen in Hudson NY he going to school she got work they have there own apt nere the school

Call me

Pot good for a ride on the bus if get boored just ask somebody if they want to get

HIGH and you have some body to wrap with. if not get high your self and fall a sleep.

Love peace

R

2.

["LETTER LETTER" is written in small block print in the top left margin, followed by LISA with a long squiggly tail rising up from the "A" like the exhaust of an airplane. Again, there is no date.]

Hay think you write back we seem to have lost communication we may say a few words but we—you don't talk. I got feeling from you that you don't want to or me to be around I guess 'I just don't know.' Lou Reed

I thought of asking

You want friendship

Nobody I can feel comfortble with

I want to know what I feel

I dont want us to stop

It wierd I like to know you

[illegible line]

Just write the end

R

in a way, of a perimenopausal woman. The opposite, because while both are frequently destabilized and even thrown off balance by wildly shifting hormonal levels, the former turns it all into a high seas adventure, a slippery decked lark, whereas the latter is hopelessly landlocked. Or beached. Yes beached might be a better way to put it, as at a certain point yours truly became stranded. Because the story of a love affair between a thirty-nine-year-old woman and a twelve-year-old boy finally can't go anywhere—finally the former finds herself lying in the dark, alone. Or in the bright, hot sun. The bright, hot sun, for finally there is a body (despite or because of all the preceding pages of words), a body that according to the above was zipped into an over-sized purple nylon jumpsuit, and which given the afore-mentioned bright hot sun, must have been sweltering.[48]

So onward, or back, to yours truly, stranded on the strand. Sweltering, in a tent-sized purple nylon jumpsuit embroidered over the right chest pocket with the legend "Lesvos is for Livers," a leopard print baseball cap, and gold platform tennis shoes. How had it come to this? Was there even a swimsuit under the jumpsuit? An attractive, fashionable swimsuit like the one described earlier on, in the "Mithymna" section of this report—an alternative to the bathos of this desperately purple ensemble? No, there was not, for in the haste to achieve a complete makeover and then to stake out a position on the beach, that detail was not planted. And it was too late to go back.

---

[48] Yes there is, finally, a body. Which is why it is impossible to proceed, as directed earlier, as if there are only words. Then again, when all is said and done, the inscribed "I" alone remains: "I want to know what I feel."

Too late to go back. Which meant that the hand dealt
must be played. Tent-sized purple nylon, "Lesvos is for Livers" jumpsuit, leopard print baseball cap, gold platform tennis shoes, in addition to dyed black hair, Ray-Ban classics and
self-tanning lotion. And a perimenopausal female body, slick
with sweat beneath the nylon suit, supine on a rented chaise
lounge. And the beach, don't forget the beach. The beach at
Eressos, the birthplace of the lyric poet Sappho, which is not
far from the beach at Lapsarna, where the head of Orpheus
washed up, still singing. Both located on the island of Lesvos,
where it is claimed that the first novel, *Daphnis and Chloe*, was
written by Longus. Details that were permissible because they
were associated through myth and legend with a setting already
established. Permissible but so far useless, in this setting that
was also flat and uninspiring, as the sand gave way to the sea
in one level plane. To be sure, there was a great hump of rock
off the shore (a half mile out, a quarter? There was no means,
at present, to determine the distance) which could lend itself to
metaphor (the skull of a sunken colossus? The half-submerged
back of some outmoded monster or leviathan?) or better yet,
serve as a place to find the boy (for small human figures could
be seen, scaling the sides). But how to get there without a boat
(yours truly is not a strong swimmer), and how to procure a
boat without resorting to contrivance?

Well, was it too late to bring up the night before? (As
mentioned above, yours truly had arrived at Skala Eressos at
10:00 the previous evening.) No, because it is perfectly natural
to recollect recent experiences without mnemonic prompts
such as old songs or childhood treats. Alright, then. Let us say,
then, that after checking into a small, affordable if mosquito

infested[49] beachfront hotel, yours truly ventured out in search of a bite, or more, to eat (since the previous day's caloric intake, as the reader will recall from the last section of this report, was inadequate). Which was found, perhaps, at a garden restaurant, two streets in from the beach, where a typical Mediterranean meal of grilled red peppers, a salty farmer's cheese, olive oil sautéed spinach and grilled fresh fish, along with a glass of ouzo, could be ordered from a dark haired, forty-something woman who possessed the authority of a proprietor. Because finally, there is a body.

Finally, there is a body, and once it is attended to, awareness may be directed outward, to the surroundings. Specifically, say, to the enchanting atmosphere of the garden restaurant, created by the slatted wood supported canopy overhead, the glowing basket lamps, the flowers both dried (bunches were tied to the wood rafters) and fresh (in clay pots on the tiled ground, in glass jelly jars on the rustic wooden tables, in the wiry black hair of the waiter/proprietor), the floral printed tablecloths and flickering votive candles, an atmosphere which undoubtedly invested the surrounding tables of women, sitting in both couples and groups, with the fictive potentiality for some sapphic romp directed by the magus. Such as, for instance, the table with the brunette with the curled, lacquered "sideburns" and mandarin jacket, the thin redhead with the pageboy and sleek, fat dachshund nestled in her lap, and the blond with the thick, Valkyrie's

---

[49] Yes, mosquito infested—despite the arid climate of the island of Lesvos, particularly on the western side. Thus the night spent at the small, beachfront hotel in Skala Eressos could have led to a case of *falciparum malaria* and ultimately to the *cerebral malaria* mentioned at the beginning of this report (see par.2 in sec. I.1; also fn. 1), if all had gone as planned.

braid, and plunging, peasant-style blouse. So that maybe, when yours truly crossed the patio of the garden restaurant in search of the WC, a long glance was exchanged with the brunette, as the latter slowly traced one lacquered curl. Thus it would not be inconceivable, were she to appear on the beach now, for her to approach (perhaps as the emissary of the trio, who bored stiff with their threesome, hoped for chiasmatic renewal in a foursome), with an invitation to "join us later this afternoon on our catamaran." But hold on. Yes hold on, because an important detail had been overlooked: the makeover, which ruled out any recognition from the night before. Without recognition, there would probably be no approach. No, an approach was unlikely, especially when the tackiness of the makeover was factored in.

OK, then what about another table? What if there was a table occupied by an intelligent-looking if somewhat frumpy woman in black plastic rimmed spectacles, accompanied by a well-tanned man who seemed to be her husband and a peaked young boy who seemed to be her son (the only males at the garden restaurant)? Say that the peaked boy vomited into his soup bowl and the tanned man carried him off to the WC for a clean up, while the intelligent-looking if somewhat frumpy woman continued, with a thoughtful expression, to eat her chicken souvlaki until her plate was not only completely cleared of food, but indeed gleamed like polished bone? She too, could appear on the beach at any moment, quite possibly alone (the well-tanned man, who did not need to become any tanner, having remained back at the hotel with the still-peaked boy), in which case yours truly could make the approach. From there, a pleasant, intelligent conversation could ensue out of a query about the young boy, a conversation that might be continued on the husband's sailboat (for that deep tan was surely a sailor's tan) later in the afternoon or early evening. And if, upon arrival at the small island of rock that was like the skull of a sunken colossus or the back of some half-submerged leviathan, there was no sign of Aslan, well maybe it wouldn't matter. Because the conversation with the intelligent-looking, if somewhat frumpy woman in the black plastic rimmed spectacles could simply resume, because at a certain point in life it is said that pleasant, intelligent conversation can provide a deeper, more abiding satisfaction than almost anything.

At any rate, perhaps it was possible, after all, to procure a boat and reach the rock without resorting to contrivance. Perhaps after all it was possible, given a precedent set last night at the garden restaurant, to strike up an acquaintance, here on the beach, that could lead to procuring a boat, and eventually, to reaching the rock, which could in turn serve as a place to find Aslan. Only the beach, unfortunately, was empty. Thus, with the exception of yours truly, there was no one on the beach, which stretched, parchment colored sand shimmering in the sun, south toward the white adobe buildings of Skala Eressos, birthplace of Sappho, lyric poet, and north, beyond rock-faced cliffs, toward Lapsarna, where the head of Orpheus washed up, still singing. Unlike the aforementioned head of the woman in the paper bag that, like a melon, was silent. And also unlike the empty beach. Upon which, because it was summer in the Mediterranean and rainfall is infrequent, the sun beat down.[50] Therefore yours truly, shrouded in purple nylon, was sweltering. Shade had to be found.

---

[50] As in Colorado, where there is not even the respite of fresh sea air.

But where could shade be found, given the emptiness of the beach? An emptiness that not only precluded other human beings (who might provide a way to reach the rock island without contrivance), but also all objects manufactured by human beings, such as umbrellas. Therefore the glare of the sun, which highlighted the emptiness of the beach, was inescapable. Then again, maybe it was necessary to think harder. To think outside the box. Or beyond the umbrella. To think resourcefully, which meant to think in terms of resources, in terms of what was already here, i.e. what already had been established, above (or as described earlier, "the hand that had been dealt"). Indeed, with a quick review, it became apparent that the beach was not empty after all: in addition to yours truly, there was, once again, the tent-sized purple nylon "Lesvos is for Livers" jumpsuit, the leopard print baseball cap, the gold platform tennis shoes, the Ray-Ban classics and in the pocket of the jumpsuit, self-tanning lotion. And the chair, don't forget the chair, the orange nylon-webbed aluminum chaise lounge, which could be adjusted to a fully horizontal position, to form a kind of platform, or low, narrow table. Eureka. Eureka, because the image of the table triggered an associated memory—a childhood memory of transforming the living room coffee table into a kind of shelter, under which a sense of privacy could be enjoyed by draping a sheet or blanket over the top. A shelter that could now be recreated with the orange nylon-webbed aluminum chaise lounge, the tent-sized purple nylon jumpsuit, and the gold platform tennis shoes (for once the jumpsuit had been arranged over the chair, the shoes would be used to anchor it—just in case a breeze struck up. Although at the time, the air was still as a cadaver).

As suspected above, there was no bathing suit, no garment

of any kind, under the jumpsuit. But there was, finally, a body. A body that, as it was slid under the shelter fabricated out of the chaise lounge and the tent-sized jumpsuit, was afforded relief. Relief from the ascending noonday sun, relief from increasing exposure. Because none of this was fooling anyone. None of this—the makeover, the report, the boy—was fooling anyone, least of all yours truly. Yours truly, who was becoming more and more tired of the whole affair, so that as the sun seeped through the purple nylon of the jumpsuit, through the orange webbing of the chaise lounge, the effect was like light coming through closed eyelids. Light that is received by the photoreceptors of the retina, at the back of the eyeball, even during sleep.[51] Until it is received no more.

---

[51] Light is received by the photoreceptors of the retina, at the back of the eyeball, even during sleep, which yours truly descended into, as people so often do when their present situation has become intolerable. Which is probably why depressed persons spend so much time in bed. The hope, of course, is that upon waking, a fresh outlook will have been acquired. And indeed, upon waking, this is what yours truly has—not only a fresh outlook, but a skiff. Yes, I have a small, flat-bottomed rowboat, perhaps because life is but a dream, but which nevertheless gives me real satisfaction as I paddle over the glassy swells that softly rise and fall, rise and fall, as if by pulmonary imperative. In my skiff, I am gliding over the glassy, seeming to respire swells toward what appears to be a very large, pocked and fissured gray rock, backlit by the orange red glow of the horizon, and I feel like I could paddle on and on. I feel like I could paddle on and on, past the backlit, pocked and fissured gray rock to the horizon and beyond, but when I dip my right oar deep, attempting to circumvent it, my course remains unaltered. In fact, as I relinquish the oars, which are secured to the sides of the skiff by metal rings, it seems that paddling makes no difference at all: the skiff continues toward the rock, carried by the glassy, respiring swells.

Yes the rock is apparently where I'm headed, like it or not. Like it or not, whether I paddle or I don't. Fortunately, there are cushions in the prow, killim pillows richly dyed in pomegranate, orange and grapefruit pink, the colors of one of the carpets J and I bought when we were teaching in North Cyprus.

Colors that are also, of course, the colors of the horizon, the limit I now know I'm not going to reach, which is just as well. Because then what? No, better just to sink back into the colorful mound of killim pillows, to let the low, slow waves carry the skiff forward toward the rock island—a place to dally, for a while.

And now the rock is looming, its great flanks curving overhead as the skiff draws alongside. Now looming, however, the rock appears unpromising as a place to dally. Its steep, smooth contours are slicked green with algae, and even if there were a place to gain a foothold, some crevice or fissure, the skiff is suddenly moving too fast, scudding the shadowy perimeter of the rock as if to do a quick lap before heading out to sea (a prospect that no longer appeals), or back to shore (a prospect that does). Yes, back to shore—a prospect that does appeal, unlike heading out to sea, that does no longer. Back, nestled in a skiff full of cushions, which have become even more colorful than before—to the point where the colors recall a bowl of Froot Loops, or the intensity of the artificial that surpasses the original. Yes, and how sweet that would be.

But as the skiff reaches the far side of the rock, away from the shore, it suddenly stops. Stops, the water sloshing beneath the hull, before a cleft of carved stone steps leading up the side of the rock island and out of sight. Which makes them irresistible—i.e., the fact that they lead up and out of sight. So that as the skiff nuzzles at the foot of the steps, I'm compelled to climb out and to ascend the cleft, my hands pressing flat against the cool, thankfully algae free, stone on either side. Will the skiff, which for now remains bobbing below, still be there when I return? Will I even be able to descend again, given the almost impossibly steep angle of the steps? Best not to think about it or to look back.

As I approach the top of the steps, I hear a voice, a voice that is light yet loud, almost as if projected for my benefit: We must be patient, Yoshiko.

Yes, Sadako. But do you think he will come out again?

I don't know.

But when I reach the top, I see no one—only a hummocky expanse of rock, as if some variety of mineral-eating rodent has been burrowing beneath the surface. And in fact, when I look down I see the stone is randomly pocked with what appear to be the prints of small paws. Only paws that oddly seem to have been toeless and clawless, as if encased in tiny moccasins. Yes, as if encased in tiny moccasins, the prints of which grow uniformly thick off to my right, coagulating into a path that leads down between two mounds of rock and disappears. And then a voice rises up: I think I just saw him!

I descend.

Squeezing out from between the two mounds, I immediately spot the two sisters, crouched before what appears to be a small cave, at the mouth of which the path of tiny moccasin-like indentations ends. Each girl is wearing some sort of school uniform—a crisp white, short-sleeved shirt, a skimpy navy skirt, and navy knee-socks with Mary Janes—dressed as if for a field trip, or, once again, someone else's psychodrama. For someone else's psychodrama, and yet, undeniably, familiar. So at some level I have to take responsibility as the older of the two sisters, Sadako, stands up and miming a microphone, brings it to her lips: This might be it folks. Have we finally bagged him? After all this time on the trail, and so far from his natural habitat?

As Sadako speaks, her eyes seem to fall on me. Then again, it's hard to say—they're inhumanly large and round, with shiny black centers, like plastic or glass. I draw back into the cleavage of rock, into shadow, while in the meantime, Yoshiko stands up and joins her sister. Her eyes are just as large and round, just as impenetrable and fake appearing as she takes hold of the mimed microphone: But what is his natural habitat, Sadako? Then she hands back the imaginary mike and reaches down to pull up her navy knee-socks.

A good question. An excellent question. We will ask him, when he comes out.

And if he does not come out? What then? Yoshiko asks, resuming her crouch by the mouth of the cave.

Sadako sits on the ground opposite her sister, legs folding into the lotus position. Her navy skirt hitches up around her narrow hips, revealing black panties as slick as her eyes. I don't know, but surely after all this we can wait a little longer.

A little longer? But dusk is falling, deepening the shadow in which I am standing, dragging the scene into darkness. A darkness that is not soft or velvety, but vitreous black. I step out. I step out, and because my feet are bare (yes, bare), I can feel the tiny indentations in the stone, polished smooth like tooled leather. Just write the end. But then the breeze blowing up from the sea smells like salt, and the girls with their shiny black eyes scuttle off like crabs. Just write the end but I don't want us to stop

It wierd I like to know you
I want to know what
I feel hair growing down
From my bellybutton
Call me
We seem to have lost
A few words
Will look like a zipper
Nobody I can feel comfortble with
You don't talk
Dose that matter or make sence
I want to know what
I feel
Just write